SAGE OF HOPE AND RUIN

SAGE OF HOPE AND RUIN

THE VEIL OF ELPIS: BOOK ONE

For the girls who were taught they weren't worthy of love, and those who struggle to find a light in the dark. To the one soul who stood by my side, even when I thought I was alone.

Map of the known world not yet consumed by the Empty

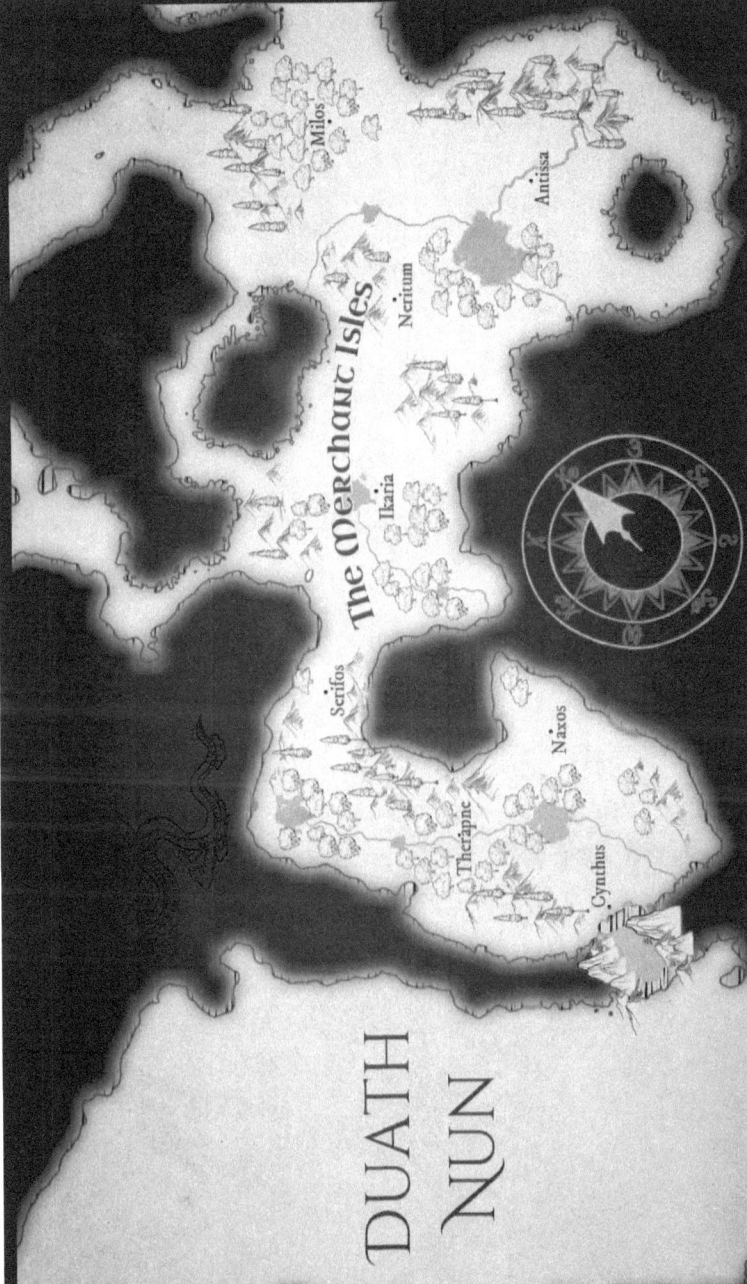

PROLOGUE

THE WORLD CARED NOT FOR people like me. For girls tossed aside by their own mothers.

Exhausted, I fell to my knees, palms rough and scratched by the forest's dense underbrush. Breath and emotion heaved in my chest as fresh tears spilled down my dirty face.

Until my tenth year, I'd clung to my mother's skirts, begging her not to leave me.

A week ago, she had vanished before I awoke. I'd chased after her, though I knew it was no use.

She was gone.

Pulling myself up, I wiped away the tears, coating my puffy red eyes in mud. Trees surrounded me in every direction. I'd trekked out here in hopes of finding berries, something—anything—to eat. My stomach groaned with pain, reminding me of my failure.

And now I was lost.

Wrapping my arms around myself, I looked around. What was I supposed to do now? Where did a girl who had nothing go?

The wilds were dangerous. I shouldn't be out here, with night drawing near.

Maybe it didn't matter. If my own mother had wanted nothing more than to be rid of me...

Who would want me?

A twig snapped nearby, and I gasped, tripping over myself and landing on my butt. A deer thundered by, paying me no heed.

Sighing, I pulled my knees up and laid my head across them.

I was to blame for everything, Mother had always said. For her lover leaving her, for her husband throwing her out. A drain on her coin purse, a poison to her life...

I should have known this day would come.

Terrible sorrow welled in my chest, forcing new tears to my eyes. If monsters did prowl the wilds, what was the point of running?

No one would care if I were to die.

A new sound from the forest caught my ear. I raised my head, looking around in worry.

I saw nothing. Heard nothing. And in that moment, I realized it had not been a sound I heard, but the absence of one.

The swaying branches had gone still, and the distant patter of small animals had ceased. Birds no longer sang.

In that unnatural stillness, I saw it: a tiny bead of darkness forming between the trees, mere paces from my eyes.

With trembling hands, I reached out. It drew me, like a moth to a flame, and I could not stop myself. My fingertip brushed the speck of darkness.

It erupted.

From a tiny bead burst pure shadow, and the forest was torn asunder. The ground caved beneath the growing void; trees disintegrated to ash. The black hole opened its maw at my feet, and I peered down a sheer cliff into an endless sea, still and unmoving.

This was the Empty. I'd heard people talk about it, heard the priests sing of the void consuming our world.

Of the void that came for people who were utterly alone.

My heart pounded, stirring my limbs to life. Gripped by all-consuming fear, I staggered to my feet and fled.

My steps made no sound, though I crushed leaves and grass underfoot. My breath heaved beneath the effort, but I could not hear it.

The void chased me through a muted world, destroying everything in its wake. Forest turned to empty air, the lush ground fell away. Everything behind me became a chasm that tumbled into that still sea.

I couldn't outrun it. Every breath, the edge of the void drew nearer. A pulsing red light brushed my face, warning me of its arrival.

It would turn me to dust—like the trees, like the flowers. Gone, like I'd never mattered.

Because I hadn't.

My limbs screamed, exhausted and starving. My lungs burned, and I felt my legs give out.

My knees struck the ground. Through the silent world, I heard my mother's voice—the hatred buried in her words, the disdain hidden in every glare.

Turning toward the approaching void, I extended my arms. Envisioning my mother—her beautiful head of curls and chocolate eyes—I embraced her phantom, pretending she had loved me, even once.

I waited for death. It struck me like a charging bull, and all sound snapped back into the world.

Pain thudded through my side as someone grabbed me and pulled me into their arms. Leaves and twigs snapped beneath their weight as they wrapped around me like a shield.

I clawed at my captor, and my hands found purchase around the folds of a cloak.

Every muscle in their body tensed—waiting for the Empty to take us.

But it did not.

I looked over their shoulder to see the void looming a mere pace away. A pebble tumbled over the sheer cliff and fell into the still sea.

If it made a sound, I did not hear it.

"What were you thinking?" A man's voice chastised. "Venturing into the wilds alone?"

Pulling my hands back, I finally looked up at him.

I knew him, his dark hair and golden brown eyes. A strong hooked nose gave him a distinctive appearance.

He had pressed coins into my palm last night, bidding me to get a warm meal.

"I thought I told you to stay out of trouble," he said.

He had. He'd pulled me away from a man who'd looked at me with hungry eyes. When he'd wrapped his arm around my shoulder and guided me down the street, hope had bloomed in my heart.

Maybe he'd take me to my mother, or the father I'd never met. Maybe he'd decide he needed an assistant or an apprentice, and I wouldn't be alone anymore.

But he'd left me there, at the end of the street. The crowd had pushed me in its tide, and the coins he'd gifted me had spilled from my grip.

"Come on," He pulled me up. "We need to get out of here."

I stumbled after him, fingers wrapped in his.

Hot tears streamed down my face, and I pulled my hand loose. Cradling it to my chest, I collapsed.

He whirled around, realizing he'd lost me.

"I don't want to go," I sniffled. "I don't want to be given hope again. Because you'll leave again."

The man slowly knelt at my side. "I live in a world of thieves, liars, and knives. It is no place for a child."

"So?" My voice trembled. "I lost your gold. Someone pushed me, and. . ."

He watched me, silent. Tilting his head, he looked over the scrapes covering my arms and knees. "The streets are no place for a child, either." Sighing, he extended a hand. "Come on."

I looked into his golden brown eyes. "Are you going to take me with you?"

"You do not even know where I'm going. Who I am."

"No, but. . . you're the only person who's ever helped me."

His eyes softened. "Alright. You can stay with me. For as long as you need."

Stunned, I stuttered over my words. "Do you promise not to leave me?"

He smiled sadly. "No girl your age should be alone. You have my word."

I stared at his open palm, and my heart tore itself in two.

One side pulsed with relief and joy, warm and gold like the first rays of sunlight in the morning.

I wouldn't be alone anymore.

The other ached with agony and nostalgia. It beckoned me to turn back to the void, whispering of the fate I'd avoided—the fate I'd been meant to suffer.

Thief, crook, murderer—I'd do whatever this man wanted if it meant someone would look upon me like they wanted me.

I glanced back at the abyss. It called to me, the still sea.

"Aethra," The man said my name gently, "I have need of an apprentice. Should she agree—I will not leave her."

He gazed upon me with a softness my mother never had. He'd asked me my name last night—and given me his.

Ainwir.

I slipped my hand into his, praying, hoping against hope, that he did not lie.

ONE

Thirteen years later. . .

ODAY WAS A DAY LIKE any other. There was no reason to rise in the morning, nor any hope for tomorrow when night fell. I pulled my dress on and examined my weary face in the dirty mirror, wondering if happiness had ever gleamed in my ashen eyes.

The man I'd loved most bequeathed to me suffering and left me behind in the dust, stealing away my chance at life.

Ainwir had lied, all those years ago.

Five paces worth of space; that's all my home could fit. A little crocheted pegasus laid on the tattered mattress I called a bed. One of its eyes was missing. Ainwir had given it to me for my twelfth birthday. Pushing it aside, I grabbed my bag and slung it over my shoulder.

I had a job to do tonight.

My life had fallen into the Guild's hands after Ainwir vanished. They gave me jobs—forgeries, deliveries, seducing men they needed information from—and I did them.

Should I refuse, they would kill me.

The lack of choice made my life simple. It was about the only compliment I could pay my sorry existence.

I fussed with the door's broken lock before finally throwing it open and stepping outside.

Ikaria was a beautiful city—if you lived near the center. Here on the outskirts, mud-mired water stained the wooden shacks resting precariously on the edge of waterways.

Most people who lived here rose before the sun had fully ascended the sky and returned after dark, traveling in groups to and from the city's sprawling farms. Deeply tanned and aged beyond their years, they barely glanced my way as I passed them.

Stepping onto the rickety wooden bridges spanning the channels, I followed my usual path to the central square.

With every step, the flimsy walkways gave way to solid stone bridges, the waters cleared, and the buildings grew in height and width. Lanterns strung over the channels glimmered on the water's surface, like beacons guiding me home.

Glancing over my shoulder, I slipped into a quiet alley and dropped my bag on a dried-up fountain. Checking to make sure no one watched, I quickly tied my thick curls into a bun and pulled a pale blue toga over my plain white gown.

I tried to see my reflection in what little water remained in the basin. It appeared little more than a brown-and-cream blur. Oh, well. Sticking a flower through my bun, I snapped golden bracelets onto my wrists before pulling out the most important piece of my disguise: a white mask decorated with soft blue flowers. Fitting it over my eyes, I took a breath.

This job was going to get me killed, but at least I would look nice.

Throwing my bag back around my shoulder, I emerged from the alley and rejoined the crowd. A stream of people funneled toward Sundering Square, and boats bobbed along the channels, ferrying nobles to the ceremony that would be held there.

Once a year, the square came alive for the Sundering Ceremony. During the height of the celebration, the clergy would bring forth their most holy relic: the Maiden's Bloodstone.

Supposedly, it was crystallized blood from the goddess herself. Should an unworthy soul so much as run a finger across it, he would have his head removed from his shoulders.

And I was here to steal it.

The Guildmaster was normally a reasonable woman. I suppose she'd decided I'd been a helpful enough slave, and killing me in an entertaining fashion was more valuable than my continued service.

'Never take a job you aren't certain you can handle.' Ainwir had always said.

Gods. What would he think of this?

Shoving the thought of the backstabbing old man from my head, I joined the crowd waiting outside the Sundering Square gates. Waiting to be allowed entry.

Lowering my head, I listened to the idle chatter around me.

Gossip. Comments about each others outfits—some scathing, some insincere. I brushed aside the useless words and focused on an interesting conversation from the couple next to me.

". . .father's been in a panic all week." A young man in a lion mask was whispering to his date. "Something's shaken the entire council."

"Maybe the king dropped dead," the woman in a deep red toga answered.

"Ha. Maybe. Father must be trying to arrange my marriage to the princess."

The woman shoved him, and he laughed.

The council was in a panic? What about, I wondered.

I'd be dead after tonight, when they cut my head off for heresy and grand theft. That made the matter quite firmly, not my problem.

Should I succeed, though, against all odds. . .

Freedom. I'd be granted freedom from the Guild if I managed to pull off this heist. The Guildmaster had promised to forgive my debt.

I had never known freedom.

The sound of metal hinges creaking drew my attention to the gates as they peeled open, allowing the crowd entry. They surged through in an eager tide.

A gondola slowed to a stop alongside the walkway, and a man in a gorgeous silver wrap stepped up in front of me. I paused, watching as he lifted his little girl from the boat and set her on his shoulder.

My fingers curled into a fist, and I scowled, though I hadn't meant to.

Wiping the expression from my face, I took a breath. Five years had passed since Ainwir betrayed me. He'd hardly acted like a father, so why did I still think of him as one?

The man had borrowed a heavy sum from the Guild's coffers, dropped the debt on my head, and run for the hills. He'd gifted them a talented slave—why would the Guildmaster suddenly have a change of heart and set me free? And what madman had commissioned her to steal such a precious relic?

The answers were none of my business. Nor did I care to know them. All that mattered was the freedom awaiting me if I could do this one thing.

In all likelihood, I'd fail. I was a con woman, not a thief. But an end beckoned sweetly, promising to deliver me from the nothingness that drolled on without meaning.

In the next few hours, my destiny would be decided— freedom, or the gallows.

TWO

HE GREATEST HEIST THE MERCHANT'S Isles had ever seen would occur tonight - assuming I succeeded. More likely, town criers across the continent would spin the tale of the idiot woman who tried to steal that which could not be stolen.

A mere three days. That's how long Laverna had given me to prepare. I'd blinked and the days had disappeared; the Sundering Ceremony was upon me.

Fitting the mask of flowers over my eyes, I smoothed down my opal gown and stepped into Sundering Square. Once, years ago, I'd attended this grand ceremony with Ainwir, awed by the beautiful ladies and their splendorous masks.

Drunken merriment clashed in an unintelligible rush of voices. Masks of every design, from animals to gilded gold, concealed the people's faces. Togas of finest silk and those of tattered tartan swathed their bodies, dividing those with wealth from those with nothing.

Lanterns glowed on the water channels flanking the long stretch of pavement. Past the rows of ancient marble buildings, peaked with bronze roofs, the channels converged into a lake that bordered the temple.

I made myself small as I slipped through the crowd, avoiding attention. Grabbing a glass of wine from a passing harlequin's tray, I sipped idly on the bitter drink while my eyes feasted on the main event.

An enormous boat bobbed on the lake's calm waters, more stage than vessel. Flat and wide, it would never be seaworthy. It was a *theater*. Atop its stage, the sermon would be held, and the re-enactment of the Maiden Brizo and the creation of her Bloodstone would be performed.

Any other night, I would have enjoyed the show. But I needed to get aboard the grand vessel and leave without being seen.

Two wooden bridges connected the boat to the square, but both were in plain view. Even a shadow could not slip across unseen. Once the show began, the crowds would flock to the lake's edge - hundreds of eyes would be watching.

Across the glowing lake, a stone pathway connected the back of the theatre ship to the temple looming over the city, its windows bright spots of gold. The Maiden's Bloodstone was stored in a vault beneath it, emerging only once a year for the festival of the Sundering.

A heavy troop of guards would escort the Bloodstone to the ship. And once the ceremony concluded, they would return it to its vault. That left but one tiny window for me to steal it.

Leaning on the stone banister guarding drunken attendants from falling into the lake, I reconsidered my plan. I was a fool for thinking this heist was possible.

Laverna probably just wanted to get me killed in the grandest way she could imagine.

"Beautiful, isn't it?" A soft voice met my ears as a masked man joined me at the lake's edge. "Though I don't imagine it's seaworthy."

I quickly scanned the stranger—shoulder-length brown hair, a simple white toga with a scarf, and a mask of owl feathers. A scholar, or maybe a priest?

Harmless, either way.

Shifting to face him, I smiled sweetly and spoke with an elegant, noble accent. "Is this your first time attending the Sundering ceremony?"

"Yes. I've never before had the pleasure." He admitted.

I glanced over his shoulder, watching a procession of women in sea-colored robes approach the bridges and kneel in silent prayer. My opening was drawing near.

"I hope you brought a suitor," I said idly. "There's a dance after the rite."

A sly smile crossed his lips. "Not this time."

"Shame." I passed him, bowing my head. "Merry sailing."

"Ah, one moment," he said, studying me intently. "I didn't catch your name."

I curtsied. "Lady Terpsichore," I offered my fake alias, and walked away.

"Merry sailing, my lady." He called after me.

A ring of guards protected the maidens and nobles from the riffraff. Standing a few paces away, the crowds jostled past me as I gathered my thoughts and prepared my lie.

Pulling an envelope from my satchel, I approached the guards: men with heavy helms covering all but their eyes and mouths, and red tabards flapping in the breeze.

Finding the youngest of the lot, I studied my nails. "When do we board?" I asked dryly.

The young guard looked me up and down. "In two chimes of the bell, madam. . .?"

"Terpsichore," I said, hoping the lady remained at home, as Cecelia claimed.

"Ah." He raised his chin, recognizing the name. "I heard you and your father wouldn't be attending."

Shit. Improvising, I pressed a finger to my lips. "I didn't want to miss this. Don't tell anyone?" Smiling sweetly, I tilted my head.

Thankfully, he smiled back. "Of course. Do you still have your invitation?"

"Right here." I handed him the envelope, heart pounding.

Would he notice it was a forgery? I watched him break the seal and unroll the letter, keeping my breathing steady. His eyes flicked over the words meant to be written by the Archon and hastily returned it to me.

"Enjoy yourself." He said. "The others should be arriving soon. You can wait here."

"Thank you," I said, bowing my head and walking past him.

Relieved, I tried to relax. Pretending you belonged fooled most people. The nobles who sat on the king's council were permitted to board the ship with the priests, allowing them to witness the ceremony up close. Hopefully, the mask concealed my face enough to fool those who'd met Lord Terpsichore's daughter.

A gaudily dressed man in a brilliant purple doublet approached the guards in the company of a flaming-haired woman. With their faces concealed by masks, I couldn't see a hint of their features. The man quickly conversed with the guards, while the red-haired woman in black regarded me.

Whether she smiled or scrutinized, I couldn't tell.

The gaudy man bowed to the guards playfully and returned to his date's side. The fox engraved on his mask regarded the priest by the waters I'd spoken with earlier.

The owl-masked man and the gaudy purple lord exchanged glances, before turning toward me. Why did they stare? Pretending not to notice, I looked away, instead watching a pair of lords dressed in glittering gold join our little group.

Another chime rang across the waters, and a hush quickly fell across the square. Bowing their heads, the maidens began their procession across the walkways, and the young guard gestured for me to walk ahead of him.

Holding my head high, I drank in the theatre boat's every detail, its soaring mast and high banisters

There. A troop of guards in heavy black armor emerged from the temple, surrounding a broad man who carried the great bust of the Maiden.

The goddess Brizo, in all her marble glory. Flowing hair spilled like water across her back, and her bare breasts were covered by cupped hands. Glowing beneath the lanterns, a brilliant blood-red stone was embedded in her palms.

Carrying the entire bust out of here would be impossible. Thankfully, all I needed was that stone.

A cluster of priests in pale blue togas and the maidens in sea-tinted robes knelt at the back of the ship. Dancers streamed onboard behind them; women in masks tipped with enormous feathers gathered around the railing, their male partners shrouded behind long, ornamental beaks.

The group of nobles stood center-stage. Following the crowd, a bead of sweat ran down my temple as the enormous man set the bust down gently on its altar.

The High Priest approached the edge of the boat, arms cast wide, as if inviting the crowd on the lake's other side. He would give a brief speech, then festivities would commence. The day was for *living*, not sharing sermons about the afterlife.

Pale blue scarf trailing in the wind like a sea current, the High Priest began his brief recitation of the verses.

"Daughter of the sea, Brizo, our savior, I pray for your continued protection. For your hand steers the ships of the ocean on their flying course, and shields our land from encroaching wars. Upon your vessel, did we escape the endless sea."

Looking down, I scanned the gaggle of performers. A troupe of musicians quietly set up in the back corner, wearing robes the color of the boat.

When the dancers spun in front of the idol, perhaps. . .

The noblewoman with fiery red hair leaned toward me. "Quiet year. There used to be more coin poured into these festivals."

Startled, I turned to the woman beside me. A phoenix mask concealed her face, save for eyes of faded blue. She stood nearly a foot taller than I, clad in a handsome charcoal gown.

Who was this? I studied the red braid tumbling down her back, but no names came to mind. Neither did I recognize the fox-masked lord with her.

"They did." I agreed. "The royal coffers must've taken a hit this year."

"Maybe." The woman agreed. "Need a partner?"

"I'm not much of a dancer." I denied. "I just wanted to watch the show up close."

"Suit yourself." The woman said coyly, turning away.

"Fear not the tide of sorrow," The Grand Priest continued, "For in life we find our salvation, the cacophony of voices, the beads of sweat borne from dance."

This concluded the short speech. The dancers stepped up, preparing to begin the play. Shadows plunged the courtyard into darkness as the lanterns were doused, forcing all eyes upon the theatre ship.

Something moved in the shadows across the waters. Leaning forward, I could see people running around near the walkways leading to the ship, but. . .

"May Brizo's light grace us this night!" The Grand Priest stepped back, and the dancers began, knitting hands with their partners, their thick skirts swirling around the stage like a whirlwind.

Lunging forward, I seized my only chance: rip the Bloodstone from its socket while all eyes were on the dancers.

But someone else seized it first.

A man yelped nearby. I spun around to see the gaudy purple noble plunge a knife into a guard's thigh, knocking him to his knees.

Fire erupted everywhere; heat struck my face like a sharp slap. Stumbling, I backed away from a circle of fire growing around the bust, trapping me inside its blazing cage.

Blood streamed through the air, whirling around the ship like red streamers. Fire followed the crimson, setting the blood alight.

Fear pounded through my heart. A chthonic mage? *Here?*

The red-haired woman stepped forward, a cut on her palm spilling fresh blood. It dripped from her fingers and hovered in the air like threads pulled by a loom, dancing in the circle of glowing fire.

Screaming consumed the boat as those aboard tripped over themselves in their bid to escape the flames.

Pressing a hand to my eyes, I blinked away the burning pain and focused on the woman. At home in her circle of fire, she sauntered up to the idol and grabbed the Maiden's Bloodstone, yanking a few times before it clicked and pulled loose.

Thundering bootfalls slammed across the bridges as guards rushed the chaos. They hesitated outside the wall of flames, unwilling to throw their steel-cased bodies into the fire.

The red-haired woman whipped around, throwing her arm. A tiny opening appeared in the fiery cage, streams of crimson whirling around it as new pillars of flame erupted from the blood. Choking on smoke, I watched the red-haired woman dash through the opening as walls of fire rose to either side of her, creating a flaming hall leading off the ship.

She was fleeing with *my* stone! Pushing past the crowd of panicked nobles, I chased after her.

Shouting and heavy footfalls pursued us. Leaping over a fallen dancer, the red-haired woman landed on the western bridge and dashed into the darkness.

Sprinting after her, I couldn't help but admire her gall. What was her plan? Pound through the crowd of people and guards and hope nobody stopped her? She reached the end of the bridge and glanced over her shoulder at me.

My foot slammed into something hard, and I tumbled onto metal. Pulling myself up, I realized what I had landed on: the crumpled body of a guard.

I caught a final glimpse of the woman's red braid before she dove into the darkness swallowing the panicked crowd in the Sundering square.

No sooner had I dragged myself to my feet than a banshee's wailing knifed into my heart. I pressed my hands to my ears, overcome with fear and an unbearable urge to run and never look back. What in the Maiden's grace was that? A spell? But from what kind of mage?

The crowd screamed, scrambling in chaos, climbing over one another to escape the noise. A flash of fire briefly illuminated the dark world. A clearing appeared at the edge of the lake, the red-haired woman at its center.

The owl-masked man from before leaned out from an alley, waving to the woman. She raced toward him. Gasping, I followed, shouting futilely at them. "Wait!"

The brief spot of fire vanished, dousing the square into shadow once more. My feet struck stone, informing me I'd stepped off the bridge. Feeling my way toward the alley, I felt a gap in the stone buildings surrounding the square and slipped through.

Light waited in the distance, where streetlamps still burned with flame. Tearing toward them, I rounded the bend into another street and found myself at the tip of a scythe.

Not any mere scythe, forged of steel. This was a weapon of flowing blood and searing flame.

The red-haired woman stared at me, even-tempered. "You're no noble." She accused.

My eyes darted to the Bloodstone clutched in her other hand.

"That's mine," I said stupidly.

The woman's eyebrows shot up. "Is it?"

"What are you doing?" I blurted out. "You'll never make it past Main Street, let alone the gates."

"Mistress!" The owl-masked man ran towards us, halting when he noticed me. "It's ready."

"Good." The red-haired woman lowered her weapon.

Shouting sounded behind us - knights hollering orders. With a wave of her hand, the flaming scythe vanished, and she turned away.

I glanced between the two thieves, wondering who else sought the Bloodstone this night.

As Ainwir always liked to say, sometimes unexpected trouble presented new opportunities. It would be far easier to rob a woman than a vault.

Hiking up my skirt, I followed the pair of thieves, glancing over my shoulder to see a torrent of guards in pursuit. Something whizzed overhead, and a javelin slammed into the pavement a few inches from my toes.

Yelping, I scrambled around it, spotting the red-braid whirl around another corner. Throwing myself around the stone to take cover, I grimaced when I realized we'd reached Main Street. A carriage waited on a wide road, doors open, and the woman flew inside, pulling them closed. A cloaked driver slapped the reins, and the horses took off.

Shit. Trying in vain to catch them, my hand wobbled for the door handle as a javelin cut a chunk of my hair loose, lodging into the door by my head.

Shrieking, I lost my footing and nearly fell face-first into the gutters. Instead, the door flew open, and a hand grabbed my collar, hauling me inside.

Scrambling for purchase, my hands found the folds of a scarf and latched on. I tumbled forward onto a man's chest as the carriage door slammed closed behind me.

Sage green eyes behind an owl mask regarded me. "Are you alright?" He asked calmly.

Lifting myself off him, I glanced between the occupants as the carriage bounced along the road.

The man in the horrific purple coat sat opposite the flaming-haired woman.

"Terpsichore." The woman said flatly. "You look different from how I remember."

The man in purple leaned forward, his low-brimmed hat falling over his mask. "Were we *supposed* to rescue her?"

"No." The owl-masked man said. "But she was going to die, so I thought we'd give her a lift."

"What do you want with the Bloodstone?" I demanded.

"You first." The woman said.

I opened my mouth to answer, but a scream emerged instead. The sound of a horse braying in pain preceded the carriage veering wildly before it flipped onto its side. I slammed into the door as the carriage slid across the road.

This time, the owl-masked man landed on top of me. Our bodies tangled as the carriage slammed into something else and came to a stop. We jolted against the seats, and pain streaked through my side. The breath left my lungs as I flailed, desperate to escape the pile of bodies. The woman kicked the door that was now the ceiling, throwing it open before effortlessly hoisting herself up.

"Sorry!" The owl-masked man breathed, regaining his feet and helping me to mine.

A flash of purple crossed my eyes as the gaudy noble climbed out. He leaned back into the hole, offering me a hand up that I took. Sweaty palms latching onto his, I hauled myself outside and balanced on the overturned carriage.

I should have expected the sight that awaited us. A line of mounted soldiers blocked the road, and a javelin had skewered one of the carriage horse's legs. Blood streamed from its leg as it writhed in pain.

Men on foot closed in from the other side, as civilians raced for their doors, shutting themselves away from the chaos.

Spinning, I searched for an exit. More cavalry galloped from the south, blocking a side street. The mounted soldiers fanned out, circling our wreck, a foot soldier braced between each horse, javelins held high, ready to fly should we resist.

The red-haired woman glanced back and flashed me a grin. She held up her hands, surrendering.

I'd always known this would end in catastrophe. The carriage and fire had been a surprise, but the soldiers approaching me with drawn spears were not. Defeated, I lifted my arms.

The woman's grin never wavered as the rest of us were pulled down to the street, and our hands were forced behind our backs and shackled. Was she mad?

Maiden's grace, I hoped we wouldn't share a cell.

THREE

I'D NEVER BEEN THROWN IN a dungeon before, despite my less-than-savory past. Ainwir had always said dungeons were not a threat; hardly anyone in the Merchant Isles was executed, allowing you ample time to prepare your escape.

An easy claim to make, a harder one to follow up on.

Exhausted from the night's events, I leaned against the cold walls, staring through the iron bars at the dim hall. The bleak sight was preferable to looking at the occupants in the bordering cells.

The shrill notes of a small flute pierced my ears. Curled in the corner of his cell, the man in the horrid purple doublet played a mournful tune, head cast down, concealing his face with the brim of his feathered hat.

On my other side, the priest I'd run into before the heist incessantly tried to talk to me.

"Are you alright?" The man with the sage-green eyes asked again.

Giving up the silent game, I stared into the cell to my left. The owl-masked man had been stripped of his belongings during our arrest, revealing his face. Gentle, with brilliant eyes, he might have been pleasant to look at had he not stolen my precious rock.

I sighed heavily. "I'm fine."

"Good. The carriage tipping wasn't part of the plan."

"I'd hope not." Narrowing my eyes, I scooted closer to the bars separating us. "What exactly was your plan?"

"What was yours?" He tilted his head. "Same as ours, no? Seize the Bloodstone in the one moment it's not under guard, using the cover of the show and darkness."

"I meant to merge back with the crowd, not make a scene."

"They would have searched everyone the moment they noticed it was gone."

I let my head thud against the stone wall. He was right. "I didn't exactly have much time to plan. And it was impossible besides."

"Mhm." He agreed, the edge of his mouth turning up.

"First, the red-headed madwoman, now you. What's so amusing about the life sentence coming our way?"

"It might not be." He corrected me. "Executions are rare, but it's always heretics who get them." He paused. "Stealing the Bloodstone is most definitely heresy."

Wrapping my arms around myself, I buried my head in my knees and started planning my escape. Maybe Laverna would never catch wind of my flight, and I could roam free, assuming I changed my name, dyed my hair, and wore a mask at all times.

Rolling my head to the side, I gazed into the darkness. Was there any difference between a dungeon and my previous life? Maybe being stuck here wouldn't be so bad.

The same darkness, day after day. No escape. No hope.

Shrill flute pierced my ears, dragging me from my despair. Wincing, I glared at the gaudy nobleman. "Why did the guards let you keep that?"

He pulled the flute from his mouth and looked up, but his hat shadowed his features. "Do you not appreciate the flute?"

"Not right now, no."

"Ah, it doesn't suit the atmosphere, does it?" He grinned. "Don't worry. You won't be in here much longer. Right, Eleos?"

Brow wrinkling, I stared at the green-eyed man, who rubbed his nose and rolled his eyes. "You weren't supposed to say anything, Perse."

"Oh. Oops."

"Wait," I interjected. "What do you mean?"

A thin line of light spilled down the hall as a door opened in the distance. Footsteps sounded on the stone floors. Leaning forward, I watched as a woman strode into view, a lantern held up to dispel the pall, casting fiery light over her red locks.

The woman who'd stolen the Bloodstone stood before my cell, comfortably unshackled, dressed in a stylish charcoal coat. Baffled, I furrowed my brow and stared at her in disbelief.

She leaned forward, face obscured behind a plain white mask. "Eager to get out of there?"

Usually, I came up with retorts quickly, but I found myself at a loss for words. Instead, I gaped at her, unable to understand why she walked free.

Pulling a ring of keys from her belt, the red-haired woman unlocked my cell and pulled it open before unlocking the men's cells. Shooting to my feet, I paused at my cell's threshold.

"What's going on?" I demanded.

Casually pushing the other cell doors open, the woman glanced at me. "Someone has an offer for you. A job, in exchange for freedom."

"Did they offer you the same?"

"In a sense." The red-haired woman said. "Getting caught was always part of the plan."

Still confused, I glanced between the men who'd been imprisoned with me.

Noticing my look, the red-haired woman smiled. "Eleos was worried you'd feel lonely if you were detained alone. Now, come." Returning the keys to her belt, she strode away.

I remained in my cell, watching the woman's heeled boots click on the stone, her coattail flapping behind her. While the gaudy purple noble chased after her, the man named Eleos paused beside me. "Are you coming?"

Nervously glancing around, I emerged from my cell and pursued the strange woman. "You thought I'd be lonely?" I asked, glaring at him.

"Yes," he said softly. "You've never been imprisoned before. It's not a pleasant experience."

"And how do you know that?"

Eleos hurriedly looked away. "I've been watching you for some time."

". . . why?"

"Mistress Seraphim will answer all your questions."

Seraphim. The name sounded familiar, but I couldn't place from where the memory stirred. I'd never met a woman of her stature and brilliantly colored hair before.

None of the dungeon guards stopped us. They nodded at Seraphim as she passed and watched me closely, but said nothing. We ascended the stairs to the palace's first floor and turned sharply down a hall before entering a door.

A middle-aged man sat at the desk inside, dressed in beautiful red robes gilded with gold. He raised his quill from a piece of parchment as we entered, dark eyes flicking over his guests. Rising from his seat, he ran a finger along the bookcases lining the back wall and pulled out a thick, ancient tome.

Seraphim spoke words of introduction, but I already knew who this man was from his uniform. Lord Atropos, the king's Archon. This was the man who oversaw the council and ran the country, behind closed doors.

Raking my fingers through my hair, I tried to straighten my ruined locks, but a glance at my torn gown dissuaded me from trying.

Cradling the old book, the Archon approached me. "You're talented. To have effortlessly blended in with the crowd and convinced everyone you belonged, with only a handful of words. To say nothing of that difficult forgery."

"Thanks." I cleared my throat. "I had a good teacher."

The Archon raised his eyebrows and flipped open the book. "Tell me. How much do you know about the Empty?" With a heavy thud, he dropped the book onto his desk.

I studied the book, reading the faded lines of text and smudged drawings: history Ainwir had taught me long ago. Everyone knew what the Empty was. Beyond the borders of the livable world, a great, unending void swallowed what once had been verdant. With every passing year, the border of the Empty expanded, and the land we called home shrank.

Most knew only that nothing could survive inside the Empty and to stay far from its bounds.

"A little," I answered. "Why?"

The Archon pushed the book closer to me. "Read this, then."

Approaching the desk, I scanned the passages, but I was already familiar with its contents. Life dispelled the Empty. Most people lived in the great cities, hubs of life that kept them safe. Roads were populated with countless outposts; people surrounded you even when you departed the gates, for the wilds were dangerous, pockets of stillness that invited the Empty's embrace.

A thousand years ago, the goddess Brizo sundered the eternal Empty and summoned the boat that ferried humanity from the still waters to the Merchant Isles. We lived in an endless cycle; when the Empty once again consumed the world, the Maiden would reappear and guide us to a new life, a new land.

A story the religious believed, at least.

Stepping away from the book, I turned back to the Archon. "What does this have to do with me?"

"We ride to the eastern farms," the Archon said. "This answer is easier shown than said." He nodded at Seraphim. "Fetch the horses."

WE RODE FROM the palace under the cover of darkness in an unassuming wagon driven by a lone guard. The Archon was trying to keep a low profile, but was he hiding us from the city or the royal family?

I received no chance to voice my myriad questions; we traveled in stiff silence until we passed through the eastern gates onto the sprawling fields pressed against the city as though clinging to its skirt for safety.

Seraphim sat beside me, and the noble Eleos called 'Perse' reclined opposite us, boots kicked up, hat tilted down. The Archon watched me, his dark gaze unwavering.

Eleos grabbed a lantern from the wagon floor and struck a fire inside, handing it to me before lighting his own. Holding the flame up to pierce the night, I searched the fields for what we'd come here to see.

Wheat waved under a gentle breeze, windmills creaked against the night, and farmhouses stood silent, their lights doused. Something churned in my heart, as a sense of unease mixed with aching nostalgia. I pressed a hand to my chest, bewildered by the strange sensation that grew stronger with each passing minute.

Disturbed by the discomfort, I flinched and looked down. The night seemed to darken around me, as though all stars had been doused.

The wagon abruptly halted; the horse drawing it reared and refused to go any further.

"There," the Archon announced.

Looking up, I gasped when I saw it.

An abyss consumed the fields before us, a sphere of darkness so deep the night seemed bright by comparison. A thin red halo surrounded the void, shimmering like freshly drawn blood. Where once had been sprawling farmlands, now a gorge plunged into the depths of the earth, where still waters rested deep below the surface.

This was the Empty. I'd seen it once before.

"How. . .?" I stuttered. "But the Empty cannot appear near cities."

"No. It should not." The Archon agreed, leaning forward. "Our time runs short. If the Empty can appear within the capital, it can appear anywhere. It is only a matter of time before it consumes us."

Swallowing, I stared into the empty void, a great sphere of nothing where life had once been. "But the Maiden Brizo will appear, right?" I glanced at Eleos. "She's supposed to rescue us."

"Should we trust that?" Eleos said. "Should we wait for her to arrive, only to realize with our last gasp she had never been real?"

"The Bloodstone is proof she's real, isn't it?"

Seraphim reached into her pocket and produced the precious relic. It glowed red beneath the fire of her lantern. "Or it's just a rock. And, as you said, it's yours, no?" She tossed it to me, and I caught it clumsily.

Running a thumb over its smooth surface, I stared at the gem that promised me freedom, hardly able to believe it was in my hands.

"You said a job for freedom." I gestured to the abyss. "What am I supposed to do about that?"

Eleos answered calmly. "If there is a means to stop the Empty's spread, we are to find it."

"This is Seraphim's venture," the Archon said. "When *this* appeared, she convinced me to aid her."

"Then what was the point of the heist?" I spluttered. "To steal a stone you think does nothing?"

The Archon spoke up. "Even I cannot access the Maiden's Bloodstone. Try as I might, I could find no way to convince the grand clergy to allow me into the vault without arousing their suspicions. Lady Seraphim suggested stealing it, allowing her time to swap it with a convincing fake."

"Funny, hm?" Seraphim smirked. "That you were trying to steal it, too."

Rolling my tongue in my mouth, I considered their words. Everyone feared the Empty, feared it would consume us. Suggesting that no salvation would come meant decrying the goddess and committing heresy. A crime that would see the Archon swiftly removed from his station.

"Surely the city knows." I bounced in my seat anxiously. "You can't hide something of this magnitude."

"Oh, but they're trying," the Archon crossed his legs. "The people have been evacuated and asked for silence until the council finds the best way to break the news. But rumors already stir."

"Then, convincing the clergy that action needs to be taken wouldn't be so hard."

Eleos laughed quietly. "You've never dealt with the clergy if you think anything less than the end of the world would make them change their minds. The Maiden will come. So it has been taught for a thousand years."

Sitting back, I rubbed my eyes. I hadn't given much thought to the Empty, not when the dangers of the city streets and the weight of debt occupied my every day.

"Seraphim and I have entered into an accord." The Archon folded his hands. "She begged my aid. In exchange for her efforts, I agreed to clear her records and those of anyone who aids her. I have the king's confidence, though he asked me to keep our alliance secret."

I turned to Seraphim. "This was your idea?"

"I believe I've found a way to save us." She said, "I may be the only one who knows of it."

"Why do you want my help?" I asked. "All I can do is talk."

"That's exactly what I need." Seraphim patted the back of the driver's seat. "But there'll be time aplenty to apprise you of the details. Are you in or not?"

Heeding her order, the guard driving the wagon turned us around, and we slowly rolled back toward the city.

"I'm in debt to the Guild," I said. "They won't take kindly to me leaving."

The nobleman named Perse finally spoke up. "We know. World-ending chaos is their business," he pointed to Seraphim and Eleos, "but the underside of civilization is mine. I can help you avoid them."

I tried to examine his shadowed face to no avail. He was a criminal, that much I knew. Maybe he could help me.

"Why trust us?" I turned to the Archon. "We're wanted men—setting us loose only promises we'll flee the first chance we get."

"Seraphim won't let you," The Archon's hand curled on his lap. "I said this was her venture, did I not? Abandon your duty, and she'll see your head removed from your shoulders."

Casting the red-haired woman a sideways glance, I recalled her flaming scythe and effortless magic.

"Of course," he waved a hand, "you'll be handsomely compensated, should you succeed."

"And, if I say no," I said slowly, "I return to my cell?"

"Mhm." Seraphim nodded.

"The clergy will realize their Bloodstone is fake," I said.

"Doubtless," the Archon agreed. "You should leave well before they do."

Sighing, I gazed into the Empty, into its still waters, writhing under the discomfort of the mixed sensations pulsing in my breast. There was no decision to be made here. Only one option existed.

"Fine," I said. "I'll go."

FOUR

THE ARCHON'S SECRET WAGON RETURNED to the palace, and we were hastily ushered out. There was no time to dawdle—a manhunt would begin once the fake Bloodstone was discovered.

Equipped only with bags of supplies and the clothes on our backs, we slipped out in the thick of night and made for a hidden exit that Ainwir had shown me years ago.

I felt silly, fleeing through dark streets wearing a noble's fanciful toga, my flower mask hanging around my neck. Four people composed our merry band: myself, Eleos, Seraphim, and Perse.

We were neither priests nor nobles, but criminals escaping our sentence by pursuing a fool's errand.

Following a channel that flowed to the city's northwestern edge, I guided us toward a large grate at the base of the walls, where refuse from the sewer trickled into the surrounding marshlands. It wouldn't be pleasant, but this was the only exit where guards did not keep rapt watch over the roads.

Though the bars of the grate were too close together for a person to slip through, one in the center was loose. Finding the rusted pole, I dragged it out of place and pushed it aside, creating a gap just wide enough to shimmy through.

I allowed the others to go first, taking one last glance at the city lights before squeezing through. My sandals sank into the marsh, soaking me to my knees.

Grimacing as the ends of my dress clung to my legs, I pulled up my skirt and trudged forward.

Everything had happened so fast. I wanted to lie down and process the abrupt change, not wander through the wilderness.

The four of us remained silent until nothing but willows and damp soil surrounded us. The man in the purple doublet fell into step with me, lifting his low-brimmed hat to reveal part of his face: affable, with a nose that curved upward at the tip. He was far paler than anyone I'd met, with a mouth curled in a permanent smile, though his hat concealed his hair and eyes.

"Apologies for the lack of introductions," he said, bowing like a stage actor. "I'm Percy. Pleasure to have you on the team, lady. . .?"

Perse must've been his nickname. Staring at his hand, I considered ignoring it. No sense being rude, I supposed. Shaking his hand, I narrowed my eyes. "Aethra. How do you people know who I am?"

Seraphim spoke without turning around. "Chance, really. I need someone skilled at dealing with nobles, and the Guild recommended you."

"So you know that I'm-"

"A con woman?" Eleos finished. "Yes. That's just what we need."

"What for?" I asked, staring at Seraphim's back.

"We'll go over the plan later," she called. "By a fire with good wine."

"Fair enough," I agreed, glancing between everyone. Much could be gleaned about a person from a cursory glance.

Eleos wore a blue scarf and white cape: the colors of the clergy, though he lacked their metallic insignia. He seemed so *soft*, a typical pretty boy I might cast as the shining prince in a play, but his hands were calloused. A frequent traveler?

Seraphim looked to be in her forties, a scar rising from her collar to caress her neck. How many more hid behind the surface?

Percy seemed like a performer; he walked with a lively jaunt, had a permanent grin etched on his face, and dressed like a blindingly colorful beacon meant to light our way.

Eleos watched me with sharp eyes. "Trying to figure out what we were thrown in the dungeons for?"

"Yes," I admitted. "The Archon implied you were already criminals."

He chuckled. "Seraphim and I had been detained for questioning when the Archon recruited us. Percy happened to be in the neighboring cell."

I raised an eyebrow at Percy, who turned several shades of scarlet. Whatever he'd done to earn a dungeon cell must have been terribly embarrassing.

"Well, spill it," I said. "What did you-"

"Sh." Eleos grabbed me and dragged me behind a tree.

The distinctive sound of horses forging through water caught my ear, and I chanced a glance around the willow to see a unit of men, torches glowing in the night, riding through fog settled on the marsh's low waters.

I snapped my head back around cover. "They're already looking for us?"

"Hm." Eleos seemed unbothered. "Two hours earlier than I expected."

"We'll never outpace them on foot," I hissed.

"Luckily, we don't have to," Eleos whispered back. "Come. Not much further."

Darting out from behind cover, we fled deeper into the marsh, listening intently for activity. Wandering west would lead us toward the world's borders and into the Empty. We'd have to wind back around to the main road, where the guards would await us.

A knoll rose from the marsh in the center of a copse, granting respite from the muck. Three horses gathered around a rather unhappy-looking older man.

Seraphim tossed the man a sack of coins. "Thank you. Take care heading back."

The old man grunted, stuffing the sack into his pack. His eyes skimmed over us before he trudged through the marsh. "You'll never hear from me again." He promised.

"Percy," Seraphim ordered. "Lay a false trail. Make them think we're heading east."

"Must I? In my finest?"

His finest? I shuddered to think what the rest of his wardrobe looked like.

Seraphim slapped his back, pushing him in the direction the soldiers had ridden. "You two. C'mere."

Resigned to his fate, Percy grabbed his horse and led it away. I watched him go, startled by a bundle of rags that struck my chest. Catching it clumsily, I turned the tattered thing over, realizing it was a patchwork bag.

"Carry that," Seraphim ordered. "Make yourself useful."

"I'm good at nothing if not being useful," I murmured.

Satisfied, she turned around and grabbed a horse, tightening its saddle bags. Glancing between the horses, I counted them again. Only two remained.

"Hm." Seraphim glanced at me with a smirk. "Seems our man miscounted. I asked for four steeds. You'll have to ride with Eleos."

Wandering over to the green-eyed man, I tugged on the knapsack's strings. "What's in this?"

"I'm, ah, not sure," Eleos admitted, untying a pretty red mare. "Percy's effects, most likely."

As I pulled the bag open to peer inside, he grabbed the strings and fastened them closed.

"Better not to look, in that case," he warned.

"Well, now I'm curious," I said, throwing the pack around my shoulder.

An enormous horse dappled with spots of white and brown sloshed through the muck to Eleos' side. I swallowed, trying to figure out how I would mount it. Ainwir had always hailed carriages. I had never ridden a horse by myself before.

Eleos always knew what I was thinking. "Don't worry," he said, grabbing the reins. "I'm experienced. You'll be safe with me."

"If you say so." I chewed my lip nervously as he knelt and made a step out of his knitted hands. Hesitating, I cautiously stepped up and floundered when he boosted me. Grabbing the saddle, I gracelessly pulled myself onto its back.

Mounting effortlessly, Eleos sat in front of me, glancing back to ensure I hadn't fallen off. "Hold on tight. You'll get the hang of it."

Sloshing water drew my attention east, as Percy rode back to the knoll. "Our pursuers have been taken care of," he announced. "If they don't hear *that*, they're idiots who won't catch us anyway."

"Hear what?" I asked, realizing I hadn't given Seraphim's order to 'leave a false trail' much thought.

"Magic, my dear." Percy smiled.

"Let's go," Seraphim said, riding north.

The dappled horse took off, and I lunged forward, grabbing Eleos's waist tightly as the horse bucked back and forth, lifting its hooves to escape the piles of mud.

The scholarly-looking man felt *firmer* than expected. Though his build was lithe, I could feel taut muscles in his arms and core. His brown hair brushed against my neck, luxuriously soft and smelling of parchment and sandalwood. An image nestled in my head of an armchair resting before the fire, warm and inviting.

Eleos tilted his head to look at me. "Not all scholars are pudgy old men."

"What?" I asked, surprised.

"Nothing," he said, turning around.

Had he read my mind? Or had my shock been apparent? Gods, had I felt up his abs like a perverted wench?

Nuzzling my face into his scarf, I blocked my view of both the horse and its rider. "The Bloodstone. Do we need it for something?"

"Yes," Eleos answered. "Supposedly, it emanates a sacred aura that protects one from the atrophying effects of the Empty."

"Has that been tested?"

"Of course not. The stone would be lost forever if it failed."

"Oh, good," I mumbled, trying not to think about it. Seraphim said she would explain everything when we stopped. Good enough for me.

Silence consumed the marsh save for the sound of crickets and the sloshing of hooves. My heart started beating faster as fear set in. Pockets of the Empty could appear anywhere in the wilderness. I'd seen one as a child. A shadow within a shadow, the world itself warping as it was torn away and turned to dust. It had spread, like hands reaching for me, trying to pull me in.

Staring over Eleos' shoulder, I watched the woman named Seraphim warily. She was a chthonic mage. Abyss-cursed, some called them. Those who used their blood and the blood of others—life itself—to fuel dangerous spells.

A deadly game, when death beget the end of the world.

"Calm down," Eleos said softly, "We'll be alright."

Were my hands trembling? Tightening my grip, I clung to him like a frightened child, though I probably should have done the opposite.

"Percy is a mage, too." He said. "We aren't helpless."

That gaudy charlatan could use magic, too? Three kinds of magic existed, each gifted by one of the gods—a rare blessing few obtained. Ainwir had been a mage, but he'd never told me which kind.

First, there were the psyches, born of Psythos, the goddess who governed and endowed humanity with their emotions. They could read minds, and alter emotions.

Then there were muses, disciples of Callesis, the god of luck, who drew magic from art into countless forms. I'd never met one and understood little of their talents.

Last were the chthonics, chosen by Haimyx, he who imbued the world with life and guided us after death into the great continent beyond the Empty.

Only the Maiden Brizo did not gift her magic to mortals. Perhaps she thought her Bloodstone enough. The other gods bestowed magic upon extraordinary individuals who had endured great struggles.

Small wonder I hadn't received the gods' blessing.

Exhausted, I counted the minutes as we rode deeper into the wilds, skirting the road to avoid the guards. The water level slowly lowered as we drew closer to the wetland's edge. We crested a high hill, where Seraphim abruptly stopped and slid off her horse.

"I think we're safe here," she said. "Get a fire started. We'll rest a while."

I glanced around the soaked wetlands. "Where are we going to find dry wood?"

"We won't," Eleos said, dismounting. "I packed some." He stepped away, but paused, eyeing me worriedly. "Do you need help off?"

Leaning left, I measured the distance to the ground. Swallowing, I smiled at him. "If you wouldn't mind."

"Slide off." He beckoned. "I'll catch you."

Grabbing the saddle for dear life, I slowly swung one leg over and held my breath before letting myself slip off. Eleos grabbed my waist and gingerly set me down on the damp soil.

"See?" He said. "Not so bad, right?" Turning around, he pulled a sack of dry twigs from his saddlebags and dumped them into my arms. "Take these to the fire."

I had been about to laud him for being a gentleman, but I quickly rescinded the thought. Carrying my pile to where Seraphim set up a stack of fat wood, I dropped them beside her before joining Eleos in his hunt for more kindling.

Picking up a twig and tossing it aside, I wiped my hands off on my upper arms. "So you're a priest?"

"No." Eleos knelt to inspect a broken branch. "Goddess, *no*. I'm a scholar."

"But you wear the scarf."

"It's comfortable."

"Did you steal it?"

He released a short laugh and met my eye. "Do I look like the kind to rob a poor, frail elder?"

"Looks can be deceiving." I shrugged. "I suppose I should thank you. For pulling me into the carriage."

"Seraphim wanted to see how you'd fare by yourself. Considering the guards weren't in on our scheme, I worried you'd be killed." He snatched up a broken stick. "Found one."

"Did she want to test me? See if I was good enough to recruit?"

"Mhm." His eyes drifted away, distracted.

I still hadn't learned anything about him. "Scholar, hm?" I tried again. "What of?"

"The Empty."

"There aren't any knowledge houses dedicated to the Empty."

"That's true." Eleos agreed, dropping a final stick into my arms. "It's considered heresy, after all, to imply the Maiden's protection is not enough."

"Is that your crime?" I tried. "Heresy?"

"How many crimes do you intend to accuse me of tonight?"

"Can you really be offended? I already know you were tossed in the dungeons for *something*."

"And here I thought Guild members didn't judge." Grabbing a final stick, Eleos returned to Seraphim's growing fire.

The heat was welcome. Twisting, I tried to dry my wet skirt by the flames. "Eleos," I said, "How long were you watching me for?"

"Not long." He answered, tending the flames. "A couple of weeks to assess your skills."

Narrowing my eyes, I checked for signs he was lying, but found none. How had he known I feared being thrown in the dungeons? I'd never told anyone before. Just another reason not to trust these people.

Wrapping my arms around myself, I glanced at Seraphim's coat pocket, wondering if I could simply pickpocket the Bloodstone and return it to Laverna.

What had the Guild master wanted it for, anyway?

Behind her mask, Seraphim's eyes were sharp and honed. She'd been through much, I could tell. Ainwir had the same look about him.

Thieves with class, he'd called us. No more evil than nobles who took everything from the poor.

My mouth twisted in disgust. Why did I keep thinking about the man fondly? The bastard was the sole reason I was in this situation.

A tickle crept up my arm, like a spider climbing to my neck. Running my fingernails up my bare shoulders, I whirled around, searching for an insect, but nothing was there.

The discomfort rose through my spine, caressing my head, rising into a pressure that felt like my eyes would be pushed from their sockets. Grimacing, I doubled over as a cacophonous sensation bloomed in my heart.

Overwhelming unease and aching nostalgia.

A horrible sound followed.

Or maybe it was the lack of sound that was most frightening. Like all life had been suddenly snuffed out.

I'd felt this in the farmlands. Panicked, I spun around to see a tiny bead discoloring the marsh, hovering in the air between the willows. Black as night, yet utterly colorless, it slowly grew in size, warping the world around it.

Without warning, it ripped open, tearing the air like a great maw, peering down into an utterly still sea beneath a dead sky.

I had seen a man enter the Empty. At first, it seemed like he would simply tumble into its depths. But he had turned to dust before his feet had departed the ground.

The maw spread, rising into the sky, reaching east and west, and carving deep into the ground. A faint blood-tinged aura bloomed around its edges.

"Again?" Eleos' voice was surprisingly even. "So close to the city?"

"Shit!" Percy cursed, scrambling toward his horse.

Grabbing my wrist, Eleos tossed me onto our horse, and I desperately grabbed the saddle and hoisted myself up. Climbing up behind me, Eleos slammed his heels into the horse's flank.

It didn't require much coaxing. Snorting, the mare bolted, tearing through the marshlands, kicking up water like waves as the world behind us was pulled into the void and disappeared.

FIVE

POCKETS OF THE EMPTY APPEARED all over the world, creating impassable seas and encroaching on what livable land remained. But the most terrifying thing about them was the lack of warning.

No tremors shook the earth. You did not feel the ground heave beneath your feet before it collapsed.

One minute, the normal world was there, and the next, it was simply *gone*.

Eleos leaned forward, pressing his legs against mine to hold me steady in the saddle as our horse flew through knee-high water. Ducking my head, I glanced behind us, watching the Empty swallow the marshlands. Blue water evaporated as the void reached it, and trees disintegrated into debris on the wind. A black line cleaved through the marsh, opening a terrible canyon that gazed upon a silent sea.

A still sea, disturbed not by the slightest ripple.

Our horse screamed, throwing itself into a desperate sprint. It bucked, almost throwing me from the saddle. Grabbing its mane, I clung on for dear life.

"The Bloodstone!" I shouted into the horse's neck.

"Mistress Seraphim has it," Eleos said.

How did he sound so *calm*?

Staring past the wildly flying mane, I searched for the other woman. I caught a glimpse of a black horse darting between two willows, kicking up water as it leapt over a fallen log. A red braid whipped in the breeze and vanished into the trees.

Glancing back, I noticed the consuming void had slowed its pace. The distance between us and the drop off into the dead waters had grown.

Maybe we wouldn't need to test the Bloodstone after all. Relieved, I tried to sit back up.

That proved a horrific mistake.

An inhuman hiss reverberated across the marsh, somewhere to our left. Frightened, the horse reared violently, scrambling right to escape the threat. One of my boots left the stirrups in the chaos, and I felt myself slipping.

Shit!

Water enveloped me as I fell into the marsh, soaking my clothes and hair. Gasping, I fought against the brackish drink, trying to claw my way to my feet.

The dappled mare bolted into the distance and vanished behind the trees. There went my ride.

The hiss sounded again, this time right beside me. I turned to see hollow, empty eyes boring into me before a claw dug into my shoulder, tearing through my dress and drawing blood.

Shrieking, I threw myself in the opposite direction, managing to break free. Grabbing my bleeding arm, I stared in horror at my attacker.

It almost appeared human. Stringy hair clung to a gaunt face set with eyes the same color as the still sea. Tattered remains of clothing hung on its body, flowing unnaturally as though suspended underwater.

A keres. Lost souls who fell into the abyss and now existed solely to drag others to their doom. I had assumed them no more than old maids' tales used to frighten children into staying within the bounds of the city.

Every bone in my body screamed for me to run. But I froze.

A second keres emerged from the trees behind me and slammed into my back. Claws hooked around my wrist and shoulders, constricting me against its frail, wet body.

Struggling to escape, I flailed against my captors. My heart pounded in my chest, feeling like it might crawl up my throat and escape. The keres' claws dug deeper, ripping through my skin.

Nothing would have stopped them from dragging their clawed hands through my neck or driving them into my heart. But they didn't try to kill me. They stood still, holding me in place as the edge of the Empty approached.

My fear vanished as I gazed into the still sea. A sense of inevitability fell over me. My life had never been kind, never been worth anything. What better end than to vanish and be forgotten by the world?

The blood-red halo surrounding the infinite darkness covered my view of the sky, bathing me in the light of death.

Someone I didn't want to remember flooded my mind. Pain ripped through my shoulder, and a splash of red trickled past my vision.

Suddenly, it wasn't about me, but the man I needed to see again. Red flashed around my eyes, like dancing lights in swirling water.

Aching nostalgia ripped through my breast, like a well of light begging to be grasped. Reaching for it, I extended my hand, willing the Empty to stop, or perhaps beckoning for it to come.

I winced, waiting for the abyss to sweep over me. But the Empty halted its advance.

Claws retracted from my skin as the keres released me. They moved like someone walking underwater, slinking past the Empty's threshold into the canyon of still water, falling over its edge and disappearing into the dark, dead sea.

Gasping, I fell backwards, landing in the murk. If I took *one* step forward, I would tumble down a fathomless canyon into the world from which no one returned.

Someone raced through the swamp toward me, but I didn't register their presence until a bright red light flooded into my eyes. Wincing, I saw Eleos kneel beside me, the glowing Bloodstone clutched in his hand.

So that was why the Empty had suddenly ceased spreading. The thing worked, after all.

I burst out laughing, an unhinged noise one might expect from a man who'd been locked in the dungeons for years.

Eleos' expression had finally changed from a calm half-smile. His sage-green eyes were wide, filled with either fear or wonder. Maybe both. Without speaking, he grabbed my arm and helped me up, guiding me away from the cliff where once the marsh had been.

With every step we took from the Empty, the Bloodstone faded until it glowed no longer.

Three horses cantered nervously in place atop a nearby hill. Seraphim leaned forward on her saddle. "It worked!"

"I don't. . ." Eleos shook his head. His eyes snapped into clarity, and he started. "You're injured." He exclaimed, as though he'd only just noticed my wounds.

Releasing me, he grabbed one of his saddlebags and tore it open.

"Can it wait?" Percy hissed nervously. "Until we put some more space between us and *death*?"

Grimacing, Eleos gave my wounds a cursory glance before deciding I was fine, for now. Dazed, I allowed him to help me onto the saddle, and he sat behind me.

Blood streamed down my white gown, though pain hadn't set in. Breathing heavily, I grabbed Eleos' sleeve when he wrapped his hand around my waist, clinging to him for dear life.

Glancing back, I tried to see what became of the keres, but they were simply gone. Our horses flew forward into the wetlands until eventually the great black hole with the red halo vanished from sight.

Percy herded us like sheep. Though calm starlight and buzzing swamp were all I could see, he urged us on, terrified the Empty would resume its pursuit.

My vision started blurring when Seraphim finally ordered us to stop. She jogged over, helping me dismount and setting me on the ground.

Eleos quickly tended to me, finding the puncture wounds and packing them to halt the bleeding.

Seraphim paced before us. "Did I see that correctly? The stone worked?"

Frazzled, the scholar looked up. "Y-yes. It must have," he stuttered, wrapping my shoulder tightly.

I winced as the bandage squeezed the gash. "That should do for now." He said. "I would rather stitch you up somewhere. . . *cleaner*." Taking my hand, he gently helped me to my feet.

The world spun. Maybe it was blood loss or shock; I couldn't tell. I took one step through the brackish mud and fell against something soft.

A bed, maybe? No, too much to hope for. But if death had removed the wretched smell rising from the marsh, I welcomed the darkness with open arms.

I ROUSED FROM a nightmare, but couldn't remember it upon waking.

I sat bolt upright, panting. Pain flared through my arm, and I flinched, remembering claws digging into my shoulder as I gazed into the abyss.

The marsh was gone. Dry grass surrounded my bedroll, not muddy water. A dappled mare grazed nearby, and a pair of boots approached.

Still groggy, I looked up to see an entire woman attached to the boots. Red hair swung down her back in a thick braid. Faint lines framed her pale-blue eyes.

"There she is." Seraphim knelt beside me. "Took long enough."

Everything came back to me at once—the Empty, the dead sea, the keres, and the glowing stone.

"You know," I pointed out. "I'm already proving I won't be much help on this quest."

"Nonsense. I think there's plenty of use in keeping you around." She pulled a waterskin from her belt and offered it. "You'll heal just fine. Eleos is brilliant. I'd trust him if he told me I was dead and just hadn't realized it yet."

My arm protested as I lifted the waterskin and drank. "I've never met a healer who was also a criminal."

"Eleos is talented in many ways." Seraphim stood. "Our Bloodstone works. Seems our faith in the Maiden will pay off."

"I guess I shouldn't have skipped church." I grimaced, dragging myself to my feet. "Where are we?"

"Halfway to the Isthmus trade post." Seraphim folded her arms, watching me as I took a few shaky steps. "You're in debt, right?"

"Yes. I thought you already knew everything about me."

"I don't know the details." Seraphim narrowed her eyes. "Did you cross the Guild?"

No sense pretending otherwise. ". . . in a sense."

"Sounds like you need coin, then." Seraphim dropped her arms. "If we succeed, the law will look the other way, but the

Guild won't forget. There'll be coin in this for you. Something to raise your spirits."

"Mm." I sat back down. "The Archon mentioned that. He's offering a lot—this job must be more dangerous than you've implied."

"If all goes to plan, we'll be doing much worse than brushing the edge of the abyss. We'll be diving into its source."

Source? Did the Empty *have* a source?

As if reading my mind, Eleos walked up behind me and answered. "Supposedly, it's in Duath Nun. A river leads into the original sea from which all pockets of the abyss are born."

"Oh," I pressed a hand to my aching head. "But Duath Nun's-"

"Forbidden." Eleos finished my sentence.

Rubbing my eyes, I remembered what Ainwir had taught me about the country of Duath Nun: almost nothing. Centuries ago, it had sealed itself away, threatening death to any foreigners who trespassed.

A lethal strait separated our two countries, encouraging the divide. My eyes darted around, observing Seraphim, before lingering on Eleos. These people wanted to invade a country that would stick our heads on pikes?

"We don't know that," Eleos said. "Duath Nun could be perfectly civilized. We haven't spoken to them in centuries."

I hadn't voiced my thoughts aloud. Rearing back, I stared into his green eyes and studied his smug half-smile. "Oh, no. You're a *psyche.*"

His smile widened, but he did not answer.

Great. He'd been reading my mind since the moment we met. No wonder he'd figured out everything about me; nobody had told him I'd never been imprisoned—he'd read my fear.

"Is the lady awake?" Percy's cheerful voice ascended the hill where the others were camped. "And she looks no worse for wear."

Rolling his neck, he yanked off his low-brimmed hat. I didn't mean to gape at him, but I couldn't help it.

Not one wrinkle marred his face, but shock-white hair brushed against his skin. Shadowed by his hat, I hadn't noticed his pale gray eyes and pallid skin.

But he couldn't have been more than thirty. Only those who'd suffered prolonged exposure to the Empty had their features warped, drained of color. Anyone who showed their face in public looking like that would be driven out of town, for fear of them spreading their curse.

Percy noticed my stare, but didn't seem to mind. "I say we get going before the world tries to eat us again."

"Agreed." Seraphim marched back to her horse. "Up you go, girly. An inn room's not far."

A hand brushed my arm. Staring ahead, I avoided Eleos' gaze. Ainwir had taught me how to block out psyches, but it required a great deal of concentration—something I lacked with a throbbing arm and a heavy head.

"Seraphim meant what she said," Eleos promised. "It's quite a sum she's promised us. I haven't decided how to spend my lavish retirement yet."

"You're getting paid, too?"

"And Percy."

Seraphim flashed me a grin as she swung over her horse's saddle.

A lavish retirement, eh? I closed my eyes, imagining presenting Laverna with the absurd sum I owed her. More likely, she'd slit my throat or sell me to a brothel for failing the job.

"Or," Eleos suggested. "They'll push more debt on your head and keep you in servitude for as long as you're useful."

"Stop that." I hissed.

"Sorry." Eleos glanced away. "Ready?"

"Yes," I said reluctantly, holding back a groan as he boosted me back onto the saddle. Still exhausted, I wobbled back and forth until he sat behind me. Appearances be damned. I slumped against his chest, unwilling to spend the hours bent over the horse's neck.

Wrapping an arm around my waist, Eleos pressed his legs against mine, securing me against him. Warmth from his body enveloped me, warding off the chill from my soaked clothes. Heat slowly trickled to my cheeks, and I turned a bright shade of red. Earlier, I'd dwelt on his pleasant scent and surprising musculature.

Oh. . . he'd read all those thoughts, too.

"I was flattered," Eleos said, unhelpfully.

Closing my eyes, I reminded myself to guard my thoughts more carefully, going forward.

"I do a lot of traveling," Eleos added, ordering the horse into a trot. "Running across rooftops, fleeing the guards. Sometimes stealing from temples or libraries."

"So that's why you're built like a thief," I muttered.

"I don't consider myself a thief." He said. "Had they less stringent rules, I'd simply borrow what I need, but-"

"But study of the Empty is forbidden." I finished his sentence.

"Are you a psyche?" He teased.

As the horses trotted across the grasslands, I stared over my shoulder, remembering my brush with death.

I'd met my master, like that. A pocket of the Empty had appeared beside me while I was playing in the woods, alone. Ainwir had appeared from nowhere, rushed to my side, and by the goddess's grace or sheer luck, the all-consuming void had halted in its tracks, sparing our lives.

Twice now, the Empty had stopped before me while I felt aching nostalgia in my breast and tugged upon it. Had that been a coincidence?

"It wasn't," Eleos said. "I saw you, the way your blood bent around the edges of the chasm. You were *channeling*."

SIX

I SAT ON A BENCH, drinking in the sight of life. Outposts were always crowded with travelers and merchants. The awning above my head beat away the glare of the sun and blocked my view of the cottages clustered down the dirt path.

A pack mule grazed beside me, tail swishing aside buzzing gnats. Holding out a hand, I focused on the creature.

Eleos claimed I'd channeled while staring into the void—into my death. Nothing sparked to life in my heart, nor did any magic swirl about my fingertips. I felt nothing.

What was the odd scholar on about? The Empty halted its advance because of the Maiden's Bloodstone, just as promised.

Tonight was my last chance to escape these lunatics. If I wanted to steal the Bloodstone from Seraphim, finding a caravan to ride back to Ikaria would be simple. I could return the stone to Laverna, pay off my debt, and run free. Doubtless, Seraphim would send word of my betrayal to the Archon, and my face would be plastered across city walls, but disguises were my forte.

Removing the sack of coins from my belt, I shook it, feeling its weight.

Fifty thousand Heschian pieces: that was my debt to the Guild. This sack held only two hundred. An amount that would make a peasant fall on his knees in prayer, to be sure. . .

I toyed with the coin purse's strings. If Seraphim paid me well for this mission, I could carve out a comfortable life for myself—assuming the Guild didn't come for my head.

Laying my head in my hands, I stared at the ground. Which was the best option?

"Let me guess," Eleos's even voice pulled me from my thoughts. "You think we stole that gold?" He sauntered over, wearing a smug little half-smile, and dropped a bundle onto my lap.

"I never said that." I shoved the coin purse back onto my belt and inspected the bundle. "What's this?"

"Clothes." He glanced at my bandaged arm. "Your current attire is conspicuous and tattered." Stretching, he sat beside me. "If you have questions, Lady Aethra, I'll be happy to answer them."

"Lady?"

Eleos ignored the inquiry. "Seraphim will go over the plan tomorrow morning, but she tends to leave out details."

"Important details, like. . ." I tilted my head. "Who knows about us? Is the king's council in on it? What about the city lords?"

"They don't know." He sat forward. "Nobility and clergy are inextricably tied. Most would not risk heresy for two reasons: to avoid sentencing, and so they won't have to face the unthinkable."

I paused to consider his words. Our mission, the appearance of the Empty so close to the capital. . . it meant the end days were closer than previously believed.

"We should keep a low profile, then." I decided, looking Eleos up and down.

He dressed like a rich man. Embroidered cuffs, a well-tailored coat. But he still wore the pale blue scarf of the clergy.

"Are you sure you aren't a priest?" I asked.

"Very sure." He stood. "I found lodgings for the night. They have decent baths, too." Offering a hand, he helped me to my feet.

A few people cast interested glances at my torn, bloody garb. Looking past them, I scanned the walls for wanted posters, lest the guard had arrived ahead of us. None appeared.

I had fond memories of this outpost. Ainwir and I had passed through often, traveling between Ikaria and Serifos whenever we started gaining unwanted attention from guards and cheated customers.

This place was cute, for a tiny hamlet tucked between enormous swathes of the Empty. Colored banners hung from roof sills and even stretched to the tops of the watch towers, shading fields of reeds growing from the damp soil.

"Here we are." Eleos stopped before an ancient stone building, its foundation sunk in the mud. "Ah. One more thing." He pressed a wrapped parcel into my hand.

The scent of sandalwood penetrated the paper. "Soap?" I chuckled.

"We may be criminals," He tutted, "But we aren't classless." Holding the door open, he beckoned me inside.

Seraphim sat at a table, boots kicked up next to a glass of wine. "Ready to be apprised of all the details?"

"Assuming you'll answer questions about yourself, yes," I answered.

"Why wouldn't I?" Seraphim shooed me away. "We can talk after you've had a bath and slept in a proper bed." Grabbing her wine, she leaned forward. "You smell like a swamp."

"So do you."

"Yes, but I didn't fall in." Raising her glass, Seraphim stared at me with twinkling eyes.

The woman had a point. Suddenly horrified, I quickly excused myself.

The baths called.

I REMEMBERED MY first real bath as if it had happened yesterday. Master Ainwir had beckoned me into a more richly decorated washroom than I'd ever seen, helped me fill the tub, and ordered me to relax.

Before that, all my baths had been taken by jumping into a river channel or by splashing my face in a fountain when nobody was looking. With that small gesture, Ainwir had won my trust.

Kindness was how con men stole your heart just before tearing it out.

Opening my eyes, I swished a hand through the bath water; it was getting cold. Had I drifted off? The poor serving boy had refilled my bath at least twice; scrubbing off the caked-on mud had been a battle in itself.

Stepping out of the bath, I unwrapped the parcel of clothing Eleos had left on the counter: a simple white toga with a golden sash. Had he read my mind and learned I preferred to be invisible?

Raking my fingers through my hair, I shook my head. Brunette curls that had never lain straight in all my life tumbled over my shoulder, dampening the gown.

Night had long since fallen. The others had probably turned in. Cracking the door open, I peered out, finding only a quiet, dim hall. Tying my hair into a bun, I stepped into the common room, but Seraphim was no longer sitting at her table.

Only a dim light spilled from the hearth, illuminating a single guest still finishing his bowl of stew. I had the night to myself. Finding the inn's back door, I stepped out into the yard.

Feeling the grass beneath my bare feet, I touched the bandages on my arm.

Chthonic mages wielded magic through blood. Through *life*. Whether their own or another's, they were harmless without it.

Supposedly, what effects they could shape from blood depended on the person. Ainwir claimed to have met someone who turned blood into sunlight. Seraphim had shaped it into solid flame.

Had my blood controlled the Empty?

Grimacing, I tugged my bandages off. Magic was bestowed upon those who experienced something extraordinary. And whatever they received would match their personality.

Reckless souls who lived violent lives became chthonic mages. Artful souls brimming with creativity became muses. And those with great empathy became psyches.

I was neither remarkable nor reckless. I'd been taught a valuable lesson by Ainwir: talk your way out of a fight. Failing that, run for your life. But never face battle if another option presented itself.

His lessons had kept me alive to date. Why would Haimyx bestow chthonic magic upon *me*?

Whimpering, I pulled my knife from my belt and stared at the stitches Eleos had carefully closed my wounds with. Holding the knife to my shoulder, I squeezed my eyes shut, hesitating.

"Fuck it," I murmured, slicing the threads apart and digging the knife into the claw-mark, reopening the gash.

Cursing, I pressed my hand to the bloody laceration and pulled it away only when scarlet coated my palm. Holding up shaking fingers, I tried to do. . .

Something. I searched for what I'd felt before—the surge of emotions roiling in my breast: nostalgia and unease.

Lowering my hand, I gasped. Was I a madwoman? What if I tore open a rift to the Empty and killed everyone in this town, myself included?

Curling my hand into a fist, I hastily lowered it. An amused voice spoke in the silence.

"You're perhaps the most timid chthonic mage I've ever seen." Eleos stepped out of the door frame and approached me. "I can't claim to be an expert on chthonics, but I've always assumed using blood magic requires. . . reckless abandon."

"Maybe it does." Pressing my hand to my arm, I tried to halt the flow of blood.

"According to every record we have," Eleos looked up at the stars, "The Maiden Brizo could enter pockets of the Empty safely, and halt its advance. And I needn't lecture you on how she sundered it in twain."

"You think that's what I did?"

"Maybe." His brow wrinkled. "Perhaps I got overexcited. It's a theory, at best."

"Hm." I flinched as blood seeped between my fingers. "I'm not sure I'd trust records claiming to have seen the gods walking among us."

"I don't either." Eleos looked down. "But if you wield magic—I'm quite certain you aren't chthonic." He glanced at my arm. "Would you like me to help you with that, Lady Aethra?"

"Why are you calling me that?"

"Is that not what you are? You introduced yourself to me as a noblewoman. I imagine you often masquerade as one."

He sounded completely earnest, but that little half-smile. .

.

"You're making fun of me." I guessed.

"Not at all, Lady Aethra," Eleos said calmly. "Would you like me to restitch that?" He asked again.

"Yes," I said, feeling foolish. A faint smirk twitched across his face before he opened the door for me.

Trying not to drip blood all over the floors, I scurried after Eleos, following him into his inn room and sitting on the edge of his cot. Last he'd stitched me up, I had been as conscious as the dead.

Pressing a cloth to my shoulder, Eleos's sage-green eyes peered into my soul. "You should've just cut a palm."

Oh. That seemed a rather obvious choice, in hindsight.

"Never mind. Perhaps you *are* reckless."

"I usually think on my feet, not beforehand," I said.

Sitting beside me, Eleos held the cloth to my wound, eyes fixed on the bloody stains. His other hand gripped my wrist, holding my arm steady.

Shifting uncomfortably, I registered how close he was, and promptly tried to erect walls around my mind.

Searching for something to fill the space, I thought of a question. "What did you do? Your crime, I mean."

Opening a small pouch, Eleos pulled out a needle and threaded it. "I figured it would keep you entertained for a while if I made you guess."

"Your insistence on keeping the secret makes me think you did something truly awful."

"That narrows it down, no? You'll get there eventually." He wiped the blood from my shoulder and set to stitching. "What about you? How'd you end up selling cheap trinkets on Ikaria's market street?"

"I was a gutter rat. My mother dumped me, and I was lucky to survive long enough to meet a tutor." I narrowed my eyes. "Why ask? Can't you just read my mind?"

"I'm trying not to." He leaned closer, focused on his task. "It's impolite." He looked up, green eyes an inch from mine. "I haven't peered into that chaotic hellscape since the marsh."

"I don't believe you." I snapped my mouth closed. "Wait, what do you mean by-"

"You should. The honesty on my face reflects my sincere soul."

"Alright, now I'm absolutely certain you're lying."

He muffled a laugh, pulling the needle through my wound.

I turned my head, nearly knocking it against his.

"Sit still." He ordered.

"Sorry," I murmured, looking ahead. "You watched me for weeks, huh? Did you learn anything interesting?"

"You have a tiny house." He said. "You pick flowers most nights when you get home. There's a step you trip on nearly every day, and you say the same curse. And," He sat back, meeting my eyes. "You think an awful lot about how much you hate a man named Ainwir."

I pursed my lips. "I can't say I enjoy being spied on."

"Sorry. Seraphim and I needed to be sure you were the one."

"The one?" I chuckled. "There are plenty of con artists better than me." Narrowing my eyes, I studied his even expression. Why *had* they settled on me?

"Who is he?" Eleos asked. "Ainwir."

"My teacher. I'm in debt because of him."

"Ah. Your hatred is justified, then." He paused his work to look into my eyes. "I know trust won't come easily, but no one in this company will betray you. You have my word."

"I. . . thanks." Trust wouldn't come easily, but it was nice to hear.

We fell into silence as he carefully patched me up. When not on the job, I rarely interacted with men. Occasionally, I found a break and visited a tavern to listen to a bard and enjoy a drink. But for all my talents with speech, sincere conversations were difficult for me, more so when the man across from me seemed a good soul.

If Eleos read my thoughts, he kept them to himself. He touched me tenderly, as though I were fragile glass that would shatter if handled too roughly. Neat little stitches closed up the ragged tear running down my arm.

"There." Snapping the thread with his teeth, Eleos sat back. "You know, psyches can do far more than read minds. Were you never told that?"

I pursed my lips, trying to remember every inexplicable thing Ainwir had accomplished. Secretive trickster, he'd never said he was a psyche, nor informed me of what magic he could conjure.

He'd hidden everything that gave him an advantage, even from me.

"What else can you do?" I asked, genuinely curious.

Eleos responded with that little half-smile. Wiping his hands off, he closed his satchel of medical supplies.

This man was going to drive me mad long before Seraphim's quest pushed me to my death. Racking my brain, I tried to recall something extraordinary Ainwir had done. Something that could have only been magic.

Nothing came to mind.

"We can tune emotions, too." Eleos stood in front of me. "It's not easy—I have to coax my target closer to my desired state before I can alter them."

"What do you mean?"

"Before, you were tense and troubled." He knelt, gently wrapping a bandage around the wound. "But you've calmed down, and now. . ." Tying the bandage, he rested a hand on my arm.

Solace washed over me, like the comfort of a bath after a long, tiring day. Every limb loosened, my muscles relaxed, and my pounding headache slowly lifted.

"Ah." I breathed. "I understand now."

"Forgive me." His brow knit. "You've lost a lot of blood and need rest."

"No, it's fine", I said, tempted to lie back and close my eyes. "Thank you."

Taking my hand, he helped me to my feet. I felt like I was floating above the clouds.

"Do you need help getting back to your room?" He asked.

"No, I'm fine." I walked to the door and paused. "You said you study the Empty. Did you find something that gave you hope?"

"I wouldn't be here otherwise."

"Whatever Seraphim's plan is, it's probably going to end in our deaths."

"Very true."

". . .you just don't seem-"

"The type who joins suicide missions?" He chuckled. "Twice a week, the people gather at church in solemn devotion to the gods. We lead them in prayer, casting their wishes toward Those who wait for us in the beyond. And in exchange for their piety, the Empty encroaches a few inches every day, cutting off land, taking more lives, until inevitably *everything* will be gone. I figured someone ought to try doing something about it."

'We lead them in prayer.' I pointed at him accusingly. "You are a priest."

Face unchanged, still wearing that little half-smile, Eleos turned away. "Goodnight, Lady Aethra."

Defeated, I walked across the hall to my room. Closing the door behind me, I ran my fingers over the new stitches.

Eleos sounded so passionate, so frustrated. Maybe joining them on a noble cause would be a nice change of pace.

But Seraphim had mentioned recruiting me for my silver tongue and experience in the underworld, which meant. . .

That little heist of theirs was but the first of many crimes to come.

SEVEN

MORNING SUNLIGHT SPILLED THROUGH THE window, a sharp reminder of the poor sleep I'd gotten last night. Seraphim rolled out her map across the inn table, weighing the edges down with bottles of wine. I glanced over it, trying and failing to read the strange shorthand scribbles the woman had riddled the parchment with.

"Here." Seraphim tapped the main road, a few miles from the outpost.

Percy leaned forward, hat tipping low over his eyes. "What's there?"

Eleos leaned on the back of my chair. "Serifos' dungeons: where those who deserve execution are left to languish."

Percy whistled. "Sounds like it'll have high security."

"I'd imagine."

Seraphim uncorked a bottle and poured herself a glass. "There's a dangerous chthonic being held there. I want to recruit him."

Leaning back in my chair, I gazed out the window. The sun had barely risen, and she was already drinking?

Percy chuckled nervously. "You know what they say—one violent chthonic is enough."

"Come, Percy." Seraphim tutted. "Two is always better than one. Not every leg of this journey can be solved by bribes and sweet smiles. Should danger come, we'll need someone to protect the three of you." She paused to drink. "Unless you *do* remember your father's lessons?"

Percy hastily looked away. "Alright, fine. *Two* chthonics."

"Forgive me," Eleos said gingerly. "But you're the only chthonic I trust."

Seraphim flashed him a smile, which did little to reassure him. Folding his arms atop my chair, he cast me a skeptical look.

Dropping my boots onto the floor, I leaned forward. "I thought you were going to share the whole plan."

Tapping the map, Seraphim drew a line between Serifos and Cynthus. "After we have the full team, the rest is simple. We travel, keeping a low profile until we arrive in Cynthus. The lords there are very strict about preventing entry into Duath Nun—they guard their borders like hawks and we won't slip by without permission."

I nodded. "You want me to convince them to let us through?"

"We'll need a story. A good one." Seraphim paused. "Luckily, it'll take a while to get where we're going. Think you can come up with a plan by then?"

I nodded, already considering a few possibilities. A royal decree from the king, perhaps? It wouldn't be a complete lie—and tales with a nugget of truth were easiest to spin.

"But let's stay focused on today." Seraphim brushed a strand of fiery hair from her face. "Serifos' dungeons are tightly guarded. How would our newest recruit suggest getting in and out?"

"Forge a transfer," I said. "Stage ourselves as guards intending to move him. Get in, get out, prisoner in tow."

"Who are we impersonating?"

"Someone that one of us resembles." I tapped my chin, trying to think of a lord in the military. Ainwir had avoided them.

Percy rubbed the back of his neck. "I. . . have an idea"

Seraphim snorted into her wine, and Eleos' eyes lit up. "Ah."

"A relative?" I guessed. "Perfect. You can impersonate them. May I?" I gestured to Seraphim's journal.

Opening the book to a blank page, Seraphim slid it across the table. Grabbing a quill, I jotted down a list of everything she'd need. Dyes, scrolls, disguises.

Pausing, I glanced up. A mind-reading psyche could make a useful sentry, searching the guards for growing suspicions. Seraphim could stay outside with the caravan, in case we needed rescue.

"Come with me." I tore my page out and beckoned to Percy. "Tell me what this officer looks like."

"Not like me," Percy replied, looking to Seraphim for approval.

"We leave tomorrow." She ordered. "Be quick."

Pressing my back against the door, I pushed it open. Percy walked past me, much less of an eyesore than when we'd first met, though he couldn't look *more* like an eccentric traveling minstrel.

A shirt embroidered with multiple bright colors lay open to his belt, and a matching patchwork of colors ringed his waist and trailed down to his knees. Puffed sleeves swept past my face as he bowed in gratitude.

The outpost bustled with activity, none of it hostile. Guards undoubtedly pursued us, but word had not reached this hamlet yet. The sun rose in a cloudless sky, drying the puddles from an overnight rainfall.

"So," I said, walking alongside him. "How did a bard get caught up with all this?"

"Didn't Eleos say?" Percy adjusted his hat. "I was in the cell beside them."

"You never said what for."

He flushed. "Bards, we. . . don't always have a lot of coin. I came up short when paying for an inn and then got into an altercation with the bartender."

"You fist fought a bartender?"

"He started it." Percy cleared his throat. "Seraphim learned I had magic and asked me to join. She paid well."

I tapped the torn page against my wrist, remembering the night we'd met. The *wailing*. Some horrible banshee scream had driven the crowd and guards away, clearing their path.

"You're a muse," I said. "I never understood how your magic works."

"That's because it's so different between us all. Some use painting as a medium, and some dance. I play music, but it's not my medium. And I doubt you'd guess what form it takes."

"You're right. I'm not the artistic type." I walked sideways, studying him intently. "You know what they say: only those who lived extraordinary lives receive the gift of magic. So what's your story?"

I asked the question with an inquisitive smile, but quickly regretted my levity. Percy's face paled, and his cheerful expression vanished.

He was touched by the Empty. Any who were discovered to be tainted faced death, for fear they'd spread the void.

Percy answered quietly. "I sang requiems for funerals. Not a conventional career for a minstrel. Maybe that's why."

I could tell he was lying. The words came out quickly, and his mouth twitched. But I did not know him well enough to press. Nothing drove someone away quicker than digging into wounds that had yet to heal.

"Let me see that page of yours," Percy asked.

Handing it to him, I watched as he leaned against a quiet wall and scribbled away. When he returned the page, a surprisingly detailed sketch of a man decorated the corner.

The older man's portrait bore a resemblance to Percy, albeit with far more hair. This would be easy enough to replicate. Looking up, I examined his features.

"Is this your father?" I asked.

"How could you tell?"

"He looks just like you."

"Oh, don't say that," Percy frowned. "Yes. He's my father."

Glancing down at the officer's portrait, my mind wandered. Lord's sons always inherited their land and titles. How had this one become a wandering bard who brawled with bartenders?

"Why not dye your hair?" I blurted out.

"We'll have to. Pops has black hair."

"No, not for the disguise. For yourself."

"Why not?" He seemed surprised by the question. "I. . . I like it this way."

"Oh." I wasn't sure what to say to that. Pushing open the door to a small fabric shop, I scanned the shelves.

Master Ainwir had taught me how to fill a basket with everything you'd need for a job without arousing suspicion. If I ever saw him again, I'd thank him for the lessons.

And then slit his throat.

LEANING AGAINST THE inn's stone wall, I slid onto the soft grass and sifted through the contents of my bag. Everything I needed to stitch together a noble's dress and an officer's cloak was here. Now we just needed a live body to strip a uniform from.

Something told me that was a task Seraphim would happily take care of.

The inn door swung open, and the woman in question emerged, bottle in hand. Dirt crusted her boots, and tears riddled her coat, but her confident stride commanded authority nonetheless.

"Drink?" She held out a glass.

"Thanks." I accepted, crossing my legs and balancing the glass on my knee.

"You agreed to help." Seraphim sat beside me, setting the bottle on the ground. "But I never asked you to join the team."

"I assumed they were one and the same."

"Not necessarily. We'll need to have each other's backs if we're to forge into the unknown."

I chuckled, sipping the wine. "I'll join."

Seraphim grinned, pouring herself a glass.

A couple walked by, laughing. The lights were still on in the tavern across the street. Shadows passed the windows. Dancing. Drinking.

It certainly didn't seem like the world was ending. All my life, the Empty had simply been an obstacle to avoid. Everyone else thought the same. To city folk, it might as well not exist.

Seraphim gazed wistfully at the night sky. "Can you imagine a time when there were still miles and miles of sprawling country? Where lords fought over land?"

The world was a straight line: a populated road connected the cities. I couldn't imagine anything different.

"There are no remnants of the battlefields." Seraphim continued. "Everywhere victory was claimed, the Empty appeared in the wake of the bloodshed and swept them away."

Shifting to face her, I tried to read her to no avail. "What's your story?"

"I'm surprised you didn't recognize my name." Seraphim tugged on her braid. "The Cynthus royal family is famed for their locks, after all."

I choked on my wine. The lord of Cynthus had cast his daughter out decades ago—since her exile, none had seen her nor spoken of her.

"No wonder I couldn't place your face," I said. "I assumed you'd died ages ago."

"Most have forgotten me." She picked idly at her coat. "But you understand how invisibility is an asset."

"Your father went to great lengths to keep the scandal obscured. What did you do?"

"That is a story for another time." Seraphim's eyes flashed. "For now, I'll tell you where I disappeared to." She leaned in, anticipating my curiosity.

"Duath nun?"

"Dammit." She frowned. "You were supposed to humor me."

"How else would you have found the supposed Source?" I gestured with my glass, sloshing some wine. "How did you get past the border?"

"My brother helped me. He'll be our man on the inside when we get there."

"Lord Phaedrus himself?" I asked. "This'll be easier than I thought."

"Not so fast. He needs the full approval of all the border lords. His vote is only one of five." She paused. "But he can arrange the meeting."

"And you trust him?"

"Completely."

Seraphim leaned against the wall, watching the stars flicker in the sky. Beneath the low glare of the lanterns, she looked somber and calm. Not the kind of calm I expected from someone contented, but rather someone. . .

Who'd lost so much they'd grown from grief into acceptance.

Or maybe I was reading too much into a simple expression.

Draining her glass, Seraphim pointed it at me. "Eleos read you like a book when he spoke with you by the ship's overlook. 'She's scared. But I don't think it's the danger she fears.'"

"Ha." I chuckled bitterly. "Maybe he knows me better than myself." I groaned. "Could you tell him to stop that?"

"Eleos is exceedingly polite and proper. He tries very hard not to pry."

"Sure he does."

"With everyone else, at least. Maybe he finds you irresistibly interesting." She leaned toward me, smirking.

"What?" I asked. "I'm an open book, and not very interesting to boot."

"Suit yourself." Seraphim stood, brushing off her coat. "I'm glad to have you on board. With any luck, we'll make it to Cynthus alive, and I can pay you the rest of what you're owed."

"Here's to living." I raised my glass.

"That's the spirit." She nodded and slipped through the door.

Sighing, I quietly finished my drink. In the unlikely chance we survived, I could return to Ikaria and resume the endless task of paying off my debt.

Or would everything change, assuming we succeeded? Would the Empty recede, and new lands arise? Or would it simply halt, and life would continue on as I'd always known it?

Shouldering my bag, I walked back inside. A quiet hum hung over the inn's common room; Percy leaned on the counter, chatting with a middle-aged barmaid.

A married barmaid, judging by the tattoo burned into her finger, but neither seemed to mind. I briefly wondered if he preferred older women, but he stood straight as a much younger barmaid walked by with a tray of drinks and winked.

Percy preferred women with a pulse, then. He noticed me and waved with enthusiasm. Raising my hand in response, I wondered if his affable nature was an act.

Nearly everyone I'd known concealed their true nature behind more palatable masks.

Trotting up the stairs, I hesitated by Eleos' cracked door. He sat inside, scrawling away at a journal stuffed head to toe with orderly notes. I raised my hand to knock, hesitated, and turned away.

"Come in," Eleos said softly.

Standing in the door frame, I cleared my throat. "Last chance to stock up before we hit the road. Need me to get anything for you?"

"I don't think so." He looked up from his notes. "Surprising, isn't it? I once gave Percy a simple math equation to solve, and it took him two weeks to come up with the wrong answer. Yet, the ladies seem to like him."

"Most ladies don't require maths from their suitors."

"Where I come from, they do." He brushed his light brown hair behind his ears. "I've never seen a forger at work. Care to show me how it's done?"

"It's boring work, really." I pulled out my journal and flipped it open, laying it on his desk. "I kept loads of reference documents on me. Eventually, you start to memorize how they're written." I shooed him. "Move for a second."

Eleos half-complied, shifting to take up only half the seat when I'd meant for him to vacate it. Shrugging, I sat on my half and dipped my quill into his pot of ink.

"Transfer orders are usually brief," I said. "I just need our prisoner's name."

"Burgundy Rose."

I snorted. "That's his name?"

"No. Nobody knows his identity." Eleos ran a hand over his eyes. "Always wears a mask, sneaks to his target's location without being seen, then disappears into the shadows. As for the name, I think it came from a famous play."

Plays were luxuries I'd never been able to afford. Wrinkling my nose, I leaned my elbow on the desk. "Who's the character? A thief?"

"Thief. Assassin. Charming rogue." Eleos said.

"Is he a murderer?" I asked, biting my lip as I concentrated.

"Depends on who you ask. Some call him that. Others, an assassin. And fewer, a hero." He watched me with interest. "Have you done this before?"

"Actually, I have. It was a much smaller prison, though, so security was somewhat lax." I chuckled, quickly scrawling a mock order. "Percy will have to show me how his father signs his name, but that's pretty much it. Seal it with wax, and most won't know the difference."

"Look like you belong, and nobody asks questions."

"You'd be surprised how well it works." Wiping off the quill, I smiled at him.

I hadn't spoken to many priests. When envisioning them, I pictured old men. Bald. Probably a little pudgy. Or, young and scrawny.

But a man with brilliant eyes, handsome features, and beautifully soft hair that fell in gentle waves around his face? Tracing my eyes over his locks, I resisted the urge to touch them.

Eleos blinked. "It occurs to me we don't know anything about each other."

"Whose fault is that?" I snapped out of my trance. "You dodge all my questions and read my mind."

"*Thoughts.*" He corrected me. "I read thoughts. They're often emotions, scattered and erratic. Even if I could peer into someone's heart, I wouldn't."

"I see." Glancing away, I studied the curtains swaying in the breeze. Did I really think about Ainwir so often? I needed a new hobby.

Expecting a smart response, I eyed Eleos. He tilted his head innocently. "What?"

"I expected you to respond to my thoughts."

"I already told you. It's not polite." He said.

Glancing between him and his notebook, curiosity swept over me. Laying my quill on the desk, I flipped the page in his journal and studied the notes. A detailed description of my encounter with the keres and the Empty's sudden stop painted the page.

Eleos leaned closer to me, reading the forgery I'd drafted up. His hips and shoulders pressed against mine, and the words on the paper blurred.

When was the last time I'd been intimate with anyone? Not sex, but simple touches like hugs or linked hands?

Years. The last had been a man I'd courted before realizing he only wanted me to warm his bed.

Gods, how long had I been this lonely? Eleos' warmth called to me like a stream after days without water.

Eleos looked up from the desk. "Do you need help sleeping again?"

"No." I shot from the chair, mind whirling as I considered every errant thought he might have overheard. "Magic is bestowed on those who experience something extraordinary. Percy won't tell me his story. Neither will Seraphim. I suppose you won't either."

"I. . ." Eleos' face was usually impassive, but distress flickered across his features. "Psyches are those with great empathy. I found myself in the company of an unfortunate soul. I suppose Psythos noticed my distress and. . . ensuing actions."

"I see," I said. He moved to speak, but I cut him off. "No, it's alright. I prefer not to pry into personal matters. What you've said gives me enough of an idea."

"I've read you correctly, then."

"And how's that?" I laughed awkwardly, tugging on a curl. "Scattered? Hopeless? Clumsy?"

"Kind." He said. "There's a hole in your heart you seek to fill, but never with yourself."

I froze, brow furrowed, unsure what he meant.

"You should get some rest, Ae-" He quickly corrected himself. "Lady Aethra."

"Great. I guess that name is stuck now, huh?"

"It's only polite to call people by the name they introduce themselves with." His sly half-smile returned.

"Hm." I pursed my lips and walked away.

Eleos must have seen someone suffer unimaginable horrors. He'd failed to save them and had fruitlessly sought revenge. At least, that's how I interpreted his vague story.

Psythos favored those with great empathy. Small wonder one of her blessed was risking his life to save the strangers he'd never meet.

Ainwir had taught me to save only myself. Once, I'd thought his words were those of a caring mentor, who didn't want to lose his apprentice.

I'd wondered countless times how he'd managed to convince Laverna to loan him such a ridiculous amount. An answer I'd never learn. Maybe she had killed Ainwir for robbing her blind, and that's why he'd vanished.

Or perhaps the bastard had gamed the system and was living happily ever after somewhere far away.

Maybe he, too, had fled to Duath Nun, and I'd see him again on its distant shores.

EIGHT

PERCY HAD ATTEMPTED TO EXPLAIN his magic to me on our journey to Serifos' dungeons. Maybe the concept was beyond me, or perhaps he was as empty in the head as Eleos claimed.

'Requiems are dirges for the departed. Everyone reacts to them differently. Some feel sorrow, others anger, and more fear. Within the bounds of those emotions, I can create anything imaginable.'

I couldn't claim to understand it, but I trusted him to watch my back. If all went to plan, we wouldn't need magic. A set of forged papers and winning smiles would suffice.

Adjusting my hat, I pulled my veil over my eyes and turned to my partner. Percy looked entirely different, with his hair dyed black and makeup that mimicked the lines of his father's face. Pulling the red-padded helmet over his eyes, he frowned at me like a lost puppy.

"You look professional." I complimented, smoothing out his tabard.

"If these people have ever *sniffed* my father, they'll know I'm a fake." He insisted.

"Why? What's he smell like?"

Percy paused, thinking. "Ham. Mm, or maybe charcoal."

"I was joking, Percy," I said, folding my hands on my lap.

83

Our carriage jostled over a bump in the road, and I grabbed the door handle to keep steady. Rows upon rows of trees streamed by outside the window, leading us toward the fort tucked safely inside their embrace. Seraphim sat in the driver's seat, guiding the horses, while Eleos sat across from Percy and me, dressed as one of our soldiers.

"So, anything we should know about our quarry before meeting him?" I asked.

"I told you all that I know." Eleos's voice was muffled inside his helm.

"Seraphim is a tight-lipped lady. Maybe you've noticed?" Percy leaned toward me. "A dangerous chthonic, one who's probably guilty of murder. Sounds like a pleasant fellow."

"She wants him for a reason," I said.

"Assuredly." Eleos agreed. "She's probably refrained from sharing because one of us will protest."

"Or all of us," Percy added.

"Ask for forgiveness, not permission," I murmured. "Is that her motto?"

"More or less."

"I hope she knows what she's doing." I peered out the window as the carriage turned down a new road.

Two towers rose from the trees, shadows stationed in their turrets. A heavy gate and high walls barred the entrance to the courtyard; men in steel armor and red tabards patrolled the parapets.

Prisoners and guards would be plentiful inside to safeguard this place from the Empty.

"You know," Percy whispered. "I haven't asked." His faded gray eyes bored into mine. "Are you seeing anyone?"

"No," I answered quickly. "Why?"

"Well, it's only polite to check. Serifos is a nice city, we could-"

"Run away and leave our woes behind?" I raised an eyebrow. "You should have asked earlier. By the time we reach the gates, we'll have a wanted criminal with us."

"We're all wanted criminals, darling. It's cozy in the shadows, besides." Percy squinted. "You actually look somewhat like my mother, dressed like that."

"Is that a compliment?"

"But of course. My mother's a goddess. What son would say otherwise?"

Eleos laughed, the sound reverberating inside his helm. "Percy. *Relax.*"

"Right." Closing the visor of his helm, Percy sat back.

I chuckled. Our carriage rolled to a stop, and Seraphim dismounted, knocking on our door before pulling it open. Her red braid was tucked neatly beneath a guard's helm.

She saluted sarcastically. "Ready?"

Percy saluted back at her. "Assuming our new recruit doesn't try to kill us, yes."

"He won't," Seraphim promised. "Let's get going before someone notices us loitering."

Fixing my hair, I exited the carriage with Percy. The knights on the walls stood at attention as all eyes fell on us.

A knight called down from above. "State your business."

"We bring orders from Lord Eusebius," I called back. "He wishes for a prisoner to be transferred to Therapne."

"Open the gates."

The easiest part of the plan was done. Eleos opened the door for us to re-enter the carriage, as the heavy metal gates slowly cranked open. Grinding chains and scraping steel set my nerves on edge. The carriage door slammed as Percy took his seat beside me, and Seraphim guided the horses forward.

"The hard part is over." Eleos encouraged. "The rest will be easy enough."

Percy frowned. "I never tire of your sarcasm."

"I'm not being sarcastic."

"Oh, come now. Even the new girl's seen through you."

I couldn't see his mouth beneath his helm, but I was certain our scholar was wearing his annoying half-grin.

The carriage stopped in the courtyard, and Percy and I exited once more. A knight approached us, the flowing red cape trailing behind him denoting his higher rank.

"May I see your orders?" He asked.

Percy handed him my forged document. "My apologies for not sending word. It was an abrupt decision."

He sounded a world different from the flamboyant bard: serious and gruff, just as we'd practiced.

The knight read the papers before looking up at us. "Has the good lord gone mad?"

"Serifos was not the only city he wronged," I said. "Many of the crimes he committed in Therapne have gone without answer."

"We could question him in your stead. Surely-"

"You have my orders." Percy interrupted. "Do you assent or will you send us back to Lord Eusebius to deliver your denial?"

Nodding, the knight gestured east. "Have your carriage follow the path to the eastern gate. We'll bring him out there."

Seraphim saluted, awaiting my word. Nodding, I turned back to the knight and followed him to the imposing front doors, into the heart of the fort. The carriage rolled down the eastern path, and I glanced back at it before the heavy doors shut behind me.

The dour dungeon I had been expecting was instead a gorgeous grand hall, with a looming archway leading into a chapel. Water trickled between the pews in decorative channels, and a statue of Haimyx rose in cracked stone from the center. He looked less like a life god and more like a death god, depicted with a bloody scythe and a funeral shroud.

Our guide led us past the grandeur to a small office, where he dropped us off with a bow. A grizzled older man who must have been the Warden sat at a positively ancient stone desk, a pile of papers and ledgers before him.

Raising his quill, the old knight waved us inside.

"Transfer orders, sir," I said politely, handing him the forgery.

The man's heavy brow knit tighter and tighter until I was sure it would cover his eyes completely. Unlike the guard, he did not question the order.

Rising, he grabbed a key ring from his desk and walked past us. "Use caution. Stay behind me and do not approach him."

"Is he that dangerous?"

"He's chthonic. If he spies a threadbare cut on you, you're dead." The Warden beckoned for us to follow.

Pausing to grab a torch from one of the sconces, he led us through the halls to a stairwell cutting down into the earth. Men lounged in the room below, playing cards at stone tables, guarding heavy iron doors locked with a chain.

They sat forward, watching intently as the Warden unlocked the heavy padlock leading to the rows of cells. A few reached for the weapons at their belts, perhaps a trained reflex, or maybe in fear of who they knew was locked within.

Several images danced across my mind. A massive man with a wicked smile, a bearded wraith with hollow eyes. Whatever this murderer looked like, it was sure to be unpleasant.

Without the Warden's torch, we would have ventured into utter darkness. Bumping into Percy, I grabbed his arm to keep myself from walking face-first into the hard stone walls.

"You hold them in the dark?" Percy asked.

The Warden looked over his shoulder. "Closest we can get to the eternal damnation of the Empty." He answered. "Drives them mad. Only a few keep their heads."

Our footsteps echoed, heralding news of our presence. Flinching with each new step, I peered into the cells, trying to catch a glimpse of their occupants. Each was sealed shut with a heavy stone door. Not even a slat allowed the occupants to gaze out, nor for those outside to gaze in.

Complete darkness and solitude. *Forever.* I shuddered at the thought.

The Warden brought us to the end of the hall, wrestling his keys out as he approached the center cell. I heard the key fit into the lock, though I could hardly see.

But the sound of a door scraping open didn't follow.

Yanking the key out, the Warden stepped back, waving his torch over the door. He cursed under his breath and kicked.

The door scraped open, revealing a stone room of featureless walls and a single bench.

An *unoccupied* bench. The cell was empty.

My stomach tumbled into my nether regions when I realized what this meant.

"Stay here." The Warden ordered me. "You." He waved the torch at Percy. "Come with me."

Percy grimaced, glancing at me, but the Warden was already jogging away. Pushing him encouragingly, I knitted my fingers together as the two soldiers disappeared into the shadows.

Great. Just great. A dangerous murderer was loose, and I was armed with a smile and honeyed words. A very useful thing in the pitch dark.

Feeling my way along the wall, I took a step forward, heard a bang from inside a nearby cell, and backtracked.

Was it safer to wait here? What if the cell's occupant returned?

How had he escaped?

I couldn't stay here. I wasn't even supposed to be here.

"*Shitshitshit,*" I muttered, running a hand along the wall to guide me through the shadows.

My hand slipped from the wall, and I stumbled forward. Had I reached the end of the hall? Turning in a circle, I strained to adjust to the darkness, but saw only vague blobs in the gloom.

Choosing a direction, I crept forward, feeling for the wall. Instead, my boot crashed into metal. Cursing, I hopped back, trying to see what I'd struck.

My back collided with a person who had most certainly not been there a moment before. A strong arm slipped around my waist, pressing me against his chest.

"Don't struggle." An almost charming voice laced with an unfamiliar accent whispered. "And I promise you'll make it out of this alive."

Before I could think of something to say, a dagger dug into my neck. Feeling cold steel, I gritted my teeth and managed a muffled, "Okay."

Fire rushed through the hall ahead as several armed men holding torches raced down the steps. An officer barked orders from above, instructing them to fan out and find the missing prisoner.

The metallic thing my foot had struck had been a collapsed guard. My captor's arm swam into view, a scarred wrist wrapped in a ragged bracer.

A soldier spun in our direction. He drew his spear.

"I wouldn't do that." My captor warned. "Harm either of us, and I'll slit her throat. I don't think you want to see what I could do with that."

A second guard joined the first. I could see Percy's dull gray eyes beneath his helm. Grabbing the other soldier, he forced the man's spear arm down.

"Idiot." Percy hissed in his officer voice. "You'll get us all killed."

"Atta boy." My captor sounded almost friendly. Dragging me forward, his grip on the dagger never wavered. A perfectly steady hand held it a hairsbreadth from my skin.

Silence fell over the dungeons, save for the sounds of our footfalls and crackling torches. Even if the men were willing to sacrifice me, a more pressing fear prevented them from attacking.

One cut of my throat, and the chthonic would have the only weapon he needed.

More guards waited in the room above, frozen, hands clasped on their sword hilts as they watched us cross the room. Trying to breathe, I floundered to find the steps while my eyes were fixed on the knife at my throat. It felt like a lifetime passed before we crested the top of the stairs.

Kicking the door closed behind us, the chthonic spun me around, knife to the back of my neck as he encouraged me to walk ahead of him. I caught a glimpse of black hair before the cold steel encouraged me to face forward and walk.

"I am sorry about this." He apologized.

I wanted to bitterly retort, but given the current situation, I held my tongue. Walking faster as he forced me forward, I gasped when he grabbed my arm and pulled me back to his side, dagger sliding across my jugular as we ascended another flight of stone steps.

What was he doing? If he wanted to escape, he needed to go *out*, not *up*.

Sunlight split through tall windows, illuminating a door as it flew open. A soldier in regal armor, a cape trailing behind him, flew out and froze when he saw us.

Recognition passed between them; I saw it on the knight's face and felt it from my captor's tensing muscles. The knight's gaze flew to the dagger at my throat.

"How did you-" The knight began, before raising a hand. "S-stay back. There's no reason to hurt her."

"Oh, Acrius," the chthonic said in a bitter, taunting voice. "I came here for *you*. Do you really think you can bargain for your life?"

Acrius's hand trembled, and his eyes widened, bloodshot. Terrified.

The dagger departed my throat as the knight turned to run. An elbow struck my side, sending me stumbling into the wall. I turned to see my captor slashing the blade across his wrist.

A stream of blood erupted, shooting across the hall like seeking daggers that far outpaced their target. The crimson blades coalesced into a scarlet greatsword that plunged through the knight's chest, rending his armor and throwing him against the wall.

I gasped as the knight hung from the stone, suspended by the magicked blade piercing his gut. A ratty cape trailed behind my captor as he stalked toward his victim and yanked the man's helm off. Graying brown hair spilled out. The assassin tilted the knight's chin up, whispering something in his ear.

I didn't realize the horror of a dying man could deepen until I saw the effect the chthonic's words had on Acrius; his mien raged with guilt, terror, and fury.

I'd never seen violent death before. Bile rose in my throat, and I ripped my eyes from the corpse, hand pressed to my neck. When I heard the knight's last gasp, I looked back up, finally seeing the face of our new recruit.

Wavy black hair framed eyes rimmed by dark shadows. Rich red irises matched the blood dripping from his blade. But he did not look at me as though I were his next target.

Thundering footsteps preceded the arrival of the soldiers we'd left behind in the dungeons. Flipping his dagger, the red-eyed prisoner turned and fled.

Iron boots pounded past me as the guards gave chase. Percy ran to my side and helped me up, dragging me behind him as he raced after our target.

The red-eyed man glanced behind him and shot us a devilish smile before throwing himself out the window. I gasped, slamming into the windowsill and looking down the multiple-story drop.

Bloody knives manifested mid-air, impaling the stone walls of the dungeon. The red-eyed man landed on one, caught his balance, and jumped down the rest, as though they were a set of bladed stairs.

Percy sighed with relief when he saw our quarry hit the ground safely. He stiffened, looking behind him as the soldiers scrambled to sound the alarm and give chase.

"Shit." Percy cursed, eyes flashing with color. A horrible wail, like an out-of-tune flute, reverberated through the hall, and deep purple mist sprang from the walls, clouding my eyes as I choked on a sudden surge of unrelenting fear.

Percy reached through the haze and grabbed my wrist. The moment he touched me, the effects of his magic fled, and my senses returned. All around us, guards writhed in a mix of pain and fear, swatting at nothing.

"Time to go," Percy announced, pushing through the dazed men.

"Percy." I hissed, chasing after him. "You blew our cover."

"The plan fell apart a while ago, lest you didn't notice."

Gritting my teeth, I tried not to look at the corpse pinned to the wall. The scarlet greatsword lost its shape, dropping the broken knight to the floor in a heap.

"Who is that?" I asked.

"I have a guess," Percy called over his shoulder. "*Later.*"

The alarm bells surged in intensity as we dashed down the stairs and fled toward the eastern exit we'd been directed to leave through. A knight sprinted toward us, yanking off his helm to reveal sage-green eyes and soft brown hair.

"This way." Eleos panted, turning around the moment he saw us.

We burst into the courtyard, but found no carriage awaiting us. Guards stationed on the walls turned in our direction, leveling bows at our heads.

Eleos tackled me, throwing us behind a pillar. I heard several arrows crash into the stone and slam into the ground.

"Why are they shooting at us?" I hissed.

"You'll see." Eleos breathed, eyes darting around.

Percy took cover behind the next pillar, hands held over his head, flinching with every impact.

"Go." Eleos pushed me, and I obeyed.

Running as fast as my skirt would allow, I stared ahead to avoid looking toward certain death. Flinching as an arrow whizzed past my ear, I looked up to see a carriage riddled with arrows waiting for us, Seraphim sitting in the driver's seat, frantically waving for us to board.

Eleos threw me in first before diving after me. Percy joined Seraphim at the front, flailing panickedly to climb onto the seat. A whip cracked, and the carriage rolled forward.

I stumbled into a man already sitting in the back. The man who'd held me at knife point.

I froze, eyes widening. He returned my shock with a sly grin.

"What-" I managed before the carriage violently rocked.

Seraphim whipped the horses into a frenzy, driving them into a gallop. Through the windows, I saw a stream of men burst through the doors, and more arriving from ahead, blocking our path.

A javelin thudded into the door, the metal point mere inches from my face. Gasping, I scrambled back, slamming into Eleos. He grabbed me, and craned his neck toward the driver's seat window.

"Seraphim!" He shouted.

I saw her arm extend, blood coating her gauntlet. Heat crackled through the air as fire erupted from her grasp. Two wings of flame tore ahead of us, cleaving through the guards blocking our path.

Our carriage screamed through fire. Hot flames crawled up the wheels and licked at the horse's hooves. Soldiers leaped out of the way of the spreading flames and careening carriage as it tore through the courtyard.

The carriage nearly tipped as the horses sprinted through the gates and turned down a sharp bend in the road before fleeing into the surrounding woodlands.

I lost balance and fell face-first to the carriage floor, covering my head as I waited for the violent rocking to finally stop. Gasping, I raised my head, noticing first the murderer we'd come here to save, then Seraphim peering through the carriage window to grin at us.

"I think that went well!"

NINE

I DIDN'T LIKE OUR NEW recruit. Maybe it was his lackadaisical attitude, or more likely, the knife he'd pressed to my throat.

Seraphim had led us far off the road, deep into thick woods dotted with white birch trees. Stalled in mud and unable to squeeze through the tightly packed trunks, we were forced to abandon the escape carriage. Leaving the wreck behind to delay our pursuers, we extracted our supplies and unhooked the horses.

We'd gained a steed at the outpost, but with a new recruit, we were still a saddle short. Eleos guided the dappled brown horse we'd shared before to me and patted its flank. "Think you can mount by yourself this time?"

"I can try," I said, grabbing the saddle and staring at the arduous climb.

A steel helm landed in the mud with a plop as Percy threw it from his head, shock-white hair spilling loose. "You." He seethed, pointing at the dark-haired assassin.

"Percy!" The red-eyed man said affably. "I never would have expected to-"

"You *rogue!*" Percy snapped. "Why didn't you say anything? I. . . I. . ." He stumbled over his words, but I couldn't tell if he was furious or hurt.

Seraphim yanked her helm off, braid frizzed. "You two know each other? You should have told me."

Flushing, Percy glanced at the red-eyed man. "He went by a different name when we met." He folded his arms. "Isn't that right? *Burgundy Rose*."

Eleos smiled impishly, leaning toward me. "I think someone had their heart broken." He whispered.

"Seems like it," I whispered back.

'Burgundy Rose' interjected. "You came to the dungeons for me. Why?"

His strange accent scratched at my memories. It was unfamiliar, yet it tugged at something deep within.

"I'm recruiting you," Seraphim said plainly.

"For what?"

She smiled wryly, glancing at Percy. "Our bard spins tales like a master and packs like a drunk." She grabbed a saddlebag from the mud. "Ask him."

Sighing, Percy ran a hand through his hair and began our strange tale. The red-eyed rogue paced around him, wrapping the gash on his palm he'd used to cast his spells.

Nervous pricks ran up my spine, and I spun to look behind me.

Nothing was there. Trees stretched on for as far as I could see.

Shaking off the discomfort, I helped Eleos prepare the horses for travel. Percy certainly made my blunder at the Sundering ceremony sound more exciting than the truth.

He won a few points for making me look good, at least.

The red-eyed man listened with an even expression until Percy caught him up to the present. He thought for a moment, then turned to Seraphim. "Getting into Duath Nun will not be easy."

"No. It won't." She agreed.

"Nor will crossing the Acheron. Duath Nun protects it with everything they have."

"I know," Seraphim said in a low voice. "You have quite a bounty on your head. Aethra here would *love* to claim it." She raised an eyebrow, and glanced at me.

Perking up, I smiled mischievously. "That I would."

"Aid me, though," Seraphim continued, "and you'll have your name cleared. A full pardon, granted by the Archon."

The red-eyed man regarded me before staring into the trees. Finally, he turned back to her. "I owe you. You'll have my aid. And my fame has grown out of hand. A clean slate would be welcome."

"Wonderful." Seraphim grinned. "Serifos isn't far. We'll restock there before crossing the isthmus." Grabbing her horse, she placed a foot in the stirrup.

"Wait," I called. Seraphim paused and stared at me. "I want something cleared up first. That knight, Acrius," I peered at the assassin. "Why did you kill him?"

"Seth." The red-eyed rogue interjected. "You can call me Seth."

Percy hummed. "*That's* the name I remember."

"What has it been? A year? Two?" Seth mused. "We need to catch up."

"Yes, I-" Percy's joy simmered into anger. "I haven't forgiven you, yet." He jerked his chin up. "Aethra's right. You owe her an explanation."

Seth stared at me intently, stepping closer. "Do you understand Serifos' order of succession?"

"Vaguely." I watched him warily. "It still functions how it did when they were an independent country, right? If the king's family falls, the highest-ranking general takes the throne."

"The king may now be a mere city lord and his general a captain, but the idea remains," Seth smirked. "You work with the Guild. You know they make great coin entertaining the city lords' petty grievances. Captain Acrius dealt with them often, in his trip to the top. Does his name ring a bell?"

Lord Acrius. . . I searched my memories for the name. Ainwir had been offered a job by someone working for Acrius—a job he'd refused.

Percy interjected. "My father hated him. Called him a corrupt, power hungry blasphemer."

"Everyone knows the young lord's heirs died mysteriously." Seth continued. "But nobody can prove it."

I glanced away, thinking. The Lord of Serifos had lost both daughters to illness in the past few years. Was Seth implying those had been murders?

"Or better yet." Seth continued. "Speak to the graves and ask Acrius' daughter who drowned her when she learned she was pregnant. Nothing makes a noble look worse than bearing a bastard. Least of all those who're aiming for the throne."

The Guild made good coin, hiding bastards away to spare their noble parents the shame. What kind of man would turn to murder instead?

Swallowing, I met Seth's eyes. "How are you so sure he was responsible?"

"I have contacts in the Guild. I pay well for my information." He stared into the night. "They keep records of who hires their services. Nobles and clergy members pay them to commit atrocities, but everyone looks the other way. At best, they languish in a cell until their family pays for their freedom."

"And you give them the punishment they're due?"

"Yes."

Words escaped me. I knew of the Guild's less savory activities, some I'd been party to, though I'd asked no questions. Ainwir had dealt with them only passingly, advising me not to fall afoul of their political dealings.

Lords did not wish to share, to play second fiddle to another king. But wars won them nothing but death, so they exerted their power in other ways. Underhanded, quiet ways. Better not to make enemies of them, Ainwir had said.

"Satisfied?" Seth asked, returning to his horse.

Percy cleared his throat. "I've met some of the men Seth. . . takes care of. You can trust him."

An elbow to my ribs drew my attention from the mud. Eleos stared intently at the back of Seth's head. "I was reading him. He's telling the truth—or, at least, what he believes to be the truth."

"You said some people think him a hero. He's a vigilante." I guessed. "That would have made me feel a little better about this."

"As I said, I wasn't sure," Eleos said

"Stop loitering," Seraphim called. "We need to move."

"One moment," Seth said, eyes darting around the trees frantically. "He should be here somewhere. I commanded him to stay nearby."

"Who?" Seraphim asked.

Seth whistled sharply, startling me.

Seraphim glared at him with the ire of a thousand suns. "What are you-" She cut herself off, grabbing her knife and pressing it to her palm as leaves rattled in the distance.

But it was not soldiers who sprinted toward us. An enormous dog raced through the underbrush, a shaggy mess of dirty, matted fur. Seth kneeled, opening his arms for the hound, who dove onto its master with joy.

Percy lit up. "Whisper! Do you remember me, boy?"

Covering Seth's face with slobber, the hound ran to Percy, eagerly sniffing his hand, tail wagging furiously. Leaning to the side, I studied the creature's features, trying to determine its breed. Tall. *Filthy.* Mud covered everything else.

Seraphim rolled her eyes. "Percy. *Later.*"

Scrambling to his feet, Percy returned to his horse. Eleos nudged me, offering me a hand. "At least we have a dog, now."

Chuckling, I let Eleos help me up and wrapped my arms around his waist when he sat ahead of me. Still not accustomed to all this running around, I leaned my head against his back, exhausted.

Our horses rode through the woods, weaving between trees to scatter our trail. The hound kept pace, trotting alongside his master, tall ears stalwartly listening for pursuit.

Dropping the reins, Eleos raked his hands through his hair, combing his waves. Leaning around his shoulder, I teased him. "Priests aren't supposed to care about appearances."

"Psythos senses vanity." Eleos finished the saying. "Luckily, I'm *not* a priest."

"Mhm," I rested my head against his back. Metallic steel infected his comforting scent. "Seth mentioned something called the Acheron," I said softly.

"Yes. There are few records of it in the Merchant Isles." Eleos answered. "That's the source. The river that flows into the heart of the Empty."

"And we cross it to get inside?" I asked. "Do you still disappear if you walk in through the front door?"

Eleos chuckled at my analogy. "That's my theory. We'll be able to *traverse* the Empty and discover what hides within." His gaze drifted to Seraphim. "If what they say is true, the denizens of Duath Nun will know more. If we can get them to talk, rather than run us through."

"Is that another task for me?"

Eleos smiled. "If you can sweet-talk Duath Nun's royalty, Lady Aethra, I'll forgo worship of the gods and bow to you instead."

THE SCENE OF bloody death replayed in my head: punctured steel, rent flesh, exposed innards, and the sheer amount of blood streaming from the dying man's body onto the floor.

Shuddering, I closed my eyes and pinched my nose. The sharp scent of wood filled the air as I leaned against a tree and wrapped myself in my cloak.

Darkness swallowed the forest. Seraphim had advised against lighting a fire lest our pursuers find us. I'd offered to take the first watch, as sleep would doubtless evade me. The others gathered in a hastily made camp, watched over by the hunting hound Seth apparently took everywhere with him.

What would Duath Nun be like? A country everyone knew of yet understood nothing of. The border lords kept rapt watch over their lands, lest anyone slip by and incite the hostile country into starting a war we couldn't afford.

The people of Duath Nun would try to kill us if we entered. More bloodshed awaited, more brushes with the Empty.

What was I doing here? I wasn't cut out for this.

Seth's voice rose behind me, startling me out of my thoughts. "You're not a very good watch, if I can sneak up on you so easily."

"I'm watching for *outside* threats," I muttered, trying to see him in the dark.

He joined my side, towering a head above me. The faint outlines of messy hair and tattered clothes caught my eye in the night.

"I, um. . ." He began awkwardly. "You seem distressed about what happened in the dungeons."

"I hadn't seen anyone die before," I answered. "Not like that." I took a step away. "And I don't particularly like it when people hold me hostage."

"I told you I was sorry." He shrugged. "I had a different plan, but then you presented yourself on a silver platter. Who makes for a better prisoner than a beautiful lady?"

"Wait. Did you get caught on purpose?"

"Yes. It was the best way to get to Acrius." He folded his arms. "How *did* said beautiful lady end up here?"

Knitting my hands behind me, I leaned against the tree. "It's a long story. Seraphim needed a con woman. I'm half decent, and had nothing else to live for."

His gaze hardened. "How long have you worked for the Guild?"

"Technically, never," I corrected, leaning my back against the tree. "I'm indebted to them thanks to the nefarious deeds of another." I paused, trying to find an eloquent way to put it. "Essentially, I'm their slave."

"Colorful word choice." Seth paced around, sizing me up. "If you need a job when this is over, Percy could use a partner."

"Ha. I'll think about it."

He cast me an odd stare, hand on his hip. As my eyes adjusted to the night, his blood-colored irises appeared as red splotches in a sea of black. "Seraphim mentioned your inability to fight. I can teach you, if you'd like. Consider it compensation."

"I think the word you're looking for is 'recompense.'" I corrected. "But, I'm not a chthonic."

"I know plenty of traditional techniques, too. It took years for my magic to manifest." He leaned back and forth, studying my belt. "You don't carry any weapons. Do you prefer daggers? Swords?"

I flexed my hands, trying to envision them holding a blade and sweeping through hordes of enemies. A laugh bubbled in my throat, and I held it back.

"Let me think about it." Staring back toward the camp, I saw Seraphim's silhouette roll out a mat. "She wanted *you*, specifically. Do you know why?"

"You haven't heard of me?" He drew blood from the bandaged wound on his palm and shaped it into a small dagger. "The infamous butcher of lords and ladies?"

"No. I try to avoid powerful people when I'm not selling them cheap trinkets." I watched him spin the scarlet blade, mesmerized.

"Perhaps you haven't noticed, but you're on a suicide mission." He flipped the blade and caught its handle. "Typically, those with blackened hearts value their lives above the world, and who besides a criminal set to die would risk their necks on a fool's errand?"

"I guess you're an altruist who makes a perfect fit, huh?"

"Well, yes." He grinned, letting the blade burst into droplets of blood that streamed onto the forest floor. Lowering himself into a bow, he spoke solemnly. "Forgive me for our unfortunate meeting. I promise to make it up to you, Lady Aethra."

"Ugh." I rolled my eyes. "Did Eleos tell you to call me that?"

"He did. Should I not?" He stood, smiling. "But I mean it. I'm not in the interest of hurting innocents. Least of all, allies."

"I'll consider forgiving you." I tilted my head toward the camp. "You're going to miss your chance to sleep if you stay here with me."

"Keep your eyes sharp. Rouse us if you hear a hint of danger." He turned to go.

"Wait," I called, and he paused, glancing over his shoulder. "What set you down this path?"

"Killing people with no promise of reward?" He tilted his head down, dark hair falling over his eyes. "I lost every reason to care about *my* life. And in the process of losing myself, I. . . I decided I could be justice, for the people who would otherwise be denied it."

Staring into the darkness, I dwelt on my mother, on my father. The man who'd beaten me in the Guild's punishment room. Ainwir.

"I can understand that," I said, looking back at him. "On both accounts."

Lifting his head, Seth nodded. He clicked his tongue, and his shaggy dog rose from its mound of dirt and padded to my side. "Keep her company, boy." Ruffling the dog's ears, he returned to camp.

The man wasn't what I expected, in more ways than one. Eyeing his dog, I bent to meet its eyes. "So, you're Whisper?"

The dog panted in response. Intelligence gleamed in its sweet eyes, and its swift arrival spoke to its training. Maybe Seth used him to track down his targets.

Sitting beside the dog, I offered a hand and petted Whisper when it didn't shy away. Wincing, I examined the sheer amount of filth covering the poor boy. Maybe I could find time to bathe it while we were in Serifos.

Rubbing its ears, I leaned forward. "I bet you'll be handsome once you're clean." Its tail swished through piles of leaves.

Sighing, I leaned back, and the hound laid beside me. Though Seth had not meant to insult me, doubt wormed its way into my heart and slowly ate away at my core as the night dragged on.

Seth claimed to kill those who avoided justice, finding vengeance for the wronged and ridding the world of hidden monsters. Eleos had devoted his life to studying the Empty in hopes of saving it, and Seraphim championed the dangerous quest to see it through.

Even Percy, small as it was, sang songs to honor those lost and comfort those left behind.

What did I do? Cheat people out of coin? Arrange meetings and deals to suit the Guild and their clients, happily shutting my eyes and ears to who they might be hurting?

"Aethra!"

Startled, I turned to see Percy walking toward me, a satchel dangling between his fingers.

"Something wrong?" I asked.

"But of course something's wrong." He frowned, looking down at me, hat pointed toward the dirt. "We were supposed to watch each other's backs in there, and I let you down."

I laughed. "You're hardly to blame for that."

"Well, I say I am." He sheepishly pulled on the satchel's strings. "I picked these up back at the outpost. It's not the greatest apology, but it does come packaged with my solemn swear."

"Solemn swear?" I asked, a smile creeping up my face.

"To do better next time." He offered me the bag.

Curious, I took it and pulled it open. The nostalgic scent of candied oranges wafted from inside. Ainwir used to buy me these little sweets during our travels.

Chuckling, I pulled one out. "Thank you."

Bowing, he grinned at me. "Keep Whisper company. He gets lonely."

Pulling out a second candy, I offered it to the dog. Despite his size, Whisper took the candy daintily from my hands. "Good boy," I whispered, rubbing his head.

Still smiling, I closed the bag, saving the rest for later. What a sweetheart. Between his tone and body language, I'd gotten the impression Percy had been utterly sincere.

A bard tainted by the Empty, with a heart of gold. All my companions were mysteries to solve, their pasts a puzzle.

Pulling my knees up, I stared forward, reminding myself I was supposed to be paying rapt attention.

Serifos awaited us, a mere stopping point on our journey. My mother had dumped me on its streets, and in its outskirts, Ainwir had found me. Most of my life had been spent in its underbelly, learning how to make dishonest coin.

Sometimes, I tried to convince myself I had no other choice. I couldn't choose my master, nor his profession. I was working with the only skill I knew.

But it wasn't true. I'd never wanted for more, never thought outside myself. And I'd never felt guilt over it until now.

TEN

WE'D ROUSED IN THE MORNING to the sound of movement in the forest to our south. I'd been dragged from my bedroll and tossed onto a horse, mind racing with fear as I wondered what would happen if the soldiers caught us.

A confrontation would beget bloodshed and death. Here, in the wilderness, that could spell our doom. The guards doubtless understood the danger as keenly as we did—catching murderers in a world where violent death was to be avoided at all costs was their job. They'd have a means to outpace us, surround us, and force surrender.

I glanced around nervously as we left the woods behind and returned to the main road. The sounds of pursuit had faded an hour ago, but my heart raced nonetheless.

Eleos turned his head. "We'll be fine. They didn't see our faces, remember?"

"Stop reading my mind."

"I'm not. You're practically carved into my back, and I can feel your heartbeat."

Realizing he was right, I sat back on the saddle and almost lost my balance. Floundering for a handhold, I grabbed him again, less tightly this time.

Percy rode at the rear of our little formation, eyes glued behind us, Whisper trotting at his side, nose to the ground. Scanning the road, I watched intently for the gates I both loathed and adored the sight of.

Serifos: the last bastion of the isthmus. A thin strip of land carved through the Empty, leading to Therapne and Cynthus in the southwest. Pearl white gates rose above the trees, visible far before you reached the city's outskirts. There wasn't space for farmlands here: ranches gathered around a river, where herds roamed the thinning trees.

Once, mountains had risen toward the sky, wrapping Serifos in their protective embrace. Hints of white rock peeked from the ranches, though the mountains had long crumbled and disappeared into the Empty.

I sat forward as we crossed the bridge into the city proper. The guards here had not yet received word of the assault on the dungeons. Hopefully, we could get lost in the streets before they did. Leaning around Eleos, I took in the sight of my old home.

Some saw this place as the pinnacle of civilization: countless waterways riddled the city, traversed by boats like horses on streets. The channels pooled into the great Empty to either side of the isthmus, their life-giving water turning to a soul-sapping void.

Lanterns hung above the water, lights glinting on their rippling surfaces. Beneath the marble, the Guild operated— tainting the underside of the pristine city with blood.

Seraphim wound us through the streets, avoiding the wealthier parts of the city in favor of the poorer fringes. Memories flooded back to me in a rush: I could probably navigate these roads with my eyes closed.

Seraphim stopped in a familiar square: a willow tree grew from the cracked pavement, crowded with citizens traveling to and from their places of work.

"I need to meet with someone," She said, turning her horse. "Grab a drink if you need one," She nodded at an unsavory-looking inn, "and refresh supplies. I'll meet you here before curfew."

"Serifos has a curfew now?" I asked.

"You didn't know?" Seraphim raised an eyebrow. "Don't worry—you'll hear it. We have plenty of time left in the day." Clicking her tongue, she rode away.

Seth dropped his reins and stretched. "Who wants what?"

Eleos cleared his throat politely. "You two have catching up to do. Tend to the horses. Lady Aethra and I will handle rations."

"Good idea." Percy agreed.

"Oh." Seth raised his eyebrows. "You want to do this in private? I thought you liked to air grievances in public."

Percy raised a finger to argue, but hesitated. Chortling, I interjected. "Eleos and I are dying to know how you two fell out. And I could use a drink."

"So could I," Percy said, angrily yanking his gaudy fox mask out and strapping it onto his face. "I've written *two* songs about it." With unnecessary aggression, he shoved his hat down, nearly flipping it off his head.

Swinging my leg over the saddle, I clumsily dismounted, dropping to the road with painful reverberations through my knees. Rubbing my thighs, I grabbed my bag from the saddle and swung it around my shoulder.

Seth took my horses' reins and led the mares away. Nodding my thanks, I trotted up the inn's steps and stepped through the door. The smell of booze slapped me across the face, and I nearly choked. Searching for a lonely table, I sat down and flinched when a splinter dug into my rear.

Sighing, Eleos sat beside me, flipping open his journal where he kept track of our supplies. Seth joined us a moment later, sitting heavily in the seat opposite Eleos and kicking his feet up on the table.

Eleos reared back, eyes fixed on Seth's muddy boots. He gritted his teeth and stared daggers at the rogue, shielding his journal from the unseemly footwear.

A hand brushed my shoulder, and I turned to see Percy standing behind me, offering a mug of ale. "For the lady." He said, smiling.

"Thanks," I said, taking the mug and downing its contents. Horrible, cheap beer. The perfect brew for my current mood.

Percy laid two more mugs on the table, and Eleos quietly accepted one, eyes still glued to Seth, glowering.

"Alright," Seth grabbed his cup. "Sing your little song."

Clicking open his lute case, Percy slung the instrument around his shoulders and cleared his throat. He raised a hand dramatically, hesitating before strumming the first chord.

Magic slammed through my bones as his song began. I gripped the mug tightly, teeth vibrating and hands trembling. Crushing weight bore down on my soul. Agony. Heartbreak. Raising the mug to my lips, I drank as though my life depended on it.

I'm not sure if the song had any words, or if I simply couldn't remember them. I heard Percy's voice, warm and comforting. Sweet chords hung heavy in the air, tugging on my heartstrings.

I felt empty. Alone. *Betrayed.* Every emotion came like a wave, crashing over me as the chords shifted. The lyrics danced at the edges of my mind, like whispers bidding me farewell. Something deeper shook in my soul, as though I'd been offered an escape from hell itself, and the person I'd loved most shut the door in my face.

Ainwir appeared in my mind. Over and over. No matter how I tried to shove him aside. *Betrayed.* Abandoned.

When the song ended, a heavy stone lifted from my heart. Gasping for breath, I glanced down to see that my mug was empty.

Lifting my head, I looked between the men. Eleos grasped his journal rigidly, glaring more intensely than before. Seth looked like a puppy who'd just been scolded, face torn by guilt. Shoulders slumping, Percy removed his lute from his shoulders and returned it to its case.

"I, um. . ." Seth cleared his throat, regaining his charm. "I didn't realize you felt so strongly about our. . . unconventional farewell." Rocketing from his seat, he took Percy's arm. "Do you need anything while we're out? It's my treat."

Percy placed a hand on his hip. "I'm not a dog you can bribe with food."

"Didn't you have a crush on that cobbler? We could go see her."

Lighting up, Percy grinned. "You mean it?"

Rubbing his eyes, Eleos drained his cup, snapped his journal closed, and stood. "Let's get going, Lady Aethra."

Standing, I shouldered my bag, rubbing my sternum. Percy's emotions had wormed their way into my heart, all too similar to my own.

Seth whirled around and caught my wrist. "The Guild favors this town. Stay with the scholar."

Nodding, I gazed into his scarlet eyes. "Do you call yourself Burgundy Rose because of your eyes?"

"Seas, no." Seth rubbed his neck. "I didn't name myself. What do you take me for?"

"I don't know. . . the winks, the smiles, all while being chased by guards? You seemed the type to bestow upon yourself a stupid name." I slipped my hand from his grip. "Wear your mask."

"Anything for a beautiful lady," Seth winked at me before covering his eyes with a black mask and following Percy.

Holding open the door for me, Eleos exhaled when we stepped outside. "You know this city best. Lead the way."

Dancing down the steps, I waited until the door slammed shut behind us. "Is Percy really that upset about Seth?"

"Yes. He's *dramatic*," Eleos said. "From what I've read of their minds, they were good friends. Percy thought they were partners in crime—the hero and his bard. Seth didn't."

"Oh," I nodded. Suddenly, their relationship made perfect sense.

Eleos rubbed his chest. "Psyches' emotions lift once we cease the spell. Muses. . . linger."

"Hopefully not for long," Retrieving my mask from my bag, I fitted it over my eyes, and Eleos quickly followed suit, covering his face with the owl-feathered mask.

Nobody thought twice about those concealed by masks. People donned them for every occasion—festivals, funerals, celebrations. Hidden behind a stony exterior, one could express their truest self and close their eyes, for only a moment, to the horrors of the world around us. Not unlike the Maiden, who sheltered, but did not save us, from the encroaching storm.

A useful tradition for those of us who needed to hide our faces.

Keeping my head down, I avoided passerby's gazes, though it didn't seem many paid us a second glance. They probably assumed Eleos was a priest. I caught a few bowing their heads in respect out of the corner of my eye.

One man drew my attention: I noticed his dark boots slow as he drew near, and glanced up to see his simple tunic emblazoned with an unmistakable insignia: a chalice overflowing with golden water.

A Guild member.

Hoping it was a coincidence, I ignored him as we passed. He glanced over his shoulder at us, but continued on his way. Relieved, I released my held breath.

"Trouble?" Eleos asked quietly.

"I don't think so," I whispered back.

Hastening his steps, Eleos walked alongside me. "By the way, what did Seth talk to you about last night?"

"I think he was trying to apologize for holding me captive."

". . . for *what*?"

"Oh, you weren't there," I realized, chuckling, "he held me at knife point to escape the guards. Threatening to kill them with my blood if they attacked."

I expected Eleos to find the story amusing, but his brows lowered and his eye twitched. "And Percy didn't stop him?"

"What was Percy supposed to do? It was dark. I don't think he realized it was his old friend."

Eleos released an exhale lined with disgust. "Knowing Percy, he was too busy envying you."

"Me? Or Seth?"

"Both." Eleos corrected. "Was it at least a decent apology, then?"

I paused, thinking. "Not really, no. I think he implied it was my fault for being so conveniently vulnerable."

"Right," Eleos said with contempt. "I'll keep that in mind." He leaned closer. "I don't know if I like him. He gives off. . . an unstable air."

"He's a vigilante murderer. I'd be surprised if he didn't."

Mouth twitching, Eleos looked away. He was upset about something, but I wasn't sure what. Seth's willingness to put innocents in danger, perhaps. Psyches were known to be bleeding hearts, after all.

My nose wrinkled. Maybe I had guessed wrong, placing Ainwir as a psyche. The goddess Psythos would never turn her gaze toward a selfish thief whose only interest was lining his pockets.

A scent from my childhood caught my nose: nuts and fresh pastry. Grabbing Eleos's wrist, I guided him toward a tiny shop and pushed open the door.

Heat wafted from the oven tucked in the back, and displays of baked goods sat on thin plates. Ainwir had taken me to this bakery often—he'd loved it.

I remembered the woman behind the counter, though her hair had grayed. Sharp nose, soft eyes, blonde hair. Every time we'd visit, she'd smile and hide an extra treat in my bag. Did she remember me?

No. Not a hint of recognition appeared in her eyes. I bought two pastries and watched her turn her back, oblivious to the little girl whose day had been made lighter by her food.

A painful reminder of how little I mattered to anyone.

Swallowing the sorrow, I handed one of the wrapped pastries to Eleos and stepped back outside. "Ever had one of these?" I asked.

"No." He turned it over. "What is it?"

"A heavenly stack of syrup and nuts," I answered, popping it into my mouth. "Nobody should leave Serifos without one."

Chuckling, Eleos savored the pastry as if it were a gift from the king. "Mm. I see why you like them."

Taking slow bites to make the moment last, I took in the city I once called home.

A towering statue of the Maiden Brizo rose above the roofs, hands spread, water trickling through her fingers in streaming fountains that framed the temple she presided over. I'd seen the elegant edifice, its vaulted ceilings and numerous pillars countless times, yet never set foot inside.

Eleos stared at it in awe. I nudged him. "Never been to Serifos before?"

"Only passed through." He confirmed. "I've heard their library dwarfs the other cities—they house every kind of scholar. Agricultural, religious, geological. . ." He rattled off a few more names, but I didn't really hear them.

The excitement in his eyes was infectious, especially since he often appeared perfectly emotionless. I wanted to pull his mask off to see his face in full; men were never more handsome than when gushing about their greatest passions.

Leading Eleos away from the market, I turned west and headed toward the library.

"Did you join a Scholarly House?" I asked. "Or did you never have a proper job?"

"History." He said. "There are fascinating stories buried in old tomes. Maps of dead countries, wars no one remembers." His sage-green eyes lit up. "Did you know Cynthus was famed for its theater? They used to perform something called 'rain dances.'"

My lips tugged upward as I watched him light up.

"They even had their own gods." He waved his hands wildly. "Most people did." His eyes locked on me. "Did you ever hear the tale of the Forgotten-" He paused. "What?"

My smile spread into a grin. "Nothing. What were you saying?"

"The Forgotten Battlefield." He toyed with his bracers. "It's the only one that wasn't swallowed by the Empty. Numerous suits of armor and old blades riddle the fields, but no one knows who the soldiers were, or what they fought for."

"Oh. I hadn't heard of that." My smile vanished. Dead men and women, forgotten by the world itself. The thought made me sad.

"I always wanted to solve that mystery." Eleos continued. "What was the war about? What would those soldiers think, to know they fought a pointless skirmish for dead kingdoms?" He looked up sharply. "Did I bring down the mood?"

I shook my head and grabbed his arm. "Look there."

Following my gaze, his back straightened. A beautiful promenade flanked by marble statues led to the library, a towering building surrounded by rows of decorative pillars.

I tilted my head toward it. "You should visit. Might be your last chance."

"But-"

"I've shopped here a thousand times. I could do it in my sleep." I nudged him. "Go on. I'll find you when I'm done."

Guilt briefly flashed over Eleos' face before he drank in the library: a simple, but elegant building whose sides were carved with likenesses of the three lesser gods.

"Thank you." Eleos nearly tripped over both his words and himself. "I'll be quick." He took a step, then whirled around and caught my wrist. "I'm not supposed to leave you."

"The Guild doesn't attack people in broad daylight. Even if they caught me, at worst, I'd be thrown in a brothel. That was Laverna's favorite threat."

My attempt to reassure him had the opposite effect. His fingers tightened around my wrist. "Never mind. I'm staying with you."

"Maiden's grace. I was *joking.* I'll only be gone for half an hour." Pushing him, I encouraged him to go.

I wasn't joking, and trying to deceive a psyche was a foolish mistake. He read the truth on my face with ease. "Lady Aethra. . ."

"I'll be fine. I promise."

His severe expression eased. "Alright," he said reluctantly. "Half an hour." He swore, finally turning away.

Smiling, I watched him run up the steps and disappear through the great doors. Adjusting my bag, I turned on my heel and returned to the markets. Balancing on the patterned stone bordering the waterway, I watched my reflection in the water.

Water. Ainwir had asked me exactly once what I wanted out of life. At age fifteen, I'd blurted out a silly answer, but in the eight years since, it had never changed.

I wanted a house on a lake, or maybe a river. A loving husband and two children. That was all.

It was such a tiny thing, but anything we'd never have seemed like a wonderful dream. Unattainable. Distant. A paradise far out of reach.

Lifting my head, my gaze caught on a stall selling flowers. Wandering over, I examined the collection of petals, noticing a pale blue bloom sitting by its lonesome, without a bouquet to keep it company.

Wishing I could justify wasting coin on frivolous blossoms, I ran my fingers under its petals and admired its beauty. As a child, I'd pick flowers and weave them for Ainwir. Sometimes he'd humor me and wear the little crowns on his head.

"Like that one, do you?"

Startled, I turned to see a man standing beside me. Wearing a wealthy burgundy coat and a matching red and white mask, it was plain to see he was a nobleman. Wavy hair the color of wine tumbled past his neck, resting below his collar in a neat bond.

Retracting my hand from the flower, I smiled, glancing at the florist. "It's beautiful."

Reaching into a satchel at his waist, the nobleman pulled out a gold coin and passed it to the florist. The woman's eyes flew open, and she happily accepted the rich payment for so small a thing.

The stranger plucked the blue flower and tucked it in my hair. I tensed when he touched me. "It suits you, Aethra."

I froze, studying his features, trying to discern if I knew him. The mask concealed his entire face, with slits for his eyes alone. Eyes that matched Eleos': sage green.

He leaned in, whispering in my ear. "Care to walk with me?"

"I'd rather not," I spoke in a whisper.

The masked man lifted his gaze to the library behind us. "Would you like your friend to return to your inn alive?"

Blood running cold, I stiffened and nodded.

"Good." He smiled. "Come with me."

Pretending everything was fine, I followed the man, eyes tracing over his back in a desperate bid to find any clues as to his identity. He did not wear the insignia of the Guild.

We stopped beside a less-traveled channel that flowed beneath bridges connecting the streets. A gondola approached, empty save for its driver, who slowed the boat until it rested before us.

Beckoning to the empty seats, the masked man looked at me expectantly.

Normally, I'd seek escape. Boarding a vessel like this would guarantee an unfortunate end. Noticing my hesitance, the masked man calmly glanced up the road toward the library, silently reiterating his threat.

I couldn't know who he worked with, how many of them hid in the shadows. Assassins could be perched all around the city, waiting to strike. Swallowing my fear, I stepped into the gondola and accepted my fate.

ELEVEN

EETING DEATH AT THE HANDS of a handsome nobleman couldn't be the worst way to go. Lowering myself into the gondola's seat, I scanned the crowd desperately, hoping to spot one of my lunatic companions—ideally one of the two who could fight.

The nobleman sat opposite me and motioned for the boatman to take us away. With a sweep of his paddle, the boat departed the walkway and drifted toward the center of the channel. I stared longingly at the library as we sailed away from it.

The nobleman brushed a lock of red hair behind his ear. "Forgive the rude introduction. You're a clever sort. I doubted I could get you alone with anything less than threats."

I studied him intently, deciding kindness was more likely to see me through this encounter alive. "You thought correctly," I confirmed. "I don't typically trust strangers, especially not those high above my station."

"Yet you trusted one before. In this very city."

My mouth warbled. Did he mean Ainwir?

Folding his hands, the nobleman crossed one leg over the other. "I hear you've had a change in profession recently."

"How would you know what my profession was?" I asked guardedly.

"Because they say you're quite good at it. Laverna recommends you to many of her clients." He tilted his head. "But this? This requires a warrior, and my dear, I don't get the impression you are one."

"Armies need more than soldiers," I chirped, eyes flicking around.

Our boat rowed beneath a wide bridge, dust drifting over our heads as boots and hooves tracked across it. Where were we headed? I couldn't tell yet.

"Why is it your concern, anyhow?" I asked. "Most would be thrilled to learn of our goal."

"No, they would not." He corrected harshly. "They would be *horrified*. They would do everything in their power to stop you. Do you know why?"

I licked my lips. "They wouldn't-"

"You have too much faith in man." He interrupted. "Your mission implies an end. It makes them consider what they've never given heed to. They come face-to-face with the inevitable. And what an end, it would be." He leaned forward, voice dropping to a whisper. "Snuffed out. And for what? For *nothing*."

I knew he was right. The Archon had hidden us from the clergy for a reason. Seeking a solution implied no goddess would be coming. No salvation. No *hope*.

Voice gentling, the masked man sat back. "Tell me. How much do you know about Seraphim?"

"Enough," I answered. "But I won't tell you anything, if that's what you're after."

He tutted. "Already, you show such loyalty to her. Haven't you learned your lesson about trusting people?"

I swallowed, straining to hide my expression. He did know Ainwir.

"Did Seraphim tell you the story of her exile, at least?"

"No." I spat. "People don't owe me their stories any more than I owe them mine."

"Oh, but I think you deserve this." He smiled wryly, and I found myself wondering what he looked like beneath the mask. "The good lord of Cynthus sired three children: twin daughters and a son. Though they wore the same face, the girls couldn't be more different. One became Seraphim, the other Themis."

Curse my lack of knowledge about lordly affairs. I knew next to nothing about Lady Themis, not even that she'd been Seraphim's twin. Women did not inherit the throne. Gossip did not care about them.

"Seraphim believed the only way to stop the Empty was to enter it." He explained. "Themis was far more pious and forbade her from exploring blasphemy. Behind her family's back, Seraphim carried on experiments only to arrive at a horrifying truth."

I narrowed my eyes. "What kind of experiments?"

"How would you learn the means required to enter the Empty?" He shrugged. "You send people in until one comes back alive."

I bit my lip. The Seraphim I knew wouldn't do that, would she? "And what was the truth?"

"That *nobody* returned alive." The masked nobleman's eyes darkened. "Lady Themis caught wind of her sister's heinous crimes and exposed the truth. Desperate to cover it up, the rest of the family elected to banish her into the Empty. A fitting end."

But her brother had saved her, helped her escape to Duath Nun instead. I could ask Seraphim about this later—I had no reason to trust this man when I couldn't read his expressions.

"Interesting," I said. "I'd rather learn who you are and why you care."

"Seraphim does not know if the Acheron River will ferry you safely into the heart of the Empty. Are you willing to be her next sacrifice?"

"Yes," I said, surprising myself with how quickly the answer came. "I'll die either way. I don't really care which finds me first."

He laughed bitterly. "You have no idea what you're getting into, do you, *Elpis*?"

I blinked at him. "What did you call me?"

"Perhaps you do not care about your fate." He shook his head. "But I do."

"You don't even know me."

"But I should." He paused. The boat drifted by the slums built along the waterline, the buildings erected on the higher level rising into the sky like guarding walls. "Have you ever wondered why Ainwir appeared in the woods that day?"

No. I hadn't. And I didn't care now. "How do you know him?" I demanded.

"Come with me and I'll tell you everything you wish to know. You'll be safe under my care—both from the Guild and harm."

I grimaced behind my mask. Ainwir had taught me to always know my enemy. But this man's voice was not familiar, and I could not see his face, nor judge his age. Plenty of people in the Merchant Isles had shades of red hair. He might not even be noble—gods knew how many times I'd dressed nicely and pretended to be one.

The only clue I had was his eyes. Sage-green. But it was just a color—a color that hundreds, if not thousands, of people shared.

Gods, I knew *nothing* about Eleos. Why had I started trusting these people? For all I knew, this could be his brother. His father. A distant cousin.

I lifted my gaze from the boat's floor, praying this man wasn't a psyche. He watched me calmly, unreadable behind his mask.

"Tell me your name," I said. "And I might consider it."

Waving a hand, the nobleman directed the boatman to stop. The gondola moored on a familiar street, one that Ainwir and I had often walked years ago.

The nobleman stepped out of the gondola and offered me a hand. I begrudgingly accepted, stepping from the boat onto solid ground.

"This isn't the safest area for you." He said. "Especially not these days."

The Guild had countless eyes and ears in this part, and I didn't want any of them to catch wind of me. Glancing around, I quickly spotted a textiles shop nearby; its back door would lead me onto an alley I could follow back to the library.

"Thank you for the conversation," I said rigidly. "I would say it was a pleasure to meet you, but you never offered your name."

Exhaling, he ran a hand through his hair. "I suspected you would try to run. It's really going to make things more difficult for both of us."

"You might've considered inviting me to dinner first."

"Did we not discuss what such a course would have yielded? You know better than to trust a man who smiles and offers you aid." His eyes crinkled. "You really are a great deal like Ainwir. Looking at you feels like looking at him."

I moved to respond, but his tone of voice caught me off guard. Affection. *Fondness.* He did not speak of Ainwir as a hated foe, but a friend.

'*Never trust a man who smiles and offers you aid.*' Ainwir had warned. '*Trust instead the man who bears his teeth and carries a knife. Only one is being honest.*'

"I can protect you, Aethra." He said, eyeing me intensely through his mask. "If you stay with Seraphim, you will not survive."

"So you've claimed, but I don't trust you either."

"Did I not reveal to you the truth?" He asked. "You didn't want to be part of this reckless mission. You became what you are out of necessity. I can offer you the solace you long for."

Had a nobleman arrived at my door a few months ago and offered to pay my debts, I would have leapt at the opportunity. His charming conman act would have worked on anyone else.

But I was a con woman myself.

"I'd say thanks for the ride," I spat. "But it wasn't exactly pleasant. Fair sailing." Turning on my heel, I strode away.

The smell of iron surged through the air as red thorns whipped around me, encircling my upper body and waist, their razor-sharp tips digging into the fabric of my dress and skin. I stumbled as they drew me back to him, spinning me around to face him.

These thorns were made of *blood*. He was a chthonic mage. The god of art and luck clearly did not favor me.

The nobleman grabbed my chin and tilted my face up. "I bear no intentions to harm you." He said evenly. "But I cannot let you return to her."

Biting my lip, I weighed my options. Follow this man to who-knows-where, or risk death to escape.

I didn't give my situation the thought it deserved. Something in me snapped, and I moved.

Grabbing the vines wrapped around my chest, I tore them away from me. Thorns dug into my hands, drawing blood. Pain ripped through me as I threw myself backward, trying to escape my bonds.

The nobleman's eyes flared, and he quickly scrambled to release me from his spell. The vines fell away, and I spun on my heel and sprinted for dear life. Glancing behind me, I saw him staring at my blood in horror. He hadn't expected me to harm myself to escape.

"Wait!" He called

Red vines grew from the blood coating my dress, whipping toward my ankle to trip me up. But they wavered at the last moment, as though afraid to touch my skin. Taking advantage of his hesitance, I slammed into the textile shop's door, fumbled with the knob, and threw myself inside. The vines sprouting from my body caught in the door and exploded into a shower of scarlet rain.

Someone shouted in horror. I ran into a stand and knocked over a bolt of cloth in my flight. Reaching the back door, I fled into the quiet dark alley and followed the sloping path north.

Before meeting Seraphim, I had never dealt with chthonics. Now, I understand why they were so feared. How were you supposed to fight someone who turned your own blood against you?

The world flew by in a blur. I was a child again, alone and frightened. My mother had dumped me on a street corner, promising to return, but she never did. A man had grabbed my arm, and though I was too young to understand his intentions, I knew to feel fear.

Blinking the memories from my eyes, I dove behind an empty wagon sitting in a corner by a small warehouse. Pressing my back against the stone walls, I ran my hand down my shoulder, checking my injuries.

It stung. There was a lot of blood, and I didn't understand enough about medicine to accurately assess myself while consumed by panic.

I pressed a hand to my chest, trying to stop the bleeding soaking my dress. Pounding drum beats thudded against my ribs as my heart raced. Had the nobleman followed me?

Footsteps sounded on the road. Holding my breath, I crept forward and peered beneath the wagon. I caught a glimpse of white pants and boots, and quickly recognized the elaborate patterns stitched up their leather.

Rising from my hiding spot, I stumbled as pain flared through my arm. Eleos spun in my direction, sage-green eyes widening in worry as he raced to my side.

"Seas." He gasped, hesitating to touch me. "What-"

"We need to get out of here." I interrupted, clutching his wrist.

I managed to drag him two steps before I faltered. Blood streamed down my dress, and everything hurt. Pulling behind the wagon, Eleos forced me down and tore my dress to examine the wound. Cuts and scrapes patterned my arms and chest where the vines had dug into my flesh, and a deep gash cut above my breast.

Eleos flinched, ripping a section of his cloak to pack the wounds before pressing down on the gash to stop the bleeding.

I wasn't proud of the whimper that escaped my lips.

"Who did this?" He hissed.

"A noble in the city," I panted, "Has it out for us. For Seraphim in particular."

"Why?"

"I don't know. I didn't recognize his face, and he didn't mention his name."

Eleos glanced around the wagon. "Nobody should know about us. Not by name." Tearing off his sash, he wrapped it around my chest and bound it tightly. "We need to get back."

He offered me a hand, but I shook my head. "We'll attract too much attention, running through the streets like this." Raising my chin, I studied a nearby street sign. "I know this place like the back of my hand. There's a brothel nearby we can shelter in."

"Is a brothel really the best-"

"The women there will help us." I staggered to my feet, shimmying around the wagon to check for a man dressed in red. A few people came and went, but none wore masks.

Taverns and whorehouses adorned this road; the crowds would arrive with the setting sun. That gave us only a few minutes before we'd find ourselves surrounded by onlookers. Limping from behind my cover, I hurried down the street.

Eleos followed me, hand hovering behind me as though worried I'd fall.

A 'closed' sign hung from the brothel's dirt-smeared door. Leaning against the stone building, I gestured for Eleos to knock. "I'll talk to them."

He hesitated before knocking heavily. A few moments passed before the door unlatched, and a woman, tangled hair bound in a bun, peered through the crack.

"I need a room and a change of clothes," I said. "I'll pay whatever you like."

The woman studied me quickly, eyes darting to my bloodied gown before settling on my face. "The second room on the left is empty. I can let you have it for an hour." She said, pulling open the door.

I HADN'T EXPECTED to lie topless in a brothel today. Stranger things had happened in my lifetime, I supposed.

Ainwir and I had hidden in this place once before. He'd taught me a valuable lesson: most women will aid other women. Learn to tell which will throw themselves into danger without a word, and which will turn you away.

I'd like to think I was the former, but had yet to find a distressed young woman at my door.

Squeezing my eyes shut, I winced as Eleos poured a bottle of cheap liquor over my gash. I took a glance at the jagged wound and decided I didn't need to see it again if I wanted to keep my lunch.

"Sorry," Eleos murmured. "You're sure you didn't recognize him?"

"I didn't exactly brush shoulders with the highest of society," I said, pointedly staring at the brothels' stained wall.

The thorns had ripped across my chest, meaning there was but a thin sheet preventing us from getting to know each other a whole lot better. Wiping off the alcohol, Eleos retrieved a bandage from the end table and hesitated.

"Do you mind?" He asked, reddening as he reached for the sheet protecting my modesty.

"I thought healers were supposed to be professional."

"I'm not a healer."

"Or a priest or a scholar."

"You remember wrong. I *am* a scholar."

"Right. The only scholar of the Empty." I said, trying to lighten the mood. "But tonight, *learned of the female form.*"

"I'm already familiar with the female form."

"Oh? Are you?" I grinned.

"Yes." He said calmly. "I studied anatomy in my youth."

"Well, that settles it," I murmured. "You *are* a scholar. No one else would phrase it that way." Turning my head, I stared back at the wall. "Go ahead. They're not bad, so enjoy."

"I, um. . ." Clearing his throat, Eleos pulled back the blanket and quickly bound my wounds.

Had anyone else been beholding my naked body, I wouldn't have cared. I laid there rigidly, intimately aware of every brush of his hands against my skin.

The last thing I needed was growing feelings for a man I knew nothing about. Had I learned *nothing*?

"There," Eleos said softly, tying the bandage and pulling up the blanket.

He turned his back to me, staring at the far wall. Sitting up, I checked the bandages, frowning. Was it better for him to say nothing, for us both to pretend this hadn't happened? Or was I upset at the silence?

Maybe he read my thoughts. Head tilting slightly, Eleos offered quite possibly the *worst* compliment I'd ever received.

"You're right. They're. . . aesthetically pleasing."

A laugh erupted from my lips, and I doubled over as pain shot through my chest, the burning only worsening as the laughter refused to cease. Wrapping an arm around my chest, I rose from the bed, half-whimpering, half-giggling.

Chuckling, Eleos nervously played with his hair. "I shouldn't have said that."

"No, I'm glad you did." I caught my breath, grabbing the black frock the girls had lent me from the wardrobe. "Have you courted someone before?"

"Yes."

"Did you use that line on her?"

"No." He blurted out. "I imagine it would've ended much quicker if I had."

"Sounds like she wasn't any fun," I said, pulling on the gown.

Most of the men I dealt with were sleazy and disingenuous. It was nice to speak to a man who was anything but.

My chest cracked in pain, and I pressed a hand to it, grimacing. Eleos flew from the bed and grabbed the sash from my hands. "Let me."

I forgot whatever I'd been thinking as he drew me close and touched my back, gently looping the silk around my waist. Over the years, I'd been with a few men. Some I'd been foolish enough to think were love, only to learn they were not. None had ever begun with something simple. All had started in lust.

Eleos tied the sash in a neat bow at my side and looked up from his work to meet my eye. Maybe he read my emotions, or perhaps he saw them on my face.

"Your eyes." I blurted out. "He had your eyes."

Brow furrowing, Eleos stepped back. "The nobleman?"

"Yes. Do you have family?"

Eleos answered hesitantly. "Yes."

"Then, maybe-"

"None of my family are nobles. Nor would any be here, threatening you." He shook his head, pulling his cloak off.

Shaking out the pale blue fabric, he wrapped it around me. "We need to get back to the others. The first curfew bell already sounded."

Oh, it had. I'd been distracted by the blood streaming down my arms. Pressing a hand to my chest, I grabbed my bag and followed him to the door, pausing at its threshold.

Gods, I was an idiot. In all the dreams where love had found me, never had I been the one to ruin the moment. Disheartened, I trudged out the door.

The brothel had come alive since we'd entered. Several patrons sat in the common room or led girls upstairs. Fishing out his coin purse, Eleos approached the counter and thanked the matron for sheltering us.

Pausing by one of the couches, I examined the room, the barely-dressed girls, and the men who eagerly sought their company.

The men were the kind you'd call neighbors and peers, not the scum I had once imagined. A girl who'd worked here years ago had given me words of advice: most of their business came from married men. Love and loyalty were delusions only naive maidens indulged in.

Someone touched my arm, drawing me from my thoughts. Eleos gently wrapped an arm around me. "Come on." He said, guiding me to the door.

A cold breeze dug into my bare skin as we stepped outside. Night had blanketed the city, save for fires glowing in lanterns. Pain throbbed in my chest with every step, and though my legs were unharmed, I struggled to move them.

Stopping, Eleos sighed, muttering to himself. "What am I doing?" Swinging his bag around to his side, he knelt in front of me. "Let me carry you. And you aren't allowed to say no."

Lucky for him, I wasn't usually the stubborn type. Relieved, I trudged forward like a shambling corpse, wrapping my arms around his neck and burying my head into his hair. Grabbing my thighs, he hefted me up.

First a brothel, now a piggy-back through Serifos' backstreets. My life just got better and better.

"It's not the best solution," Eleos whispered. "I know you didn't want to draw attention."

"No, it's fine," I said. "At this time of night, everyone will assume I'm your drunken lover."

"Good point. It's not far from the truth."

Had I more energy, I would have contested the egregious line. Closing my eyes, I tried to ignore the throb of pain with every step, instead focusing on his hair.

The *hair*. I'd wanted to touch it for ages now, and it proved as soft as I'd hoped. It even smelled good, though I was too woozy to place the exact scent. Had he snuck out of camp every morning to bathe in a nearby stream?

Stupid scholar. Why hadn't he taken me? I probably looked like I'd just rolled out of the sewers. It had been a mistake to assume he wasn't vain.

A mistake borne from knowing nothing about him.

I wanted to change that. I wanted to glance over a market stall and effortlessly pick out something he'd like. Come the evenings, we could sit together in companionable silence, each aware of the others' hobbies and quirks.

Not since Ainwir betrayed me had I shared my soul with another. The loneliness had grown into an all-consuming hole.

"Are you alright, Lady Aethra?" Eleos asked.

"No," I murmured into his hair.

"I can put together a proper painkiller for you when we get back." He said. "Oh, and you aren't going anywhere alone anymore."

I turned my head, watching stores and houses pass us by. "Can psyches fight?"

"You'd be surprised what we can manage in a scrape." He said, releasing a soft snicker. "Perhaps I can demonstrate on Seth."

"Don't jump to judge—maybe he's a nice guy."

"Hm."

Wind swept over the streets, blowing strands of his hair across my face. Lifting my head, I opened my eyes and noticed him looking back at me.

The expression he wore fractured the solace I'd slipped into. Worry darkened his face, but not for my safety.

I'd seen that expression before. Men wore it when closeness had grown between them and someone they had not wished it to. Because they could not be together, or because the woman had not learned the depths of his sins.

Eleos quickly looked away, and my mind reeled. Day after day, he'd shown me kindness. Reading insincerity came easily to me—and he'd displayed nothing but genuine compassion. Any doubts I'd harbored about his character had faded at the outpost.

He feared I would learn a secret he kept hidden. A secret that would make me hate him.

TWELVE

HE SECOND WARNING BELL WOULD sound soon. Those comfortably in the middle class hurried to finish their work and scurry home, while those in the slums made no fuss about the curfew. The Guild owned those streets, not the guards.

Eleos carried me through cozy cobblestone roads, occasionally saying something to convince onlookers I'd merely had too much to drink. Letting myself drift off, I closed my eyes and tried to relax.

I roused from my daze when Eleos gently set me down in the square centered by an old willow. The place where Seraphim had wanted us to regroup.

"Shit." I cursed, eyes adjusting to the darkness. We were late.

A man paced the far side of the square with an agitated gait. Noticing us, he turned on his heel and ran over.

I didn't recognize him at first. A tall man with silken black waves stood before me, his tanned skin marred by a scar across his cheek. A scowl twisted his mouth, but I focused instead on his strong jaw and the hints of stubble that remained after a fresh trim. The sleeves of his black coat were rolled up, revealing defined forearms criss-crossed with scars.

Was that *Seth*? Bathed and newly dressed, I hardly recognized him. Had he always been that attractive under the grime?

"Finally," Seth folded his arms, scarlet eyes glowing with exasperation. "You're late. I thought you were *dead*." His eyes traced over my arms and studied my new gown. His scowl vanished. "You certainly look like it. What happened?"

"Aethra was attacked," Eleos said coldly. "Is the inn safe?"

"By who?"

"We don't know. A nobleman wearing a mask."

"Great." Seth spread his arms. "Your leader hasn't returned, either. Percy ran out looking for you guys, and told me to wait here in case you returned."

Eleos ran a hand over his eyes. "Do you know where he went?"

"It's Percy. He doesn't know where he went."

Eleos made a sound of distress. "Gods, you're right." He shook his head. "But Aethra's injured. I need to get her to safety."

"I'll search for them," Seth walked around us. "If enemies lurk in the city, Percy's an easy target."

"Wait," I called. "We'll go with you. None of us should be alone." I took a step after him and flinched. "But, can we take a horse?"

Without missing a beat, Seth spun on his heel and swept me into his arms. Gasping in surprise, I locked my hands around his neck as he marched down the street, heading for the stables.

Seeing him up close confirmed my suspicion: Seth was undeniably attractive, when he didn't wear the caked-on mud and tattered rags of a deranged murderer. The stylish collar of his jacket framed his prominent collarbone and sharp jaw quiet nicely. . .

Eleos jogged to catch up with him. "What are you doing?"

"She's injured," Seth said matter-of-factly. "Making her limp is cruel and a waste of time." His brow furrowed. "Tell me about this attack."

"I didn't get a good look at him," I explained. "He dressed like a noble, wore a mask. He said he wanted me alive, but I didn't get the impression the same extended to the rest of you."

"Aren't we doing the entire world a service?" Seth scoffed. "Who would want to stop us?"

I looked down, remembering the nobleman's words. Why did he want me alive and no one else?

A towering, muddy hound sat patiently outside the stable doors; his tail wagged furiously when he noticed us. Seth set me down gently beside Whisper and hurried inside. Unsteady on my feet, I gratefully leaned on Eleos when he offered his arm.

"Are you sure you won't stay here?" He asked.

"If he finds me, I won't be able to defend myself."

Eleos sighed. "You're right."

The stable doors flew open, and Seth led two mares out. "Nobles." He spat, handing the reins of the red mare to Eleos. "Why is it *always* nobles?"

"I take it you have a history with them?" Eleos asked, helping me onto the horse's back.

"Who doesn't? They trod over the people for leisure every day." Seth swung himself into his saddle. "And still, they haven't had their fill of pain." Clicking his heels into the horses' flanks, he rode north. Whisper rose and followed him.

Sitting behind me, Eleos flicked the reins, and our mare followed. "If he thinks nobles are bad," he muttered, "he's clearly not dealt with the clergy."

"I haven't either," I said. "The Guild stays away from them."

"I don't blame them."

Shifting to make myself comfortable, I leaned against his chest, a warm, comfortable seat. Eleos wrapped an arm around me, carefully avoiding my wounds.

Stiffening, I fought a war in my head. I yearned to trust him, but couldn't let foolish infatuation lead me to ruin again. Convincing myself the closeness was necessitated by my injuries, and we could return to simple friendship afterward, I relaxed.

Trying to be useful, I scanned the streets for Percy, hoping we'd find him alive and unharmed.

As a child, I'd run afoul of a crowd of panicked, angry people. Curious what might be happening, I'd strayed toward them. Ainwir had caught my hand and barked a harsh whisper: *Stay away from the tainted.*

A woman with snow-white hair had stood in the middle of the throng, her face buried in her hands, sobbing. The last I saw of the unhappy event was the guards arriving to drag her away.

Tainted were cast out, driven to the edge of the Empty by armed guards. Bound in shackles, they were left to die. If anyone caught wind of Percy's condition. . .

We rode back to the markets, hoping he'd gone to search for us there. The streets had emptied since the first bell had chimed. In the shadows of night, the Maiden Brizo's statue looked more ominous than holy; the black water trickling through her fingers bore an uncanny resemblance to the still water of the Empty.

Lonely lanterns shone down on us, guiding us through the market stalls towards a crowd gathered near the temple.

Whatever had drawn people here was already over. The throng broke up as a pair of guards marched through the promenade, torches held aloft, shouting for the crowd to disperse. Fear and anger painted the people's faces as they fled.

Seth cursed under his breath. "What's going on?"

Pulling out of Eleos's grip, I dropped off the horse and caught up to a woman, who clutched a young child by the hand, desperately leading him away. Catching her arm, I spoke to her in a friendly, concerned tone.

"What happened? Is it safe that way?" I nodded my head toward the temple.

"You didn't see?" She gasped, whirling around. "A tainted. Here!" Her hand trembled on her child's.

Blonde hair flecked with gray fell to the woman's shoulders, framing her sharp nose and soft eyes—the baker I'd been so fond of as a child.

Collecting myself, I shrank away in feigned fear. "Did-did they get rid of it?"

"Yes, thank the Maiden." Her bulging eyes darted around. "Get away from this place. It needs to be cleansed."

She pulled from my grasp, and I let her go. First, she hadn't remembered me; now, she condemned one of mine. Everything I'd once loved had lost its luster.

Eleos rode up beside me. "How did anyone notice?" He wondered. "Percy's always exceptionally careful about concealing himself."

"I doubt there's another tainted in the city," I accepted his hand back onto the saddle. "The guards are taking him to the Empty. They might've only just left."

Yanking the reins, Eleos rode toward Seth, who'd paused on the bridge beneath the maiden's left hand. Water trickled to either side of the passage, tumbling into the channels below.

Seth turned toward us, red eyes laced with concern. "If we're lucky, they'll leave him bound an inch from death. If we're not-"

"The bounds of the Empty aren't far." Eleos interrupted. "We can catch them."

"We'll be branded heretics for trying to stop them."

"Then we *won't* stop them," I said. "Can Whisper track Percy? We'll wait until the guards leave, and then untie him."

Eleos's eyes darted around. "Do you have a plan for getting out of the city? The guards aren't going to let us saunter through the gates past curfew."

"I know a way. It's guarded, too, but members of the Guild are easier to bribe."

Seth grinned. "Lead the way."

Taking the reins from Eleos, I directed the horse south, fleeing the temple and traveling along thin roads pressed against the empty waterways, driving us into dark alleys. Retracing the path Ainwir and I had walked once before, I stopped outside an unassuming-looking wooden shack resting along a dirty channel.

Eleos took the reins back when I dropped them. "What's this?"

"There's a tunnel inside." I nodded at the house. "The Guild uses it to smuggle goods and people out."

Seth dropped off his steed. "I'll convince them to let us by. Wait here."

"Don't kill them." I pleaded.

"What do you take me for?"

"An assassin?"

Winking, Seth drew a knife from his belt and leaned against the door, listening for activity inside before knocking.

When no one answered, he glanced at us before throwing the door open and stepping inside. A few moments later, he re-emerged, grabbing his horse to lead her through the door.

"No one's home," he said.

"No one?" I repeated, slipping off the saddle and limping through the threshold.

A musty scent clung to the tattered curtains and threadbare quilt. Dust gathered on the wardrobe, but not on the desk. Running a finger along the old wood, I wrinkled my brow in confusion.

Had this place been abandoned? When Ainwir had taken me through here, a man had stood guard inside, keeping record of comings and goings. More Guild members had guarded the passage, both ensuring the safety of their clients and preventing unwanted shadows from haunting their territory.

Seth threw open the back door and carefully descended the dirt slope into the underground. The *lovely* scent of sewage emerged from the tunnel, and I pinched my nose to keep it out.

The horses protested vocally as they were led down the slope into the old sewer system. Dark stone surrounded us on all sides, cracked and crumbling in places. Pulling his lantern from his saddle, Eleos lit a fire to guide our way.

Whisper ran ahead of us, scouting the path. With every step, I grew more concerned. Why did no one guard this passage? Whisper never returned to warn his master of danger, never barked to alert us to another's presence.

When faint moonlight spilled in from outside, Seth narrowed his eyes. "Seems it's unguarded." He said, whistling for his dog.

Whisper rose from his seat by the tunnel exit and returned to Seth. Kneeling, the assassin reached into his bag and pulled out a crumpled ball of colorful fabric. He offered it to the hound and let him thoroughly sniff the cloth before stuffing it into his pack.

Eleos raised an eyebrow. "Is that Percy's?"

"Who else's?" Seth answered.

Nose pressed to the ground, Whisper ran outside, seeking the bard's trail.

"Where is the Guild?" Eleos muttered.

"I don't know," I said. "I don't like this."

Seth remounted. "Take the blessings while they last." He said, riding after Whisper.

We emerged from a hole in the ground, neatly obscured by fallen leaves and piles of tree branches. Thin woods and sloping hills surrounded us, dotted by chunks of white rock.

Closing my eyes, I flinched as our horse stepped over the rocky terrain and slowed to weave through the trees. My chest ached every time I was bounced around on the saddle. The glow from Eleos's lantern painted an orange halo against the black of my closed lids.

My mind wandered. Why had Seraphim been late? She'd mentioned needing to meet someone before we parted. Had the red-haired man found her?

The horse stopped abruptly, and my eyes flew open. Whisper had paused, nose buried in a bush.

"He's lost the scent." Seth dropped off his horse, guiding the mare as he walked alongside the dog.

Eleos slipped off the saddle, sweeping his lantern over the dirt. "They're bound to have left tracks." He paused, glancing back at me. "Can you handle her alone?"

Balancing in the saddle, I took the reins and pressed my thighs to the mare's side. "How hard could it be?"

Eleos flashed me a smile before continuing his search. "So, Seth," He said quietly. "What made you decide killing people would be your life's decree?"

"Is this really the time?" Seth called back, unamused.

"On a mission such as this, there will *never* be a good time."

"I thought I already explained myself," Seth said. "You can only stand by and watch cruelty unfold so many times before you can't stand it anymore."

"Who were you before that?"

"You first." Seth prodded. "All four of you were in the dungeons before being promised a pardon. So what's *your* crime?"

"Don't bother," I said. "I already tried asking them."

Seth snorted. "I can tell you Percy's at least." He glanced back at us. "He's got a good heart. It was probably something ridiculous like tax evasion."

Eleos quietly corrected him. "Disturbing the peace. He fist-fought an innkeeper."

A wicked grin tugged at Seth's mouth. "I didn't think he had it in him."

Snap. Sitting up, I whirled around, searching for the source of the noise. Shadowed woods surrounded us, and infinite black beyond. Taking a breath, I tried to relax. It had probably just been a rabbit.

Seth's voice drew my attention back ahead. "So, you're all keeping secrets from one another? A perfect start to a functional team."

"I don't owe you my past," Eleos said guardedly.

"What about her?" Seth grabbed my horse's reins. "Is she owed your past?"

Hesitating, Eleos' eye twitched.

Seth looked up at me. "How much blood have you left in your wake?"

"None," I answered. "I have nothing to hide."

"Few can say that with certainty," Seth said in a low tone. "We'll never make it far without trust. Luckily, I know a good bonding exercise."

"I shudder to think what an assassin considers bonding," Eleos said.

"Training. Every loss is a secret owed." Seth smiled cheekily. "Are you in, scholar? I doubt you know your way around a blade."

"So, we'll beat the answers out of one another?" Eleos sighed. "Mistress Seraphim will be thrilled."

"Ah. . ." I swallowed nervously. "I've never been trained to fight before. Does it hurt?"

Seth eyed me like I was a lost puppy. "That might be the cutest thing I've heard a hardened criminal say."

I exhaled with frustration. "I'm a con woman. We don't knife people in back alleys. We're thieves with *class*."

He dropped the reins and held up his hands. "I didn't mean any offense. Training leaves us all with bruises. But you'll be grateful for them when you survive your first fight." Grabbing his horse, he returned to Whisper's side.

Nudging the mare forward, I caught up to Eleos. He glared at Seth before looking up at me. "Are you doing alright, Lady Aethra?"

"I'm fine," I assured him. "Do you sense something. . . *off* in Seth's emotions?"

"The opposite." Eleos stared at the man's dark shape through the trees. "He's put up walls that keep me out, save for surface-level thoughts. Only intense training can repel psyches."

"Is that a bad thing?"

"Not in itself. But nobody trains for that unless they have something to hide, and a very good reason to keep it hidden."

"Found it!" Seth called. "This way."

Eleos swung himself into the saddle and took the reins. Whisper must have picked the trail back up; the hound flew through the underbrush, tail pointed skyward.

A familiar sensation bloomed in my chest: unease and nostalgia. A strange cocktail of emotions that made me feel both like a small child and a woman moments from facing her death. Writhing beneath the growing pain, I gritted my teeth.

"Stop!" I hissed.

Seth whistled to Whisper, calling the dog back. He turned to me, but froze. In the silence, we all heard the same thing: men speaking and twigs cracking.

Leaping off his horse, Seth tied it to a nearby tree and crept forward, taking shelter behind a trunk and peering into the darkness.

"Stay here," Eleos whispered. He moved to dismount, but turned back to me. "Do you trust me?"

"For the moment, why?"

"Because I'm worried about you." He gently brushed my cheek, and for a moment, I thought he intended to kiss me. Leaning forward, he cupped my face in his hands and pressed his forehead to mine.

A strange sensation sparked between us, a slight pain beneath the surface. Releasing me, he leaned back.

"*Can you hear me?*"

I started, realizing his mouth had not moved. He'd spoken into my mind.

"*I'll take that as a yes.*" Dismounting, he hurried after Seth.

Eleos' voice rang against my skull, jarring but not unpleasant. I touched my head. Psyches were more dangerous than anyone had led me to believe. Closing my eyes, I tried to think at him.

"*Could we do this all the time?*"

"*No. It's taxing for both of us.*" He responded, though his shadow had disappeared into the trees.

"*Can you hear all my thoughts right now?*"

"*Only if you shout them at me.*"

Trying to put a clamp on my whirling mind, I caught my breath, deciding how I felt about this revelation. A useful skill, to be sure, but I didn't trust anyone enough to let them fully into my mind.

Wincing, I leaned forward, hoping to make out anything in the dark. A horrible realization struck me: Seraphim still had the Bloodstone. We had no defense against the Empty.

Pulling my leg over the saddle, I managed to drop off the horse, though the landing sent painful reverberations through my wounds. Catching myself on the tree, I tied the mare's reins to Seth's and limped after the men, crouching beside Eleos. He didn't look surprised to see me.

"Stubborn one." He spoke into my mind. "*Just stay behind us, alright?*"

Shadows danced in the distance. I could make out four or five men in the glade ahead, one kneeling or perhaps forced to his knees and bound. The distortion in my chest grew, suffocating me.

Seth pressed his back to the tree and motioned for Whisper to lie down. "Now we wait." He whispered.

The guards quickly finished the unpleasant work. Two seemed nervous, eagerly backing away from the glade, hands on the hilt of their blades. One turned around and perhaps gave an order. Two men practically turned tail and fled, the third marching behind them.

The fourth remained, standing before the bound captive. If he felt guilt, said a prayer, or spat in Percy's face, I couldn't hear. Eventually, he turned away and hurried to join his brethren.

Seth waited until the sounds of their footsteps disappeared. Bolting from our hiding spot, he drew his dagger and rushed to Percy's side. Eleos motioned for me to remain behind, but my fears over the damnable rock we *didn't have* sent me chasing after them.

Eleos' lantern illuminated the chains bolting Percy to a stump, the splotches of blood on his face, and a gash across his brow. Relief flooded his face when he saw us. "Seth!" He whispered. "I can explain."

Grabbing the chains, Seth scanned them for a lock. "You idiot. I don't need an-"

"We're in danger," Percy panted. "Someone targeted me. He knew who I was. Knew who you were."

Shit. Another snap sounded behind us, and I whipped around, scanning the trees.

Slitting his palm, Seth drew blood and shaped it into a thin pick. Biting his lip, he fitted the makeshift lockpick into the shackles.

Overcome with a mix of emotions, I backed into Eleos. "What's wrong?" He whispered.

The Empty loomed behind us, a terrifying few paces away. Blinking my eyes, I realized the oppressive dark behind Percy wasn't the night: every living thing ceased at the edge of a cliff and disappeared into the void.

"Got it," Seth muttered, pulling the shackles loose and helping Percy to his feet.

Bloody vines shot through the underbrush, wrapping around us like a constricting viper. Eleos pulled me back as they surged through the air, blocking our way forward and back.

The nobleman in red stepped from the darkness, blood dripping from his palm. His sage green eyes gazed at me with disappointment through his concealing mask.

"You just had to run, didn't you?"

THIRTEEN

A FLASH OF SCARLET WHIPPED across my sight as a longsword formed from the droplets falling from Seth's hands. My heart pulsed, watching the lifeblood spill from his palm, a twin echo to the Empty thrumming behind me.

The masked nobleman raised a hand in peace. "Two chthonics clashing so close to the Empty will bring nothing good. For either of us."

The bloody long sword hovered by Seth's side. "Agreed. You don't make a move, and I won't either."

A hand wrapped around my elbow, yanking me back. Eleos stepped in front of me, shielding me. Whisper lowered himself to the ground, teeth bared, a snarl ripping from his snout.

Shadows moved in the woods as more people emerged, forming a line between us and the forest. I squinted, trying to make out their features and count their numbers. Ten or so, each dressed in leather emblazoned with a goblet. Though I couldn't see the colors of its stitching, I had a feeling it would be gold.

Guild members.

Pulling arrows from their quivers, the Guild's assassins knocked their bows and pointed them at us.

"How nice of you to bring company," Seth said, his voice friendly. "I take it *you* attacked our con woman and arranged Percy's mob?"

I glanced at Percy, who nodded stiffly.

The nobleman stalked forward, his red vines coiling around us like snakes. "There is a good reason I brought you here. So long as you drop your weapons, we will all walk away from this alive."

"I'm not sure I believe you," Seth said. "Normally, people get to know me before cornering me in the woods with hired thugs."

"I would have invited you for dinner had we the time." The nobleman sounded like he was smiling. "My only interest is in the lady, and not because I wish her harm." He turned to me. "There is something here you need to see. And when you do, you will thank me for it."

"What do you want me to see?" I asked.

Behind the mask, sage-green eyes swept over us, drinking in our every detail. "One of you will turn and walk into the Empty. And you will do so knowing you saved your allies' lives."

Seth scanned the woods, counting the enemies, one hand curling behind his back, fingernails digging into his palm. Spots of blood appeared on his skin.

Eleos squeezed my wrist and spoke in my head. "*I think we can take them. Between the three of us, we can carve a path to the horses.*"

"*What if the Guild members are mages?*"

"*I doubt they are. They would have flaunted their advantage.*"

The nobleman's gaze darted to Eleos. He peered at us as though listening to our conversation. With a horrible gurgle, the blood vines surged upwards, wrapping around Eleos and me, a thorned tendril brushing against Eleos' neck, drawing blood.

"If you have faith in the Maiden," the nobleman said calmly. "There is no cause for fear."

Eleos tensed, watching the vines scrape his skin. "I have no faith in the Maiden." He said harshly.

The nobleman's sage-green eyes landed on me. "*What happens next depends on you.*"

I flinched, touching my head. Had he spoken into my mind?

The hand Seth had curled behind his back flexed, and blood poured from his palm, gathering into a jagged blade. His eyes focused on the nobleman's neck as his fingers grasped the blade's handle.

Percy noticed Seth's actions and shot to his feet. "I'll walk into the Empty. It's not like I haven't spent enough time around it already."

"Percy," Seth hissed. "There's no need. We can-"

"What? Start a fight and let the Empty spawn under our feet?" Percy snapped. "The moment one of you strikes, we're all dead."

"You don't know that-"

"But I'm not willing to risk it." Percy stared at the nobleman. "You said something good would come of it. Let's see what, then."

"Good lad." The nobleman commended, nodding for him to go.

Brushing himself off, Percy stood and took a step toward the Empty. Both Seth and Eleos lunged for him, trying to pull him back.

Splintering sorrow like I'd never felt tore through my heart, and my world darkened as my vision saw only streaming tears and tearing agony. My knees hit the dirt as the will to continue on fled my body. Haunting music sang through the air, like the sound of a wailing mother turned to song.

Eleos and Seth crumpled under Percy's spell. Pressing my hands into the dirt, I tried to regain my mind, shaking off the music he'd forced upon me. My vision steadied, and I raised my head. The nobleman watched me intently. His vines parted, allowing a man wearing a white tunic to pass by, his colorful patchwork sash flapping in the breeze.

Percy walked toward the dark, towards an inevitable, instantaneous end.

The pain of my wounds vanished. A newfound strength surged through my limbs, and I stumbled to my feet, taking two uncertain steps before finding my stride. I paid no mind to where the nobleman's deadly vines blocked my way, not caring if they tore me open.

But they receded in my wake, shrinking away to allow me past. So little space separated us from the Empty. Merely a few strides. I reached for Percy, but I was too late.

One step separated Percy from the bounds of the Empty. He glanced over his shoulder at me as he took his final step.

Aching nostalgia filled my breast, like a siren song calling me home.

"Percy!" I shouted, throwing myself across the distance between him. My fingers caught on his shirt as I clumsily tackled him.

The surprise of my weight threw him to the ground. He landed on his back noiselessly, and I collapsed atop him, fingers ripping through fabric.

The sensation in my breast ceased. Air fled my lungs, and sound could not reach my ears. Raising my head, I stared into the great void, the endless canyon that dove miles below the earth into a still sea.

A sea that rested quietly below me, so still it appeared like glass. Glass that did not reflect anything above it, a stagnant pool that could have been boundless as the ocean or thin as a sheet. Only a thin red halo, shining around the Empty's borders, pierced the fathomless dark.

Percy sat upright, grabbing my arm, eyes widened in shock.

Nothing separated us from the fall into death. The edge of the Empty's canyon was behind us, a steep tumble unto death, but we did not fall. Something held our weight, barely visible, like a film of transparent thread. It looked like we simply floated in a great void, leagues above the sea.

We were *inside* the Empty.

My head pounded. Everything hurt. I felt like the twine that made up my bones was coming unwound, and my skin was being torn off, piece by piece. Writhing in agony, I doubled over, fingernails digging into my palms.

Percy's dull gray eyes brightened. Staggering to his feet, he wrapped his arms around my waist and threw us both back toward the cliff.

Everything flooded back in an instant. Sound, breath, life. I gasped as I struck dirt and heard the heavy thud as Percy landed beside me.

"*Aethra!*" Eleos' voice rang sharply in my mind.

Bloody thorns still surrounded the men, though they'd found their feet. Seth's intense gaze caught my eye first; he gaped at me with abject horror, a stark contrast to the euphoria I could feel radiating from the masked nobleman's eyes.

"*Move!*" Eleos' voice scraped across my mind.

As though the Empty were an ocean, keres emerged from its bounds like swimmers breaking the water's surface. Ragged clothing clung to their sallow limbs, torn by their long claws. Their hollow eyes fixed on Percy and me.

The Guild members pointed their bows at the creatures. An arrow sailed over my head and struck the keres behind me, steel sinking into its chest. The creature staggered, its head thrown back by the force of the impact. The sinewy neck snapped back into place a moment later, and the keres trudged on, undeterred.

Percy grabbed my arm and hauled me to my feet. Instincts kicked in, and I fled toward safety, ignoring the pounding pain in my chest.

Whirling around, Seth grabbed the long sword that had been hovering beside him and threw the dagger he'd clutched in secret. It soared through the air toward the nobleman's throat while he cut through the bloody vines with his chthonic blade.

Ducking out of the way of the dagger, the nobleman drew a rapier from his belt and cut his hand. Thorned vines burst from his palm, wrapping him in a protective embrace as the bloody dagger arced past him and swung around mid-air, circling back to slam into his back.

It connected with the vines, blood merging into blood before the two separated, and the knife whirled back to Seth's hand.

Steel rang across the forest as several Guild members drew their blades, and arrows arced through the air.

Shit shit shit! I cursed in my head, turning back to look at the Empty worriedly. The edges of its border pulsed, unstable, drawn to the violence. Nostalgia and unease burst to life in my heart.

A keres charged me, slamming into my back and knocking me to the ground. Covering my face with my arms to shield myself from its claws, I tried desperately to summon whatever cursed magic I possessed, but nothing answered my call.

A flare burst through the night sky, searing the land with a red glow. The keres' sunken eyes lifted from my face to stare toward the battle raging behind us. Taking advantage of its distraction, I shoved it off me and crawled away.

Pounding hooves alerted me to a charging horse: a black mare bolted toward me. Shrieking, I pressed my head to the ground and shielded myself, but the mare leaped over me. Fire streaked across my vision as a scythe of burning radiance spun through the air and cleaved the keres' head from its shoulders.

A bright red braid swung behind the woman on the horse, a scythe made of blood and flame clutched in one hand, a shimmering red stone in the other. *Seraphim*. Hope flared in my heart for a fleeting moment before I noticed a shadow closing in on me.

Gods, why hadn't I taken sword lessons? Bolting to my feet, I found myself face to face with a Guild member, his blade arcing for my head. Back-stepping, I avoided his first swing and managed to block his second with my gold bracer. The jewelry wasn't meant to be armor. It dented and pain racked through my wrist.

The black mare charged between us, forcing the Guild member back. It kicked, hooves connected with the man's chest, sending him flying backwards. He struck the bounds of the Empty and disappeared into a sea of dust.

I'd seen someone touch the Empty before, but the experience did not spare me from the shock and horror.

Life, extinguished, leaving nothing behind.

"Stay down!" Seraphim shouted. An arrow flew past her head, soaring into the Empty and crumbling. Hooves pounded past me as she rode back towards the remaining enemies.

Heeding her order, I ducked, trying to take stock of the chaos. Seraphim's flames burnt a path through the trees, and I could faintly see Seth's bloody blades whipping through the air, but the night and the Empty made it impossible to keep track.

My attention was drawn to a white coat and a blue scarf. Eleos. He stood where he'd been before, gaze locked with the masked nobleman.

What were they doing? The nobleman didn't move either, rapier clutched in a frozen grip.

Keeping low, I hurried toward him, intending to push him down to better avoid flying arrows, if nothing else. The masked nobleman's head jerked in my direction, and his voice sang in my mind.

"*We will meet again. And you will understand everything, then.*"

Eleos pressed a hand to his head and staggered to a knee. The nobleman stepped back, a little unsteady, but found his footing and quickly turned, disappearing into the trees. Running to Eleos' side, I put a hand on his back.

"Are you alright?"

Shaking off whatever had stunned him, he wrapped his arms around me, shielding me with his body as he pushed me back towards the horses. An arrow whizzed past, scraping a gash across his cheek.

The sound of our horses, frightened and distressed, guided us to where we'd tied them up. Sliding behind the trees, Eleos grabbed one of the mare's snouts, trying to calm her. "Cut her loose." He snapped.

Fumbling with the rope, I managed to unfasten them. Fire blazed through the woods as Seraphim rode toward us, strands of red hair clinging to her face. Yanking the reins, she halted beside us.

"They're retreating." She said, "Ride to safety. I'll catch up." Kicking her heels into her horse, she turned around and bolted back into the chaos, grabbing Percy by the neck and hauling him onto her steed.

Eleos wrapped an arm around my waist, picked me up, and threw me onto the red mare's back. He climbed up behind me, tugging the reins to turn the horse around.

"Wait." I gasped, reaching for the other steed's lead. "Seth!"

Teeth gritted, Eleos looked as though he was going to suggest abandoning the assassin, but he closed his eyes and sighed before turning the horse around. We bolted across the fields, across pools of blood left behind in the chthonics wake.

A flash of crimson streaked through the night ahead as Seth disarmed a Guild member and drove his sword through the man's gut. Yanking the blood blade out, he turned toward us, ready to strike, but lowered his weapon when he recognized us.

I dropped the other mare's lead as we reached him. Seth grabbed the horse's saddle as it ran past, managing to climb onto its back mid-stride. Whisper ran after him, clinging to the horse's hind legs.

The Empty pulsed behind us, the depths of its void slowly marching forward.

"Seas." Eleos cursed, staring daggers at Seth. "Are you asking for death? Why did you attack?"

"You're going to scold me now?" Seth yelled. "Save it."

Writhing emotions spun in my chest. Doubling over, I grabbed at my breast, unable to tear my eyes from the void and its still sea as it slowly consumed the world where we'd been fighting only moments before.

I saw the corpse of the man Seth had killed be consumed, turned to unceremonious nothingness as his existence was swept away.

And then it stopped. The bounds of the Empty halted and quickly fell out of view as we galloped into the trees.

FOURTEEN

URING MY LIFE IN IKARIA, when stress seized my soul and pounded against my skull, I'd walk along the waterways and pick flowers. Flowers that would die by the morning, but would brighten my tiny home for a single night.

Tonight, I relieved stress by washing a muddy dog. Whisper stood in the brook, brown murk washing from his coat and drifting down the stream. I shivered in the cold water, rubbing soap between my palms before running it down his fur.

Scrubbing the dirt from his snout, I smoothed back his wiry fur and beheld his handsome face. Tongue flailing from his mouth, he tried to lick the soap from his tall, pointed ears.

Leaping from the stream, Whisper shook himself dry, throwing water and suds everywhere. His tail whipped violently across the river stones, alerting me to someone's approach.

A black shadow ducked between two trees and descended upon the hound. "Did she wash you, boy?" Seth cooed, rubbing the dog's ears.

Smiling, I rinsed off my hands as Seth joined me at the riverbank. Blood soaked his arm and dripped down his forearm. Examining the wound, I met his gaze.

"Shouldn't you wrap that?" I asked, gesturing.

"Hm?" Seth raised his arm. "It's probably fine. Chthonics get used to bleeding."

"It's *not* fine," I said, hiking up my wet skirt and reaching for my bag hanging from a branch. Pulling out a roll of gauze, I flicked my fingers at him. "Take your shirt off."

"I thought Eleos was the resident healer." Seth loosened his cloak and pulled off his tunic.

"He's a scholar." I corrected, unrolling my bandage. A jagged wound similar to the scar on my breast snaked down his bicep. Grabbing a handful of water, I washed the laceration off and set to binding it.

Seth stared quietly at the top of my head as I worked. "You entered the Empty." He said.

"I did," I confirmed, fingers trembling on his skin.

"Who are you, really?"

"Nobody," I said earnestly.

The stern gaze in Seth's eyes softened, but I couldn't read him. He guarded his expressions as tightly as his mind, barring both psyche and con woman out.

Stepping away, I checked over my work. Good enough. My eyes quickly drifted to his bare chest, tracing the myriad scars crossing his back and abdomen. Tattoos painted his uninjured arm, black swirling patterns I didn't recognize. They rose from his elbow, caressed his shoulder, and covered his pec, as though vines reaching for his heart.

My gaze lingered on his defined chest and the way his arm muscles flexed as he shook out his shirt. Forcing myself to stop ogling, I pointed at the scar crossing his rib cage.

"Where'd you get those?" I asked.

Shoving his tunic over his head, Seth straightened out his black waves. "The scars? From a fight with a dragon."

"Very funny," I splashed water across my face and stood. "You lectured Eleos about keeping secrets, but I think you have more to hide than he does."

"I have every intention of being truthful," he slung his cloak around his shoulders, "once I know I can trust you."

His words sounded like hypocrisy to me. Shaking my head, I retrieved my cloak from where it hung from the trees and wrapped myself in it. "And how long does that take?"

"Depends," Seth said, the corner of his mouth turning up, "Percy? He knew all about me in only a couple of days. But he was a trained warrior, so I imagine it'll take much longer for *you* to best me in battle."

I'd almost forgotten his offer to trade secrets over sparring matches. "Sounds like you never intend to tell me who you are," I said, slipping through the trees. Whisper trotted at my side as we returned to camp.

Seraphim had suggested we stay away from the city. Instead of a warm inn, we nestled between two ranches in a rocky depression hidden from sight.

I felt a little better about my disheveled state: everyone now shared a few cuts and scars. Seraphim's hair had flown loose from its braid, Percy's ridiculous outfit had been torn in several places, and Eleos's collar had been ripped in half. Gratefully warming my hands by the fire, I sank to my knees.

"Feel better?" Eleos asked, offering me a wooden bowl filled with some kind of stew.

I chuckled, taking the food. "Yes. He needed a bath." I glared at Seth.

"He's a hunting hound," Seth said, dropping beside me. "Not a prince's show dog."

"Why can't he be both?"

Seraphim paced around us. "Did the cold water jog your memory?"

"No." I shook my head. "I'm certain I've never met him, and I don't have family or old friends."

Running a hand across her forehead, Seraphim stared into the fire. Concern bloomed in her eyes, and a slight tremble shook her fingers. But the moment passed, and her confident stride returned as she paced the camp.

Eleos stood, tying his cloak around his shoulders. "At least we know why he tried to kidnap you. He wanted to drag you out here and see if you could weather the Empty."

"Which you could," Percy added quietly, plucking at the strings of his lute.

Red light bounced off the fire as Seraphim pulled out the Bloodstone. She palmed it, sighing. "The Maiden's Bloodstone shields us from the Empty. Everyone knows that. But few heard the rumors of a little girl who'd commanded the Empty before it was forgotten."

I stared at her, the meaning behind her words slowly taking root in my mind. "What?" I said softly. Realization struck me like a hammer, and I flew to my feet. "You *knew*?"

Eleos flinched. "I wouldn't go that far-"

"Why didn't you say anything?" I demanded.

"We thought it was a pointless hope," Seraphim admitted, palming the stone. "Honestly, I thought they were baseless rumors, but Eleos was insistent on tracking you down."

"Our best leads guided us to you," Eleos said. "A woman with talents we needed. It worked out nicely."

I chewed my bottom lip. "That's why you were watching me! *You* paid Laverna. *You* asked her to send me on that mission."

Seraphim raised an eyebrow. "I thought that was obvious."

Throwing my arms wide, I repressed a manic laugh. "Why didn't you just knock on my door and hire me? Why did you try to get me killed first?"

Eleos flinched again. "I wanted to knock, but Seraphim-"

"I thought Eleos was chasing delusions." Seraphim folded her arms. "I wanted to test you, see if you were as good as Laverna claimed."

I ran my hands down my face, trying to decide how I felt about everything. From what I understood of Seraphim thus far, testing me by throwing me into the fire was precisely her style.

"And the stone?" I gestured to the Bloodstone. "Does it do anything?"

"I certainly hope so." Seraphim tossed and caught the precious relic. "Though I'm not keen to test its talents until absolutely necessary." She stared at me gravely. "Nor am I keen to test yours. The Empty is not to be taken lightly."

On that, we could agree. A sharp stab of pain radiated through my chest, and I sat, regretting the way I'd flailed my arms about.

"Seraphim," I asked, "Who were you meeting in Serifos?"

"My brother's contact," She said, "He'll send word of our arrival, so my brother can prepare the border lord's meeting."

"Why were you late?"

"The Guild held him up," She dipped her head, "I had to swoop in and rescue him. They must have wanted to delay me, keep me from you."

Seth waved a hand over the fire, sending embers flying across the night. "Let's focus on the present. Our masked nobleman followed your little rumor, too, but clearly doesn't seek the same goal."

"So what goal does he seek?" Seraphim muttered, pacing.

"We should avoid him at all costs," Eleos said, staring into the fire. "He's chthonic and psyche both."

I'd guessed as much when he'd spoken into my mind, but I'd never known someone could inherit more than one god's magic.

Neither had Percy. "Both?" He echoed.

"It's rare, but it happens," Eleos confirmed. "I tried to alter his emotions, get him to pull his men back. We clashed as he tried to dig into my thoughts, and I into his."

Seraphim looked up sharply. "Did you learn anything?"

"No. He was the stronger of us." Eleos's brows drew together. "Though. . . I got the impression he knew me, even if the recognition wasn't returned."

Seth's head snapped up. "Where are you from?"

"Therapne."

"Then we can start our investigation there." Rising, Seth grabbed his bag and approached Percy. "Are you alright?"

"Fine as any of us are," Percy responded, shrugging. "I'm still. . . processing the revelation."

His nonchalant shrug was a poor attempt at hiding his frayed nerves. I glanced over his tainted features, trying to decide if I owed him an apology or thanks.

Seth turned to Seraphim. "We should get moving."

"We're leaving?" I asked.

"Staying here invites another attack," Seth said. "Leave now, and we might shake them."

"I suppose he's right." Percy rose, rubbing his back. "Especially now that we know the Guild wants our heads. That being said," He counted the horses. "We're down to three. Traveling will be slow going."

Seraphim chuckled, shouldering her satchel. "And here I thought muses were supposed to be creative." She gestured to the rolling hills. "Where are we, Perse?"

His eyes narrowed, then widened. "Oh. We're to play the part of thieves again, then?"

I choked on my stew. After breaking a dangerous assassin from a heavily guarded dungeon, horse thieving seemed trite by comparison.

Seraphim caught my gaze and smiled softly. "Aethra. Go with Seth. Find a good one. Eleos, with me. Percy. . . take a breather." Turning on her heel, she marched off.

Eleos looked at me somberly. "Be careful. I'll leave the fire burning. Maybe it'll throw them off our scent." Stepping around the flames, he followed Seraphim.

Running a hand across my aching chest, I limped to Seth's side. "So," I said, hoping to lighten the mood. "Are we stealing one for you or me? Because there are these beautiful blond horses with white manes. . ."

Seth glared at me, eyes the color of blood.

"Something wrong?" I asked, hesitating.

"No." He said quickly. "Come on. I'm sure we can find one of those."

Breaking my gaze, he led the red mare away, Whisper trotting behind its hooves. Exhausted and aching, I trailed after him, adjusting my eyes to the night as we approached a nearby field to rob the poor farmers of their steeds.

Seth halted abruptly. "Thanks." He said quietly. "For saving Percy."

"It wasn't the most elegant rescue." I huffed, glad to be stopping. "We were supposed to be sitting by a fire with wine right now, listening to Percy slander you in a heart-wrenching ballad."

"He did mention having a second song, didn't he?"

"A more traditional crooning over your break-up, I'd imagine."

The corners of Seth's mouth twitched. "I do feel. . . a bit bad about what happened."

"What did happen?"

Seth paused, tugged the horse's reins, and continued walking. "I abandoned him."

"I gathered as much." Burning pain traced across my chest as we walked. "Why?"

He sighed. "Percy shouldn't be out here. He should be at home. I thought I'd be doing him a favor, but I should have known he'd be too stubborn to do the right thing."

"What do you mean?"

Seth's brow lowered in thought. "It's not my place to spill his secrets. Ask him. He'll tell you."

I tried to read between the lines of his words and expressions, wondering if Percy had a family or obligations he'd left behind. Seth's tone revealed little save a worry for his friend. Pain flared in my chest again, and I doubled over, face torn in a grimace.

Seth grabbed my arm, steadying me. "Are you alright?"

"No," I choked. "Hurts."

He tilted his head. "Have you ever moonlit as a horse thief?"

"Surprisingly, no." I gasped. "I didn't leave the city much."

Nodding, Seth whistled. Whisper's ears shot up, and the hound hurried to my side, sitting on my feet. "Protect the lady, boy." He released my arm. "I'll steal your horse for you."

Handing me the horses' reins, he jogged into the night. Grateful, I sank to the ground and tried to sort through my thoughts.

I could stop the Empty. I could *enter* the Empty. Why?

And how had rumors about me spread? As a child, I'd been stupidly wandering the woods when the Empty had cleaved across the land toward me. Ainwir had appeared in the nick of time, sweeping me into his arms and carrying me to safety, running far faster than my short legs could have managed.

I'd sworn the Empty had receded from my touch, but I'd never shared my flights of fancy with anyone but. . .

Ainwir.

The masked nobleman had implied that Ainwir's timely intervention was no coincidence. But. . . what did that mean? If Ainwir had known about my magic, why had he simply taken me on as an apprentice, nothing more?

My head hurt too much to think right now. Wrapping my arms around Whisper, I tried to drown out the sound of the wind, the insects, the distant rushing of the stream.

Pure silence had enveloped me in the Empty, devoid of senses, of breath. In a way, it had been. . . comforting.

The keres beckoned us to join them in oblivion. Free from suffering, from strife.

Whisper growled, and I raised my head to see Seraphim's black mare approaching. Eleos slid off its back, a flurry of words tumbling from his mouth.

"I'm sorry! Seraphim and I remembered you're injured, and aren't fit to ride, and. . ." He closed his eyes, rubbing the bridge of his nose. "With everything that's happened, I've been distracted."

I almost didn't recognize his voice. No matter the danger we'd faced, Eleos' voice had always been even and calm. Though hints of worry or anger had crept into his tone, never had it overtaken his unflappable attitude.

For the first time since we'd met, he finally sounded shaken. Worried.

"It's alright," I said, laughing. "I forgot, too. And I'm the one with the wounds."

Eleos dropped beside me, sitting with the heaviness of someone utterly overwhelmed. "A chthonic psyche. Callesis must hate us."

"He blessed Percy."

"Did he?" Eleos spat. "Callesis gifted him magic, but little else." He paused. "If the other gods give their blessings, why not the Maiden Brizo? Maybe we just don't understand her magic, I thought. Maybe there's still hope."

Turning my hands over, I studied the lines of my palms. I'd spent so long living in a hovel, surviving on scraps, the mere thought I could be capable of anything more struck me as ridiculous.

"Everyone wants to believe she'll come." Eleos continued, staring forward into the night. "But nothing in this world happened without people. Everything we have blossomed from us. Parents toil for children who'll long outlive them, and architects work on grand edifices they'll not live to see completed. Why should salvation be any different?"

Frowning, I recalled how harshly he'd denied belief in the Maiden. Those who spurned the gods often drew their spite from tragedies the gods should never have allowed to pass.

Flexing my hands, I recalled the moment I'd halted the abyss, and the churning emotions in my chest. "Do you think there are others who wield the Maiden's blessing?"

". . .I don't know. I hope so."

"I don't know how to control it."

"No mage does, at first." He smiled. "We have plenty of time to learn."

Twisting to face him, I scanned his features, the dark lashes and soft brown waves. "How long were you stalking me? Was it *really* only two weeks?"

"I was not stalking you, Lady Aethra. Frankly, it's a miracle I ever found you."

"Hm. Alright." I chuckled. "I wonder what would have happened had you knocked."

"So do I."

Closing my eyes, I collapsed against his side, burying myself in my cloak. Eleos fell silent. A calm breeze stirred the hills, tugging my curls away from my shoulders.

Forgotten magic, the end of the world. . . topics too grand for a simple con woman.

"Do you have a hobby?" I blurted out.

"What?"

"A hobby. Something you do when you find yourself with unexpected free time."

Taken aback by the sudden question, Eleos stared at me like I'd hit my head before answering. "I read."

"You read?" I arched an eyebrow. "That's it?"

"Yes. What did you want me to say? That I carouse at the local taverns?"

"I would be *very* surprised to hear that."

He laughed. "There's so much more in this world than any man could hope to learn in a lifetime. I never tire of it."

"Okay." I closed my eyes. "What did you read about last?"

I felt the muscles in his arms relax. "It's been a while since I've had the time. I think it was about the history of leather-working in northern Cynthus."

Snorting, I leaned off him.

"What?" Eleos demanded. "They have a unique technique there. Clearly, you've never had the pleasure of buying one of their cloaks."

Giggling, I unfolded myself and stood. "Nothing. You're just cute."

Frowning, he rose and planted a hand on his hip. "Fine. What do you do for fun?"

"I pick flowers," I said, shrugging. "Not very exciting, I know. But it's all I have time for." Taking a deep breath, I brushed off my dress. "We should get back to the others."

When I looked back at Eleos, his eyes had drifted away. Distracted, he strode a few paces down the hill and knelt before returning to my side. A little red poppy, freshly plucked, was tucked between his fingers.

"Flowers suit you." He said, brushing aside my curls to tuck the flower into my hair. He parted my strands gently, folding the stem into a little braid to keep the blossom steady.

My hand trembled as I reached up to touch it. A swell of emotions washed over me, and tears burned in my eyes, though I had no reason to cry. Swallowing, I glanced away, hiding my face.

I knew how to read people. Attraction, most of all. Whether it was lust or a more innocent interest, I could see it in men's eyes. But even when off the job, such gazes had been shallow, intended only to lure me into their bed. What did a man look like when he yearned for something more?

No, I was reading too far into things. Feelings followed lust. Never the other way around. And I'd never seen Eleos look at me with a hint of desire.

"Are you alright, Lady Aethra?" He asked gently.

"Mhm," I nodded, wiping my eyes. He stared at me in concern, brows lowered. He didn't understand.

I didn't either.

Whisper's tail thumped against my leg. The dog stood at attention, tail flying furiously, gaze fixed at the lone rider galloping toward us.

Mounted atop a gorgeous blonde mare with a flowing white mane, Seth guided the stolen horse to me and gestured with playful theatrics.

"Well, princess?" He asked. "Will this steed do?"

Wiping the moisture from my eyes, I laughed. "She's perfect."

FIFTEEN

RIDING A HORSE BY MYSELF felt like a greater hurdle than all the trials preceding it. Worse still, Seraphim had decided Seth would start training me to fight tonight.

Pressing my thighs against the saddle, I sat rigidly, grasping the reins for dear life. The blonde mare with beautiful white locks had a gentle personality, at least, and heeded commands with little fuss. Eleos had thoroughly tested her before allowing me to ride her alone.

Trying to relax, I admired the scenery. Ainwir had taken me to Therapne when I was twelve. It felt like a lifetime ago. I had no memories of this road, nor of the city where the seat of the clergy was built.

Red-leafed trees dotted the mountains like fire burning in high pyres. Steep ridges collapsed into deep gorges, and waterfalls trailed from the highest peaks into the lowest valleys.

What lovely scenery—a pleasant backdrop for the beating I'd receive tonight.

Someone snickered, and I looked over to see Seth laughing at me.

"What?" I demanded.

He effortlessly pivoted in his saddle. "I thought the destitute of Ikaria were all farmers. How have you never ridden a horse?"

"I stayed in the city. There was no reason to leave."

"Just balance, princess, it's not that hard."

Twice now, he'd called me that. I hoped he hadn't decided it was my nickname.

Eleos glanced back from where he rode ahead. "The princess can take however long she needs to learn."

"She most certainly can." Seth agreed jovially. "And I can laugh at her, just like I laughed at Percy."

Twisting to look over my shoulder, I spied an unamused expression etched on Percy's face. He leaned forward on his stocky mare. "The Merchant Isles don't have a cavalry, Seth. I was a *foot soldier*."

The horse lurched beneath me as she stepped over a crevasse. Panicking, I grabbed the reins and leaned forward, legs squeezing the horse in a death grip. Seth chuckled again.

Galloping hooves thrummed behind us, like heavy drumbeats. I wanted to turn around, but I didn't want to risk falling. Tilting my head every so slightly, I watched Seraphim ride past on her black steed, turn, and circle around me until she rode step in step.

"Looks like you can ride after all." She admired, grinning.

"Does it?" I asked.

"We're not being followed," Seraphim announced. "Close as I can tell. Maybe they lost our scent."

"Here's hoping," Percy grumbled.

Biting my lip, I recalled what the strange man had called me. 'Elpis.'

No matter how far I reached into my memories, the word meant nothing. Though I wanted to chalk his actions up to the hubris of a madman, I couldn't. He'd known I could step into the empty and survive.

Sitting back up, I focused on riding. Everything could come one step at a time, starting with keeping my seat. Chthonic madmen who were also psyches? I'd worry about them when I could ride a horse.

The sun began its descent through the sky, illuminating the mountain pass in orange light. We'd be stopping soon, thank the Maiden.

"Ah!" Seraphim called. "There's a nice spot to camp."

She rode to a cliff overlooking a lake and swung out of the saddle. A river cut through the pass, plunging into the waters below. Clopping through the shallow water, my horse stopped at my command and patiently waited for me to dismount.

Oh, gods. This was the hardest part. Psyching myself up, I muttered under my breath, telling myself the task was simple, and I was just overthinking it. Slipping one foot from the stirrups, I dragged it over the saddle, and. . .

Losing my balance, my other foot departed the stirrup, and I crashed to the ground, landing on my ass with a surprised yelp.

Like it was the easiest task in the world, Seth leaped off his horse and offered me a hand. "Color me impressed, princess. I thought you'd need help." He tilted his head. "Help *off* the horse, at least."

Begrudgingly accepting his hand, I brushed my toga off. He clicked his tongue.

"Don't bother." He suggested. "I'll have you rolling in the dirt plenty tonight." Patting my shoulder, he retrieved a bundle of supplies from his saddlebags and joined Seraphim by the fire pit.

Rubbing my eyes, I imagined what life might look like right now, had I never left home. Market Street would close with the setting sun, and I'd be trudging toward the bar to hand over my day's earnings to my collector.

Maybe sword lessons weren't so bad. Anything was preferable to my old life.

"How'd it go?" Eleos asked, holding the reins of his horse.

"Better than I thought," I admitted, looking up at my stolen steed. "I can't say I'm a fan of riding, though."

"Neither am I. Short rides are wonderful, but long ones?" He shook his head. "Camping's the best part of traveling, anyway. Especially when you have good company." He smiled at me. "And a bard."

Chuckling, I touched the flower he'd woven into my hair. Seth had suggested I ask Percy his story, and I'd yet to find the courage. Perhaps I'd finally catch a moment of his time tonight.

Laying a hand on my horse's neck, I gazed into her intelligent eyes. Horses deserved names, didn't they?

"Eleos," I called. "Does your horse have a name?"

He patted the dappled brown mare. "Yes. Artemis." Stepping back, he studied the other stolen mare, a black and white draught horse. "She'll need a name, too. Percy will come up with one in no time, I'm sure."

Seth returned from the fire, carrying a sheath. Drawing the blade, he spun it gracefully before offering me the hilt. "This is a side sword. I think it'll suit you."

Taking the blade, I held it up to the fading sunlight and studied it. An intricate sphere of thin, metal circles protectively shielded the hilt of a slender, elegant blade.

"Pretty," Percy commented, walking by with a bag filled with tonight's dinner. "He never got me anything."

"Your father was a vaunted officer, Percy," Seth called. "You had a spear worth more than a small army."

"Yes, well, I don't have it anymore."

Rolling his eyes, Seth led me to an open stretch of dirt near the fire. "I'm not teaching you how to fell armies, only how to defend yourself. That blade is made to point and fend off attacks while protecting your hand. So all you need to do is parry."

Eleos sat on a rock nearby, flipping open a journal as he watched us. "Hold it away from you." He instructed.

Thrusting the blade forward, I glanced between them. "Like this?" When Eleos nodded, I narrowed my eyes. "Wait. I thought Seth was supposed to teach you, too."

"Psyches can fight." Eleos deflected.

"How, exactly?"

Eleos moved to respond, but Seth cut him off. "Don't worry. The scholar's next." Dragging a dagger across his palm, Seth shook his hand, sending droplets flying. Each speck of blood grew into a crimson dagger. Shooting forward, the daggers slammed into one another, seamlessly merging into a larger broadsword.

A broadsword that then sang through the air, aiming for my heart. Gasping, I ducked, shielding myself with my arms.

The broadsword effortlessly reached its target, swiveling at the last moment to strike me with the handle rather than the blade. A punch of pain rang through my ribs, and I landed in the dirt on my back.

I squeezed my eyes shut as I tried to breathe. When air flooded back into my lungs, I opened them to see Seth standing over me, twirling a bloody dagger between his fingers.

"The *sword* is your defense." He said gently. "Throwing it away rather defeats the point."

"I can't help it," I said, taking his offered hand. "My first instinct is to run."

"Well, you're backed into a corner with nowhere to go. So," He leaned in. "Parry."

Picking up my sword, I settled back into a defensive stance as Seth stood across from me. Studying him intently, I searched for a crack in his persona.

I couldn't read him. Sometimes, he was the picture of politeness; other times, he struck me as harsh. One moment, his mouth curled in a snarl; the next, he grinned and winked.

Seth's blood blade shot through the air again. This time, I held my ground, blade pointed forward, and managed to knock the incoming sword off its course. Reverberations rushed through my blade, and I shook my hand in pain.

"Perfect." Seth commended. "Just like that."

"This works against weapons, sure," I said. "But how am I supposed to defend against chthonics?"

"One thing at a time." He said, grabbing his scarlet blade from the air before he charged.

An entire man throwing his weight behind the blade made the impact altogether more difficult to parry. I flinched again as Seth reached me, barely managing to scrape his oncoming sword. Losing my footing, I tumbled backwards, desperately trying to keep my grip on the hilt.

We landed on the ground in a tangle of limbs, a bloody blade pressed to my neck while his other hand restrained the wrist holding my sword.

Finding myself at his mercy, fear trickled down my spine, just as it had on our first meeting.

"I thought you were teaching me to parry," I said, twisting my head away from the blade.

"I am. But," he glanced over me. "I saw an opportunity. If that nobleman wants you alive, you should learn to *escape*."

Before this journey, I hadn't thought much about strength. My arms could lift little more than small boxes, and physical feats were beyond me; usually, I batted my eyelashes at a strapping lad and got him to do it for me.

Seth wasn't holding me tightly; I could breathe easily, but my wrist felt like a stone was weighing it down. I couldn't see anything besides his, admittedly, handsome face.

"Whoa!" Percy's voice sounded somewhere to my left. "I thought you two were training."

Heat rushed to my face as I realized our position. Seth crouched over me, face an inch from mine, strands of his hair brushing my cheeks. One of his legs was planted firmly between mine, holding me in place.

Which meant one of my legs was between *his*. Perfect. Jerking my knee, I tried to ram it into his weak spot.

I was denied revenge for his grievances against me. Seth noticed what I intended and quickly released me, narrowly escaping my knee. Eleos snorted and hurriedly buried his nose in his journal.

Seraphim leaped over the rock Eleos sat on and plopped down beside him, grinning brightly. She looked like a noblewoman who'd acquired a personal box to watch her favorite play.

Sighing, I grabbed my sword and stood. "How's that?"

"Hm." Seth frowned. "I was hoping you'd discover more of your magic. Peril encourages it, usually."

I turned my palm over. "Were you hoping I'd disintegrate you? I wield the *Empty*."

Seth opened his mouth to respond, then snapped it closed. "Ah, hm. Good point."

Eleos snorted. "Perhaps leave study of the strange new magic to the scholar?"

"Sorry, princess," Seth said, twirling his blade. "We've no choice but to train the old-fashioned way until you can parry with your eyes closed."

Sighing, I lifted my sword and retook a defensive stance.

Training proved to be as miserable as I'd feared. Seth beat me with the blunt end of his blade, correcting errors in my stance and offering advice. Whenever I managed to parry or block his attack, he'd smile like a bright-eyed child and attack me with renewed fervor.

Most assaults ended with me lying in the dirt and him explaining what I'd done wrong. Each time, I'd hope for release and greet disappointment when he hauled me back up and instructed me to retake my stance.

Night had settled over the land by the time he finally released me. Doubling over, I caught my breath and longed for a bath.

"Not bad." Seth commended, running a hand along his blade. "Tomorrow we can tackle something more difficult."

"I don't think I'm cut out for this." I huffed.

"No one is, at first," he flicked his hand, and the crimson sword shattered into red droplets. Grabbing the sheath from the ground, he offered it to me with a smile.

Twirling the blade slowly, I attempted to mimic his fanciful blade work. I failed spectacularly, dropping the sword instead.

Seth laughed, retrieving the sword and sheathing it for me. "Not a bad first attempt." He offered me the side sword. "It's yours."

Tilting my head, I stared into his scarlet eyes, trying once again to read him. Eleos was right. Even though I wasn't a psyche, I could see the walls he built around himself to keep everyone else out. The smile seemed fake.

"What?" He asked.

"Just trying to figure you out," I admitted, glancing down with a frown. I didn't have a belt to sheath my blade on.

He chuckled. "Remember what we discussed? You never won a training bout, so I don't owe you any secrets. But," he grinned. "You owe me a few."

"Ugh. I lost count of how many times I fell on my ass."

"Start with one, then." He ran a hand under his chin, cocking his head as he looked me up and down, focusing on the features of my face. "Why did you never try to escape? With your skills and looks, couldn't you have charmed a nobleman and taken shelter in his estate?"

"Charmed, like married him?" I asked. Nose scrunching, I studied the dirt. Why hadn't I taken advantage of some lonely, gullible noble?

"Surely he could have paid your debts." Seth continued.

"I guess," I said, swallowing. Buried in my foolish heart was a yearning for. . . *more.* I wanted a house by a lake. A loving husband and two kids.

"Well?"

I didn't want to tell him the truth. Stalling, I studied the silver buttons on his coat, and the detailed embroidery on his collar.

Seth knelt, bringing his face into my line of vision. "You won't steal any of my truths, if you don't share yours."

Sighing, I supposed fair was fair. "I didn't want something fake," I said quietly. "I wanted to fall in love."

Seth regarded me quietly. "Did you?"

". . .no. Considering our course, I suppose I never will."

"Hm." He looked away. "Romance is something fools dream will fill the void in their heart. But it doesn't." He said shortly. "Take a rest. You've earned it." Turning stiffly on his heel, he marched away.

Had I said something to offend him? No. Something in my words had drawn forth unpleasant memories.

Dusting myself off, I slid my sword into my saddlebags and pulled out my bedroll. Eleos followed me, snapping his journal closed as he reached my side. "You alright?"

"Yeah, why?"

"It looked like something he said upset you."

"I think you have it backwards," I said, finding a spot by the fire to roll out my mat. "And I can't read him, still."

Eleos watched Seth across the fire. "Neither can I. But, he's been an ally, and it's rude to pry. . ."

"You're not going to try and catch him in a moment of weakness?" I guessed.

"You read my mind." He said, wearing a little half-smile. "Some people bury their heart not to hide it from others, but to shield themselves from reliving the pain."

He was right. Maybe the secrets this group kept were not born of malice or shame, but *pain*. Maybe we were all just broken inside.

THE STARS HID behind a blanket of clouds tonight. I watched the gloomy sky, searching for a hint of light behind the black canvas. Myriad thoughts raced through my head, keeping my eyes open and awake.

Sitting up, I glanced around our camp. Percy had taken the first watch, and I'd been assigned the last. A dim lantern glowed in the distance, where he kept vigil over the mountain pass. Dragging myself from the sleeping roll, I pulled a cloak around my shoulders and wandered toward the light.

Soft lute twangs reached my ears, a gentle lullaby. Perched on a rock, Percy idly strummed a song while staring forward into the night, his white hair hanging into his eyes. Noticing me, he quickly brushed back his hair and smiled.

"Aethra. What are you doing up?"

"Can't sleep," I said, sitting beside him. "What are you playing?"

"A song my mother liked." He set the lute aside. "She used to sing me to sleep with it."

Percy had changed from his tattered tunic into equally garish garb. A ridiculous V cut his tunic in half, cinched by his colorful patchwork sash. There must've been a story behind it for him to wear it so often.

"Did she make you that?" I asked, nodding at the sash.

"Yes." He sat forward eagerly. "It was originally a doublet. My first proper bard outfit." Nostalgia warmed his eyes. "I was six, in case you were curious."

"She must have been proud." Folding my arms, I tucked myself into my cloak. "How did you and Seth meet, anyhow?"

"Chance." He crossed a leg over the other. "He needed information from the town guard. Of all the men he could've chatted up, fate chose me."

"I take it he was asking about a target?"

"One I didn't much like. I ended up helping him." He leaned back, watching the stars. "The old codger had it coming. Some madams treat their girls like people. Others, like refuse." Percy's head snapped back down. "Gloomy tales won't help you sleep. The story of how he abandoned me is funny, in hindsight."

Shifting, I clasped my hands in my lap. "Seth mentioned that. He said you should've stayed home. That he was hoping you'd turn back."

"Ah. . ." Percy's brows fell. "He's probably right. But there was nothing for me at home but despair, and I've never much liked songs that sound like it."

"Do you have a family?"

"A mother and a father." He chuckled. "Not the wife and children you're thinking of." Pausing, he sighed heavily. "You're trying to figure out what Seth meant, aren't you? I have an illness. There's no cure."

"Oh," I said, surprised. "Do you mean the taint?"

"No." He breathed. "No, that's a different story entirely."

"Is it bad? You *seem* alright."

"Most days, I am. It's not at its worst, yet." He explained, almost cheerfully. "Every year, I feel a little weaker. Every month, my joints stiffen a little more. Eventually, they'll stop working. Most people don't live long after that."

I sat silently, unsure what to say.

"It developed around the time I met Seth. When he learned of my ailment, he tried to get rid of me." Percy huffed, offended. "He wanted to keep me safe. To prolong my life. But who gets to decide that but me?"

"Is that why you agreed to join Seraphim?"

"Isn't it grand?" He grinned. "I can't think of anything better: a mission worth dying for, that'll claim me before I'm spent." Sorrow washed over his feigned joy. "There's no other point to living a life with a deadline. No point in waiting for a slow death. At least now I can go out on my own terms."

"I. . ." Floundering for words, I offered only stillness.

"It's okay," Percy said gently, meeting my eyes. "Most people don't know what to say. I wouldn't either. We're all living on borrowed time now. Might as well enjoy the ride, together, no?"

"You're right. We should." I glanced away. No wonder he'd so readily offered himself as the sacrifice.

Guilt tore through my heart. I'd had the gall to feel sorry for myself, yet here was a man who was condemned to an early death through nothing more than a stroke of ill luck. I wanted to say something. But what words would suffice?

"Hey," Percy took my hand. "It's okay. Really. The last thing I want is for people to feel bad for me. I'm at peace with it. Really."

He was lying. The truth was written on his face, plain as day. Fear flickered in his eyes, regret creased his brow, and sorrow tugged at his lips. I squeezed his hand, trying to offer what little comfort I could.

Releasing my hand, Percy picked up his lute. "Are you sure you don't want that lullaby?"

"And distract you from your vigil?" I asked playfully.

"I owe you for saving my life, don't I?"

"The way I see it, you saved ours."

"Then *that*, my dear," he strummed a happy chord, "makes us even. Now, go get some sleep. Eleos will kill me if I keep you up."

Nodding, I stood and returned to my bedroll, idly playing with the strings of my cloak. Sitting on my mat, I stared into the night, more awake than I'd been before.

Life was unfair to those who deserved joy, and fortune was spilled on those who didn't. For some reason, the thought made me burn with fury.

SIXTEEN

IFE DISPELLED THE EMPTY. For hundreds of years, the clergy had promised as much in prayer, and in all our history, never had they been proven wrong.

A sprawling town covered the mountainside, with marble buildings stark against the brown stone, their roofs tiled a deep red. Herd animals followed sheepdogs and ranchers across dirt roads, weaving through merchant caravans and travelers.

The road to Therapne had brought us through many outposts, but this one was unusually crowded. I hardly found space for myself on its congested streets. My blonde mare nuzzled my head when I stopped to let a wagon pass, and I felt her saliva dampen my curls.

"Eugh." I rubbed my head, wiping off the slobber.

Eleos smiled at me, rubbing his mare's snout. "She loves you."

"Already?" I flicked the saliva from my fingers.

"Horses are intelligent creatures. She knows she's safe with you."

Frowning, I stared into the horse's eyes. Maybe Eleos was right. A deep well of intelligence seemed to lurk beneath the surface. Eleos' dappled brown horse nuzzled him, much more gently and without coating his neat brown waves in spit.

Of course, his horse would be as polite as he was.

Seraphim and her black horse shook their thick manes at the same time. She glanced between us. "I hear the markets here are great for souvenirs."

Percy tipped his hat over his eyes. "You want to go shopping? Shouldn't we stay together?"

"I'll watch over you." She nodded at Percy. "And the boys can watch Aethra. We'll only be across the street from one another."

"But-"

"Take a moment to breathe. We'll meet back up by that tree." Nodding, she pointed out a canopy of red leaves looming over a small church atop a nearby cliff.

Taking Percy's arm, Seraphim dragged him away. Seth furrowed his brow, shifting from foot to foot, as though intending to chase after them.

I nudged Seth. "You can go with them."

"Percy doesn't need me hovering over him like a worried mother." He peered down at me. "Besides, he can hold his own in a fight."

"I can, too."

"Is that right, princess?"

"Mhm." Leading my mare away, I flashed him a cheeky smile. "I disarm them with a smile and then run away."

Rolling his eyes, Seth muttered under his breath. "I'm training her for nothing, aren't I?"

"Well," Eleos turned to look at us. "Did any of you forget something at home?"

Chuckling, I glanced over the shop signs. "My sorry excuse for a mattress."

"Want a new one?" Eleos asked. "An aching back might get you out of bed earlier."

Seth snorted.

"Hey," I protested. "It's not my fault that none of you wake me up." Glancing across the street, my gaze lingered on Percy as he waved his hands around in enthusiastic conversation.

Face falling, Eleos watched Percy and Seraphim disappear into a textile shop. "You've been looking at him differently. I know how you feel. I didn't know what to say, either."

"What can you?" I muttered.

"Nothing," Eleos said plainly.

"Don't say anything," Seth called from behind us. "Percy *hates* being treated differently." Skidding to a stop, he gasped, staring at a sign across the street. "Wait a moment."

I followed his gaze to a smithy, where a variety of knives hung on display behind the forge. Dropping his reins into Eleos' hands, Seth darted away, though Whisper remained behind with us. Finding a tree in the center of the road, I ducked beneath its boughs to escape the crowd while we waited.

Whisper sat on my foot, his wiry fur tickling my skin. Petting his underbelly with my shoe, I flicked a few new clumps of mud off the poor boy.

Leaning against the trunk, I watched Seth hungrily eye the collection. "Does he have any hobbies besides blood?"

Eleos stood beside me, pulling out his journal and flipping through the pages. A quill was tucked into its binding, worn down and feather frayed. One heavy day of writing, and it looked like it might fall apart entirely.

"Eleos," I said. "Something you said back in Ikaria's been bothering me."

"What?" He muttered.

"What did you mean?" I asked. "When you said, 'I seek to fill my heart, but never with myself?'"

Eleos snapped his journal closed and looked up. "Tell me something good about yourself."

Snorting, I brushed my hair behind my ear. "You ask the impossible."

"That's what I mean." He said. "You never afford yourself grace, but you'd happily give it to others."

"I think you have a much higher opinion of me than you should."

"See?" He raised an eyebrow.

Pursing my lips, I stared back at him, wondering what he saw within my mind. I was envious of psyches. Right now, I'd give anything to peer into him and learn what dwelt beneath the calm surface.

"You're a psyche." I waved a hand idly. "Can't you fix my head, or something?"

"I could make you feel happiness, or pride, but it would be fleeting and fake."

"Give it a try. I'm curious what it feels like."

Taking my hand, Eleos cupped it between his. "I have to lure you toward the emotion I want, remember? What draws you toward happiness?"

I thought for a moment. "Tell me I'm pretty."

"You're very aesthetically pleasing to look upon, Lady Aethra."

I laughed. "I've never heard that said less romantically."

He smirked, a tiny half-smile, barely there. Slowly, my troubles washed away, tossed into the depths of my memories and forgotten. Warm, bubbling joy swam to the surface, a sea of yellow against the night. Pleasant humming sang to me at the back of my skull, like a melody my mother might have sung, had she loved me.

It lasted only fleetingly. Though the sensation was wonderful, it fell into a maelstrom of sorrow, unable to escape the storm. My face broke as tears brewed at the corners of my eyes, though I wasn't sure what had summoned them.

Eleos released my hand. "Something fake only magnifies the truth."

"Maybe," I murmured, longing to feel his fake joy instead of my own sorrow. Year after year, my hatred had grown tiresome.

Wretched girl. Hopeless. *Meaningless.*

"Besides," Eleos mused, "Happiness is better found the old-fashioned way."

"There's an old-fashioned way?" I raised an eyebrow. "Why didn't anyone tell-"

Eleos cut me off, gently cupping my face and kissing my cheek. His fingers traced my cheekbones, slowly drawing a line across my skin. Grabbing a loose lock of my hair, he gently tucked it behind my ear and returned to his journal, flipping it open again.

Startled, I raised my hand to pull him back, but then lowered it.

A tiny half-smirk curled his lips. Bastard.

Whisper barked, alerting us to his master's return. Seth twirled a new knife between his fingers. "What do you look so happy about?" He asked.

"Nothing." Eleos tucked his journal away. "Found yourself a reward for your good deeds?"

"Isn't she beautiful?" Seth unsheathed the little blade, but it didn't look much like a weapon of war. It was all handle, no blade. A tiny speck of steel emerged from a curved wooden hilt.

"It's a little small." I offered.

Seth bit back a laugh. "Do you say that often?"

"Unfortunately."

"Your turn, princess." Seth gestured for me to lead. "Shall it be a frumpy mattress? Or something more luxurious?"

Strolling down the crowded street, I stopped outside a building whose sign read 'Cynthus Exports.' Remembering something Eleos mentioned back in Serifos, I tied my horse outside and pushed through the door.

A tiny bell jangled. An assortment of luxury items lined the shelves, most crafted from leather. Tufts of feathers caught my eye, where a box displayed a small assortment of quills. Perfect.

A rack of leather cloaks drew Eleos like a moth to flame. Seth joined him, whistling. "I've always wanted a Cynthus-made cloak."

"So have I." Eleos agreed.

Backing toward the quills, I watched them, curious if leather, of all things, would bond them.

"Percy had one, before he fled home." Seth continued.

"What?" Eleos gasped. "He left behind his spear *and* Cynthus leather?"

"The man's an idiot, I've tried to tell you." Lining his voice with a flamboyant tilt, Seth mimicked Percy. "Material goods bring no joy, for a wealthy man carries gold in his heart."

Shaking his head, Eleos inspected the price: far more coin than I was willing to spend. Only a nobleman or wealthy merchant could afford one of these cloaks.

"Think we can haggle it down?" Eleos asked.

"You're a psyche." Seth mused. "I'm charming. We could manage."

"Charming?" Eleos raised an eyebrow.

"You don't think so?"

"Maybe to women," Eleos said dismissively, turning his head. "Let me get a read on the shopkeeper."

Leaving them to their leather, I examined the box of quills, landing on one whose feather was painted a beautiful green, the same color as Eleos' eyes. Picking it up, I turned it over, admiring the craftsmanship and words carved into the pen.

'*May written work protect what time forgets.*'

The creed of the Scholarly Houses, if I wasn't mistaken. I wondered if Eleos had sworn these words when he'd been instated.

I tried to envision a young Eleos joining the Scholarly House of History; doubtless, he would have been an awkward, lanky teenager. The thought made me smile.

Shaking my head, I watched Eleos and Seth across the shop, ensuring they were busy arguing before I approached the shopkeeper at his counter. Graying hair flecked his black locks, and surprising muscle defined his arms. Setting the quill down, I balked internally at the price. Ten Heschian coins.

A few weeks ago, I would have died on the spot at the mere idea of buying a quill for that price. My hovel of a home cost half that much for a year's rent.

Without a hint of jovial cheer, the merchant took my coin and moved on to the next customer. Wishing the boys luck with their haggling endeavors, I tucked the quill into my satchel and stepped outside, leaning on my horse as I waited for them.

When the two men finally emerged, I stood straight. "Any luck?"

"That merchant's made of steel." Seth marveled. "I admire his tenacity."

Eleos sighed. "Maybe we can find a better deal in Cynthus."

"Well, I'm content," I said. "Shall we head for the tree, or did you need something, El?"

"El?" he repeated.

"Nobody ever called you that before?"

"Only one." His face flickered, briefly touched by nostalgia. "No, I'm alright. Let's get away from this crowd."

Jealousy flashed in my heart, but I shoved it down. He could be talking about anyone—a parent, a sibling, a friend.

Grabbing my horse, I followed him down the street, but a malaise grew in my bones. Rubbing my neck, I tried to place the sudden discomfort. Flinching, I looked around wildly as the sounds of chatter and footsteps muted, as though plunged underwater.

Unease blossomed amidst the silence, and nostalgia heightened in my breast. Halting mid-stride, I gasped in terror.

Seth grabbed my arm. "What's wrong-"

I stared into his eyes, seeing only the red of his irises and the disaster behind us.

A black spot appeared on the dirt road, a perfect contrast to the beautiful marble stores. Red haloed its infinite embrace, casting light on the single drop of water sitting quietly at its base.

Everything fell silent. The birds stopped singing, and the people's voices ceased. Everyone halted, the world stilled, life and time froze for a fleeting moment.

It all burst back to life, far too loud, all at once. Screams tore through the air as the people noticed the pocket of Empty.

The abyss surged in all directions, buildings disintegrating beneath its touch, roads collapsing into the sharp canyon, people vanishing into specks of dust. Chaos erupted as people scrambled to escape.

Seth's horse reared in fear, tearing from his grasp and charging forward. It clipped me as it ran past, throwing me to the ground. My head struck the stone steps of a shop, and the world blurred.

Screams echoed through the fog.

Sheer terror captured their voices. The screams of the dying.

Someone grabbed my wrist and hauled me up. The world spun before my vision snapped back into clarity.

Seth yanked me roughly, spinning me around to face the void. "Stop it!" He shouted.

Focusing, I thrust my palm forward, fingers trembling. The void advanced, dropping the city into a chasm filled with still waters. The blackened sky consumed the clouds, tearing the very aether asunder. But nothing happened. Nothing in my breast stirred, no magic sparked at my fingertips.

The Empty advanced, uncaring of my futile attempts to stop it.

"I. . ." I stuttered, watching our doom approach.

Seth pulled me away from the Empty and pushed me ahead of him. "*Run.*" He barked.

Finding my footing, I sprinted away from the growing void, glancing over my shoulder to see a child trip. My heart pounded, but the horror was over in an instant. The bounds of the abyss reached the boy and turned him to dust before his mouth had fully opened to scream.

A solemn weight crashed through my body as I stared at the spot where the child had been. Throat going dry, I forced myself to keep going.

Where were the others? My head snapped forward, but all I could see was a throng of people, loose horses, and cattle. Relief sang through my heart when Eleos pushed through two men ahead of me and dashed to my side.

He touched my arm, and his voice rang in my mind. "*Can you stop it?*"

"*No.*" I thought back at him, nearly screaming the word aloud.

Seth slammed into us from behind, propelling us forward. Keeping his grip on my arm, Eleos heeded the order and ran.

The ground quaked beneath our feet, tossing me off balance. Tremors raked through the mountain as the Empty destroyed it. Cracks ran through the road, and I looked up to see boulders falling from the cliffs above.

If the Empty didn't reach us first, the landslide would sweep us away.

A baby's cry rose above the cacophony. Just another noise, to me.

But not to Eleos.

He stopped. Dropping my arm, he spun on his heel, quickly finding the source of the noise. A pregnant woman had tripped, a swaddled infant clutched in her arms. Resigned to her fate, she buried her face against her child, shrouding it with the falling locks of her blonde hair.

I reached out to stop him, but my fingers grasped air. Eleos flew to her side.

Another thud shook the road, and the dirt ripped apart. Seth grabbed me, pulling me back as a boulder crashed into the store behind us, splintering its roof before tumbling onto the road. I ripped from his grip, only to see a growing crevasse separating me from Eleos and the young mother.

No! Raising my hand, I stared down the approaching abyss, willing myself to do something. How had I stopped it before? How had I saved Percy and me from certain death? How?

Nothing happened. Nothing. Why? Beads of sweat ran down my forehead as the Empty closed in. All I could see were its endless shadows.

Ten paces away. Eight. Six.

"*Aethra!*" Eleos' voice screamed in my head, at once with a noise beside me.

"Aethra!" Seth shouted.

Something slammed into my stomach, shaking me from my trance. Seth roughly threw me over his shoulder as he sprinted down a side road. A horrifying wall of darkness closed in on the spot we'd been standing, tearing asunder the building I'd leaned on but a few moments ago.

It would have consumed the spot Eleos had been standing, too.

"*Eleos?*" I shrieked in my mind, hoping he heard. Hoping he could answer.

But I heard only silence.

"Shit!" Seth cursed, glancing behind him as the Empty pursued us. "Shitshitshit."

Gods, was it moving quicker? I hung uselessly over Seth's shoulder, watching the abyss in despondent horror.

Seth slammed into something, crashing through wood. I was jarred loose from his grasp and rolled over tiled floors, landing on my back to see a statue of the Maiden looming above me.

Water trickled through her fingers into a basin at her feet—water meant to represent the Empty she could destroy.

Whisper leaped onto my chest, furiously nuzzling my face. Snapped out of my trance, I grabbed his neck to let him know I was alive.

Shooting to my feet, I dashed through the pews, catching up to Seth in time for the bounds of the void to crash through the far wall. Still cursing under his breath, Seth rammed through the other door, grabbing my wrist to haul me out with him. He paused, whistling urgently for Whisper, who shot between our feet.

From the top of this cliff, I could see the crowds of people and animals fleeing through every street in every direction. One beast broke from the throng and raced up the road towards us: A blonde horse with a flowing white mane.

Seth intercepted it, grabbed its reins, and reached for my hand. He threw me up first before mounting behind me, jerking the reins to turn my mare around as the church splintered into dust and fell away into the silent sea. Slapping the reins against the horse's neck, he drove her into a frenzied gallop.

Spinning in the saddle, I stared at the Empty, trying again to stop it. My fingers trembled, my shoulders shook. Fear raced down my spine in sharp splinters, and worry pounded at my heart.

I couldn't think. Couldn't focus.

I couldn't do a damn thing.

My head whipped violently around as the horse took a sharp turn, fleeing from the village down a steep road leading into the wilderness.

"What are you doing?" I shrieked.

"Getting us out of here!" Seth snarled.

"We can't-" I stuttered. "We have to-"

"Go back?" He barked. "To what?"

A building high on the cliff crumbled as the landslide swept over it. I watched the debris rain down the mountainside, striking people and buildings in its path. Meaningless destruction and death. The Empty was upon them a moment later, turning their blood and rubble into nothing.

Raising my palms, I stared at them in horror.

I was supposed to wield the Maiden's power.

I was supposed to stop the Empty.

But when it mattered most, I failed.

SEVENTEEN

RAIN DRIZZLED FROM THE HEAVENS. Maybe the gods mourned the tragic loss of life. Drops traced down the sharp cliffs, like tears falling down a cheek.

If others had survived the catastrophe at the outpost, Seth and I had yet to encounter them. We'd ridden into unfamiliar territory, a valley tucked in the mountains through which no roads crossed. The underbrush grew thick, tangling around jagged boulders and red-leafed trees.

I could see the Empty behind us, a speck of black against the dreary sky, where the bounds of the abyss rose to touch the sun. Placing a hand on a tree, I pulled my foot from the tangled vines growing beneath it. Something snapped behind me—a person stepping over fallen leaves and branches, but I paid them no mind.

An assassin come to slit my throat would be welcome.

Seth joined my side. "I don't see anything or anyone. My best guess is we're east of the road."

"Are you any good with maps?" I asked.

"Yes." He took the blonde mare's reins. "But Eleos had them."

Ice shot through my heart at the sound of his name. I touched my cheek, remembering the panic and despair I'd felt when he had not answered my call.

I'd tried to reach him a few times, shouting into the void, hoping he'd hear me, or read my mind like he always did. Nobody answered.

"Let's get moving." Seth yanked the reins and walked away. Whisper followed him, pausing to sniff my hand before plodding on.

Running a finger across my palm, I remained frozen, unable to rip my eyes from the Empty.

"Are you coming?" Seth barked. "Or are you determined to be a burden?"

His sharp words snapped me out of my reverie. Turning on my heel, I trudged after him.

Seraphim had the Maiden's Bloodstone. Maybe. . . maybe she and Percy were alright. They would've shielded Eleos, too. After all, the two had only been across the street from us, a mere twenty paces away.

We walked in silence. Anger bristled off Seth like waves of heat, and I kept my distance. Well-deserving of his ire, I kept my head bowed and stared at the rocky path, looking up only when my horse struggled to cross the mountainous terrain.

The clouds in the sky darkened as thunder rumbled and lightning flashed above. Heavy raindrops plummeted over the mountain, picking up in speed and intensity as a storm swept over us.

A bolt lanced through the air, striking the mountains ahead of us. The blonde mare reared, and Whisper ducked between my feet, trembling. Reaching down to soothe the hound, I wiped rain from my eyes, but the relentless wind only blew more into my face.

Seth halted, cursing, head whipping around. "We should find shelter."

"It's just a storm," I shouted over the howling gales.

He glanced back at me, flinching as another lightning bolt struck the ground behind us. Whisper shot out from between my feet, disappearing into a shadow painted across the mountainside.

"Maybe you're brave enough," Seth calmed the horse and guided her to the cavern Whisper had found. "But the dog isn't."

Cavern proved too strong a word. The entrance was barely large enough for the horse to fit through, and by the time she'd fled into its safety, there was scarcely enough space for one person, let alone two.

Darkness closed around me as I ducked inside, pressing myself against the cold wall. Seth sidled in across from me, chest a mere inch from mine. I watched the pounding rain and flashing lightning for a few moments before noticing him staring at me.

His jaw tautened, and his eyes twitched. He looked primed to explode.

"I thought," he snarled. "You were supposed to control the Empty. The Maiden's chosen, or some rot."

"I. . ." I trailed off, looking down.

Percy and I had survived falling into the Empty. Had that only been because Seraphim was near, and the Maiden's Bloodstone with her?

"That's all you have to say?" He said. "Gods know how many people just died, and *that's all you have to say*?"

"I couldn't- Nothing I did worked!"

"Of course it didn't." He spat. "They're fools for thinking some knave is going to save them. Nobody has power over the Empty. *Nobody*."

Seth's voice fractured on the last word. I hesitantly raised my eyes to meet his. Why did he speak as though he'd long known about the search for someone who could wield the Empty?

And why did he sound so brokenhearted?

"Seraphim's theory was a good one." Seth leaned back, staring at the rain. "It might have worked. But now they're dead."

"They might not be," I said. "They Maiden's Bloodstone-"

"Is probably as useless as you."

Thunder crashed overhead, and I flinched. My hand brushed my satchel, where I'd tucked the quill I'd meant to surprise Eleos with.

Everything in life ended so suddenly. One morning, I'd awoken to find Ainwir gone. A few nights ago, I'd sat by the fire with Percy and learned of his illness, seen the fear in his eyes. This morning, I'd planned to catch Seraphim alone with a drink and ask her about her storied past.

Just *gone*. Blinked away as though they'd never existed. Never mattered.

All my fault.

The entire outpost had perished because of *me*.

Choking, I fled the cavern and ran into the storm. Pounding rain washing over me, soaking my hair and toga. My foot caught on a boulder peeking out from thick grass, and I tripped, landing on my knees.

My fingers dug into the mud, and water gathered in the gouges. Lightning struck nearby, blinding my eyes with a bright white flash.

I don't know why I ran into the storm, why I couldn't find the strength to move. All I'd wanted was to get away from Seth and his accusing glare. The rain was frigid, and chills seeped into my bones, but any sensation was preferable to the nothing I'd been feeling before.

All I wanted was for the storm to sweep me away.

Back to the Empty's silent embrace, where everything lay still.

"Aethra!" Seth ran towards me, a blur of black in the storm, boots sloshing through the mud. "I—I shouldn't have said that."

With his words, I realized I wasn't mad at him. How could you hate someone who spoke the truth?

Seth knelt beside me. "The storm is going to blow you away." He flinched as thunder boomed above us and a nearby tree splintered beneath the wind. Cursing, he grabbed my arm and hauled me up.

I didn't resist. Stumbling over the rocks, fighting against the gale, we returned to the tiny shelter, where two cowering animals awaited us. Pressing my back against the stone, I slid to the floor, water dripping everywhere. Wrapping my arms around my knees, I stared at my horse instead of the man.

Seth sat beside me, far too close. "It's not your fault." He said softly. "I was just. . . lashing out." He shifted, resting an arm on his knee. "Maybe we shouldn't have run. You and Percy managed to walk through it okay."

"For only a moment," I said, finding my voice. "How am I to assume from that mere second that I could just, what, hold everyone's hand and guide them to safety?"

"We don't know enough about how it works," Seth agreed. "It's not an easy thing to test." He gritted his teeth. "It's not a thing that *should* be tested."

"Someone has to." I raised my head, watching the storm. The Empty wasn't far. I could return to its border and test my supposed magic in full.

Pressing a hand to the cavern wall, I tried to rise, but Seth yanked me back down.

"*Stop*," he said sharply. "You're no good to anyone dead."

"I thought I was useless."

"I. . ." he exhaled heavily. "I'm not mad at you. I couldn't control my magic for months, either."

Shivers ran down my arms and shook me from within. Pulling my cloak around my shoulders, I tried to warm myself, but frigid air swept in on the breeze. "What came first?" I asked. "The assassin or the blessing of Haimyx?"

"The former, I suppose." He said, eyes fogging.

"So you were an assassin first? Why are you judging me, exactly?" I said, face tightening in anger. "You're a murderer."

"Only to those who deserve it." He snapped.

"How do you know?" I pressed. "How can you be sure? And what if their death invites the Empty and kills an innocent?"

"Innocents are being hurt either way. You agree with the lords, then? We should look the other way and let evil carry on atrocities because something *might* happen? Because it's inconvenient to deal with the fallout?"

Swallowing, I broke his gaze. "Percy told me how you met. But he didn't say much about the target he helped you find."

"Tale as old as time," Seth said in a clipped tone. "The madame ran a whorehouse where men could buy the girls as young as they liked and beat them until they bled, so long as they paid extra." He paused. "I think that's what broke Percy. What made him lay down his helm and fall out with his father: taking the hands of those little girls, and telling them it would be okay."

Before Ainwir had found me, a man had tried to trap me in his brothel. I'd been too young to understand, then. A sudden stop from the Empty was a mercy in comparison to a life in chains, preyed upon by monsters.

How could anyone look a girl in the eye who'd been through that, and tell them it would be okay?

"What happened to them?" I asked. "The girls?"

"Girls don't end up there because they have someplace to go," Seth said quietly. "I hope we saved them, but I'm not so naive as to assume."

I don't know why I asked. I already knew the answer.

Frigid wind blew in again, showering us with a deluge of cold rain. Squeezing my eyes shut, I curled into a ball as the shivers grew into violent shakes.

"Great," Seth muttered, "now you're going to freeze to death." Shifting closer to me, he extended an arm. "Here."

"I don't," I chattered, "want to be warmed by someone who hates me."

"Would I have carried you to safety if I hated you?"

Bereft of a good answer, I pursed my lips and shivered pathetically.

Slipping an arm behind my back, Seth pulled me against his chest and wrapped his arms tightly around me. Feeling the warmth of another body, I instinctively pressed myself closer to him, inhaling the scent of rain permeating his clothes.

Noticing us, Whisper stood and curled up by our side, a pile of wet fur I'd need to wash again. Seth shrugged his cloak around both of us. The black fabric tumbled around my shoulders, sealing out the biting wind.

I could feel his heartbeat, slowing from a rapid thump to a steady beat. Strands of his hair brushed my face, and his chest rose and fell beneath me. It was far too intimate a moment for my liking, but such times were the perfect chance to ask questions otherwise ignored.

"When I saved Percy," I said quietly, "You looked horrified."

Seth's muscles tensed, his arms tightening around me.

"Why?" I pressed. "That madman looked elated. Eleos was awed. So was Percy."

I felt Seth's chin brush over my hair as he looked away, but he remained silent.

"You're very impassioned about what you do," I continued, "And my magic proving to be false made you-"

He exhaled heavily. "People want a savior they can foist their burdens onto. They would martyr you in an instant to save themselves." He laughed bitterly. "They'd martyr you even if you had no magic at all—just to see if it worked."

Reading between his words, I twisted to face him. "You knew someone. Someone who supposedly-"

"Yes." He barked harshly. "I don't want to talk about it."

Shifting away from him, I fell silent. Water dripped from my hair onto the cavern floor, a sound swallowed by the raging storm. Hardly anyone in the Merchant Isles studied the Empty, let alone theorized it could be channeled by mages.

Who had he known before?

Everything in his past was still a mystery.

Wind howled into the cavern, digging into my soaking back like a volley of arrows. Shaking, I wrapped my arms around myself.

Scowling, Seth leaned forward and grabbed my waist. "Stop trying to freeze to death." He murmured, dragging me back under his cloak.

He wrapped his arms around me, tucking me safely against his chest. Trapping my legs between his, he left me without an inch of space to myself, but with his heat radiating over me like a furnace, I decided I didn't mind.

"I don't know why I was angry," his voice was soft, "I'm glad you aren't what they think. Let the people go back to hoping their Maiden will save them. At least they aren't hurting you."

"The nobleman," I said, "He thought they'd hate me, not celebrate me."

"He's right. The clergy would be divided, I think." Seth leaned his head against the wall, thinking. "A schism would form. Some would brand you a heretic. Others would proclaim you chosen of the Maiden, not a defiance of her existence. Half the world would kill you, half would martyr you. Dead, either way."

Closing my eyes, I listened to the rumbling thunder. "Do you think it was all a mistake? Or did I fail?"

Seth pondered my question quietly. "Magic requires a state of mind. Intent." Lifting his right arm, he turned over his palm. "Chthonics cannot merely spill blood and cast what they like."

"How does it work?"

Flexing his hand, Seth wrapped it back around me. "I'm sure Seraphim's is different. Everyone's is. For me, I remember the way I felt when magic first came to me." He paused. "The risk of death didn't matter. Submitting to the void was better than lying down and doing nothing."

Whisper crawled forward, laying his big head on my foot, ears soaked and pressed to his head. Feeling a little better, I tried to relax. "Do you know how Percy's magic works? He tried to explain it, but. . ."

Seth chuckled. The rumble in his chest was comforting. "He's horrible at explaining *anything*. Best I can tell, he creates sound and controls people with it. Mournful dirges, terrifying noises, haunting chants. . . save we feel the effects tenfold."

"I'm still not sure I understand."

"Ask a different muse. One who thinks about more than whichever woman happened to pass him last."

Extracting my arm from his grip, I held it out. "How would mine work, then?"

"I don't know," Seth admitted. "To stop the Empty. . . would you need to embody life? Or, maybe hope?"

Hope. Eleos had spoken to me of hope in the fields around Serifos. His eyes had shone with faith rarely glimpsed in others. I couldn't let him down.

Resolve washed over me as I stared at my palm. "When the storm clears, I'm going to try again."

"Aethra-"

"What does the danger matter? They're all gone. Like you said, the Maiden's Bloodstone was probably as false as I am."

He sighed. "I didn't mean that."

"Yes, you did."

He tensed beneath me and slowly relaxed. "Fine. But if I think you're in danger, I'm dragging you away."

"I'll never learn if you stop me from trying."

"I don't care." He said curtly. "And you don't stand a chance against me in a fight, so it will be all too easy to manhandle you. There's no point in arguing."

I opened my mouth *to* argue, but snapped it closed.

Dammit. He was right. If only I'd been a traditional thief, adept at scaling walls and fleeing from guards, maybe I'd be a half-decent fighter.

Exhaling, I buried myself against him, craving warmth, wanting nothing more than to collapse and pretend nothing had just happened. Laying my head against his chest, I listened to his heartbeat.

Memories swirled in my head. The screams, the child, the deaths.

Eleos. He'd risked his life to save another, and I'd abandoned him to his fate. Tears brewed in my eyes, and I sniffled, desperately trying to wipe them away.

Seth ran a hand through my hair and tucked my head beneath his chin. "The scholar's right. You're too hard on yourself," he sighed, "and my inability to express myself isn't helping."

"You expressed yourself just fine."

"No. I said everything but what I meant," he paused, nudging me in an attempt to cheer me up. "Percy used to call me emotionally constipated. You would have loved watching him try to get me to open up. Did you know he serenaded me, once?"

I chuckled, wiping the last tear from my eye. We listened to the storm in silence until he spoke again.

"I stole you a damn good horse, princess."

Breaking into a grin, I opened my eyes and stared at the blonde mare lying beside us. "I suppose she's earned a name."

THOUGH I FELL asleep in frigid cold, I woke in pleasant warmth. Heat surrounded me like an inviting blanket, and I longed to simply close my eyes and drift off again. Consciousness found me, despite my wishes.

Blinking the sleep from my eyes, I slowly roused, stretching my limbs. My leg swept over someone else's, and my fingers flexed around what felt like a firm bicep. The mattress beneath my head rose and fell. Breathing.

Pressing my palms to the cold cavern floor, I raised myself up off of Seth and glanced around. Our tiny cavern weathered the storm, and rain had ceased falling. Yellow light rose over the horizon as morning arrived.

I should have moved, but I loomed over him like a creeping witch come to steal his soul. Morning sunlight danced across his tanned face, drawing my attention across his sharp features and prominent collarbone. An impulse to trace a finger across his jaw and down his neck consumed me. I gasped when I noticed my hand had lifted from the ground to do just that of its own volition.

Seth woke, eyes drifting from my face to my chest. Still soaked through, my dress clung to my body, leaving little to the imagination.

"Not a bad thing to wake up to." He mumbled, openly ogling my breasts.

Crawling off him, I nearly hit my head on the opposite wall. Cursing, I stumbled outside, wringing the water from my hair and clothes. My curls fell in limp, pathetic clumps at my shoulders when I finished, and I felt like a sorry, wet mutt.

Seth emerged after me, shaking his hair and brushing it back. His ebony waves fell neatly around his face, curling around his ears and framing his eyes perfectly. A smirk traced his lips, as though he were well aware of his effortless perfection.

"You know," I said, brushing my hair out with my fingers. "You never apologized for the way we met."

"Didn't I?" he tilted his head, thinking.

"Not well."

"Hm." He smiled. "I'll do you one better. Thank you for being such a good hostage. You performed your role admirably." He bowed his head respectfully.

". . . why does Percy like you?"

"You should drink with us sometime. I've been told I'm *hilarious*."

"It takes more than words to impress me. I was raised to have a silver tongue." Not the best retort, but I wasn't in the mood for clever words. Ducking back into the cave, I took my horse's reins and led her outside.

Seth patted her neck. "What's the good steed's name, then?"

"Athena."

"It suits her." He rubbed her nose and studied me. "You know, mounting and riding would be easier if you wore pants."

"I am." Parting my skirt, I revealed the thin hose that covered my upper thighs.

"Those are *not* pants, princess. We're traveling. Fighting. Shouldn't you wear something more practical?"

"Can't a girl feel pretty in the middle of the woods?" I asked, hiking up my skirt as I attempted to mount by myself. Sticking a foot in the stirrups, I bounced on my other leg, building, if not momentum, then courage.

Hauling myself up, I managed to swing my leg around and seat myself in the saddle. Seth whistled. "Maybe she doesn't need pants, after all." Throwing his pack over his shoulder, he mounted behind me.

I leaned forward when his chest touched my back, and his legs trapped mine against the horse's flank. "Eleos said the one not holding the reins sits behind, not in front."

"Normally, I'd agree." Seth took the reins and gently ordered Athena forward. "But it's easier to stop you from recklessly throwing yourself into danger if you're in front of me."

Shifting awkwardly, I tried not to notice every inch of him touching every inch of me. We'd been too close for too long, and I was starting to like it.

Seth hummed. "Now *you* look emotionally constipated."

Chortling, I sat back against him. We'd both woken this morning and attempted levity, but our words felt hollow. Knitting my fingers together, I stared up at the faint smudge of black I could see in the sky.

"Do you think. . ." I trailed off.

"We can try, princess. Nothing more."

"And if it doesn't work? If I'm a farce?"

"We look for the others."

Biting my lip, I asked the question I didn't want to consider. "What if they're gone?"

"You saw what happened back there," Seth said softly. "Life no longer dispels the empty. Our time runs short. We carry on in their names, or we perish with everyone else."

EIGHTEEN

SETH STOOD ATOP A HIGH ridge, cape billowing in the breeze, overlooking the most terrifying sight I'd laid eyes on.

The Empty spread before us, in every direction. The black void pressed against the sheer mountainside to our east and reached toward the canyon plummeting to our west. A thin woods separated us from the impassable abyss.

We were trapped.

Seth's hand tensed on the pommel of his dagger as his gaze swept over the landscape. Releasing Athena's reins, I climbed up beside him and glanced over his back.

"You wouldn't be able to make little blood wings, would you?" I asked.

"Good question," he murmured, distracted. "I've never tried before."

"Because if you can't," I said, "We have two choices: scale the mountain behind us with no gear, or-"

He interrupted me. "Don't use this as an excuse to be reckless."

"I'm not. You learned how to wield magic. If I truly have any myself, you'll be able to teach me."

He grumbled. "I don't have a teacher's patience."

"It's not that hard." I knit my hands behind my back. "All you need to do is give clear instructions and provide an incentive."

He raised an eyebrow, looking me up and down. "And what would you consider a proper incentive?"

"Gold", I answered readily.

Chuckling, Seth whistled for Whisper to follow and descended the slope. Taking one last look at the bleak vista, I followed him. My foot caught on an uneven rock, and I stumbled the last few steps to the bottom.

Seth caught my hand, steadying me. Brushing myself off, I laughed. "Thanks. Maybe you were right about finding pants."

Looking up, I met his gaze: an intense, piercing stare. His fingers caressed my hand gently, the way I might expect a nobleman to take his date's arm.

Tilting my head, I stared back. "What? Something on my face?"

Dropping my hand, he grabbed Athena's reins. "Be careful. The path ahead is treacherous."

"Okay", I muttered, trailing after him. After last night, I thought I'd begun to understand him—evidently not.

Whisper stuck to my side as we descended the mountain's slope, finding ourselves in a sea of red trees buried in slanted earth. With every step, the unease in my breast intensified—a feeling I knew well meant the Empty drew near.

The mix of emotions confused me. Nobody else felt what I did. The unease, I could understand. But what was this aching nostalgia I sensed as well? It wasn't unpleasant, far from it. Had I a home and family to return to, I imagined this nostalgia would warm my breast as I walked the road back to them.

A great wall of black barred our path forward. I traced its edges, following the faint glow of red that crested the mountains and reached for the heavens. Steeling myself, I joined Seth by its border.

Wind tore through the trees, stirring Seth's hair. He stared into the void, eyes focused on the still sea resting below the sheer cliff.

"I've never known," I mused, grabbing my elbow. "How long does it take to become tainted?"

"I'm not sure", Seth answered, gaze fixed ahead. "A long time. Days."

"Why would anyone subject themselves to that?" I wondered. "Why would Percy?"

"He hasn't told me. But I have a guess." Seth turned toward me. "Give me your hand."

Tentatively offering my hand, my breath caught when he gently took it and ran a finger up my palm.

"Magic needs intent." He said. "That's true for all of us. You cannot create that which you don't *intend*."

I closed my eyes, remembering the last two times I'd encountered the Empty. "But the times when I stopped the Empty, I wasn't trying. When I did, I failed."

"Perhaps. But you were missing something yesterday."

A sharp nick of pain flashed across my palm. Gasping, I pulled back my hand to see he'd driven his knife across my skin, drawing a few flecks of scarlet. Cupping my hand, I stared at the pooling blood.

"Chthonic magic is simple," Seth said. "Haimyx governs life and death. Our magic is no different. We risk death to chase life. But it's a gamble we believe is worth taking." Placing his hand under mine, he guided me forward. "Do you understand?"

"I think so", I said, looking up. "Like leaping into a fire to save someone."

He nodded, releasing my hand and stepping back. Taking a deep breath, I studied the blood on my palm. My life was a small price to pay. Extending my arm toward the abyss, I focused on that: my desire to destroy the Empty, to warp it to my whims. In exchange, I offered my life.

Nothing happened.

I bit my lip, willing the blood welling in my hand to shoot forward and do. . . *something*.

Lowering my hands, I glanced at Seth.

"Did you feel anything?" He asked.

"No. Am I supposed to?"

"Yes." He returned to my side. "When you first earn your magic, it swirls within you, like a storm begging to be released."

"I don't feel anything like that."

"Maybe it isn't blood you need." He leaned on a tree and folded his arms. "Think back to when you saved Percy. When you stopped the Empty in the marshlands. What were you doing? Thinking?"

Wiping my hand off, I ran my fingers through my hair, straining to recall. I'd been panicked, no? Both by my imminent doom and Percy's.

But so had I panicked at the outpost, and no magic had answered my call.

"I. . . I don't know." I said. "Maybe we're all wrong. Maybe it was just a coincidence."

"You should at least try. Exhaust every possibility."

"Give me a moment to think."

Seth shrugged, rolling up his coat's sleeves. "It's not like I can go anywhere."

Pressing a hand to my head, I paced through the trees, struggling to recall what I'd done. Magic came with intent. But I had not meant to stop the Empty. Not tried to survive it.

Whatever cursed magic had been bestowed upon me, it didn't work like that.

Halting in my tracks, I reached for a different memory. A long time ago, a little girl had run through the woods, aimless and lost. Mother had abandoned me, and my father had never been in the picture. I'd been crying. I'd given up searching for her.

The Empty had appeared, reaching toward me like a warm embrace. At first, I'd tried to flee, but my legs couldn't carry me fast enough to outpace its spread. Falling to my knees, I'd given up.

Given up.

Gasping, my eyes shot open. In the marshlands, I'd ceased fighting the keres and gone limp in their grasp. My life had never been worth anything; what did it matter if I died?

Panic had consumed me as I'd rushed for Percy outside Serifos, but only briefly. Once I'd realized I wouldn't reach him, despondence had taken over. I'd launched myself at him, believing it a futile attempt that would see us both dead.

Jogging back to Seth, I approached the bounds of the Empty, reaching my hand towards its shadowed realm.

Fighting the Empty was *pointless*. I'd never save everyone, never push back enough to spare our lands, our people. To enter the void itself, I had to *become* it. Empty myself of all feeling, all desire, all hope.

Trapped in the tiny hovel I called home, my days had drolled on without meaning. Every morning, I'd stare into the mirror, meet a hollow-eyed gaze, and drag my feet out the door.

All hope had fled the day I realized Ainwir wasn't coming back. Embracing the Empty came as naturally as breathing.

"Aethra," Seth called. "What are you doing?"

I didn't answer. Spreading my fingers, I advanced toward the abyss. Realizing my intentions, Seth lurched off the tree, trying to stop me.

He didn't reach me in time. Lifting my foot from the living world, I stepped into the void.

Silence enveloped me. A muted world bereft of color swaddled me in a suffocating embrace. Pain rattled through my limbs, as though my skin was coming unwound.

I didn't want this to be like last time. I didn't merely want to sustain Percy and me for a mere moment.

Hoping to dispel the Empty was pointless. But I wanted to try.

Light sparked on my fingertips and shot through the shadows. The sound of birds and howling wind burst to life as the abyss around me shattered. Where once a steep canyon plunged into the still sea, flowers grew beneath my feet.

"Maiden's grace." Seth cursed, eyes flashing around my pocket of safety.

"Stay close," I called. "I don't know if it'll close behind me."

Whistling for Whisper to follow, Seth yanked Athena's reins and joined my side. Walking forward, I let the magic stream forth. Seth had been right. Now that I understood its call, something roiled within me, a raging storm unable to be quelled.

Like a splitting sea, the Empty parted for us, pale blue flowers growing where once nothing had reigned. The black pall receded, and blue skies shone overhead. A grin spread across my face, admiring my pointless venture, and the magic only seemed to intensify in response.

A bridge of life extended across the chasm, far above the silent sea.

"Is there an end ahead?" Seth asked. "Can we reach the main road?"

"I don't know," I answered in a trance-like voice.

"It can't be far," he said, glancing behind us. "We're headed away from the outpost. The Empty would have stopped, eventually."

Maybe it hadn't. Maybe it had spread forever, this time. The thought didn't stop me.

A new sensation joined my thoughtless charge. Pain simmered beneath the surface, unlike anything I'd felt before. At first, I couldn't describe it—a malaise radiated beneath my skin, though I couldn't place its cause.

Eventually, it grew into a distracting ache, like the abyss was seeping into my soul and turning me to dust—just like it did with everyone else.

Stumbling beneath the agony, I gritted my teeth, maintaining my grip on the magic.

Seth caught my arm. "What's wrong?"

"I don't know." I hissed through gritted teeth.

"Don't let go." He ordered. "You're okay. I've got you."

Wrapping my arm around his shoulder, he supported my weight as we trudged on through the endless black. Was this how sailors once felt? When they'd set sail into the fathomless seas, unsure if their boat would ever reach another shore?

Like the Maiden, when she'd split the endless Empty for the first time. . .

Biting my lip, I desperately tried to keep my footing. But the pain grew until I could bear it no longer. I looked down, expecting to see myself crumbling away.

My knees gave out, but Seth caught me before I fell. Sweeping me into his arms, he whispered gently to me. "Don't let go, princess. I've got you."

Hand trembling, I grabbed his collar, but the touch of leather faded from my skin. With every passing moment, I felt him less and less. It was like I floated alone in the darkness.

Closing my eyes, I imagined the vast emptiness and my single point of light. The flowers spread faster than before, cleaving through the Empty and racing out of sight. Straining to keep up, Seth broke into a jog. Leaning my head against his shoulder, I drew upon the well of magic swirling in my breast until the final wisp of light faded, leaving me with an empty, hollow void.

Had we made it? Or had we faded into dust? A thousand years might have passed, or only a single moment. When I opened my eyes, it felt like I broke the surface of an ocean I'd been submerged in for a lifetime.

Seth stared down at me, face creased with worry. He sat on a bed of patchy grass, cradling me in his lap. A blue sky crowned the world, and red trees swayed in the breeze, painting colors against the backdrop of the Empty, looming behind us like an oppressive wall.

We'd made it.

Sitting bolt upright, I quickly regretted my actions. My body felt like its threads had come unwound, and pain splintered through me. Leaning my head against Seth's chest, I grinned like an idiot and looked up, expecting the same expression on his face.

His worry softened into a smile. "Fine. I was wrong. There are mages of the Empty, after all."

Laughter escaped my lips, and Seth chuckled with me. A wet muzzle nudged my hand, and I reached out to ruffle Whisper's ears.

"How did you manage it?" Seth asked.

"I gave up," I said. "I knew it was pointless to try. Even if I could carve a path, we had no idea if we'd reach the other side."

Seth furrowed his brow, not entirely understanding. "Did it hurt?"

I grimaced, echoes of the agony radiating in my bones. "Yes. I don't know how to describe it."

"Then it should be used sparingly."

Nodding, I closed my eyes again. The Empty had been lifeless, cold. Seth was warm, alive. My hand curled into his tunic, pulling me nearer to him, as though closeness could infuse me with the life beating beneath his breast.

Seth wrapped his hand around mine, trapping it against his chest. "Don't tell anyone about this."

"What?" I gasped, eyes flying open.

"Do you remember what I said? They'll turn you into a martyr."

"But I can save everyone! What if I can travel through the Acheron and destroy the Empty entirely?"

"I see two futures for you," Seth's gaze hardened, "The clergy and a mob of angry people force you to the Empty, and you tear yourself apart trying to appease them. Or. . ." He trailed off.

"Or what?"

Seth inhaled and closed his eyes. "Promise me you won't use this magic where anyone can see. Promise me you won't tell anyone."

The energy he usually radiated washed away. Lines of sorrow riddled his face, and his teeth dug into his bottom lip. Memories danced behind his eyes, and I could but wonder what he saw.

"Seth?" I reached out and gently cupped his face.

I wanted him to open up, to tell me the truth. But he exhaled and looked away instead.

"Can you stand?" He asked, brushing my hand away. "We should look for the others."

"Give me a moment," I breathed. The pain I'd felt while casting slowly faded away, until only a bearable ache remained.

Finding my footing, I slipped from his grasp and stood, wandering back toward the Empty to examine the hole I'd cleaved in the abyss. A thin strip of life bloomed between the endless nothing, verdant grass flecked by pale blue flowers. Kneeling, I plucked a flower from its stem and lifted it to my eyes, turning the petals over, half-expecting them to simply vanish.

"Incredible," Seth marveled. He nudged me. "I bet you can't wait to tell Eleos all about it."

Eleos. Hope dared to bloom in my chest. Maybe. . . maybe they were okay. Maybe they were waiting for us, somewhere.

"You-" I whirled around, jabbing my finger into his chest. "I thought you said to keep this secret?"

"Not from the others," He shook his head. "I'm worried you'll tell Seraphim's lordly brother and his border hounds."

Retracting my hand, I pursed my lips. A hundred years had passed since anyone had been granted the authority to travel to Duath Nun. In an effort to persuade them, I probably would have embellished my talents and insisted I could save them from doom.

"Mhm," Seth's eyebrow shot up. "I'm right, aren't I?"

"I have an excellent poker face. How did you read me?"

"You've lost every training bout, princess. I'm gathering your secrets like gold."

"Yeah? And what have you learned?"

Tilting his head, he brushed a leaf from my hair, fingers lingering on my curls. "If something threatens our goals, if someone hurts us? You'd trade your life to save ours in a heartbeat."

A lump formed in my throat, and I tried to swallow it. Had he really seen through me from a few silly secrets I'd shared at camp?

Seth stared at me in silence, shoulders tautening. He leaned closer, and I gravitated toward him.

Though our trip through the Empty had been hazy, I remembered one thing clearly—his gentle voice, promising me he would protect me.

A strange magnetism drew me toward him. His fingers slid through my locks to my cheek. Our noses brushed.

The soft expression on his face vanished, and he pulled back. Dropping his hand, he stepped away.

Tension fled from my body, and my muscles relaxed. The air felt thick when he drew near, and breath flooded my lungs when he left.

"Let's get going," I said, clearing my throat. "We should backtrack to the outpost and then follow the road."

Nodding in agreement, Seth found a hill and clambered up, using the vantage point to discern our location and find our destination. Hanging back, I tucked the flower behind my ear, hoping it would live long enough to show Eleos.

As I removed my hand from my hair, I gasped and stumbled backward. The skin on my arm had become translucent, allowing me to see through my own body—the shapes and colors of the grass and dirt were barely visible through my skin.

Panicked, I raised my other hand to see the same thing. My dress turned translucent, my legs but ghosts beneath it.

I was fading away.

My affliction passed. As though an imagined illusion, I was whole again. Gasping, I ran my fingers over my arms, catching my breath as my heart pounded against my ribs.

No magic came free. It required intent, a medium, a price.

Was mine to fade away?

NINETEEN

Seth

LETTING MYSELF GET SO CLOSE to Aethra had been a mistake. She sat in front of me on the saddle, quiet and withdrawn. I tried not to dwell on her, on the night we'd spent sharing each others warmth.

It was impossible.

I was painfully aware of her every curve, of every place where our bodies touched. The scent of flowers clung to her long curls, and I longed to bury my face in the nape of her neck.

Getting close to her was a mistake. Leaning in to kiss her had been catastrophic.

I squeezed my eyes shut, letting her guide Athena. We could not be together. I could not let myself fall in love.

Aethra sighed and leaned her back against my chest. Every muscle in my body seized.

This was torture. I needed to put distance between us—and soon.

An elbow whacked into my side. "Look!" Aethra said.

Opening my eyes, I peered through the trees and saw a bard.

A bard, wearing a patchwork sash and a sharp feathered hat. He pulled a paring knife from his belt and took a defensive posture.

Even without the garish clothing, I would have recognized Percy. Only he would try to fight bandits off with a fruit knife.

Percy gasped as we drew near and pointed at me. "You. . . You're alive?"

Gods, it was a relief to see him alive. And he was the perfect excuse to get away from Aethra. Sliding off the saddle, I extended my arms.

Laughing, Percy tossed aside his knife and sprinted at me. He struck me harder than expected—tackled me, really—and we both landed in the dirt.

I didn't mind. My best friend was alive.

Percy wrapped me in a vice grip and refused to let go. Humoring him, I let him hold the embrace for a few seconds longer. "Alright, alright," I muttered. "Get off me."

Pushing the bard aside, I rose and dusted myself off. Percy shot to his feet, grin widening as he locked eyes with Aethra. He tackled her next, picking her up and twirling her around.

She laughed. My heart fluttered at the sound.

A grimace twisted across my face. We couldn't be together. We couldn't.

Grabbing Percy's arm, I pulled him away from Aethra. "Are you alone?"

"No!" Percy looked elated at first, but his joy quickly faltered. "No. Come with me." Tone growing grim, he beckoned for us to follow. "I was keeping lookout. I was hoping you'd turn up, but I can't say I expected it."

"What happened?" I asked, leading Athena over the rocky soil.

"We ran for our lives." Percy walked backward to face us. "Seraphim grabbed the horses, threw me onto one, and slapped its hindquarters. The rest is a blur."

"You had the Bloodstone," Aethra said. "It must have saved you."

Percy made a strange sound under his breath. "Ah. . .Seraphim could tell the story better."

Aethra's face twisted in fear. "Did. . . did you find Eleos?"

"Yes," Percy said. "I'd say he's alright, but. . ."

"But what?"

"You'll see," Percy said quietly, turning around.

Terror shaded Aethra's face. She cared deeply for that smug, irritating scholar.

Though Eleos had an eye for Cynthus leather. Maybe he wasn't all bad.

If only I could chase away the jealousy in my heart with a blade. Life would be so much easier if I could solve all my problems with swords.

Percy ducked through the trees and stepped off a ledge onto a wide, dirt path—the main road.

A bleak sight greeted us. Canvas and tents were scattered around the hillside, livestock roamed free, and wagons in various states of repair littered the road. A few men in armor patrolled the rough camp's perimeter, guarding the haggard and frightened people within.

I glanced across the area, quickly noticing a great many injured sprawled across bedrolls. Some were missing arms, others looked like they'd been trampled underfoot, crushed.

"A lot of people were injured in the chaos," Percy explained. "Others brushed with the Empty, and. . . not all of them made it out."

A woman in a charcoal coat emerged from one of the threadbare tents, red braid waving behind her as she barked orders at a pair of guards. Aethra stood on her toes and waved an arm.

"Seraphim!"

Her faded blue eyes darted toward us and lit up. "Aethra!" She gasped, jogging over. "We thought we'd lost you two."

"We thought we lost you." Aethra countered, scanning the camp. "How did you escape?"

"The Empty stops eventually." Seraphim turned, and I noticed a streak of silver running the length of her braid. "Those closest to the town's perimeter made it out, but not all in one piece."

Looking up, I traced the path they'd taken, descending the mountain from where once a lively town had rested. Now, a hint of black colored the mountain's peak, warning of the void you'd find in its place.

Seraphim grabbed Aethra's shoulders and whirled her around, pointing her toward one of the medical tents. "Go see Eleos. You'll do him good."

"Is he injured?"

"No," Seraphim said softly, gently pushing Aethra forward.

The princess didn't need any further prodding. She raced off and disappeared through the tent.

Seraphim watched her for a moment, then turned to me. "Thank you for keeping her safe."

"How do you know she wasn't protecting me?" I asked with a sly grin.

"Ha," Seraphim wiped her brow. "Aethra's not quite a warrior yet. But she'll get there." She took a step away. "There's still much to be done. Take a rest, get something to eat—then come find me."

My eyes lingered on Seraphim's back as she disappeared into the sea of tents and wagons. Death and suffering surrounded us. But these people had nothing anymore. The world would deem them worthless and cast them aside.

It was a sight I'd seen all too often—a reminder of home.

I shook myself out of my bleak thoughts and turned to Percy. His hands were planted on his hips, one eyebrow was arched—he looked at me as though awaiting an explanation.

Of what, I had no idea.

"What are you looking at?" I asked.

"A very broody Burgundy Rose," Percy said. "I know you—stuff like this doesn't show on your face."

"Don't you dare start calling me that again," I said, turning on my heel. Seraphim had mentioned food, and I intended to find it.

Percy trotted along at my side. "Is it Aethra? It's Aethra, isn't it?"

I stopped and glared at him. How did he manage to see through me so easily?

"What happened?" Percy asked. "You were out there alone for a couple of days. . ."

Whatever expression crossed my face, Percy learned everything from it.

"Oh, no," Percy breathed. "Did you kiss her?"

"No," I retorted. Glancing away, I added, "Almost."

"I thought you couldn't–"

"I can't," I grabbed his shoulder. "I need to stay away from her. Make me stay away from her."

Furrowing his brow, Percy looked me up and down. Then, he winced, hand flying to his shoulder.

I yanked my arm away. "Did I hurt you?"

"No, it's just," Percy rolled his shoulder, "Running from danger, getting jostled around. . ."

Sometimes, it was easy to forget about Percy's illness, that his limbs fought against him, that his joints were wearing down. My heart sank each time I was reminded his time was short.

"Don't look at me like that," Percy slapped my back and kept walking. "We don't understand each other, but we understand each other." He turned, walking backward. "I keep you away from Aethra; you stop mothering me."

I chuckled. "Perse, you are by far the least eloquent bard I've ever met."

"It's part of my charm," Percy winked and turned around. "The people here are scared. A big man with a big sword will make them feel safer. Come on."

Swallowing, I wrapped my hand around my dagger hilt.

Tragedy walked in step with me, wherever I tread. Percy, Aethra. . . My heart yearned for people I'd inevitably lose.

For people I could not protect.

TWENTY

Aethra

ELEOS WAS ALIVE. So why did everyone act like the Empty had taken him?

Heart fluttering with worry, I hurried toward the medical tent, ducking under the rough canvas. My stomach churned as I looked over the patients. One man looked like he'd fallen from the cliffs; his bones were broken in several places. A young girl's arm was crushed entirely, likely by a horse's hooves.

I saw one of the people Percy had mentioned: a young man with a soft face whose left arm was completely missing. Even some of his shoulders had been consumed by the void. Faint flecks of white appeared on his tan skin and banded through his black hair.

When he awoke, would he be glad he survived?

Raising my eyes from the dismal sight, I noticed Eleos, who knelt over a young boy, gently talking with him as he set the boy's broken arm. A horrible snap sounded, and the boy shrieked, all while Eleos quietly commended him for being brave.

I leaned on the tent's support beam, waiting for him to finish. He wrapped the broken limb and pulled a blanket over the child, ordering him to sit still and rest.

Standing, Eleos ran a hand through his brunette waves. Blood splotched his white robes and stained his pale blue scarf. He glanced in my direction, sage-green eyes tracing over my face like he peered upon a ghost that haunted his every night.

"I'm glad-" I began.

Tripping over himself in his haste, Eleos crossed the gap between us, hesitating just before he reached me. Touching my cheek, he traced a hand down my face before pulling me into an embrace.

Overcome with relief, I melted against him, wrapping my arms tightly around him, fingers curling into his scarf.

I thought I'd lost him. Holding him now, I realized just how much I didn't want to.

Eleos' fear ran deeper than mine. I could feel it in his trembling fingers, in the desperation with which he clutched me. No one had ever held me so tightly.

"I'm sorry," he whispered.

"What for?" I asked gently.

Composing himself, Eleos pulled away. He ran a hand across his eyes. "We need to talk, but—" He looked around. "Not here."

Nodding, I followed him outside, letting the tent flap close behind me. "I know a bit about healing herbs," I said. "Want me to help gather some?"

"Good idea." He touched my shoulder, leading me behind the tents into a patch of woods, where the foliage grew thick beneath the red canopies.

Kneeling, I scanned the grasses, spotting patches of gray-green leaves. Ainwir had plucked these whenever one of us was wounded. Unsheathing my blade, I carefully cut a few handfuls.

"I feel like I'm dreaming," Eleos said, crouching by a cluster of wild sage. "Life dispels the Empty. That's always been true."

"Not anymore," I said. "Which means—'

"Even the cities aren't safe," Eleos interrupted. "Nowhere is safe." He stood, staring at me. "I hoped we could fix this. But what if we don't have time?"

Remembering my flower, I shot to my feet and plucked the pale blue blossom from behind my ear. "There's still hope," I promised him, offering the blossom. "Look."

Brow furrowing, Eleos inspected the flower. "Where did you find that? I've never seen one with that patterning."

Flecks of red dotted the blue, like drops of my blood had fallen upon them. "Because I made it," I said, tucking the flower into his scarf. "I destroyed the Empty. I made a path for Seth and me to escape."

"You did?" he asked blankly.

I nodded, stepping back. "It's still there, I think. A little trail of flowers through the dark."

The glimmer of life returned to his beautiful green eyes. Beaming, he stuffed the sage into his pocket. "Can I see it?"

"It'll have to wait." Seraphim's sharp voice sounded behind us. She stepped over a thick root. "We need to get these people moving."

"Already?" I asked.

"Yes." Seraphim dipped her head. "Come with me. I could use your help."

"Where are we going?"

"Therapne." She answered. "This place isn't safe, and getting this sorry lot up won't be easy."

"Why do we have to rouse them? Surely the lord could order his men to form a caravan."

"He's dead. The lord's estate was at the mountain's peak. We're all that's left."

Seraphim turned and strode away. I had to jog to keep up with her pace. "Listen, I have good news—"

"Will it save these people?"

I hesitated. "No."

Seraphim smiled grimly. "Then it can wait. Wrangle the guards if you can; I'll ignite the uninjured."

"Lady Seraphim," Eleos called. "Can. . . can Aethra stay with me?"

Pausing, Seraphim stared at him over her shoulder. She looked between us, pale blue eyes softening. "Alright. Percy can assist me, then. Why don't you help Eleos arrange wagons for the wounded?" Touching my shoulder, she marched away.

Clutching my bundle of herbs like a bride's bouquet, I cocked my head at Eleos. "Why do you need me?"

"I don't," he admitted. "But right now, I can't let you out of my sight."

"Afraid I'll run off?" I joked. His dour expression didn't lift, so I changed tones. "Are you alright? Percy said—"

"I'm fine," he said. "Especially now that you're here."

"Alright . . ." I said, though I didn't believe him. "Let's go get those wagons, then."

Stranded bands of refugees were tales often told in the Merchant Isles. Whenever a rural settlement fell, those who survived would funnel toward the nearest city. Year after year, the cities swelled as the rest of the world disappeared.

Never before had an outpost or a capital fallen to the Empty. This would mark a new, frightening chapter in history.

Rousing the injured and the despondent was not an easy task. Coordinating a confused, frightened group of people who had lost their leadership was entirely more difficult.

Not all of them had come. Some we left behind, for they refused to move. They'd given up.

Sighing, I traced my thumb across my brow. The noise and weeping from the camp had become overwhelming, and I'd needed a moment to myself. Our little band of thieves had been so busy becoming the new stewards of the refugees, we'd had no time to talk.

I stood by a small pond, watching ripples form on its surface. Living water, a pleasant shade of blue, giver of life. Mirror of the Empty, where in stillness nothing resided.

The smell of iron drifted on the wind. Startled, I stepped back, spotting a stream of blood curling through the air around me. A rush of heat brushed my cheek as fire streaked across the blood, creating a stream of light that coalesced into a little floating ball of burning red.

Seraphim appeared from the night, hand twirling as she controlled her magic. "There you are." Joining me by the water's edge, she lifted the ball of fire to rest above the pond. "Eleos is going to steal you as soon as he's free, and I wanted to catch you first."

I chuckled, rubbing my arm. With her light, I could see my reflection in the water.

Gods, I looked horrible. Scraped, muddy, bruised.

Lifting my eyes, I studied Seraphim, her tall, regal form a stark contrast to mine. Now was the perfect time to ask her about the masked nobleman's accusations—the story of her youth and heretical crimes.

"Are you alright?" Seraphim asked, lifting my chin to inspect my face. "You look whole on the outside, at least."

"On the outside." I agreed.

"I called a meeting," she continued. "I hope you don't mind. But I got here first, in case you needed a little girl time."

Breathing a laugh, I smiled. "I've never had it. But from how others talk, it sounds like I'm missing out."

"You are." Seraphim placed a hand on my shoulder. "I figured I should tell you something, because Eleos won't. He bottles everything up. Nothing I learned about him came free."

"You and Percy had me worried." I knit my hands together. "I thought something horrible happened to him."

"We saw the three of you just before we were separated." She removed her hand and stood across from me. "Eleos darted away, trying to help a poor woman and her child. We lost sight of you and Seth after that."

"I remember."

"I. . ." She ran a hand along her braid. "I saw the writing on the wall. I grabbed Eleos and dragged him away. The mother and child died a moment later. Had he stayed, so would he."

"Does he blame you?" I asked softly.

"No. He blames himself." She sighed. "Coupled with losing you, he took the events hard. Do you know what he said?" She spun the fire above the water, creating dancing lights on its surface. "He was more upset that trying to help two innocents cost him you. And realizing the selfishness in that thought, his guilt only deepened."

A thrum rang through my heart, like the strings of a lute being plucked. Part of me felt a rush of joy; the other, a cold wave of grief.

"I'm glad you're here." Seraphim smiled. "For many reasons. As for our scholar, try to tell him he did the right thing."

"I will," I promised, studying the creases of age around her eyes. "Do you regret it? Leaving that woman behind?"

"Of course." Seraphim's eyes lowered. "But you grow numb to it, eventually. Not everyone can be saved. You have to pick and choose who gets to live, as cruel as it might sound."

"You've seen a great deal of loss, then."

"Yes. Too much." Seraphim gazed at her reflection in the water, her thoughts drifting to someone in her memories.

I debated questioning her—some people's wounds deepened when they spoke of those they'd lost, others reveled in a chance to remember their loved ones. Which was she?

"Seraphim?" My voice emerged as a nervous squeak. Settling my nerves, I looked down. "If you ever need someone to talk to, I'll listen."

Grinning, Seraphim tilted my chin back up. "You're adorable. No wonder you have the boys enamored."

"Hm?"

"I'll take you up on that offer, next we have peace and quiet and a good bottle of wine." Seraphim punched my shoulder lightly, turning to watch the approaching lanterns. "And so our time ends."

Following her gaze, I counted three figures approaching through the night.

Percy swatted bugs off his exposed chest. "Why are we meeting out here?"

Seth joined my side, laughing at his friend. "If you didn't dress like that, they wouldn't bother you so much."

"I'm not compromising sex appeal for comfort." Percy planted his hands on his hips. "You're one to talk, considering the scandalous outfit you used to run around in."

"Hold on," I said, eyeing Seth. "Scandalous, eh? Like how Percy dresses? Or how-"

Seth interrupted. "He's exaggerating."

"I am not. He—" Percy tried.

"Later," Seth said in a low tone.

Rolling his eyes, Percy found a rock to sit on as Seraphim retrieved her ball of fire from the pond and hovered it above her palm. Seth folded his arms and stepped closer to me. He'd found time to scrape the mud from his coat and had unlaced it to show off his collarbone and a hint of his tattoo.

I stared longer than I should have, remembering waking curled up on his chest. He met my gaze. The depths of his scarlet eyes consumed me, as though I'd been cast into an endless fire.

The air felt thick. Struggling to breathe, I shimmied away from him.

Eleos joined us last, the briefest flicker of a smile touching his face as he stood beside me, and gently touched my arm.

Silence fell over us like a heavy blanket. There wasn't any need to say what we all knew.

Seraphim chose a different topic instead. "We'll need to be careful in Therapne. Two of us are wanted there, and our faces are well known."

"Right." Percy cleared his throat with noticeable guilt. "We could wear our masks, but the refugees present a problem. Arrive with them, and we're sure to fall under scrutiny."

"We can't abandon them." Seraphim shook her head. "We'll guide them in, and hope the clergy sees them to safety. Can you think of a cover story, Perse?"

"Easily. We're traveling for a funeral." He offered. "But that's not the problem. My father knows me all too well, and Eleos. . ."

I stared into the fire, brow furrowed. Percy called Therapne home, and so did Eleos. I could muster a guess as to why Percy would be unwelcome—he'd deserted the army and his father was an officer, after all—but why Eleos?

I looked to him for answers, but he remained silent.

"Well," Seth rolled his shoulders, "I say we forego disguises. We'll drop the refugees off and skirt around the border."

"Agreed," Eleos said.

Reaching into her coat pocket, Seraphim produced the Maiden's Bloodstone. "If this thing shielded us from the Empty, I couldn't tell."

"It didn't." Eleos spat harshly. "It's a religious relic, propped up as an excuse for stagnation."

"Rumors and legends come from something." Seraphim turned it over in her palm, the scarlet stone catching the light of her fire. "It doesn't look like any normal rock. It has to be something."

"But what?" I asked.

Eleos chuckled harshly. "Who knows? Lying comes easier to clergy than even nobles."

The bitter hatred in his voice was unlike him. I blinked at him, surprised.

Percy removed his hat, shaking a bug out of it. "Who cares? We have Aethra."

"Don't get too excited," Seth said. "We'd need a legion of mages like her to push it back any meaningful distance. The short path she made for us nearly knocked her out."

"Still," Percy marveled, "It's incredible. I don't think anyone believed the Empty could be erased."

"Aethra," Seraphim said sharply, "Don't overexert yourself. The Acheron will take us where we need to go. Save your strength for when we find ourselves in a bind."

"Trust me," I said, "It wasn't exactly pleasant. I'm not in a rush to repeat it."

"Good." Seraphim cupped her ball of fire, letting it dance around her fingers. "We're all exhausted. Get some rest. If all goes well, we'll be in and out of Therapne within a day."

"Hm." Percy tilted his head. "I think I'll stay out here. Compose a song."

"Another tragedy?" Seth guessed. "The Empty's going to appear and swallow you."

"Someone has to remember those who died. That's what dirges are for." Percy said somberly, pulling his lute off his back. "Want to keep me company?"

Seth glanced at me, tracing my figure longingly. Heat rushed to my cheeks when I realized what he was thinking, though I got the impression his impure thoughts had been subconscious.

Realizing what he was doing, Seth quickly turned away. "I suppose. Gods know you'll get kidnapped, otherwise."

"By who, exactly?" Percy scoffed.

Leaving the boys to patch up their relationship, I followed Seraphim's fire back to camp. Eleos stuck quietly by my side until we found ourselves beneath the light of numerous torches, guarding the refugee camp from the dark.

Squeezing my shoulder, Seraphim took her leave. "Goodnight, you two."

"Goodnight," Eleos said distractedly, guiding me toward a lonely tent nestled against the trees. "Describe the pain to me again."

Following him inside, I combed out my hair. "From the magic? It's hard to describe." Closing my eyes, I recalled the sensation. "Like my soul was being siphoned out."

"I've never heard anything like that." He dropped his bag in the corner. "Magic doesn't hurt. Even chthonics grow so accustomed to spilling their blood that it becomes subconscious."

"Maybe it was only because it was my first time," I suggested, watching him roll out his sleeping mat. "I should let you get some sleep."

"Lady Aethra," Eleos said quietly. "Would you stay with me tonight?"

"Are you sure?" I tried to lighten the mood. "I thought you liked your space. You always put your bedroll well away from ours."

"Normally, I do." His eyelids drooped heavily. "Tomorrow, we run back into danger. The one bastion of safety is gone." Terror pooled in his irises. "Life doesn't dispel the Empty. Not anymore. Nowhere is safe."

I swallowed. We traveled to Therapne for shelter. But would it protect these people?

"I just want to hold you tonight. To know for a few hours, you're safe." He said, voice cracking.

"I don't want to be alone either," I said quietly.

Relieved, Eleos pulled off his cloak and dropped his satchel as though merely preparing for bed. Nothing in his body language indicated he intended to do anything but sleep.

Men had asked me to share a bed countless times. But never simply because they cared about me.

No one had ever cared about me.

Exhausted, I shrugged off my cloak and added it to the scant bedding, collapsing into a grateful heap. Eleos blew out the lantern and knelt beside me, draping his cloak over me like a bed sheet. Crawling onto the bedroll, he nestled beside me, arm wrapped tightly around my waist.

Twisting onto my back, I sought his eyes in the darkness. "You don't need to feel guilty, El."

He laughed breathily. "Seraphim got to you, didn't she?"

"It's true. You did the right thing."

"I've never been particularly. . . moral, I suppose." He pulled me closer, tracing a thumb across my stomach. "Had I saved that woman and her child, and lost you? I would've made the wrong choice."

"But. . ."

"Some people weigh life on a scale." Eleos continued. "No matter how much they love someone, the life of five strangers weighs more. The greater good supersedes desire." He ran his fingers through my hair. "But we each have something we live for. Something that makes tomorrow worth seeing. I'd rather save those I love and lead this world to ruin than lose them and succeed."

His words weighed heavily on my chest. What did I wake for? Before meeting Seraphim, I had roused for nothing and no one.

Did I want to protect the people I loved?

Or save this world?

Ideally, both. But I had little hope for either.

In the darkness, feeling the warmth of his body, I wondered if I should turn and kiss him. Say something. But the longer I lay there, in the comfort of his arms, I realized the last thing I wanted to make tonight about was sex. Rolling over, I felt his comforting presence against my back and closed my eyes.

Sex could come in better days, with smiles and laughs. Right now, all I wanted was this.

To be loved.

TWENTY ONE

Seth

PERCY HAD BEEN A GUARD when we first met, before his illness had taken over his life.

Even then, I could tell he wasn't fit for the job. Too cheerful, too kind.

Too easily broken by the evil lurking in every corner of this world.

I'd been surprised when he pivoted to singing dirges at funerals. His easy smile vanished, and he sang with deep emotion that stirred even my jaded heart.

I stood beside him, listening to the mournful twangs of his lute. He sang of the beautiful town atop the mountain, and the life we'd glimpsed before it had been torn apart.

My head dipped, and I saw my reflection in the pond. Red eyes stared up at me. Red eyes that I hated.

I lifted my chin as Percy set aside his lute. "How do you do it, Seth?" He asked, voice quiet and somber. "How do you carry all that sorrow around with you?"

Surprised, I turned to him. "Do I seem like I'm handling it well?"

"Most of the time." Percy leaned his head against his lute and stared into the water. "Do I seem okay, most of the time?"

"On the outside," I said, sitting beside him.

Percy plucked an aimless tune, filling the silence.

The past weighed on my heart. It always did. My mind drifted to Aethra, and I swatted her away.

It didn't last. Within moments, I was dwelling on her brilliant smile, the sound of her laugh. Her wit and dry humor always brought a smile to my face. And, she looked so sad sometimes. I wanted to wrap her in a hug and tell her everything would be okay.

Percy glanced down at me. "Stop thinking about her."

"We've gotten drunk together too many times," I said, looking up, "If you're reading my mind, now."

"Humor me. What am I thinking?"

A somber furrow creased his brow. "That you feel worthless. That you wished you had more than songs to give."

"Ouch," Percy rubbed his chest. "Maybe we have gotten drunk one too many times."

I chuckled. Sitting forward, Percy snatched a branch from the ground and tossed it to me. "Here. This should make you feel better."

"What am I?" I asked, picking up the stick. "A dog?"

"You like to whittle, don't you? Make something for me."

Shaking my head, I reached for my carving knife. A twig snapped behind me, and I shot to my feet, hand on my blade.

Seraphim stalked toward us, fire dancing in her palm. She flicked her wrist, and it grew into a blazing scythe. "Glad to see Percy hasn't been kidnapped."

"Ha ha," Percy rolled his eyes, plucking at his lute. "Care to join our pity party, Seraphim?"

Seraphim looked me up and down. "You look like a man who works through his emotions with blade work. Care to spar?"

Yanking my dagger from my belt, I slashed it across my palm. Blood poured from the wound and gathered into the shape of a blade. "I thought you'd never ask."

Percy leaped from his rock and staggered back. Just in time, too. Seraphim flew at me, and our weapons clashed.

She fought with ferocity, and I responded in kind. Ducking beneath a swing of her scythe, I cleaved at her side. The magicked blood of my blade sang against hers.

Listening to Percy's dirge had brought everything back— the grief, the loss. Every day, I'd felt utterly useless, broken, and spent. Unable to save anyone. Not even those who mattered most.

Here I was again, surrounded by death. Unable to do a damn thing.

Percy's illness could not be cured. And Aethra. . .

If I did not pull myself away from her, she would die, too.

My heels ground into the dirt as my blade blocked Seraphim's scythe. Twisted rage curled her lips, but it was not directed at me. Beneath the burning fury in her gaze, I saw the tearing cracks of a woman barely holding herself together.

We broke apart, panting. Sweat trickled down my brow, and I wiped it away. "You needed that, too," I observed.

Seraphim straightened out and flicked her wrist. The scythe vanished into embers and drops of blood. She cast me a sad smile. "I did. It's strange. You and I are so different, but I see so much of myself in you."

Seeing that we were done, Percy returned to his rock. "You're a brooding rogue, too?"

She cackled. "If you ever see me brooding, Perse, you'll know the world has come to an end."

Tucking my blade under my arm, I tilted my head. "Why are you doing this? There's a hell of a hole in your story, and I'm curious of its details."

"I have nothing left to lose," Seraphim said. "That's what we share in common, no? What threat is certain death when the pain we suffer every day is so much worse?" A wan smile tugged at her lips. "Might as well try saving the whole of the world."

There was more to it than that. Seraphim liked to deflect. I was beginning to see what she meant.

We did share much in common.

"Who did you lose?" I asked quietly.

She broke. Moisture gleamed in the corners of her eyes. "Did I not say? Everything." Wiping her face, she turned away. Within moments, her confident bravado was back. "Aethra is staying with Eleos tonight. I think I'm glad for them to find some joy amidst all this."

Percy sat forward, grinning. Then, he glanced at me and grimaced.

Jealousy stirred within me again, snaking vines around my heart.

"I am, too," I said, staring at the ground.

This was for the best. I couldn't let my feelings for her bloom. Letting her get so close had been a mistake.

If Aethra was with Eleos, everything would be easier. She'd be taken. There would be no risk of me giving in to my foolish heart.

Steeling my heart, I locked the memories of my past within. Dropping my blade, I let it tumble away from me.

Like everything I'd claimed to love.

TWENTY TWO

Aethra

I DREAMED OF A SIMPLE life. Sequestered in an idyllic plain, I tended the garden of my little house, watching the lake sparkle beneath the sun. Two children, their faces blurry, ran around the yard, and the door swung open. Joy bloomed in my heart as I stood to greet my husband.

My eyes shot open. I lay on hard, cold ground, wrapped in a thin blanket and cloak. A pleasant breeze ruffled my hair, and light spilled in through the tent flaps. Sitting up, I noticed Eleos lacing on his bracers, bag already packed.

"Morning." He said softly. "I figured I'd let you sleep in a bit. You needed it."

"And you didn't?"

"I've always been an early riser." He deflected, just as Seraphim promised he would.

Pulling up my knees, I studied his face. "I've never had this sort of thing before."

He looked up, interested. "What's that?"

"Someone I felt I could trust."

"I did once." He picked up the other bracer and slid it on. "But it's been some time."

"You don't trust Seraphim?"

"As a leader. As a companion. But not like. . . " He trailed off, searching for the right word.

I knew what he meant: someone you spilled the inner workings of your heart to.

Rising, I grabbed my sash from the ground. "Was it the girl you courted?"

"Which one?"

"Oh, so he is a skirt-chaser." I teased.

He chuckled, shaking his head. "No, neither of them. It was my sister."

"You have a sister?" I asked, tying my sash.

"I did." He said quietly. His sage-green eyes glistened with nostalgia. "She was the one who called me El."

"Oh," I said somberly. "I wish I could have met her. I bet she had one hell of a sharp wit."

A smile bloomed across his face. "Oh, she did." He confirmed, sweeping his cloak over his shoulder.

Grabbing my bag, I reached inside. "I wanted to give this to you under better circumstances, but," my eyes fell to his journal as he tucked it into his satchel, "I think you need it now." Pulling out the quill, I placed it into his hand.

Eleos turned it over, admiring the words carved into the leather. "Ah!" He gasped softly. "This is Cynthus leather. When did you. . .?"

"When you and Seth were fawning over the cloaks."

He grinned. "Thank you, Lady Aethra. It's beautiful." Tossing aside his broken quill, he tucked the new one safely into his journal. Cupping my face, he kissed me on the forehead. "Go help Seraphim. She's probably getting impatient."

He strode outside without another word. Playing with the clasp of my cape, I loitered in the tent. After what happened last night, I'd expected more than words between us. A kiss? Or, maybe an amorous embrace?

Perhaps Eleos was more traditional and preferred a formal declaration of courtship before engaging in anything intimate.

Stepping outside, I shielded my eyes from the rising sun. A streak of light illuminated Seraphim's fiery hair as she roused the camp, snapping orders at the guards and able-bodied men, stopping briefly to help a young mother tie their cargo to a pack mule.

I didn't believe the masked nobleman—not a word of the slander he'd tried to sell me. Seraphim had started this endeavor, risked her life for the Bloodstone, for Seth, for all of us. She strode with the confidence of a leader, guiding these people though it hadn't been our plan.

And here I was, having spent most of this journey thinking it was pointless. Wishing I could flee.

"Morning, princess." Seth walked by, tossing and catching an apple. "You're late, as usual."

"And you could've woken me up." I pointed out.

"And rouse the sleeping beauty?" He smiled mischievously. "Want to fit in another training session before we take off?"

"Yes." I declared, marching up to him. "You owe me secrets, remember? I'm going to *beat* them out of you."

"Are you sure about that? I'm fairly sure I'll be beating them out of you."

"I've been studying your weak points. You're as good as mine."

"Am I?" His gaze swept over me again, quickly darting from my hips to my breasts before settling on my face. I'd heard the tone in his voice a thousand times from other men.

Should I tell him I intended to court Eleos? Maybe that would only make things awkward. He'd figure it out soon enough.

Seth's smile vanished, and he stepped back. The amicable warmth he'd exuded but a moment ago turned icy and detached. "I hope El knows what he's doing."

"What do you mean?" I asked.

"Women like you are only good for fun."

I blinked, wondering if I'd heard him correctly. "What did you say?" I asked, eyes narrowing.

He turned his head, sharp jaw tensed. "We'll find time to train tomorrow. Seraphim wanted to see you."

Spinning on his heel, Seth stalked away. Bewildered, I watched him go, then turned my gaze to the ground, as though the dirt could provide answers.

Men. I could read their thoughts and lust like an open book, but when it came to their inner feelings?

I was utterly lost.

I'D NEVER TRAVELED with such a large group before. It was agonizingly slow. With children, elderly and wounded, our pace slowed to a crawl. We crept through the mountain road, following it into the verdant basin where Therapne, home of the clergy, awaited us.

Eleos was quiet for most of the journey, tending to the wounded where he could. I wasn't sure how to act around him, how to bring up the night we'd shared when he wouldn't.

Seth started avoiding me, too. If I approached him, he'd exchange curt words and find an excuse to get away from me. After the third time he gave me the cold shoulder, I gave up any attempts to speak with him.

Instead, I devoted myself to being Seraphim's assistant, or Percy's, should she shoo me away. The bard had somehow become the camp cook.

After a final, steep path down the mountainside, we left the treacherous roads behind and entered the beautiful land Therapne called home. Grass so green it almost didn't seem real grew in lush waves over the hillside, flecked with countless wildflowers. Fruit trees sprouted in abundance, and birds flitted through the skies, beckoning us to follow the river toward civilization and safety.

We were supposed to reach the city by nightfall. Riding at the head of the company, I leaned forward on Athena's saddle, watching the horizon for life.

Percy trotted up beside me, a ridiculous collage of color on his simple brown mare. "Look at you. Already a professional rider."

"Only if she's not galloping." I corrected, sitting back.

Frowning, Percy rode closer to me. He tilted his hat up so I could see his gray eyes. "Are you alright?"

"I think so. Why?"

"No, not physically." Glancing back, as though worried someone eavesdropped, he hushed his voice. "I noticed you seemed shaken when I found you. And now Seth's avoiding you."

"I've noticed that," I tilted my head toward him. "And Eleos is being distant. I've done something to offend the menfolk."

He chuckled at my verbiage. "Take my word for it: Seth thinks you're pretty."

"Is that why he's avoiding me?" I raised an eyebrow. "What is he, twelve?"

"Twenty-eight, last I checked." Percy corrected. "No, I mean." He huffed, frustrated. "I think he doesn't like that he thinks you're pretty. Inside and out."

I blinked at the bard a few times, trying to decipher his words. "I thought bards were supposed to be eloquent."

"Only when I'm performing." Percy rolled his shoulders. "Trust me. In matters of the heart, I'm an expert—if you need advice."

"Seth insulted me last time we talked. Are you sure about that?"

"*Exactly*. He doesn't like that he likes you, so he's pushing you away."

"Hm." I sized the bard up. "You're a man."

"That I am."

"If you were Eleos, how would you want to be courted?"

"Stiffly," Percy answered readily. "Formally. But also, understated. A simple gesture of love in a beloved location."

I nodded. His advice made sense to me.

"Oh!" Percy's head jerked back, and his hat fell back over his eyes. "Are you going to woo our scholar?"

"I'm going to try."

He clapped giddily. "Do you need help? Advice? A new outfit?"

"If we stop in Therapne," I said, "I'll take you up on the offer."

"There's a dress Therapnen women wear that would be gorgeous on you." He touched his belt. "I hope we have the coin."

Smiling, I sat upright and cast my gaze ahead. A statue rose above the trees, and I could see a few farms ahead. Therapne.

"Oh, boy." Percy tipped his hat down.

"Think we'll see Officer Percivus?" I asked, a sudden realization striking me. "Oh, are you Percivus the Second?"

"Yes." Percy said flatly, eyes carrying a clear warning: *'Don't say that name again.'* Clicking his tongue, he turned his steed around. "That's our cue to fall into the shadows." He strapped his mask on and rode back through the caravan.

Pulling my mask over my eyes, I gently tugged Athena's reins, turning her around. Something on the horizon caught my eye, and I swiveled in the saddle, watching.

The city rode out to meet us. A small company of armored men approached, pale blue tabards marking them as temple knights. A high-ranking priest rode at their center, swathed in elegant white robes and a sweeping blue cloak.

Well, shit. There went our attempt to slip away unseen.

A knight in a red surcoat broke from the party to intercept the refugees. His gaze settled on me. Cursing under my

breath, I turned to meet him. I had never been to Therapne—
he wouldn't recognize me.

The insignia emblazoned on the man's tabard was familiar:
I'd stitched it onto Percy's disguise—the one meant to imitate
his father.

Sir Percivus—senior—addressed me. "What is the meaning
of this? We received no word of such a large group."

"The outpost at Red Bluffs has fallen," I said gravely. "We
come seeking shelter."

"Fallen?" He repeated in disbelief. "To what enemy?"

"The Empty," I said. "Please, we have many injured.
Children among them."

Sir Percivus rode closer, gaze sweeping over the
procession. I glimpsed a hint of his face behind the helmet,
stern with harsh, sharp features. His features matched his
son's—but little else.

"You speak true." He guessed, seeing the wagons filled with
wounded. "Why, then, do you conceal yourself?"

Using Percy's drafted story, I pushed melancholy into my
words. "I was traveling for a funeral. I mean to honor him,
regardless."

Narrowing his eyes, Sir Percivus directed his horse to
circle me. His eyes scoured every inch of my face and body.

"You think you can fool me?" He growled. "You think I
haven't heard of the Bloodstone's thieves? Of the
impersonators who stole my name?"

"I don't know what you're talking about," I said.

"Perhaps some time in the dungeons will jog your
memory."

A brown mare broke from the caravan, riding to my side.
Percy lifted his hat, revealing his face. "Father," He said
cautiously, before enthusiasm flooded his tone. "Father! It's
been so long. Why don't we just calm down and talk about this,
like civilized folk?"

"I should have known." Sir Percivus eyed his son with disappointment. "Arrest them!" He barked. "Search the caravan—there's more of them."

"Wait," I called. "We have royal immunity. By decree of the king, you can do no harm to us."

The bullshit flowed smoothly from my mouth. Sir Percivus held up a fist, ordering his men to halt. "Speak."

"We're under the service of the Archon." I continued. "We've been granted pardon from our sins in exchange for our labor."

"Really? And what has the Archon ordered you to do?"

"Warn you," I said. "Of our impending doom."

THINGS HAD GONE better than I expected. Sir Percivus had ordered his men to guide the refugees into the city, sending one man back to the gates to deliver word of their forthcoming arrival. The five of us were instead shepherded away by the officer himself and a unit of temple knights, dressed in glittering steel and sea-blue tabards.

We were to be brought before the governor. But in Therapne, the governor was also the Grand Cleric. The truth would fall upon his ears like flaming coals. *Heresy.* My mind whirled as we rode, coming up with a story to see us from his chambers in one piece.

Seas, Therapne was beautiful. And distracting. The buildings were tall and thin, elegant shafts of marble supported by beautifully carved pillars and beams. Rivers and streams rushed through the plains, cutting through gardens of flowers with quaint stone bridges crossing the drink.

Four statues stood watch over the city, one for each of the gods. The Maiden, foremost of them all, stood facing north, her hooded countenance watching over our arrival.

Sir Percivus led us to the grand temple, an even more impressive edifice than Serifos'. I marveled at the high ceiling and the ancient murals carved into the stone: an entire tapestry, portraying the tale of the Maiden, wrapped around the building.

The officer's heavy boots clinked on the stone path as he dismounted, and he ordered us to follow suit. Climbing off Athena, I hurried to Seraphim's side. She looked down at me and winked, perhaps pleased with the story I'd woven. The three men joined us. Corralled into the center of the knights, we were guided inside.

An enormous antechamber greeted us, lit by a chandelier the size of a carriage hanging above a statue of the Maiden pouring water from an urn into a basin. News of our arrival must have preceded us; several members of the clergy already gathered around the statue, clad in white with pale blue scarves.

A middle-aged man with graying black hair was the most senior of the lot, denoted by a wide-brimmed hat decorated with dangling tassels. His harsh green eyes settled on Sir Percivus.

"What is the meaning of this-" He trailed off, face blanching when he noticed Eleos. Silence overtook him before anger prevailed, his face trembling with rage. "How *dare* you set foot in these halls again?"

Eleos glared bitterly at the Grand Cleric. "I didn't have much choice. Your men dragged me here."

Any plans I'd made shattered. Whirling around, I stared at Eleos in shock.

The Grand Priest pointed at him, hand shaking with fury. "*You.*" He seethed. "You were the ones who stole the Maiden's relic. We heard the news. Read your descriptions. I should have known!" He glanced around, eyeing the pair of guards with the officer. "Search them!"

"You've misunderstood." I blurted out as one guard seized Eleos, and the other grabbed Seraphim. "We didn't steal the Bloodstone—we were ordered to bring it to you."

Sir Percivus glanced at me before addressing the Cleric. "She claims the Archon sent them, your holiness. Coupled with the news from Red Bluff, we should hear them out."

"Red Bluff?" The Grand Cleric repeated. "What of it?"

"The Empty has taken it," Seraphim said, ripping from the guard's grip. "The few who survived have come here seeking refuge."

The Grand Cleric's eye twitched. Focusing on me, he pushed past the others and towered over me. "You have one chance to explain."

"The Bloodstone has lost its power," I said, speaking before I'd fully formed my lie. "We were ordered to bring it here, in hopes it could be restored. Ikaria's High Priest opposed the idea, and-"

"The Bloodstone has not waned in a thousand years. What could have possibly caused such a tragedy?"

"But it has!" I protested. "Every year the Empty closes in, its power diminishes-"

"*Heresy.*" The Grand Cleric hissed. "The Bloodstone will remain pure until it shields the final city from the end. From its lifeblood, the Maiden will rise anew."

Falling silent, I tried to maintain composure. The final city was spoken of in prophecy, but rarely mentioned in sermons. I'd slipped up.

Gods, why hadn't I gone to church more often?

"Take these *thieves* to the dungeons." The Grand Cleric snapped.

A temple knight grabbed my arms, but I fought out of his grip. "You don't understand. The Maiden's blessing has departed the Bloodstone—and entered a new host."

Gasps rose from the priests before a hush blanketed the chamber. Seth's molten gaze burned into my back. I stiffened, trying not to look at him.

Lines of fury painted the Grand Cleric's face. "And what do you claim bears her blessing?"

"Me," I said.

Stepping back, the Grand Cleric snapped at the temple knights. "Did you find it?"

"Your holiness." The guard who'd apprehended Seraphim bowed, offering the Bloodstone.

Taking the relic, the Grand Cleric studied the red stone with hazy eyes. Snapping from his thoughts, he glowered at me. "You dare claim to grasp the Maiden's grace? You? A mere mortal?"

"I. . ." I floundered, searching for a path forward. "No one expected-"

The grand Cleric seized my wrist and yanked me toward him. "Let's test your claims, then." Pulling me painfully, he dragged me toward the statue of the Maiden rising from the center of the room.

"Don't touch her." Eleos snarled, fighting against his guard's grip.

"If you speak the truth," The Grand Cleric beckoned for one of the guards to approach. "Your blood flows with her blessing." The guard drew his blade and bowed, offering it to the Grand Cleric. "And the Maiden will save you."

Percy tried to stop Seth as he lunged forward. Guards fell upon both of them. One crashed into Percy, restraining his arms behind his back. The other tried to tackle Seth, to no success.

Ducking out of the knight's grip, Seth bit his knuckles, and blood trickled down his hand. A scarlet blade grew in his palm as the temple knight drew his spear.

Their clash lasted only a moment. Seth batted away the knight's spear and twisted the shaft from his grip before slamming his blade into the knight's helm, sending him to the ground. Whirling around, he raised his sword to throw at my captor.

A blade touched my throat as the Grand Cleric grabbed my collar. "Stop," he shouted. "Or I'll kill her outright."

Seth's grip tensed on his blade as he eyed the Grand Cleric's sword. Snarling, he released his spell, letting the blade fall. Lunging forward, a second knight quickly restrained Seth, but I couldn't tell if the hatred twisting his face was meant for the Grand Cleric or me.

How quickly I'd walked back on my promise to keep my magic secret.

"Good." The Grand Cleric dragged the sword to my shoulder. "Now let the goddess reveal your blasphemy."

Wincing, I tensed as the Grand Cleric slashed the blade across my arm. Blood poured from the wound, spilling into the basin at the Maiden's feet. A few splotches landed on the hand restraining me, dripping from the Grand Cleric's fingers onto the Bloodstone he clutched in his palm.

A faint glow emanated from the stone. A soft thrum. The wrath etched on the Cleric's face vanished, and he paled, dropping my arm as he held aloft the Maiden's Bloodstone. He blinked at it in awe before whirling around and staring in horror at the blood streaming from my arm.

Eleos spoke up, his voice filled with a hatred I'd never heard. "You've spilled the Maiden's Blood. Get on your knees before her and beg her forgiveness. *Heretic.*"

TWENTY THREE

INWIR HAD ALWAYS SAID NEVER to pull a con masquerading as someone bigger than yourself. During our time together, he'd avoided the clergy and shied away from nobles close to the city lords. Now, I understood why.

I'd successfully convinced the clergy to consider the possibility I was the Maiden's vessel, or chosen, or something to that effect. And now that I'd gotten us into the Temple's good graces, I had no idea how to get us back *out*.

Standing before the tall mirror, I stared at my reflection aimlessly. Horrified by what he'd done, the Grand Cleric had ordered me to be stitched up, bathed, and properly dressed. Turning, I watched the thin fabric of my elegant white gown swirl across the floor.

Flopping onto the guest chamber's soft bed, I watched the sun rise outside the window. The clergy had called an emergency conclave to discuss the implications of my situation. I was expected to attend.

A unit of temple guards had dragged Seraphim and the others away to be confined until the clergy came to a decision, but I had not been informed of their prison or condition. Worry gnawed at me, evidenced by the dwindling nails on my dominant hand.

Running my fingers nervously through my plaited hair, I stared at the ceiling. A mural of the goddess Psythos looked down on me, perhaps judging my sins. Short, cloud-like hair coiled around her shoulders and shrouded her body, encircling the hand she extended as if beckoning me to join her.

I frowned at her. How *dare* she gift her blessing to Ainwir? The more time I spent with Eleos, the more certain I became of my master's hidden talents.

A sharp rap sounded on the door, and I sat up, calling for them to enter. Eleos quietly entered, dressed in clergy robes with a new blue scarf trailing down his back. Two temple guards accompanied him, their faces concealed by their helmets.

Shooting to my feet, I rushed to his side, but he held up a hand for silence.

"The conclave is underway," he said calmly, taking my hand and gazing into my eyes, "Your presence has been requested."

Glancing at the guards, I nodded quietly and followed him into the hall. Eleos grabbed a pale blue shawl from a hook inside the room before tapping the door closed behind us. His voice rang softly in my mind.

"*Are you alright?*" He wrapped the shawl around my shoulders.

"*I thought you were detained with the others,*" I thought back.

"*I was,*" Eleos thought. "*But they realized something terrible: a heretic brought the Maiden's vessel safely to Therapne. They offered me a chance at 'redemption,' so they could wash clean the scandal.*"

So his crime *had* been heresy. I wanted to press, but Eleos claimed communicating like this was taxing, so I held my curiosity for when we could speak normally.

Temple knights flanked us as we walked, their pale blue surcoats brushing against the gray stone floors. Murals of the gods gazed down from the walls, as though observing our every step.

Callesis' wicked grin and golden lyre caught my eye, and I thought of Percy. A knight's son, receiving the art god's blessing. The gods had a funny sense of humor.

Rounding a bend in the hall, Eleos guided me toward a grand archway leading into a vast chamber.

Lifting my head stiffly, I gave him a side-eyed glance. "*I haven't thought of a story that will save our hides.*"

"*Neither have I.*" Eleos thought back. "*But neither have the clergy. We'll have to improvise.*" He offered me a tiny half-smile. "*Think we can play off each other well enough?*"

I smiled back. "*I guess we'll find out.*"

Holding my head high, I strode through the archway into the clergy's meeting chamber. A towering vaulted ceiling loomed above my head, and each staggering wall was carved with the likeness of one of the gods. Several men and women in white robes and blue scarves gathered around an enormous round table centered by a basin of clear water.

Place me in a room of nobles and I could name most by their faces, dress, or dialect. But the clergy? Beyond the Grand Cleric, I had no idea who any of these people were, nor their rank in the hierarchy.

A shriveled woman tucked behind a cowl pointed at Eleos. "Why is that heretic here?"

The Grand Cleric gritted his teeth. "My son has been falsely slandered. His appearance here proves as much."

My son? I gawped at Eleos briefly before remembering to stitch my mouth shut.

"Heireia," Eleos said politely. "I believe you recall the reason for my excomm-"

"Who here doesn't?" She spat. "You-"

"Have been proven right." Eleos interrupted.

Retracting her hand, the Heireia fell silent.

I wanted to throw Eleos across the room. He swore up and down he wasn't a priest, let alone an excommunicated one. Had he not kept everything secret from me, perhaps I wouldn't feel so lost.

"*I can hear your thoughts*," Eleos spoke in my mind. "*You couldn't pick me up, let alone toss me.*"

That did it. I was going to kill him after this.

"Enough, Heireia," The Grand Cleric rested his palms on the table, "We must decide our next course of action."

"Are we certain of these claims?" A wizened man at the end of the table questioned. "There is no doubt of her connection to the Maiden?"

"I am certain." The Grand Cleric said firmly. "I saw how the Bloodstone resonated with her. And I will not harm her again for your benefit."

Snapping his mouth shut, the old man sat.

"But," a younger woman said, "but wouldn't her appearance mean. . ."

Silence blanketed the room until all voices rose at once. My eyes flashed between the clergy, trying to keep track of their argument.

"The end days cannot be upon us." One barked. "The Maiden is supposed to appear only when the final city remains."

"You heard what happened at the outpost." Another argued. "We might have little time left."

"What if it consumes us next?"

"The Bloodstone wards the Empty, it *cannot*."

"They claim it's now useless! This woman stole its blessing."

"Why are we even considering such a ridiculous story? One spun by thieves, at that!"

I retreated into my mind, thinking. The last thing we needed was for them to stick me like a pig and create a new

Bloodstone from my corpse. But convince them I was their goddess, and nothing good would follow.

"No." Eleos agreed, reading my mind.

"*You were the one who sought me,*" I thought. "*What do you think I am?*"

"*I think you bear no relation to any god.*" Eleos thought. "*Because they are mere figments conjured by desperate men.*"

Blinking rapidly, I gazed at him in shock.

Shaking his head imperceptibly, he spoke in my mind, "*Perhaps claim to be her envoy?*"

"*I come bearing a warning, before the end approaches?*" I thought. "*Stoke their egos, say Therapne will be the final city where the believers gather?*"

"*Can you sell that?*"

"*Haven't you seen me act?*"

Clearing his throat, Eleos addressed the room. "If I may?"

The arguing slowly died down until all eyes rested on the former heretic.

"She is right here, false or true. Why not ask her?" He looked down at me.

Putting on my best doe-eyed maiden impression, I met the expectant gazes. "I've felt the Maiden. I. . .I don't know how to explain it. I think she sent me as a warning."

"*Nothing,*" The Heireia articulated, "in the Scripture speaks of a warning."

"Her message is not entirely clear," I said, "It's like she's trying to reach me through the Empty itself, and. . . and it's fighting her at every turn."

"What do you mean?" The Grand Cleric pressed.

"I feel something." I said, lacing lies with the truth, "When I gaze into the abyss. Her presence. And her grace allows me to step into the Empty and survive."

One of the younger clerics rocketed from his chair. "You can survive the Empty?"

"Yes," I said, raising my voice over the growing murmurs. "Just as the Bloodstone can."

"I've seen it myself," Eleos added.

The Heireia raised her chin. "Let's test her, then. Shove her through and see if she disintegrates like all the rest."

The younger priestess looked at her in horror. "But what if she speaks the truth? You'd dare disrespect the Maiden by doubting her envoy?"

"She doesn't speak the truth." The Heireia snapped.

Studying her wrinkles, I tried to remember what duties the Heireia attended. Did her word carry significant weight, or none?

An argument broke out again. Eleos glanced between everyone at the table, gaze falling on his father last. The Grand Cleric stared back, his steely gaze dropping from his son to me. As the cacophony grew to a boiling point, he slammed his fist on the table, shattering the noise into silence.

"Enough." He shouted. "We have no reason to believe, or disbelieve her claims. They are to be treated with the delicacy they are due." He stood straight, folding his hands before him. "She will remain here, under scrutiny. We will double our prayers and seek a sign. Heireia, send word to our brethren to ask their counsel."

"Of course," The Heireia said.

"Wait," I interjected. "Can you afford to waste time praying? There's a great many refugees out there who need help."

"A problem for another day," the Grand Cleric dismissed. "This requires our full attention."

"Indeed." The Heireia agreed. "Assign a guard rotation to watch her at all hours. One of us should stay with her. Monitor her."

"My son will." The Grand Cleric said. "As penance for his crimes, he will serve the Maiden's chosen, or suffer alongside her should her heresy be revealed."

THE CRACKED STONE bench resting beneath the orchard looked like a gift from the gods after such an excruciating day. Falling onto it, I rested my chin in my hands and stared despondently across the garden.

Eleos sat beside me, eyeing the guards who watched us from across the path. "Do you see now why I dislike the clergy?"

"A little," I admitted. "How long will it take for a 'sign from the gods' to arrive?"

"Forever," Eleos said quietly. "There are no gods. No one to answer them."

I sat back, staring at him. "But I thought–"

"I believed there was magic connected to the Empty," He lowered his voice so the guards couldn't hear. "But I think the gods either never existed or abandoned us."

I couldn't claim to be pious, but I'd always believed in the gods. "Why?"

"Because gods worth worshiping wouldn't let. . ." He trailed off, abruptly changing tone. "I came here often in my youth. It's nostalgic to be back."

Sitting back, I glanced at the guards. Speaking of heresy was probably a bad move, right about now. "It's beautiful."

Unripe fruit hung from the trees, their branches flecked with pastel flowers. Neatly trimmed grass grew around staggered stone pathways, circling fountains made of natural piled stones. I tucked my hands between my legs, resisting the urge to pluck the lilies growing around the bench.

They might be holy, after all.

"So," I gripped the edge of the bench and leaned forward. "You're the Grand Cleric's son?"

"Adopted son ." He corrected. "I was left at the temple steps."

"Oh." I breathed. The Guild always left noble bastards on temple doorsteps. Doctrine required them to take in the child and raise it as a nameless disciple.

"My sister was his blood daughter." Eleos continued, closing his eyes as the breeze swept over us.

"You're still hiding a lot from me," I said.

"I know. There's a lot in my past. I've never shared it with anyone before." His eyes snapped open, and he quickly took my hand and released it. When he next spoke, it was within the safety of my thoughts. "*I can find a chance to speak with the others tonight. But it might be my only chance.*"

"*You want to plan an escape?*" I asked.

"*I know my Father. He's reeling.*" Eleos thought back, pretending to be admiring the scenery. "*None of them are prepared for the end. Nobody thinks it will happen in their lifetime. I suspect the Heireia will win out, and you will be driven into the Empty, to 'prove' yourself.*"

"*But I can survive-*"

"*You can,*" He agreed. "*But we have a mission, and we're running out of time. We cannot be tied down here, and,*" he glanced at me, "*I doubt they'll be so kind to the others when their identities are discovered.*"

I rolled my tongue in my mouth, standing. "*A daring escape it is, then.*" Knitting my fingers behind my back, I strolled to the fountain and peered into the water. "*My talents will be of little help. This might be something better suited for Percy and Seth.*"

"*You do me a disservice.*" Eleos thought, humored. "*I can hear all these guards' thoughts.*"

"*. . .What are they thinking?*"

"*They're terrified. They hope—and pray—you're false.*"

Raising my head, I stared at the shorter of the two guards, a young woman whose face I couldn't see. She stared back. Even with her face concealed, I could read her distress: her hand danced on the hilt of her blade, she bounced nervously on her heels.

Was she wondering the same thing I was? Had the gods abandoned us?

Were we truly alone in this wretched world?

Turning away, I stared into the water. "*Tell Seth not to hurt them.*"

"*I thought our vigilante didn't hurt innocents?*" Eleos rose and joined me by the pond, switching to speaking aloud. "My sister used to drag me from that very bench, close my books, and force me to train with her."

"Really?" I asked, smiling.

"She wanted to be a temple knight, not a priestess." He confirmed, smiling at her memory.

"And you've always been a bookworm?"

"I prefer to call myself an academic."

I chuckled, dropping my arms. Our hands brushed. He reached back, running a finger across the back of my hand before retracting his arm.

Nerves fluttered in my heart as I remembered Percy's words: Eleos would want to be asked to court in a beloved spot. The setting sun dipped behind the trees, spilling evening light across the fountain, and dousing the garden in romantic light.

I'd miss my chance if I didn't leap at it now, good timing be damned.

"Um," My voice cracked, and I snapped my mouth closed.

Raising an eyebrow, Eleos turned to look at me. "Yes?"

Swallowing, I tried to summon my courage. What if he said no? What if everything I wanted to say came out all wrong? Lost in his soft green eyes, I rehearsed the words I wanted to say, but couldn't voice them.

"Can't you," I croaked, "read my mind?"

"I try not to, Lady Aethra." He reminded me, stepping back. "We were only allowed a moment's respite. The guards are getting restless." He touched my wrist. "We should go."

The moment flew over my head and landed in the dirt behind me, squandered. Nodding my head absently, I followed him down the stone path back to the Temple's doors. Maybe that hadn't been the best time, anyway, what with guards staring daggers at our backs.

Lowering my gaze, I returned to the guest quarters I'd been assigned, though perhaps 'confined to' was a more apt description. Eleos held the door open for me while the guards took up station on either side of the hall.

I furrowed my brow when Eleos entered and closed the door behind him. "Are you supposed to be in here with me?"

"Yes." He said, approaching the bed, "I'm to serve you, remember? That includes preparing your chambers and ensuring your comfort."

Chortling, I followed him to the edge of the bed, watching him fold down the quilt. "So I can ask anything of you?"

He sighed heavily. "Yes. What would you have of me, Lady Aethra?"

Bouncing on my heels, I glanced around the room, thinking. "Can you put a kettle on the stove?"

"You're enjoying this, aren't you?" He dutifully grabbed the kettle from the mantle and hung it over the fire. "What did I do to deserve that?"

"Kept secrets from me," I said, turning. "Can you unbind my hair? It takes forever when I do it myself."

"Anything for you, Lady Aethra," he said politely.

Grinning, I exhaled as he gently ran his fingers through my hair, carefully loosening the braids and pulling out their pins. Shivers ran through my spine with every touch.

When my hair fell loose around my shoulders, I spun around, my face a breath from his. "Do you want to stay the night?"

"I wouldn't be allowed." He said quietly, glancing at the door.

"Not even for a little while?" I asked, tilting my head up, bringing our lips a whisper apart.

Eleos stiffened and stepped back.

"Sorry," I blurted out, "I meant to, in the garden. . ."

"Meant to what?"

"I. . ." turning red, I swept my hair behind my ear and looked down. "I've never had anyone I could really trust, and you said you've been alone, and. . ." Gathering myself, I raised my head. "I want to know you. To trust you. And I figured maybe you wanted it done formally, so. . . I'm trying to court you."

None of it came out right. As the jumble of words fell from my mouth, Eleos' smile faded. Casting his eyes away, he said two simple words.

Two words that shattered my heart.

"I'm not."

Stunned, I froze, staring at the ground as he closed the curtains and placed a hand on the doorknob.

"Do you need anything else, Lady Aethra?" Eleos asked.

"No," I muttered.

His voice chimed in my thoughts. "*Stay awake tonight. I'm going to inform the others.*"

Nodding, I kept my gaze on the floor, listening to him exit and walk down the hall. Wringing my hands together, I lifted my head and approached the fire, watching the water in the kettle slowly rise to a boil.

Pouring myself a mug of tea, I sat on the edge of the bed and watched the swirling herbs.

Gods, I felt like an *idiot*. Pain thrashed in my chest as I choked back the tea.

Why had Eleos been so kind to me? Why had he held me that night if not because. . .

I bit my lip and looked away. Ainwir had taken in a girl of eleven and raised her for seven years. Seven long years. And for what? To toss her by the wayside, his troubles dumped on my head.

I'd been betrayed once before, and had learned nothing from Ainwir's final lesson.

I was truly alone in this world.

An unlovable, wretched girl.

TWENTY FOUR

Eleos

I RACED DOWN THE DARK halls, heart hammering.

Guilt sank deep into my bones. I shouldn't have left Aethra like that. She deserved better than to be spurned so cruelly.

This was my fault. I'd been leading her on. But the two of us could not be together.

"Eleos," Father's voice echoed across the walls.

Setting my jaw, I lifted my head. The Grand Cleric stood before me, surrounded by the shadows. He stepped forward, hands folded behind his back.

"Father," I said, seeking his thoughts.

They were tucked safely behind the walls he wore around his mind. A chaotic din was all I sensed, several emotions entwining together.

Worry sang loudest above them. Beneath his impassable facade, my father was reeling from uncertainty.

"Always with that look," Father said, stepping closer. "You still think I wear the robes of a pretender."

"I have met many in the clergy. They are more concerned with power and appearances than the gods." I said stiffly.

Father's eyes flicked over my face. "Where did I go wrong? What made you like this?"

"You know damned well what made me like this." I hissed.

Father did not respond with anger. Grief tugged at him, pulling his eyes to the floor.

He recovered quickly, gaze hardening. "I did far more for you than was needed. I could have left you to rot."

"Do you wish you had?"

The sounds of distant footsteps echoed through the silence. It hung thick and heavy between us.

"No," Father finally answered. "Whatever you may have done, however you may have disappointed me. . . I am still proud of you." He stepped back. "You are not the man I wanted you to be. But you are still a good man."

I blinked at him in surprise. "I thought-"

"I never blamed you for what you did. Not all crimes should be condemned."

My wanted posters painted a thief. Therapne had cast me from its streets for heresy. But I would have rotted in a dungeon long before that had my father not covered up my first crime.

It was the only reason there was still peace between us.

"If you wish to repay me," Father said quietly. "Stay here, whatever comes. Repent." When I met his words with silence, he leaned in, voice but a whisper. "Whatever you may think of me, I care for the people I lead. Were you at the helm of this dying world, perhaps you would understand."

Swallowing, I nodded. Father met my gaze and stalked past me.

Breathing out, I glanced behind me, watching him disappear down the hall into darkness. Reaching into my pocket, I palmed the key tucked safely within.

I'd rescue the others in a moment. There was something I needed to do before I left this place for the last time.

I knew these halls by heart—I could have walked them in my sleep. Following the south corridor, I exited into a grove of tall grass and a single, towering tree. The stone pathway here led to death. To the remnant of the day, I'd come unwound.

Thin mist covered the ground, hugging the gravestones buried beneath the tree. Fresh flowers rested beside each. Stepping past the first two rows, I knelt beside a grave decorated with white petals.

The name carved into the stone had begun to fade.

'Hyacinth'

I traced my fingers over her name. What would my sister think to see what I'd become in the wake of her death?

If she heard the tale everyone believed, she'd be proud. The scholar trying to save the world.

Father knew a piece of the truth, but even then. . .

So many secrets weighed on my heart. Would I carry them to the grave?

During my stroll with Aethra, I'd plucked flowers from the northern garden. Bright orange tulips—my sister's favorite.

I laid them across her grave and bid her farewell. Once I left Therapne tonight, I'd never return. This would be our last goodbye.

I didn't believe in the gods, but. . . I hoped she was at peace, wherever she was.

My gaze shifted to the grave beside my sister's—the grave of her husband.

Of the man who'd murdered her.

The clergy had gone to great lengths to cover up the truth. The world believed my sister had passed in her sleep.

He was buried here because of me. Because I'd refused to let him live, after what he'd done.

These graves had turned me into the man I was today. The real Eleos—the one nobody knew.

Turning on my heel, I stalked through the grove and pushed through the temple doors. Pulling the key from my pocket, I turned it over in my hand as I found my way back to the chambers where the others were detained.

Murmurs carried through the door: Percy and Seraphim. Ripping a page from my journal, I jotted a quick note, then wrapped the key in the parchment.

I slid it under the door and walked away.

Seraphim could rescue Aethra. I doubted she wanted to see me, right now.

Thinking of Aethra, I faltered. She thought the world of me, just as Hyacinth had.

How wrong she was.

Murals of the gods watched me, the blasphemer, as I stalked through their halls. But they were not real.

And they had no power over me.

TWENTY FIVE

Aethra

SHORTLY AFTER ELEOS LEFT ME in ruins, someone returned and knocked on the door, rousing me from my thoughts. Setting aside my empty mug, I approached the door, hesitant to open it lest Eleos waited outside.

Yanking it open, I was met instead with his father.

The Grand Cleric stood in the hall, hands clasped behind his back. His fanciful hat, denoting his rank, was gone, allowing his neatly combed dark hair to fall free around his shoulders. I could have guessed from a glance that he and Eleos weren't related—this man was everything harsh: hard lines and stern gazes.

"You're awake. Good. Come with me." The Grand Cleric ordered, turning on his heel.

Grabbing my shawl, I followed him out the door, glancing over my shoulder to notice neither of the guards followed us. Touching my arm where bandages bound my wound, I eyed the back of his head wearily.

"Where are we going?" I asked.

No answer came. Worried, I searched the shadows for hidden assassins. Hurrying my steps to keep up, I felt a rush of relief when he brought me to an empty prayer chamber.

The Maiden loomed over an altar, hair spilling from her hood onto her dress. Her hands were spread, water cascading through her fingers into the basin at her feet. Kneel sheets spread before her, but none were occupied.

Halting before the altar, the Grand Cleric turned to me. "Much is known about the Maiden Brizo. She lived among us for a short while, to cleave a path through the Empty and give us her blood."

"Yes," I said tentatively. "What's your point?"

"The scripture is quite clear. She will return when again the Empty destroys the world, to guide those who remain to safety." He took a step toward me. "Perhaps you have not realized, but there is still plenty of land left, filled with people and life."

I glowered at him. "Did we not arrive with refugees from a destroyed outpost?"

"A small loss." He waved a hand. "No lords have been claimed, no cities ruined. Another road can be drawn between us and Serifos."

"How can you say that?"

"Because it is *true*." His eyes flicked over me. "You arrived with my son. How much do you know of him?"

"Little," I admitted. "Eleos doesn't like to talk about himself."

"Unsurprising." His father's mouth drew into a hard line. "You claim to be under orders from the Archon himself. But why would the Archon choose a man like Eleos?"

"Because we had something to gain," I said, taking a step back. "Pardons, in exchange for service."

"Is that right? And what was *your* crime?"

"I was an orphan, enslaved by the Guild." I lied, offering a hint of the truth.

"A simple, unfortunate offense. But Eleos is far more than a mere heretic." The Grand Cleric's voice lowered. "The depths of his sins run deeper. And when I covered his crimes to save him? He blasphemed for all the world to see."

"What. . . what did he do?"

"Do you know the truth of psyches?" The Grand cleric approached until he stood a breath away. "Their darkest, most difficult power? They control people. They slip inside your mind like puppeteers, steering your thoughts and emotions for you." His eyes narrowed. "I must consider the possibility that you merely dance to his tune."

"I. . ." I met his harsh gaze. "No! He's done nothing of the sort."

Mouth twitching, the Grand Cleric backed away, turning to regard the statue.

"You covered for his sins?" I followed him down the aisle. "Why?"

"Because he targeted someone I too loathed. Their death was most welcome." The Grand Cleric muttered. "But I don't know what the years have made of him. Our 'incompetence' and his obsession with a 'solution' drove him away. Have the years taught him that the solution is *faith*? Or has he strayed further from the path?"

Was the Grand Cleric saying Eleos had *murdered* someone? I wanted to press for details, but the Grand Cleric spoke again.

"Tell me what's become of my son."

"He's. . ." I struggled to explain the man I knew. He could not be summed up so easily. "He's the kindest person I've met. He cares for people and wants nothing more than to save them."

Eyes closing, Eleos's father dipped his head. "Then nothing has changed. But so too is he vengeful and bitter." His hands flexed, and he whirled around. "What about you? You spoke of the Empty. You claimed you felt a call from within." His eyes narrowed. "But the Maiden Brizo is not of the Empty. She opposes it."

Shit. Scrambling for an explanation, I stepped back. "I didn't mean to say-"

"You feel nostalgia? A comfort? A yearning?" He spat. "For our *demise*?"

"No, you misunderstand-"

"This is what led Eleos down the road to heresy. The belief we could wield our greatest foe. But if magic comes from the gods, tell me, what god blesses us with that evil?"

"I don't wield the Empty." I raised my voice. "I destroy it." Steadying my panic, I studied his demeanor, but I couldn't read him. "What are you telling me all this for?"

"Closure?" He waved his hands idly. "Whatever he's done, he's still my son." The Grand Cleric's eyes dropped to the floor briefly before rising to meet mine. "The news of your abilities would send a wave of panic through the people. No one is prepared for it."

"Then let me prove it. Let me show you what I can do."

"Prove it?" He echoed. "Perhaps I'll drag you to the Empty and find you powerless. We could condemn you and move on. But what if you succeed? What then?" He pressed a hand to his chest. "*What then?* I return to tell my people their time has come."

"But there's still hope-"

"Hope?" The Grand Cleric laughed bitterly. "Eleos' favorite word."

Fear bristled in my heart as his body language became clear to me: he was terrified, and guilt surged beneath that terror.

"You need me to be a heretic," I whispered.

"I do." He confirmed. "You care for my son. I see it in your lingering gazes. I can promise his safety if you aid us." He took my arm. "Go to the Empty. Fail, where you might have succeeded."

"But won't that paint Eleos a heretic again?"

"I want nothing more than to redeem my son," He said sadly, "But to do so would have unimaginable consequences. An escape is all I can offer."

I backed away from him, noticing shadows looming in the door. A tall woman strode through the archway, red braid dangling down the back of her charcoal coat. "An escape is all we need," Seraphim said, joining my side. "Tell me, did you bring Aethra here because you hoped the Maiden would give you a sign?"

The Grand Cleric backed into the statue in alarm. A quick expression of shame crossed his face—Seraphim had struck the truth. I almost felt bad for him, knowing he longed for his goddess to confirm he was doing the right thing—a luxury none of us possessed.

"I'm not here to hurt you." Seraphim lifted a hand. "Assuming you don't call the guard."

My racing heart settled beneath Seraphim's comforting presence. Seth's warning returned to me—his insistence the clergy would fracture as half sought to kill me. If I could con half as well as my master, I might have the perfect solution for us all.

"I know you. . ." The Grand Cleric pointed at Seraphim. "You're the exiled Cynthus daughter."

I interrupted before he could take the thought any further. "The Archon didn't send us to deliver the Bloodstone. He sent us to stop the Empty's spread." I stepped forward. "And if you let us go, you won't have to deal with the implications of my appearance."

"Let you go?" He balked. "How-"

"Claim heretics kidnapped me. You want to keep Eleos' name clean? Say he chased after me, as part of his penance. We can continue on our path to heal this world, and the clergy can unite in their fervor to regain the stone. If we're lucky?

We'll succeed. And if we don't?" I paused. "All of us will be dead, and out of your hair."

The Grand Cleric drank in my words, his stance slowly settling. "The story can shift. You are no vessel—merely an envoy sent to declare the location of the final city. But such a heinous act requires a face, not nameless heretics from the gutters."

"Mine," Seraphim suggested. "The crazed Cynthus daughter has returned to continue her profaned worship of the void."

Nodding, the Grand Cleric looked to me. "Eleos is responsible for this, isn't he? He found the solution he's always sought."

I nodded.

"Then, succeed." He said gravely. "*And do not return.*"

"Agreed." Seraphim touched my shoulder. "Give us a head start, would you? When you alert the guard, make it a big scene."

"The largest this city has ever seen." He promised. "Hurry."

Another shadow darkened the hall behind me. I whirled around, expecting trouble. Seth leaned on the wall, tossing and catching his dagger. "I hear we're kidnapping a princess?"

"And stealing her magic rock," Seraphim confirmed.

"Do you want to play the villain, Seraphim? Or shall I?"

"Drag her kicking and screaming," Seraphim ordered, squeezing my shoulder before stalking away.

"What are you doing?" I asked as Seth approached. "I- *oof.*" He threw me over his shoulder, cutting me off.

Sheathing his blade, Seth pulled out his mask and fitted it over his eyes. "Don't worry, princess. I play a damn good villain."

WHEN I'D BARGAINED with the Grand Cleric, I hadn't imagined leaving the temple slung over a ruffian's shoulder. Seraphim ran ahead of us, pausing at every corner to check for guards. The halls were eerily silent—we were alone.

"Where are the guards?" I hissed, trying to hold my head up to look behind us.

"Percy got them," Seth responded. "But they'll be back before long."

"Got them?"

"Listen," Seraphim whispered.

Seth paused beside Seraphim, and I listened. Distant, haunting music drifted down the hall. An overwhelming desire to approach the source of the noise consumed me, but I managed to snap out of it.

Sometimes I wondered if Percy wasn't the most dangerous of our group.

"This way." Seraphim spun around the corner, and Seth followed.

Grabbing onto his cloak to steady myself, I twisted my head. "Put me down!"

"No." He responded curtly.

"I'm fine! You're making this more difficult than it needs to be."

From what little of his face I could see, a smirk tugged at his lips.

Seth was enjoying this.

Resigning myself, I went limp, dangling despondently as they fled through the halls, footsteps echoing on the stone.

Seraphim stopped at a set of heavy wood doors. "I need to get the stone. Meet up with Eleos."

"What?" I asked, twisting to look at her from my unflattering position.

"I need to be seen, if I'm to bear the weight of the crime." She said, "I'll be fine. Go."

"Good luck," Seth said, pushing through the doors. Seraphim darted away, and I lost sight of her.

The music ceased. Though it had seemed faint, distant, I could instantly tell Percy's spell had faded—the tug on my heart vanished, and the ensuing silence felt deafening.

Seth set me down, and the world spun for a moment. We stood in the gardens Eleos and I had passed through earlier, their lanterns barely beating back the depths of night.

"Why'd you put me down?" I asked, following him across the grass.

"To take you on a romantic stroll before I roughly shove you into a carriage." He said.

"I didn't take you for a gentleman."

"All the best thieves are," he said with a smile, moments before stalking toward me like a hungry wolf.

"Seth?" I managed to get out.

He pushed me against the temple wall, slamming a hand beside my head. "What were you *thinking*?" He growled.

Eyes widening, I stared up at him. His dark brows wrinkled in anger, and his black waves hung like curtains around his face.

"What are you talking about?" I asked.

"I told you not to reveal your magic, and you went and told the bloody *Grand Cleric*."

"What was I supposed to do? We were about to be thrown in the dungeons!"

"We could have escaped, with the world none the wiser to your predicament."

"Or we wouldn't have." I set my jaw, reading between his words. "What do you mean 'predicament?'"

Seth's red eyes darted around my face. "Your magic is not a blessing. It's a *curse*." Shifting closer, he lowered his voice. "I knew someone with your magic. Do you know why you've never heard of her?" His fingers dug into the stone wall.

"Because she's *gone*. Torn apart by the very thing she was supposed to wield."

He spoke of someone he loved. A family member, or a lover. Grief had fractured his voice when he'd asked me to keep my magic secret—he'd buried someone who hadn't. No wonder he'd been horrified, the day I'd discovered my abilities.

Seth feared the same fate would befall me.

Touching his cheek, I forced him to meet my eyes. "I'm sorry. But I can't shy away from my magic just because of what *might* happen."

Relaxing, Seth's hand slipped from the wall. "We'll be in Duath Nun soon, and it won't matter that they know. Godsdammit," He cursed. "Why did it have to be *you*?"

"Why not? Better a nobody like me than someone of worth."

"Someone of *worth*? Aethra, you're-" He bit his lip, cutting himself off.

Pressing a hand into his chest, I pushed him away. "We're fleeing a temple full of knights, remember? We can argue about this later."

Snapping to attention, Seth looked around. "Percy's song. . ."

"You only just noticed?" I picked up my skirt and darted around him.

"Oh, no, you don't." Seth stalked after me. "This is a kidnapping, not a romantic stroll."

"You *just* said it *was* a romantic-" I turned and gasped, managing only to take a single step back before he grabbed me and threw me over his shoulder again.

"Seth!" I hissed, curling my fingers into his cloak.

Ignoring me, he ducked between two trees, and I flinched as branches swung past my face.

A black shape darted through the grass, scaring me half to death before I realized it was Whisper. The hound happily greeted his master, who shooed him off.

"Take us to Eleos, boy."

Turning around, Whisper led us back to the temple road where our horses were tied up under the shade of an enormous tree. Athena raised her head and shook her white mane when she saw me, tail swishing.

Eleos was untying the horses, oblivious to our presence until we were upon him. "Lady Aethra!" He said, voice strained with worry. "Are you alright? When you weren't in your room. . ."

A flood of emotions rushed through me at the sight of him. Curiosity, concern, relief. *Fear*. But mostly, I heard two words echo in the back of my mind.

'*I'm not.*'

"Cover your face," Seth ordered. "You can't be seen."

"Why not?"

"You're not one of the kidnappers." Seth pulled me off his shoulder and boosted me onto Athena's back.

Eleos looked between us, nodding. Maybe he'd read my mind. Grabbing a spare cloak from his saddlebag, he covered his clergy colors and lowered the cowl around his face.

The trees near the garden rustled as Percy burst through. He sprinted to Seth's side and doubled over to catch his breath. "My spell worked a little too well."

"Good." Seth turned toward the Temple doors. With a heavy scrape, they opened, and knights in blue surcoats flooded out. "Sorry, princess." He said.

Mounting behind me, Seth twisted my arms behind my back and pushed me down, making it look—and feel—more like he'd slung me roughly over the saddle, rather than daintily helped me up.

Gritting my teeth, I stared behind us, watching the flood of knights scramble to grab their own mounts and give chase. A few drew their bows and aimed for our heads.

Athena reared as an arrow landed in the dirt at her feet.

"Where's Seraphim?" Eleos asked.

"Stealing the stone," Seth said, turning Athena toward the gates.

"Wait!" I gasped. "We can't leave without her!"

Fire sparked in the distance, traveling up a tree rising behind the temple. Another roared to life beside it, glowing orange against the night. Sparks flew through the air, scattering like rain over the temple.

A few knights twisted to look at the fire. Their armor glowed red beneath the living flame that ascended the heavens before sharply descending upon them.

Great wings of blood and fire cleaved through the black of night and slammed into the temple road in a great conflagration. Seraphim rose from the embers, the wings retracting into her back before crumbling into ash. Spinning on her heel, she darted toward her horse.

I lost sight of her as Seth urged Athena into a gallop. We flew through the gates, the sound of pursuit hot on our heels. Bells rang urgently through the Temple yard, fading into the distance as we rushed through dark streets.

Seth released me and helped me sit up. Wrapping my arms around Athena's neck, I turned to see Percy racing alongside us, mounted on the little red mare.

"What's going on?" He shouted. "This was supposed to be a *simple* escape."

"Our luck's never simple," I said. "Seraphim's kidnapping me and the stone. The temple is chasing us down."

"What?" Percy gaped. "*Why?*"

"I cut a deal with the Grand Cleric." I hesitantly glanced back at Eleos. "The world would collapse into chaos if they believed I was real, and the end was nigh. I offered a solution to help us both—heretical thieves, stealing the stone."

"Oh." Percy blinked. "You know who they're going to send to kill us, right? They're going to send my *father.*"

"Who they send doesn't matter. If we outpace them to Cynthus, we'll cross the river to Duath Nun, and the chase will end."

"It's a good plan." Eleos agreed. "Assuming we don't get caught in Cynthus."

"We'll need to hide our presence," I said. "Nobody can see us enter. Seraphim." I called, searching for her behind us. A fresh wound bloodied her cheek. "Can your brother help smuggle us in?'

"Why ask him?" She called back. "We'll petition the Guild."

I sat back, wondering if that was a bad idea. The masked nobleman had worked alongside them and ordered them to attack us. Had they been paid mercenaries or loyal servants?

Percy leaned forward, scowling. "Oh, this'll be interesting."

Offering Percy a reassuring smile, I turned my head and caught Eleos' eye. Before I had a chance to read his expression, I quickly looked away, staring at Athena's thick mane instead, studying every strand of blonde hair.

I didn't want to see what Eleos was thinking, what expression he wore. I wanted to shrink into the saddle and disappear.

My emotions were ridiculous. The temple knights sought our heads, and the world itself might be ending, but the heartache throbbing in my chest was all that seemed to matter.

TWENTY SIX

KNIGHTS HAD CHASED US INTO Serifos, and now out of Therapne. If the two groups met up, we'd have a veritable army at our heels. Should they corner us in Cynthus before we could depart for Duath Nun?

No plan existed that could save us from the gallows.

Straying away from our camp, I stood on the edge of a bluff, overlooking the sea. I'd never seen the sea before. Most people feared it. The still water resting at the bottom of the Empty colored our nightmares. Our cities were built upon channels, a reminder of how the Maiden carried us to safety across the still sea, a reminder we had the power to conquer it.

The setting sun sparkled on the waters, coloring them a gorgeous shade of deep orange. Endless waves crashed against the rocks below, ever moving. I was fascinated by the surges, wondering what propelled them and from where they came.

Seraphim touched my shoulder, drawing me from my thoughts. "We can't stop for long. Take a breather, grab something to eat. Once the horses have had time to rest, we're moving on."

I nodded blearily. Hunger didn't trouble me, though I hadn't eaten today. I could hear Percy and Eleos talking behind me, distant murmurs I couldn't make out. Footsteps approached, and I looked up to see Seth standing at my side, dagger pressed into his palm.

Blood welled on his skin. "We have time to train." He said. "And considering the circumstances, you need to learn. Quickly."

Training sounded like a fantastic way to take my mind off everything.

Off *Eleos*.

Straining not to glance at the scholar, I drew my side sword from its scabbard and followed Seth to an empty field a few paces from the shore.

Mind blank, I listened to his instructions and followed his orders, copying his movements as I practiced swings and thrusts. I focused only on the man and his blade, pretending they were soldiers come to execute me for heresy.

Seth's blade clashed against mine, and he attempted to disarm me. I managed to keep my grip on the hilt and stepped back, anticipating his next attack.

But he lowered his blade. "Are you alright, princess?" He asked quietly.

"Yes," I said stiffly.

"You're focusing for once. A little too intently." He stepped closer. "Did something happen? You seemed fine before our. . . unceremonious capture."

"How would you know?" I spat, more harshly than intended. "You were avoiding me."

"I wasn't–"

"Yes, you were. Even Percy noticed." Lowering my sword, I exhaled. "Then you almost get yourself killed trying to save me, and then you yell at me during our escape. Do you have a problem with me, or not?"

Seth glanced away. "I'm just trying to give you space. I can tell something is brewing between you and Eleos."

The irony of his words forced a short chuckle from my lips. Was it relief I felt, to know others had been under the same delusions as I?

"Oh," Seth muttered, glancing behind me, where Eleos and Percy fed the horses. "I'm. . . quite wrong, aren't I?"

"I asked him to court. He said no." I said, sheathing my blade. "I don't want to talk about it."

"Did I not tell you romance was a fool's game?" He said.

Lowering my head, I reluctantly agreed. I'd caught glimpses of real love that others shared, whether romantic or familial. But it would never be mine.

"Don't beat yourself up over it," Seth said softly. "The kid clearly cares about you. Some of us have known loss, and are. . . reluctant to lose anything again. Maybe that's true for him."

"Maybe," I said, turning and walking away. Following the sea breeze, I returned to the bluff.

Whisper followed me, tail thumping against my leg as he peered up at me. Unable to resist his big brown eyes, I reached down and ran my hand over his fur.

Someone marched toward me. I whirled around, intending to tell Seth to *go away*, but instead found Seraphim standing behind me, a frown etched on her face.

"I hope you'll forgive me." She said. "I listened in."

Embarrassed, I looked down, but Seraphim gently tilted my chin back up.

"It's true. Love *is* a fool's game." She said, staring into the sea. "Some think it makes you whole, but it doesn't. It creates a new warmth, nestled deep in your breast. And, losing it rips a hole of its own. Death and parting are inevitable. Who but fools would pursue it nonetheless?"

"Are you saying it's not worth it?" I asked.

"No, dear. The opposite." Seraphim lowered her hand and kneeled, plucking a dandelion from the bluff. "What do you want to see, when you look back, at the end?"

I blinked, watching the waves. In my dreams, I saw a house, a family. But it was a dream, faded, foggy. What did I want to see with my waking eyes?

"I don't know," I admitted.

"Not this, I'd imagine." Seraphim turned, twirling the flower between her fingers. "Not a life enslaved to the Guild. Not one full of regrets, of emptiness." She raised the flower to her lips, blowing its petals across the water. "There will always be pain along the path. But I would not trade my time with her for anything. Nor would I undo my regrets, or forge a different course. This is *my* life. What, when all fades to naught, I can claim made me *Seraphim*."

Touching the flower, I repeated her words in my head, deciding if I felt the same.

She touched my cheek. "The pain of today will not define tomorrow. It will still come." Dropping her hand, she tilted her head. "C'mon. You should get something to eat before we move on."

Nodding, I watched her walk away, stealing a few more moments by the shore. What *did* I want to see, when I looked back, at the end?

My life had been meaningless, but it needn't remain that way. We walked towards oblivion, wielding magic that seemed to cost my very life. My end was inevitable, and it was coming soon.

But I could go out with *purpose*. I could, at the very least, help Eleos find the cure for this world's decay, even if I could not stop it myself.

A shadow fell over me, and I looked up to see Seth standing at my side. Burying his hands in his pockets, he pulled out the strange little knife he'd bought at Red Bluff Outpost.

I no longer wanted him gone. Seraphim's words had blanketed me in a sense of finality. Of solace.

"You spend a great deal of time worrying," Seth said, fishing a stick from his other pocket. "What you need is a *hobby*. We can't fill all the idle hours with training."

"I never had time for hobbies," I said, watching him with interest.

"Well, now you do. Hours of camp," He studied the stick and scraped the little knife along it. "Night watches. Long rides." The knife dragged down the wood again, peeling off the bark. "It'll help calm you on days like these."

"You carve wood?" I asked, raising an eyebrow.

"I whittle." He corrected, shrugging. "It gives the hands something to do."

Folding my arms tightly, I watched the waves. "I have no idea what I like. As a child, my every moment was focused on surviving, and as an adult, I spent all day working."

"Hm," lowering his knife, Seth studied my face. "I should get you a book, next time I get a chance."

"A book?"

"A story, an epic. A knight and his princess falling in love. You could use an escape from your dreary life."

Cocking my head, I considered his suggestion. Would I enjoy slipping into a dream?

Every night in my tiny hovel, I'd drift off, imagining the house by the lake and the loving husband I'd never have.

Maybe he was right.

"I'd like that," I said.

"Your wish is my command," Seth said with a smile.

"Will you show me what you're whittling when it's done?"

"Mhm. I have big plans for this little stick," he nudged me. "We should get ready to leave."

Swallowing my pain, I turned from the shore and returned to the others. Percy hovered behind Eleos as he prepared the mounts, flinching every time Eleos yanked a strap in anger. Watching them curiously, I grabbed Athena's reins and fished through my bags for a hunk of dried meat. Tossing it onto the ground, I smiled as Whisper happily snapped it up.

Eleos tightened his saddle and stepped away, jaw tightly set. "That's so typical. Of course, they'd rather keep the status quo than lift a finger and *do* something."

"Are you at least glad?" Percy asked. "That he wanted you to escape?"

Realizing they were talking about the Grand Cleric, I listened in.

"No." Eleos ran a hand through his hair. "He was going to kill Aethra. He's as much of a coward as I remember."

Seth tossed Percy a fresh waterskin. "Do you think dear old dad will spare you?"

"No." Percy angrily shook out his hat. "My father despised everything you stood for, remember? He's loyal to a fault, and thinks peace means no one's stirring the pot."

Seraphim's head sharply whipped around, and I followed her gaze. A few silhouettes flecked the distant shore—men on horseback.

"Time to go," Seraphim announced, driving her heels into her horse and riding south.

Mounting Athena, I directed her to follow. A tiny hint of pride warmed my breast; I'd climbed into the saddle and found my balance without aid. Perhaps I could learn to be of use, after all.

I kept pace with Seraphim as we diverted from the shore and dove into the trees. "You mentioned using the Guild to enter the city."

Seraphim nodded. "Every city has smuggling routes. We can enter using one, and remain unseen until my brother shelters us."

"And," Percy called, leaning forward in the saddle, "What then? The Therapnens will follow us to Cynthus. Are we not to step foot outside?"

"Maybe not," Seraphim said. "We'll have to play it by ear, once we arrive."

I pursed my lips, thinking. "The Guild worked with that masked nobleman. They abandoned the tunnel so we could leave unfettered and walk right into his trap. What if the Cynthus Guild are enemies, too?"

"We play it by ear," Seraphim repeated.

"I'll approach them, then," I said. "The rest of you remain out of sight. Once I broker a deal for safe passage into the city, I'll come get you."

"What?" Seth barked. "You're not going alone. I'm coming with you."

"Don't they know your face?"

"Maybe? I'm a beloved client, if anything. They fed me most of my information."

Seraphim leaned toward me. "Take him. You're not going alone."

"Alright, mother," I muttered, and she smiled.

Twisting in the saddle, I watched the trees behind us, searching for signs the search party had seen us. My gaze swept over Eleos, and I noticed him pull out his journal and flip through the pages, occasionally glancing up to guide his horse.

Swallowing, I looked down. He was acting perfectly normal, like nothing was wrong. The knife in my heart twisted deeper.

"Hey," Seth pulled his horse along mine. "I got something for you."

"Where?" I asked. "In Therapne?"

"Mhm." He leaned over, rifling through his saddlebags. "Well, I stole it." Flipping the bags closed, he offered me a bundle of cloth.

Keeping one hand firmly on the saddle, I took the strange bundle of brown fabric. "Why does this worry me?"

"It's pants."

Flicking my wrist, I shook out the fabric. Sure enough, it was pants: plain leggings someone might wear under robes.

Realization dawned on me. "Did you steal a *priest's* pants?"

"Yes," Seth admitted. "I took it from his wardrobe. They detained us in someone's quarters."

Percy rode up to Seth's other side. "Is *that* what you were rifling around for?"

"She needed pants." Seth shrugged. "I found some."

Laughing, I rolled them back up and stuffed them into my bags. "How fitting, for my first pair to be filched from a priest."

Seth grinned at me with a radiant, mischievous smile. Rubbing his nose, Percy chuckled with me. For the first time, I felt a sense of camaraderie, like I was among people I could trust.

With friends, if not anything more.

"Thanks, Seth." I shook my head.

"Anything for you, princess." Taking my hand, he gingerly kissed it and winked at me.

His hand lingered on mine, thumb caressing my palm. I glanced down, reminding myself I knew nothing. If I had mistaken Eleos' intentions, I couldn't imagine how wrong I was about Seth.

Dropping my hand, Seth turned to Percy. Focusing on the path ahead, I dragged in a long breath.

We were nearly at the end.

TWENTY SEVEN

THE TRIP TO CYNTHUS HAD been exhausting. We hardly stopped to rest, riding well into the night and quickly packing up camp whenever we thought someone drew near. Sleep was scarce, and our food rations had dwindled. Moods had gradually soured until we spoke to one another only when absolutely necessary.

Worn down, I ran a hand across my eyes, hoping to scrub the exhaustion from my body. I had important work to do tonight.

Seth and I were to approach Cynthus's outskirts in the thick of night, leaving the others behind in an overgrown copse. My feet protested the walk ahead of me as I emerged from the trees.

Leaves rustled behind us, and Seth grabbed the hilt of his dagger. Percy emerged from the wood line, carrying his lute case. "Wait," He called, catching up. "Let me come with you. My magic is suited for quick escapes."

Raising an eyebrow, Seth released his blade. "I suppose it's been a while since you've had a chance to perform."

"I'm not following you just to perform," Percy sounded exhausted. "But. . . it would be nice."

"You can come," Seth pushed Percy's hat down over his eyes. "Just don't get seen."

Grinning, Percy fell into step with me. "Which tavern are we going to?"

"I'll know it when I see it," I mumbled, exhausted.

Ainwir had apprised me of all the Guild's hideouts, should I need smuggling in or out of a city. Though we'd never traveled to Cynthus during our time together, I'd written down his list of contacts and locations for the border city.

The buildings here were positively ancient—their marble had browned beneath dirt and debris. Most of the tiny homes looked ready to fall apart, and some stood abandoned, their roofs caved in or walls shorn. My vision blurred every time I tried to read a sign as my body beckoned me to sleep. Faltering, my feet dragged through the rough dirt road.

"Tired?" Seth asked.

Rubbing my eyes again, I looked up at him. He cut a villainous figure, shrouded in a hood and concealed by a black mask.

"Aren't you?" I asked.

"A little. Maybe I've gotten used to sleepless nights." He paused, nudging me. "Is that it?"

Blinking, I strained to read the rickety sign he pointed at. 'Lady Luck.'

"That's it," I confirmed, pulling open the door and stepping inside.

The place wasn't the shady hole I expected. A perfectly ordinary tavern greeted us, its bar stocked with cheap liquor and tables devoid of decoration. Several people gathered inside, poor workers, judging by their dirty tunics.

We fit right in, dirt-smudged and dark-eyed.

Touching my back, Percy slipped past me, heading for the empty corner where a chair was set aside for performers.

Finding a seat at the bar, I patted the counter and hailed the bartender. A middle-aged woman with curly ginger hair wiped her hands on her apron and approached. "What can I get for you?"

"The house special," I said. "With a shot of *old* whiskey."

The woman's chin tilted up, and she nodded, "Might be a while. Grab a drink in the meantime." Turning, she walked through the back door.

Seth shifted in his seat, leaning over. "Not the most creative code."

"They shouldn't be." I studied him. "I thought you spoke with the Guild often?"

"I did. The code I was taught was much more colorful."

Music filled the tavern as Percy began to play. A grin brightened his face, and he tapped his foot with enthusiasm. I drummed my fingers on the bar, enjoying his pleasant voice and lively tune.

Seth spun to face me, leaning an elbow on the bar. "Here we are, alone in a tavern. I think this is our first proper date."

"You don't strike me as the kind of man who courts."

"Why not?"

"You said yourself romance was for fools." I reclined on the bar, matching his pose. "I presume all the girls at the brothel knew your name."

"You're thinking of Percy." He said, crossing his legs. "Here I thought I'd been romantic, but you think me a common philanderer?"

"Mhm." I nodded.

"What about the time when I carried you to safety?"

"Any good comrade would have done that."

"Pff," He rolled his eyes. "She's hard to please."

"I don't understand you." I stared into the red eyes behind the mask. "You think courting is for fools, but you keep flirting with me."

"Because it's fun," he said. "Surely a con woman like you enjoys a spot of banter."

His words flew out quickly, and his shoulder twitched. Classic signs of lying.

"That's what I thought," I said, turning away. Biting my lip, I resisted the urge to look at him again.

After Eleos broke my heart, the last thing I needed was to be toyed with, dragged on a string only to be thrown away.

Falling into silence, I studied the shelves of liquor and listened to the music, eager to get this over with. Percy finished his first song and began another.

"I know this one," Seth sat up. He flashed me a smile. "Want to dance?"

I shook my head. "I'm not in the mood."

"Are you sure? This might be our last chance to share a dance."

"There are plenty of women around for you to carouse with. Pick someone else."

"Why would I want anyone else," he said with unusual intensity, "when *you're* sitting in front of me?"

"I'm only good for fun, remember? You said as much back in the refugee camp."

Seth grimaced. Usually, his guard was iron-clad, but a moment of weakness gripped him. I read him like a book. He did not remember speaking those words, and was horrified at the thought.

Percy had been right. Seth hadn't meant his insult—he was trying to push me away before something deeper developed between us.

He needn't bother. I wasn't the kind of woman who could be loved. Seth would learn that soon enough.

"You know what? Sure," I stood. "Let's dance."

Flipping back his hood, Seth pulled off his mask and fixed his shoulder-length black waves. Offering me a hand, he pulled me to an empty corner. We passed an older couple laughing as they shared a dance, and I managed a smile.

Wrapping an arm around my lower back, Seth pulled me against him. I knit my fingers through his and laid a hand on his upper arm, but my knowledge of dance ended there.

Ainwir had never taught me.

We took a few steps, following the quick tune Percy played. I stepped on Seth's feet multiple times and stumbled when he pulled me in a direction I didn't anticipate.

Stopping, Seth peered down at me. "Aethra. Do my eyes deceive me, or can you not dance?"

"I can't." I shook my head. "I grew up in the sewers."

Glancing at Percy, Seth nudged my foot off his. "Go limp."

"Isn't that going to make things worse?"

"Just go limp."

Obliging, I relaxed my muscles and lolled my head to the side. The sudden whirl of movement that followed made me gasp.

With the grace of someone well-practiced, Seth spun me around so quickly the room blurred. Percy's song picked up in pace, and I felt myself being twirled around to its rhythm. Desperate to keep up, I frantically tried to match his feet lest I trip and spill across the floor, and found myself dancing better than when I'd been putting in a concerted effort.

"See?" Seth whispered.

Dazed, I didn't answer. All that existed was him and me, and the effortless way he controlled me like a puppet on strings.

My imagination wandered, pretending a beautiful gown swirled around my feet, and a princely cape danced around his. The heirs to rival nations, we'd sneak outside onto the balcony and steal a kiss.

A smile touched my lips as Seth pulled me back to him, his hand grasping my waist tightly. His guess had been correct—I did enjoy indulging in fantasies.

The bard's lute strummed faster and faster until he sang the final note. Seth twirled me one final time before dipping me. Floundering, I grabbed his neck, holding on for dear life.

My hair hung to the floor, brushing against the wooden slats. Seth's face loomed an inch above mine, our lips a breath apart. Warmth bloomed under my fingers, and I could feel his heartbeat rapidly thumping beneath my touch.

Wrapping his other arm around my waist, Seth lifted me back to my feet. His scarlet eyes bored into mine, hauntingly beautiful. Fingers traced my spine as his hand slid up my back to grasp my neck, pulling me closer.

Breathless, I let my eyes flutter closed.

The arms around my back dropped, and I stumbled as Seth stepped away. Cheers rang around the tavern as the people called for another song. Grinning brightly at us, Percy lifted his lute and strummed a new tune.

Playing with my bangs, I hid my face. Why would I expect Seth to kiss me after everything he'd said and done?

The tavern's back door swung open, and an unassuming man with brown hair emerged. Meeting his gaze, I walked to an empty table and sat, quietly tapping the seat beside me.

Seth followed me, laying one hand on the back of my chair. The other slipped beneath his cloak and brushed the hilt of his dagger.

Pulling out the chair beside me, the man looked me over. "You're new to these parts."

"We are," I confirmed, pulling my coin purse out. "I have orders from Laverna. I need entry into the city for five people—no witnesses. And no questions." I pushed the coin purse towards him.

Grabbing the bag, the man felt the contents. "Laverna?" He said. "You've come all the way from Ikaria?"

"No questions." I reminded him.

Satisfied with the pay, he pocketed the purse. "How deep into the city are you wanting to go?"

"As far as you can take us."

"Five people on foot?"

"We have horses," I added. "And a dog."

"I can manage that," He ran a hand across his beard, thinking. "Meet me outside the flagon in two hours. Miss that window, miss your shot."

"Done." I offered my hand, and he shook it. Once we dropped hands, we both stood and went our separate ways.

Seth watched the man depart through the back door before hurrying to my side. "That was quick." He paused. "Almost like you've done this before."

"Almost," I said sarcastically, pausing at the door.

Catching my eye, Percy nodded, quickly finishing up his song and packing up his lute. Pushing the door open, I held it open for the bard as he rejoined us and stepped outside.

A pleasant breeze carried from the sea, tousling my hair. Enjoying this moment of respite, I shut the tavern door behind me.

"How'd it go?" Percy asked. "I expected it to take longer."

"Our princess is a professional, Perse," Seth said. "Everything's taken care of."

"But she's *not* a dancer," Percy beamed at me.

"No," I confirmed. "I don't exactly infiltrate lordly balls."

"Never say never."

Seth groaned. "If I never have to see a garish ball again, it'll be too soon." He turned to me. "Need a lift back?"

"Last I checked, my feet work fine," I said.

"But, it's a lovely night," Seth stared up at the bright moon and its twinkling stars. "Besides, what man would pass up a chance to hold you in his arms?"

"Again with the flirting." I frowned.

"You called me a base philanderer. I need to restore my honor."

"What kind of assassin cares about honor?"

"Me." He said plainly, wrapping an arm around my back. Before I could escape, he swept me off my feet, cradling me against his chest like he wanted to shield me from the world.

Was this to be our relationship? Invisible threads bound our hearts, dragging us closer together, but fate would never let us touch.

The throbbing ache in my feet seemed all the more apparent now that they'd been lifted from the hellish dirt. Sighing, I leaned against Seth's shoulder. "Alright, fine. Take me away, *villain.*"

"As you wish, princess." He paused in the middle of the street, looking around. "What's the flagon, by the way?"

"Code." I flashed him a grin. "For the gallows."

TWENTY EIGHT

ETH STOOD BEFORE THE GALLOWS, wearing the grim countenance of a man who had often wondered if he would face them one day.

Once upon a time, gallows had been the center stage of every city. People would gather in the heart of town to watch criminals hang. I couldn't wrap my head around it—the desire to see someone die. Nowadays, hardly anyone was executed. The gallows were shoddy nooses hung on the edge of town, far, far from life, reserved for the occasional heretic or traitor the crown and clergy deemed worthy of death.

Snapping his head down, Seth looked to me. "Are you sure they'll come?"

"Nothing's worse for business than a bad reputation," I said, pulling my cloak around my shoulders as I paced. Wind howled through the branches, rattling the dried leaves scattered under the nooses, and tousling our hair.

Eleos gazed at them, transfixed, hood flying off his head. Shutting his eyes, he looked away, and I could but wonder what thoughts plagued him.

Thoughts of the man he'd murdered, perhaps?

"Um," Percy called, "I think they're here."

Seraphim strode up beside me, placing a hand on my back as she watched the approaching shadows. Two small wagons laden with cargo rolled toward us, pulled by scraggly mules.

A thin young man jumped out of the driver's seat and counted our number. "Hook your horses up." He said. "Then find a spot in the back."

"Wait," Percy held up a hand, "We're not riding *under* the cargo, are we?"

Seraphim smiled at him as she led her horse toward the wagon. "How else do you think we slip in unseen?"

Shoulders slumping, Percy guided his horse to the first wagon. Leading Athena to the second, I handed her to Seraphim to be hooked up, while the young man tied the mules up near the edge of the woods. Stepping back, I glanced over the cargo. Rolls of textiles, a few rugs, crates, and barrels. Hopefully, I could find a spot nestled beneath fabric and not wood.

"Well," Seth placed his hands on his hips. "Which wagon do you want, princess?"

"This one, I guess." I nodded behind me. "Percy and Eleos can take the other one." Turning to face them, I focused on Percy. "And hide yourself *completely*."

Percy toyed with his hat. "I can weather discomfort. I was a soldier, you know."

Eleos pushed him toward the wagon. "I'll tuck him in." He whistled. "This way, Whisper."

Chuckling, I sorted through the cargo, creating holes for the three of us to bury ourselves in. Seraphim grabbed a loose tarp and tossed a section to each of us, bidding us wrap ourselves in it like a cloak.

"Ugh," Seth grimaced, pulling his hood up. "This has got to be the second-worst entrance I've made to a city."

"Don't leave us hanging," Seraphim said, stepping up onto the wagon bed. "What was the worst?"

"Well-"

"Not now." I pushed him toward the wagon. "We're to remain utterly silent." I paused. "But I am going to ask you later."

Grumbling, he climbed aboard, and I followed suit. Seraphim tossed various crates and rolls atop us, burying us in goods. My vision darkened when a long roll of textiles fell upon my face, and then something heavier weighed me down. The young man walked over, adjusting the cargo to ensure we were hidden.

Gods, it wasn't easy to breathe under here. I couldn't tell if I was touching one of my companions or an errant sack. Sealing my mouth closed and ignoring the urge to kick around until I hit Seth, I listened as the young man retook the driver's seat and our wagon started rolling back toward the city.

The wagon jolted over a bump in the road, and a crate shifted, digging into my shoulder. Great.

The ride was as uncomfortable as expected. The silence was irritating, the urge to call out to someone overwhelming. Steadying my breathing through the thick pile of fabric, I tried to close my eyes and relax, remembering the sole time Ainwir and I had left a city in a corpse cart.

That journey had been much worse. Covered in heavy bodies, I'd wanted to bawl and wretch, overwhelmed by the stench of decay. Ainwir had held my hand, promising that getting caught would be worse.

Come to think of it, I couldn't remember what we'd been fleeing, and why our desperation had led us to lie among the dead. Ainwir had only just taken me under his wing at the time. . .

Pushing aside the unpleasant memories, I recalled the night after, instead. Cozy in a blanket beside a mantle, he'd poured me tea and asked if I knew how to play cards.

That was the Ainwir I liked to remember.

The wagon rolled through the outskirts and eventually stopped at the city gates. I heard footsteps around us, the sound of armored boots on cobblestone streets, and someone exchanged a few words with our driver. A moment passed, and we started moving again, rolling onto a solid road.

Exhaling quietly, I counted each turn we made, trying to map our route in my mind. Half an hour of discomfort later, the wagons slowly came to a stop, and I heard our driver dismount, tapping the wagon a few times to signal the all clear.

Seraphim burst from the pile first, followed by Seth. I struggled to find where the textiles covering me started and ended, and felt someone eventually pull them off me. Seth looked down on me, hair frizzed and frayed from its time buried under a rug.

"Thanks." I croaked, running a hand through my destroyed locks.

"That rug," he choked, "was worse than the dungeon."

Giggling, I took his hand and stood, bruising myself off before dropping out of the wagon bed. We'd parked in a small warehouse, the rickety wooden shelves lined with similar crates and barrels.

Percy and Eleos emerged from the second wagon, the bard looking relatively calm as he seated his hat back over his white locks. "That wasn't so bad."

Eleos looked at him like he was mad. "What did you get buried under? *Silk*?"

"I think so."

Rubbing his nose, Eleos flipped open his journal and pulled out his map. "We still have a ways to travel. How are we going to reach the lord's manor unseen?"

Seraphim twirled her hair, tying it into a taut bun and shoving it under her hood. She pulled out her mask and fitted it over her face before pulling her cloak tightly around her, shrouding her figure entirely.

"Keep close. Do as I say." She said quietly.

Pulling my hair up, I tucked it inside my hood.

"Well," Percy said, fitting his mask over his nose. "Now we look like a proper band of thieves."

Grinning, Seth touched my shoulder, asking me to walk ahead of him. Drawing his blade, he stuck close to my side.

I followed Seraphim outside onto a quiet alley and, for the first time, beheld the city of Cynthus.

Stone buildings, centuries old, rose from thick foundations to protect them from the sea's wrath. Unlike the slums, these buildings were well-maintained, their stone polished to a bright white rather than a faded brown.

Built upon a sloping hill, the streets cascaded downwards toward the sea, and the lord's palace loomed above them. Aqueduct bridges fanned out from the center, streaking past my head toward the sea.

A lighthouse peeked out above the cluttered streets, once a beacon for trade ships traveling to Duath Nun and nations that no longer existed, from a time no one remembered.

This street was dark. I could see the glow of lanterns in the distance, but Seraphim kept to the shadows. We pressed ourselves against the walls as we navigated through the maze-like streets.

The relative safety didn't last long. Our destination was the lord's estate: guards patrolled the streets in greater numbers as the homes became more lavish. Eleos served as our guide, searching the streets for guards and their thoughts, informing us when their backs were turned or when we needed to hide.

My heart thumped in my chest every time we ducked behind a wall and raced across a corner. Eventually, Seraphim held up a fist, instructing us to stop under the awning of a public bathhouse.

"We're here." She whispered, feeling around in her bag for a tiny key. Fitting it into the double doors, she pushed them open and ushered us inside.

Slick tiled floor nearly tripped me up as I entered the dark baths. A lone light gleamed across the room, where a lantern rested on a counter. The man dozing behind it shot to his feet, grabbing the lantern like it were a sword he could defend himself with.

Seraphim approached him, finger pressed to her mouth. "The lord's kin seeks entry." She whispered.

Rubbing his eyes, the middle-aged man gaped. "By the gods. I never thought you'd actually-" He fumbled around his counter, grabbing a ring of keys and hoisting his lantern. "This way. Keep quiet."

The man's light illuminated the baths, preventing any accidental dips into the water. I admired the spacious pools and decorative tile. This must be an establishment for the affluent—I'd never laid eyes on anything half as extravagant.

Percy bumped into me, similarly admiring the baths. "Seraphim? Do we have time for a-"

"Sh." She hissed.

Holding back a laugh, I followed Seraphim through a back door into a store room, where our guide leaned down to fit a key into a trap door. Pulling it open, he climbed down first, then beckoned us to follow.

Shimmying down the ladder, I dropped down into a tunnel carved in soft earth. An escape tunnel for the royal family, back when this place had its own king, I'd imagine. Breathing in the stuffy air, I hurried after the guide as we fled beneath the city and the manor's well-guarded gates.

Another rusted ladder waited at the end of the tunnel, and the guide crawled up, asking me to hold his lantern while he fitted his keys into the hatch above. It swung open into a shadowed pantry, his lantern shining on sacks of wheat and baskets of oranges.

Our guide waited until we'd climbed out before hurrying us through the door, past the kitchen, and into a dark dining hall. Setting the lantern down on the long table, he bid us wait. "I shall fetch the good lord. Stay here." He said quietly before slipping away.

Sighing with relief, Seraphim pulled down her hood, red locks spilling loose. Percy collapsed into one of the dining chairs, perking up and feeling the cushion. "Wow." He murmured.

"Here at last," Seraphim said. "We should be safe now."

I paused in the pantry door, watching Seth haul his dog up the ladder. Setting down the shaggy mutt, he exhaled from the effort. Tapping the dog's rear to get Whisper away from the lord's food stores, Seth touched my arm as he entered the dining room and anxiously paced around the table.

"Are you sure your brother's people can be trusted?" He asked.

"They've served my family for decades," Seraphim said. "They're loyal to him."

"Hm," Seth peered out the door. "You'd be surprised how little decades can matter to some people."

Eleos stood beside me, and I stiffened. "I read his thoughts. He was relieved to see Lady Seraphim unharmed."

"Of course he was." Seraphim pulled her mask off. "He was steward when I was a child."

Hurried footsteps echoed down the hall, and a man stepped through the door—Seraphim's brother, Lord Phaedrus. Fiery red locks tumbled around the shoulders of his luxurious silk robe, a beautiful black garment trimmed with silver. His features matched his sisters': sharp and handsome, but it was his eyes that drew my attention.

Sage-green. Blinking, I rubbed my weary face and met his gaze.

He smiled. "You're late." He tutted, striding to meet his sister. "I was beginning to think I'd need to go in your stead."

Seraphim embraced her brother. An exuberant grin stretched across her face. Genuine happiness. "Sorry. There were a few bumps along the road." She stepped back. "There is much to tell-"

"Tomorrow." Phaedrus interrupted. "These are your people? And you trust them?"

"With my life."

"I'd praise the gods if you didn't look half-dead." He said. "I'll prepare rooms for you. Wait here. And, help yourself to the pantry in the meantime." Bowing his head, the lord turned and departed.

Percy whistled. "A noble larder *and* room?"

Seth rolled his eyes as he threw open the kitchen door. "Percy, *you* were a lord."

"Only a minor one," Percy grumbled, chasing after Seth.

My appetite withered into nausea. Wondering what had come over me, I wandered down the dark hall and reclined against the wall, waiting for the steward to return.

Eleos followed me, hands knit hesitantly before him. "Lady Aethra. . ."

Summoning a smile, I folded my arms. "What is it?"

"I can read your thoughts." He reminded me. "I know how much I hurt you." He wavered, playing with a strand of his hair. "I've been trying to figure out what to say."

"It's alright." I lied. "You were quite clear."

"No, I. . ." He sighed. "I didn't mean to hurt you. I didn't want to hurt you. But you caught me off guard, and. . ." He stared at me intently. "To say yes would have been cruel. Not when you don't know the truth about me."

Shifting, I dropped my arms, remembering what the Grand Cleric had said about psyches' dangerous abilities. "Your father mentioned some of it."

"He doesn't know the full story." Eleos avoided my gaze. "Far from it. He would lose the last shred of sympathy he still bears for me, were he to learn it." Blinking, he stepped back. "But it's more than that. I'm. . . *broken*."

His voice cracked, and I stepped forward. "I'm broken, too. Whatever it is you think-"

"You're not broken, Lady Aethra." He shook his head. "Not the way I am."

Grabbing his hand, I cradled it between mine. "Everyone thinks they're worse than they are. I won't think any less of you. Tell me the truth. It'll take a weight off your shoulders."

"My burdens aren't yours to bear."

"Neither are my burdens, yours. But you've listened, nonetheless." I tilted my head, trying to meet his eye.

Eleos finally lifted his head. "Did you often deal with noble bastards?"

"Occasionally. I never transported them myself, but I would oversee their deals."

"Then you know what happens to lords who consort outside the nobility. What if you had been born a lord's daughter and fell for a common man?" He asked. "Would you pursue him, putting your child and love in danger?"

"You're not a lord, Eleos, and neither am I."

"I know," he said quietly. "Just answer."

Lowering my lids, I considered the question. Would I pursue him, knowing how the nobility viewed forbidden affairs? Would I choose my selfish desires over his safety?

"No," I said. "I wouldn't."

Slipping his hand from mine, Eleos gently touched my cheek. "Sometimes, even if you love someone, it's best to only watch them from afar."

As his fingers trailed over my skin, my emotions shifted. Buried deep in my breast, Eleos found the nugget of hope I'd been carrying. Hope that he might return my feelings. Hope that we might succeed. It bloomed within me, swelling my chest with boundless light.

Exhaling, I felt like a thousand pounds had lifted from my shoulders. But they'd come crashing back the moment Eleos' spell ended.

A lantern shone through the hall, matching my fake emotions. The old steward returned. "The first room is ready." He said.

Eleos gently pushed me. "Go ahead. You need rest."

Frowning at him, I dragged my heels as I followed the steward, gaze fixed on the scholar behind me. I looked away only when we turned a corner and ascended the grand stairway. In the darkness, and in my exhaustion, I paid no mind to the details around me: we might as well have been walking through a featureless, black space.

My eyes drooped and my steps slowed as we walked down a hallway. Eventually, the steward stopped, pulling open a door and beckoning me inside. A candle glowed on a nightstand, illuminating a bed. Overcome with fatigue, I limped toward it, yanked the sheets off, and collapsed on the pillow.

The door clicked behind me, the last noise I heard before darkness consumed the world.

Eleos had never looked at me the way Seth did. *Never.* Maybe romance wasn't in the cards for us.

But I wanted to protect him. To hold him close, listen to his troubles, and tell him it would be okay.

Two words echoed in my dreams, fractured and painful. "I'm broken."

TWENTY NINE

I HARDLY REMEMBERED WHO I was when I woke. Sitting up, a mess of drool and tangles, I took in the strange chamber.

By Callesis's luck, had I gained a fortune while I slept? Luxurious silk sheets caressed my skin, beneath a canopy of silver. Gorgeous dark wood furniture rested on tile decorated with carvings of Psythos, the goddess of emotions.

Everything rushed back to me in a flood. Tangled in the sheets, I rolled onto the floor, taking half the bed with me.

Someone knocked, and I looked up from my pile of fabric like a wild-eyed animal. Seraphim's voice carried through the thick oak door. "Baths are ready. Don't miss out."

"I'm coming," I shouted, scrambling to my feet and adjusting my dress to actually cover my indecency.

I flew outside and found Seraphim waiting for me in a thin white robe. "There you are." She smiled. "Come. I have something special in mind." Turning around, she beckoned for me to follow.

Padding down the hall after her, I admired the stunning home. Though such opulence was to be expected of a city lord.

Everything was silver. Marble tiles veined with silver threads, silver-painted walls, and delicate silver decorations lined up along dark-wood tables. Several pieces of fine porcelain tea pots and ornate vases caught my eye, and I bumped into Seraphim's back as I stared in awe.

Chuckling, she ushered me through a door into a glorious bathroom, complete with two enormous baths, separated by a beautiful, carved-wood folding wall.

"In Cynthus," Seraphim pushed me toward the bath. "We once worshiped a goddess of water. The sea was sacred. To express our deepest trust, our most hidden vulnerabilities, we bathed together. That tradition has lived on."

"Ah," I nodded, vaguely remembering someone mentioning the 'Cynthuns' perverted baths.'

Shrugging off her robe, Seraphim gently lowered herself into the bath. I stared rudely at her body, counting the scars crisscrossing her abdomen, arms, and legs. Beautiful tattoos in black ink traced up her thighs and down her arms, patterned her breasts and back. Covered at all times by a coat, Seraphim had never displayed them to me.

'Our most hidden vulnerabilities.' Realizing the depth of the gesture, I undressed and lowered myself into the water, sighing as the warmth enveloped me, stealing away the aches of the previous day.

"Don't panic," Seraphim leaned forward, wearing a wicked smile. "But Cynthuns do not consider bathing to be sexual."

"Why would I panic?" I asked as the door flew open.

Percy strode through, utterly unbothered by our presence. "Glorious baths." He groaned. "Not as glorious as that other bathhouse, admittedly." He glanced at me. "Should I move the divider for you? Shield you from the boys?"

"If you would." I squeaked.

He snickered. "It's considered rude to diminish a bath with lewd thoughts, Aethra."

"I'm not diminishing it, I just. . ." I trailed off. What did I care if they saw my tits? Eleos already had. "Never mind. I'm fine."

"That's the spirit." Percy grinned, dipping behind the folding wall. A white shirt flew over it, draping over both sides, and a loud splash followed.

The display that followed was a sight to behold. The door opened again, and Eleos steered Seth through, mouth twisted in a grimace. Seth tried to look in my direction, but Eleos shoved him behind the folding wall.

Seraphim chortled. "Everything alright, Eleos?"

"Just controlling the lecher," Eleos said calmly.

Seth tried to defend himself. "I was only joking."

"Mhm." Eleos sounded unamused. His tone changed to lighthearted curiosity. "What is *that*, Percy?"

"Oh, you haven't seen it?" Seth asked. I heard him undressing, and found myself envisioning what he might look like naked.

No lewd thoughts. Dipping my head in the water, I regained my purity.

"Oh, not this again," Percy lamented.

"What are you boys talking about?" Seraphim called.

"Percy's tattoo," Eleos answered.

I pressed a hand to my mouth, trying not to laugh. Seth laughed in my place.

"I regret it, alright?" Percy said. I could hear the water splash as he threw up his arms. "Leave me be, I've been through enough."

"We can cover it," Seth suggested. "Duath Nun is known for its tattoo artists."

"How would you know that?"

"Seraphim." He said quickly. "Look at hers. Where do you think she got them? Therapne?"

Eleos chortled. "The priests would faint."

Tilting my head, I studied the tattoo painting Seraphim's chest: two wicked horns curled up from her sternum and caressed her collarbone. "What does that one mean?" I asked.

She traced the black ink. "So many things. Motherhood, life, song, and dance. She's Duath Nun's chief goddess."

"They have different gods?" I asked, intrigued.

"Many, many different gods." Seraphim quietly confirmed.

"Hm," Eleos grunted, unhappy. "You should have told me. I would have been fascinated."

"Why listen to my poor tales when you could see their temples in person?"

"Fair." Eleos conceded.

Dipping my head below water, I grabbed a bar of soap and lathered it through my locks. "So, what is your tattoo, Percy?"

He sighed laboriously. "Tits."

"Really? How bad could that be?"

"Bad," Seth said.

"Well, now I want to see them," I said.

"Ogle me all you like," Percy said, "if you get out first."

"I'm sure I'll see you naked later." I said, "Right now, the baths call."

"Oh? And why are you so sure of that?"

"We're traveling together, sleeping in piles, patching each other's wounds," I shrugged, figuring the rest was obvious.

"Oh," Percy said, noticeably disappointed.

Seraphim lifted an arm, displaying the tattoos running down her bicep. "Want to see the rest?"

Shimmying closer, I sat beside her, marveling at the ink. They bestowed an unusual beauty upon her, painting her as a goddess of war who could shield me from any threat.

Duathian symbols covered one arm, fascinating runes I couldn't decipher. Snakes entwined the opposite arm, entangled in leafy vines. Flaming wings grew from her spine, my favorite of them all.

"We should get you one." Seraphim decided.

"Won't we be hunted? Will we have time?" I asked.

"We'll only be hunted if they know our identity. Speak their language, dress like them, keep your head down, and you won't rouse suspicion."

Something she'd said on the road returned to me. '*What do you want to see, when you look back, at the end?*'

"It's a deal." I decided. "I'll have to consider what I want."

Sighing in bliss, Seth emerged from the bath with a loud splash followed by wet footsteps. I peeked around the dividing wall, expecting him to pull a towel around himself before stepping into our view.

Instead, he strode by, completely naked.

Once, I considered myself a woman of class, unmoved by pretty faces and charming words. Maybe in a few hours, I would think back to this moment and have the decency to be ashamed of how I gaped.

Water droplets trickled down his tanned muscles, outlining a deep scar running down his side. A pleasant V-shape beckoned my eyes to fall from his abs to his waist, and below.

Grabbing a towel from a hook on the wall, Seth swung it around himself, warding away my depraved eyes. He smirked at me. "See something you like, princess?"

I opened my mouth to say no, but changed my mind. "Yes, actually," I said.

A smug light gleamed in Seth's eyes as he glanced back towards the men's bath. Percy scoffed. "Shove off. Take your vanity elsewhere."

Beaming, Seth winked at me and swung out the door. Eleos groaned. "He wanted to enter that way, too."

"Of course he did." Percy audibly rolled his eyes.

Eleos breathily laughed. "Well, Percy? Want to grandstand for the ladies?"

"I *respect* the ladies, thanks." Percy denied.

I turned back to Seraphim to see her grinning at me. "Life's all too short." She shrugged. "Why not take what we want while we still have the time?"

Sinking into the water, I pushed the soapy bubbles around. Did I want lust and simple fun? Maybe once we reached Duath Nun and the end grew near, I would change my mind.

Foolish and stubborn, I still desired love.

THE HOUSEMAIDS HAD gifted me a beautiful gown upon my return from the baths. Feeling like a proper princess, I strode down the grand stairwell, gleefully watching the skirt flow behind me. Jumping the final two steps, I grinned as the fabric swirled around my sandals.

A golden clasp secured the over-the-shoulder, pale blue gown in place, and flowers adorned the layered skirt. Adjusting the ribbon binding back my curls, I walked into the dining room, where the lord of the house awaited me.

Phaedrus leaned on the back of the head chair, red locks tied in a half-bun. A silver cloak draped his shoulders, framing the deep blue vest he wore beneath. With the chandelier burning bright above the dark wood table, I could see lines of age framing his eyes, but like his sister, they did not diminish his beauty.

"Good morning, Lady Aethra." He said warmly, his voice deep and inviting. "I hope the traditional Cynthus bath didn't frighten you too much?"

"No." I laughed. "It was kind of nice."

"Seraphim used them as excuses to bring other girls home." He shook his head.

"Did you not?"

"Themis was an uptight statue. Seraphim was a depraved maniac. I tried to be the *normal* child." He picked idly at his fingernails, gazing behind me. "I, of course, say that with love, dear sister."

"Mhm." Seraphim touched my shoulder as she passed, grabbing a honey cake from a plate and popping it into her mouth. Her charcoal coat once again concealed the tapestry of art she'd painted on her skin.

Folding my arms, I raised my eyebrows. "Baths aren't sexual, hm?"

Growling between mouthfuls of crumbs, Seraphim glared at her brother. "I was a teenager."

Seth snuck up behind me, wet hair clinging to his face as he rolled up the sleeves of his tunic. He glanced down at me. "Don't you look cute?"

"We're attending a council full of lords," I said, trying not to remember the sight of him naked. "You could stand to dress nicely, for once."

"Oh, there's no need," Phaedrus waved a hand idly. "I only need you and the psyche to come."

"Are you sure?"

"More faces will draw more eyes. You will pose as my advisor, and the psyche as a steward. The two of us will focus on sweet-talking the council, while our psyche reads the room and feeds us cues."

My shoulders tensed. Phaedrus' voice sounded familiar. Why?

Eleos and Percy joined us, freshly cleaned. Percy appeared to have found a new cloak, its vibrant red color matched the feather in his favorite hat.

"Bringing only Lady Aethra and me makes the most sense," Eleos said, tying his blue scarf around his neck. "We don't want to arouse suspicion. Obviously, it won't be Seraphim we suggest sending across the border."

"Oh, no." Seraphim agreed, mouth half-full.

"Who, then?" Percy asked.

I thought for a moment, considering various angles of approach. "The Red Bluffs outpost." I blurted out. "We share the tale of its tragedy to incite urgency, insist an envoy be sent to Duath Nun to restore relations and beg their aid, should we need more land in the near future."

"Hm." Phaedrus stared at me with sage green eyes. *Familiar* sage-green eyes. "That could work. What do you think, sister?"

"She's the con woman. I trust her."

Dipping my head, I tried to shake the sense of nostalgia. The masked nobleman had sage-green eyes, yes, but his hair had been much darker, his voice lighter. Why would Seraphim's brother have been in Serifos?

Besides, she would know if her brother was a psyche *and* chthonic, and would have recognized his magic. It was a coincidence, nothing more.

Phaedrus drifted to the center of the table, where a beautiful ivory chessboard sat on a raised display. He pushed the pawns forward, forming a circle. "The lords have been called. When they arrive, we will entreat with them, insisting someone be sent to Duath Nun. Who?"

"Themis?" Seraphim suggested.

"Hm." Phaedrus raised an eyebrow. "Do you think she'd agree? If I'm to offer her as a sacrificial lamb, I'll need her to be present."

Eleos cleared his throat. "Mistress Seraphim is Lady Themis's twin, no? Could she not stand in for her sister?"

Phaedrus stepped back, holding back a laugh. "We'd need a talented hairdresser for that. And even then. . ." He scanned his sister, grimacing. "It would be a challenging task."

Shoulders slumping, Seraphim cradled another honey cake in her palm. "I'd hate every moment of it, but I could probably play a decent Themis."

"Then it's settled," Phaedrus said, pushing the queen pawn to the center of the chessboard. "We cannot predict how the lord's will react, but expect resistance to the idea. And there's, of course, the matter if they refuse. . ."

"Right." Percy tilted his head. "What do we do, then?"

"The only ship that can safely cross the Lethe strait is under lock and key, guarded by the border lords." Phaedrus shrugged. "But every lock can be picked, every vault robbed. It would be taxing and time-consuming, but possible."

Seth rubbed his forehead. "It would be nigh impossible."

"Much like stopping the Empty." Phaedrus agreed. He stood straight, head snapping toward the hall.

The sound of heavy knocking carried from the foyer, followed by a steward rushing to answer.

"Hide," Phaedrus ordered, straightening his cloak and departing the room.

Everyone scrambled. Seth grabbed my arm and dragged me down the opposite hall into a broom closet, shutting the door behind us. Darkness trapped me in a tiny corner with him standing across from me.

"Ugh," I whispered. "Are you intent on finding every opportunity to shove me in a tiny hole?"

"Sh." Seth hissed. "Would you rather hide under the table?'

Tensing, I felt my breasts brush his chest, my knee graze his leg. His body heat radiated over me like a furnace, and the hairs on my neck stood on end.

Ignoring his own command to remain silent, Seth leaned forward. "Did you and El work things out?"

He reached past me, pressing his hand against the wall by my shoulder. Trying to ignore that, I stared at his collarbone. "No."

"Did you not talk?"

"We did. But I haven't convinced him to tell me the truth." I looked up at him. "Why? Did he talk to you about it?"

"Rather freely, yes."

"What did he say?"

"That he's torn apart by guilt for hurting you."

I pursed my lips, finding his red eyes in the dark. "It feels like you want us to end up together."

"I do," Seth said quietly. "It would make everything easier if you were taken."

"What's that supposed to mean?"

"No romantic falls in love with a woman they know is married."

I furrowed my brow, trying to read his expression. Hadn't he claimed romance was for fools? Now, he professed himself a romantic?

"Sh." Seth hissed. "Listen."

Falling silent, I pressed my head against the wall, uncomfortably aware of his body across from mine.

From here, I could barely make out what was being said at the door. I heard a familiar, harsh voice, but his words were mere murmurs. Seth sucked in a breath.

"Percy's father." He murmured.

They'd already found us? I tensed, listening, but Phaedrus' tone was even and calm. The heavy thud of armored boots didn't race down the hall toward us. Perhaps they intended to warn the city lord and request permission to disseminate orders to the local guard.

Leaning toward the door, I strained to make out the words. My head brushed Seth's chest, and he shifted closer to me, laying a hand on my back.

Seraphim's words returned to me. Seth was attractive, and I liked him. His lingering gazes shattered any doubt that the attraction was mutual. But did I want this?

Eleos insisted we couldn't be together, and the heartbreak from his refusal still throbbed in my chest.

But last night. . .

I'd wanted nothing more than for Seth to kiss me.

He turned his head, chin brushing the top of my hair. "You really do look beautiful in that dress."

". . . Seth?"

"Yes?"

"You're confusing."

He sighed. "I know."

A door slammed in the distance, and a single pair of footsteps returned. Feeling for the doorknob, I hurried outside.

Lord Phaedrus strolled back into the dining hall, running a hand through his fiery locks. "The hounds are on your tail." He placed a hand on his hip, eyes falling on me. "They seek a band of thieves who've stolen away the Bloodstone. I doubt they'd imagine finding you here."

Percy emerged from the pantry and slumped against the wall. "I thought my father had already sniffed me out."

"Not quite yet." Phaedrus' eyes lingered on me. "I've given them permission to use my men. Within days, they'll have scoured the city and will return here."

"Well," Percy rubbed his neck, "I say we get these keys and *leave.*"

Phaedrus nodded. "You'll need to wear new faces at the meeting, to diminish any possible suspicion. I'll tend to my sister, dire as her condition is, but you look like a woman of class. Think you can manage a new look?"

"I can." I nodded, looking over as Seraphim and Eleos entered the room, returning from wherever they'd hidden. "Think you can transform Eleos, Perse?"

"Easily." Percy stood straight. "I'd rather dress him up, but I can also turn him into the most mundane steward you've ever laid eyes on."

"How long do we have?" I asked.

"A day and a night," Phaedrus smirked. "I did say you were late. The border lords will arrive *tomorrow.*"

THIRTY

DRESSING LIKE A NOBLE AND dressing to be beautiful were vastly different things. New trends rose and fell each year, and anyone who failed to keep up was shunned. Considering recent events, I hadn't been paying lordly fashion much mind.

Lord Phaedrus described his sister Themis as a chameleon. Everything she displayed on the outside matched those around her, concealing the truth within. A truth even Themis had long forgotten. He'd given me a quick summary of everything she'd worn in recent weeks, and I'd managed to piece together what Cynthus nobility favored these days.

Eyes twitching, mouth set in a grimace, I tied the last braid and carefully wound it around the bun resting atop my head. Exhaling, I dropped my hands and admired the hairdo.

Oh, it was awful.

Turning away, I grabbed the dress lying across the bed sheets and pulled it on: a simple red toga with a gold leaf belt and matching armbands. Grabbing the receptacle of powder I'd been lent, I returned to the mirror to complete the look.

A soft knock echoed on my door, and I called for them to enter. Expecting the maid, I nearly dropped the container in surprise when I saw Eleos standing behind me in the mirror. Whirling around, I looked him over.

Percy had already finished his task. With his hair oiled back, spectacles set on his nose, and encased in a frumpy brown robe, Eleos looked the very definition of 'mundane.'

"Oh," I said. "You look. . ."

"I can't see with these on." He pulled off the spectacles and folded them. "Thankfully, I don't need to read anything." Tapping my door closed, he leaned against the wall beside the vanity. "Are you ready?"

"I think so," I said, leaning forward to apply the golden makeup to my eyes. "Hopefully, the lords will be more willing to listen than the clergy."

"I have hope. We're only offering to send a messenger. They can foist blame onto her."

"True." I winced. This color didn't flatter me. "It's hard to believe we're mere days from sailing for Duath Nun."

"I can't wait," Eleos said dreamily. "To see a country that's been isolated for *centuries*? There might be flora and fauna there we could only dream of."

The excitement in his eyes was so cute—just one of the reasons I'd fallen for him. Snapping the container of makeup closed, I turned to him. "Eleos. When the meeting's over, can we talk?"

He sighed. "I've been thinking, and. . . you deserve the truth. All of it."

"I promise you, I won't hate you once I know. If anything, I'll feel the opposite."

"I. . . I know I'm not that man anymore. But that doesn't mean I deserve your forgiveness." He tilted his head. "That color doesn't suit you."

"I know." I frowned at my reflection. "It's terrible, isn't it?"

He laughed quietly. "I'll see you downstairs, Lady Aethra."

Flipping his fake spectacles back on, he walked out the door. Relieved we were on track towards reconciliation, I spun before the mirror to ensure everything was in place, and followed him outside.

Quiet blanketed the manor. Everyone was downstairs preparing. I paused in the hall, stopping to look at a family portrait.

Seraphim looked like a young teenager here, positioned next to her twin. They wore starkly opposing expressions: Themis sat rigidly, holding an elegant smile, while Seraphim grinned toothily. Phaedrus stood with a hand on their seat, a few years older. He looked less like a lord and more like a fiery-haired troublemaker, wearing an imperceptible half-smirk.

Their parents seemed grander than life, clad in opulent jewelry and layered cloaks. What had Seraphim been like back then, a young noble heiress destined for marriage to another lord?

"You look horrible." Seth's voice dragged my attention from the portrait.

He leaned on the wall beside me, tugging on the collar of his stylish black coat. Percy loitered a few paces away, playing tug-of-war with Whisper, a frayed old rope clenched in the dog's jaw.

"This is what's considered fashionable." I said, smoothing my gown.

"It doesn't look like *you*," Seth pushed off the wall. "Are you sure you want us to wait upstairs? I'll be too far away to help if something goes wrong."

"The nobles aren't going to attack us."

"But their guards might. What if one recognizes you?"

"You'll hear the commotion and my frantic screams."

Seth chuckled. "I'm starting to see the benefit to your cowardice. Makes it easier to protect you."

"Is that a compliment?" I raised an eyebrow. "I need to get going. Go hide."

Furrowing his brow, Seth opened his mouth to protest again, but Percy snuck up on him and grabbed his arm.

"Don't worry, Aethra," Percy winked, "I'll make sure our assassin behaves."

Seth stumbled as Percy yanked him. "Good luck. And be *careful*." He called.

Watching until they vanished up a stairwell, I hurried downstairs and found my way to the meeting chamber. A circular table, much like the one in Therapne's temple, centered a grand room covered in beautiful paintings of the sea and Cynthus' port.

My eyes followed the wall of art, eventually landing on the woman standing at the head of the table. Elegant as a goddess, her thick red hair plunged down her back in a neat plait, a splash of color against her white gown. Heavy makeup painted her face, shadows and golden light dancing around her eyes like artwork in itself.

I gasped. "Seraphim?"

Raising an arm, Seraphim scowled at herself. "He did an amazing job. Look." She wagged her arm at me. "You can't even tell there's black ink under it."

Approaching her, I marveled at the concealer. Not one hint of ink peeked through. "You look. . ." I tried to find the words. "Remarkably like your sister."

"Strange, isn't it?" She grinned. "I can mimic my sister with ease, but I could use some direction."

"Themis is pious, right?"

"And obedient. She's never let one toe slip out of line. Never."

I ran a thumb across my chin, thinking. "Say the Archon spoke to your husband about his worries. The state of Duath Nun needs to be assessed—whether it's gone, or thriving."

"And if it's thriving. . . " Seraphim nodded. "I can work with that."

Lord Phaedrus entered with Eleos. Folding his hands on the back of his seat, the lord glanced between us and nodded, satisfied. "Good. You don't look a thing like your wanted posters, now. Ah, but have you made yourselves comfortable? We'll be here for hours."

"I'm ready," I said.

"Very well," He said. "Time to set the stage, and summon the actors."

FOUR BORDER LORDS protected the strait separating the Merchant Isles from Duath Nun. The Lethe was a death trap: no ordinary ships could weather its tumultuous seas. Each lord held one of five keys that anchored the only vessel capable of crossing the strait intact.

The lords themselves were nothing impressive to behold. The oldest of the lot, Lycus, was a gray-haired man who'd spent time in the army before his father passed. Broad and weathered, he seemed the only soul paying the situation the gravity it was due.

The youngest, Kasos, imbued within me an urge to punch him across the mouth. The brat reclined in his chair, more interested in examining his nails than participating. Every time someone addressed him, he made a halfhearted joke and urged them to lay the silly matter to rest.

A middle-aged woman sat directly across from us, sour-faced with a taut bun. I couldn't blame Lady Maera for her severity: women who inherited their father's seats were no more respected by their peers than a lowly peasant.

The fourth, Crios, reminded me of Ainwir: sharp, well-dressed, with a hooked nose that imbued him with a unique presence. Though not handsome naturally, he outshone the pretty boy beside him with his neatly trimmed beard, styled dark hair, and elegant black cape.

We'd been talking in circles for an hour now. Red Bluff's situation had shaken them, but it had not been the trump card we hoped for. While they argued amongst themselves, I glanced at Eleos, who sat behind me, recording notes, eyes flicking up to occasionally read the lord's thoughts.

Lord Phaedrus ran a hand across his brow, his clipped tone barely concealing his annoyance. "So, you'd have us do nothing?"

Lord Kasos shrugged. "It's not our responsibility. If the situation is dire enough, the church will send word."

"The church will wait until it's too late." Phaedrus snapped. "Just as they were too late to save Red Bluff outpost."

"Who cares about Red Bluff?" Kasos sneered. "It was a tiny ranching village. Another road can connect Therapne to Serifos."

"You might be safe in your city now, but if all the outposts fall, we don't have the resources to survive for long," Phaedrus said, jaw grinding. "We must reach out for aid."

"You're looking in the wrong place. Duath nun isn't protected by the Maiden. What salvation could it offer?"

Lady Maera looked sharply at the young man. "Scripture states all lands are watched over by the Maiden."

"Precisely," Phaedrus said. "What if the final city is in Duath Nun? If we don't reach out, well, none of us will be there."

"True enough." Lord Crios had a deep, velvety voice. "But no one has crossed the Lethe in a century. Should we not await the crown's word?"

"And we circle back to the beginning." Phaedrus sighed. "The matter of *time* seems to be lost on you."

"I agree." Lord Lycus sat forward. "Fifteen meetings like this one have been called in the past century, yet no ship ever departed for Duath Nun. To await consent from the crown and church, we'd wait until our dying day."

At least one lord was on our side. Seraphim stepped forward, speaking in a light, elegant voice that sounded nothing like her. "The consequences would be on none of you. I would lead this envoy. If the crown disapproves, they can take it out on me."

Eleos' voice whispered in my mind. "*Maera and Crios aren't worried about consequences; they think there's not enough cause.*"

Thinking on my feet, I glanced at Seraphim. "Have you mentioned the Archon's concerns?"

Wrapping her arms around herself, Seraphim paced around the table, swaying with a feminine stride. "My husband is rightfully concerned about our dwindling land. Nobody has returned from Duath Nun in centuries. We sit in ignorance, oblivious to what their situation might be."

"Are you suggesting we aid them?" Lord Crios raised an eyebrow.

"No," Seraphim purred, lids falling. "I'm suggesting they might be thriving. What if they've kept the Empty at bay? What if they have land and resources to spare?"

"Does it matter?" Maera snapped. "They killed everyone aboard the last ship. That's precisely why we forbid travel."

"That was a hundred years ago," Seraphim said. "How many heirs have inherited the crown since then?"

"We have to assume they're hostile," Lycus said firmly. "Conquering them is not an option."

"There are many ways to tie nations together. The Merchant Isles once joined hands after years of bloody war." Seraphim reminded them.

Her graceful poise and sultry, yet demure tone sounded nothing like the woman I knew. I almost believed this was truly Themis.

"*Better,*" Eleos whispered. "*Everyone but Kasos, whether they realize it or not, took the bait. They're wondering if Duath Nun isolated itself because it's safe.*"

Perfect. Clearing my throat, I drew the room's attention. "What of the thieves who took the Maiden's Bloodstone? You have heard of them?"

"Of course." Lord Kasos crossed his legs. "They say the ghost of House Cynthus returned." He chuckled. "What of it?"

"What of it?" I repeated, furrowing my brow in worry. "It has everything to do with this. They say Seraphim lives. You do know how she survived her exile, yes?"

"Foolish hearsay," Maera said in a clipped tone. "By all accounts, she was sent to the Empty and perished."

"Word reached me yesterday," Phaedrus announced. "Therapne's clergy names Seraphim the Bloodstone's thief. It is not hearsay."

Seraphim glanced at me, picking up on my course. "Rumors swirl about her return. Some whisper she fled across the Lethe. No one's sighted her in twenty years, after all." Her face twisted in anger. "I wasn't present at the exile. I cannot confirm if they ensured her demise. If they hid that she escaped. . ."

"They might well have," Phaedrus said quietly. "To save themselves from a severe punishment."

Lord Crios caught on. "Are you suggesting she will take the stolen Bloodstone back to Duath Nun?"

"What if she does?" I said. "If we do not send someone after her, the Bloodstone will be lost forever."

Lady Maera sat back, and silence hung over the table. Eleos spoke in my mind. *That did it.*

Placing a hand on the table, Lord Lycus studied Seraphim. "In that case, you would need a capable unit sent with you."

"Arrangements have already been made," Phaedrus assured him. "I would not send my sister without proper protection."

"Let me offer some of my men. You'll need mages if you expect to face a chthonic."

"Thank you, Lycus." Phaedrus nodded. "But your support won't matter if the rest let the thief slip away. Tell me. What do you think the church will say when they learn the border lords neglected their duty?"

Lady Maera drummed her fingers on the table. "If the thief took shelter in Duath Nun and seeks it again, does that not suggest they feed her orders?"

"We don't know." Lord Crios said. "They might be oblivious to her presence. Or, they seek the Bloodstone to save themselves."

"And condemn us," Seraphim agreed, speaking with unusual gravity. "Be they friend or foe, we *must* know."

"Very well." Lady Maera sat back. "I agree. Circumstances require haste. But the ship must be fully prepared to face whatever threat. We will not receive another chance."

"Agreed." Crios nodded. "My key is yours, on the condition I examine the crew before they depart."

"Of course." Phaedrus agreed, eyes drifting to the youngest of their group.

Glancing between his fellows, Kasos cleared his throat. "You're absolutely right, of course. We should give chase. The crown will be positively thrilled should we solve their problems for them."

Relieved, I stepped back. Eleos's voice hummed in my mind. "*Shame. I was almost looking forward to planning that heist.*"

With my part finished, I joined Eleos on the bench, watching the lords rise to do what had not been done in a century.

Each had brought with them a small chest. Within rested a remarkably ordinary-looking key, bronzed by age—one for each of the five padlocks preventing the ships' anchor from being raised.

Phaedrus collected the keys, adding them to his chest. A sense of finality coursed through me when he closed the lid. This is what Seraphim had hired me for.

The ship was ours. And before the lords realized our falsity, we'd be sailing across the border in the only vessel fit to weather the Lethe.

NIGHT HAD FALLEN before the border lords departed the manor. Lord Phaedrus had cracked open his most valuable bottle of wine to celebrate the occasion, a gift that snapped Percy and Seth out of their annoyance at being shoved in the attic all day.

Swirling my wine, I stared into its rich ruby depths. One last sip of luxury before we set out for lands unknown.

Eleos sat beside me at the dining table, paying more attention to his hair than his food. Though we'd washed off our disguises, he was adamant that lingering traces of Percy's 'wretched oil' remained in his hair. I reached out to brush out his bangs, but retracted my hand.

We'd talk tonight.

"Hm." Seth reclined in his seat. "I'm a bit disappointed, honestly. Breaking into four separate manors sounded fun."

"Eleos said the same," Seraphim said, draining her second glass of wine.

"Mad men," Percy murmured, pushing his food around. "We're going to be descended upon by crazy Duathian warriors, and you wanted *more* strife?"

Chuckling, Phaedrus met my eye. I shifted in my seat, unable to shake the feeling I'd met him before.

"So," Eleos raked his hair behind his ears, "What did you two do in the attic all day?"

"Trained Whisper," Seth said.

"Wrote a song," Percy spoke over Seth. A heavy thud followed as Seth stepped on his foot, and Percy cursed.

"Well," Eleos picked up his wine, "Those were lies."

"It's a secret." Percy insisted, lifting his head to stare at me. Seth followed suit, his red eyes darting over my face. They realized they both stared simultaneously, and quickly looked away.

Eleos glanced at me, eyebrows raised.

"And it's not important," Percy stabbed his fork into his cut of lamb. "What's Duath Nun like, Seraphim? Is it paradise?"

"Hardly," Seraphim answered, folding her arms on the table. "It's vastly different from the Merchant Isles—in every sense. But it is much safer there than here."

"Really?" I asked.

"Yes." She nodded. "For whatever reason, the Empty doesn't plague them the way it does us. Oh, it clings to their borders and locks them inside its walls, but its wilderness? Perfectly safe." She paused, rolling her tongue in her mouth. "For now."

I leaned back. The very idea was impossible to imagine. Sprawling fields and vast woods? *Safe*?

The old steward emerged from the pantry with a fresh bottle of wine and refilled Seraphim's glass. She held it up with a smile, and I noticed something she missed.

Though the steward managed to hold the bottle steady, his fingers trembled. Guilt creased his face when he retracted the wine and stepped away.

Glancing at Seraphim, I tried to draw her attention, nodding my head toward the steward and gripping my glass, but she didn't notice.

"But enough business," Seraphim leaned forward. "You mentioned this was only your second-worst entrance to a city, Seth?"

"Oh!" He grinned. "I'd almost forgotten. Perse, you want to tell this one?"

"I can't believe I haven't." Setting aside his glass, Percy tilted his hat up. "This was back when we first met—before Seth's wanted posters hung on every wall."

Feeling woozy, I rested my head in my hand. Was I drunk already? Black spots colored my vision, and I shook my head, trying to drive them away. Percy halted mid-sentence and braced a hand on the table.

"Perse?" Eleos asked. "Are you. . ." He trailed off, pressing a hand to his eyes.

Seth leaped from his seat, knocking the chair over. He placed a hand on his dagger before his knee gave out, and he dropped, grabbing the table to catch his fall. My vision blurred as I tried to stand, and I collapsed back into my seat.

Phaedrus stood, a red and silver blur beneath the flaming chandelier. "I really do appreciate your help." He said, pacing around us. "It gives me no pleasure to stab you in the back like this, but. . ." he chuckled, "You've lost your edge, sister. You made this far too easy."

A shadow loomed behind me as he placed a hand on the back of my chair.

Seraphim grabbed her dinner knife and raked it across the back of her hand. Fingers curling, she tried to form her blood into a scythe, but I could see her body trembling. Folding. Losing consciousness.

Phaedrus leaned forward, whispering in my ear. "I told you we would meet again, Elpis. It's a shame, too. You were so close to figuring it out."

Bloody vines rose from the darkness, like horrors in a nightmare. The doors flew open, and guards burst through, surrounding the table. I reached out for the fading figures around me, and felt Eleos's hand brush mine before I fell backward into shadow.

THIRTY ONE

I WOKE IN THE EMBRACE of silken sheets, the light of the setting sun spilling in through the window. Head groggy, I sat up, memories resurfacing from a deep fog.

Someone had dressed me while I slept. My hair was tied with a neat ribbon, and I wore the pale blue dress patterned with flowers. Sliding out of bed, my feet touched the cold floor, and everything came back to me at once.

My breath came in jagged spurts, and my hand trembled on the bedpost as I stood. Heart weighed down by worry, I ran to the door and grabbed the knob, expecting to find it locked.

But it wasn't. The door swung open freely, revealing the quiet hall of the lord's estate. Nervously gnawing on my lip, I stepped out, every muscle in my body tensed as I quietly padded down the hall, wondering if the night before had been but a dream.

We'd been drugged, hadn't we? Should I not have woken in a prison?

"Awake already?" Phaedrus' voice came from behind. Startled, I spun around to see him leaning in a doorway, light faintly shining on his back. "I thought you might be out until tomorrow."

"What did you do?" I sputtered.

"Come." He beckoned. "We have much to discuss."

He ducked back into the room, and I peered inside. A fire crackled in the mantle, casting cozy light over an opulent parlor decorated with soft white couches and an elegant silver and gold rug. Phaedrus leaned on the back of a chair, beside a table set with a jug and two small glasses.

Had I caught him in a moment of weakness? Strands of his fiery hair escaped his bun, and his collar was unbuttoned and hung open. Shadows darkened his eyes.

"The others are fine." He said, preempting my question. "Confined to the dungeons under tight watch, but unharmed."

"So, you're the masked nobleman," I said, fingers digging into my arm. "Are you some kind of actor? Familiar with dying your hair and using different voices?"

"You could say that," Phaedrus lifted the jug. "We had the same teacher, you and I."

My breath caught. "That's how you knew Ainwir. But you're a nobleman! Why would he. . ."

"How little you know about your master." Phaedrus poured amber liquid into the two glasses. "Ainwir was House Cynthus's spymaster, long ago. I learned a great deal from him." He lifted a glass. "But we aren't here to talk about him. You want answers, and I have them. Answers Seraphim would never give you."

Overwhelmed, I stepped back, bumping into the wall. "He was your spymaster? Why? When?" Questions tumbled from my mouth. "Do you know where-"

"Questions for later," Phaedrus said sharply.

Swallowing, I bit my tongue. Trapped in a nobleman's estate with no allies. . . what would Ainwir have told me to do?

Closing my eyes, I recalled his face. The harsh gaze above a hawk-like nose.

Resistance and ugly words earned ire and death. Amicable cooperation lowered their guard.

"Alright," I said, approaching Phaedrus. "You said you'd tell me everything. Let's start with this: you helped Seraphim flee to Duath Nun after her experiments came to light. Why, if you intended to betray her?"

"I didn't, back then." Phaedrus swirled his drink, staring into the liquid. "My sister and I were united in our beliefs, even if I did not like her methods. I wanted her alive and safe. We had every intention of reuniting, down the line."

"So, what changed?"

Grabbing the second glass, Phaedrus offered it to me, and I accepted. Sniffing the liquor for any unusual scents, I took a sip. A warming burn ran down my throat. Phaedrus watched me carefully.

"*Everything* changed." He said quietly. "I was neither chthonic nor psyche when my sister left." He turned a hand over, where a scar glinted on his palm. "One extraordinary event is rare enough, but two? I realized then, the gods had long abandoned us, and only their cursed magic remained."

"You suffered tragedy." I guessed. "That doesn't explain why you seek to undermine your sister's efforts."

"Not undermine," Phaedrus muttered. "Undo. *Prevent.*" His eyes traced the flowers stitched into my skirt. "Here stands the one creature who can brave the Empty. Who can *control* it. Seraphim would risk your life to seek a cure when you should be used to ensure its finality."

"I don't understand."

"The Empty should not be stopped, Aethra," Phaedrus said harshly. "It should be welcomed with open arms. Cruel is its slow approach, its torturous spread. Let it swallow the world in one fell sweep."

"But, I can't-"

"You *can*, Aethra." He said firmly. "The psyche can imbue happiness and sorrow. The muse can create sweet music and dreadful screams. Chthonics can shape both terrifying weapons," he pinched his palm with his fingernails. Scarlet seeped from the cut, gathering into a blooming rose in his palm, "and declarations of love."

Nostalgia and unease plagued me near the Empty. Fear of the abyss, and a beckoning to become one with it. He was right.

My fingers tightened around the glass. "Are you mad? The last thing I'd ever do is help you *kill* everyone."

Drinking heavily from his glass, he slammed it onto the end table and stalked to the fire, eyes ablaze. "Come here, and I'll show you why."

My stomach dropped. What did he intend to do? I felt like a lead ball weighed me down as I joined him by the mantle. He took my hand gently, pulling me to his side.

"Think of your companions. Take the bard, for example." Phaedrus brushed back his bangs. "Did he ever tell you why he's tainted?"

"No," I whispered. "I didn't want to pry."

"Nor should you have." Phaedrus lifted his chin. He slowly twisted my hand.

Aches grew in my joints, and my muscles throbbed. Despair raked at my brain, whispering my time was running short. I stared at my palm, terrified it would disintegrate and be gone.

"I read his thoughts," Phaedrus said. "When he learned of his illness, his slow decay? When he learned he had been condemned to a short life of suffering, he did what any sane man might do. He sought a quick, painless end."

A hollow formed in my chest. The distress and desperation passed into apathy. I wanted everything to *end*. Wanted the pain to go away. Wanted anything but to suffer and *suffer* until the gods decided to cease my torture.

The Empty beckoned. A simple, instant end. Painless. All I needed to do was step forward into its shadowy embrace.

Fear twisted in my gut. I couldn't go through with it.

I wanted to *live*.

My heart flipped. Phaedrus was a psyche. He was controlling my emotions—making me feel what Percy did.

"But this is perhaps the kindest tale," Phaedrus said in a hushed tone. "Reflect on the path you took to reach this place, and recall the thread connecting each day."

My memories whirled past, like the pages of a book flipping in a stiff breeze. The heavy emotions Percy carried with him lifted from my soul as Phaedrus took them away.

"Your tale began with a wretched young woman," Phaedrus laid his blood rose atop the marble mantle. "Enslaved. Forced into a life of servitude, allowed not even the glimmer of hope. Your sorry tale would have ended when a deal went wrong, and a client you should never have crossed slit your throat."

"You're probably not wrong," I agreed.

His hand tightened around mine. "Seraphim buys you from your owner, offering you freedom in exchange for your life." He paused. "I need not say what punishment some think my sister deserved. The lives she took."

Pain laced through my lungs, stealing my breath. Tears glimmered in my eyes as grief like I'd never known ripped through my entire being. I wanted to sob, to expel the anguish, but my throat went dry.

"The world took first her wife and child, but refused to stop there." Grabbing a log from the edge of the mantle, Phaedrus tossed it into the fire, showering sparks across the stone.

I flinched from the rush of heat. Pain flared across my back, as though from the sharp sting of a whip. A horrible sinking sensation swallowed me, as though high walls confined me within their grasp.

Stuck. Tormented. Denied an end.

Gasping through the pain, I tried to meet his eye. "Shouldn't you want to help her?"

"I do." He said earnestly, tilting my hand. "Just as I imagine you want to help that poor scholar."

Rage bristled through my veins, like fire setting me alight. I wanted to scream, to tear out someone's throat. But beneath the anger, frigid sorrow encased my heart.

Disoriented under the assault of foreign emotions, I tried to back away from Phaedrus, but he only pulled me closer.

I wanted to kill him. I wanted her back. I should have protected her. Words that didn't belong to me circled in my head.

Loathing consumed me. For *him*. For myself.

I would make them all pay. Their lives belonged to me. Under my control, the sinners would become sacrifices for the worthy.

Were these Eleos' emotions? I bucked under the weight of his fury, of the unrelenting terror at what he'd become.

"And the assassin?" Phaedrus's sage-green eyes narrowed. "Do you know anything about him?"

A different emotion bloomed inside my heart. *Love.* I felt it so deeply it ached. The sudden rush of a pleasant emotion took me off guard, and I looked up in surprise.

Warmth tucked me in its embrace, like wings folding around my shoulders. I was loved. *Safe.*

A grimace twisted across Phaedrus's mouth as his fingernails dug into my skin. A cold hand reached into my chest and ripped the warm love from my heart, tearing it to shreds, leaving nothing behind but a gaping hole.

I bled out from wounds I couldn't see, wracked by the misery of grief.

I whimpered, and it almost looked like Phaedrus took pity on me. The agony relented, patched up by bandages that did not mend my wounds, but staunched the pain. Love once again warmed my soul, like a soft caress, like a radiant sun.

This was a different kind of love. The first had been innocent. Desire surged beneath the passion—desire for her, and her alone.

A half-smile tugged at Phaedrus' lips as he stole the warmth away again. The lacerations reopened, cutting deeper than before. Claws dug into my chest, smashing the light that had kept me alive.

Anguish overwhelmed me, and a sob burst from my lips. Gasping, I pressed a hand to my chest, where an unbearable pang tore my heart apart.

"Will you make Seth lose you, too?" Phaedrus asked.

"Stop." I whimpered, crushed beneath the agony.

"You can make it stop, Aethra," Phaedrus said softly. "For everyone. Bring their suffering to an end."

The grief Seth carried with him lifted as Phaedrus dropped my hand. Catching my breath, I grabbed the mantle, trying to still my shaking legs.

"Why would I hurt them when I could *save* them?" I said. "Maybe some yearn for release, but so many more want to live. And-"

"And if you defeat the Empty, they'll gain the life they're owed?" Phaedrus gazed down on me like a bird of prey. "What in your life has shown you this world deserves to be saved? Was it the crowds who shrieked and panicked, pushing the poor tainted to their deaths? Was it the officer who consorted with the Guild to murder the lord and steal his throne? Was it the father who enjoyed the pleasures of his daughter's flesh and threw the child into the wilderness to hide the truth?"

I tried to respond, but he advanced, forcing me to back up. Grabbing my arms, he assaulted me again with his magic.

"Was it the parents mourning their children, taken young by disease? Or perhaps you thought the lords in their gilded castles deserve your pity? They who live in luxury, stealing every scrap from those they trod upon in the dirt below? Or maybe the clergy, in their endless hypocrisy, who use their station to escape their crimes?" He paused, eyes searching my face. "Your assassin has the right of it. The world chooses the status quo. Why lift a finger to help the helpless when you could look away and be blissfully ignorant of their fate?"

Every horrible emotion the world had ever felt ripped through my body. Aching hunger of a starving, dying child. The panicked throb of a man watching his love die in childbirth. The quivering hands of a parent unable to afford healing for their child.

Terror. Helplessness. Grief. The world went dark as its emotions buried me. I screamed, unable to make it stop. Pain. Hollowness. Desperation. Fury.

The spell lifted. Dragging open my eyes, I found myself curled in a ball by the fire, head buried in my arms. Shaking like a leaf, I pulled myself into a sitting position and saw Phaedrus sitting on the armchair, watching me expectantly.

"It's cruelty." He said. "No doctor of conscience would force a wounded man to lie in misery while he succumbs to wounds medicine cannot mend. They would close his eyes, sparing him inhumane torture."

"What. . ." I gasped. "What made you this way?"

"My first error was love." His eyes stared into the distance, recalling old memories. "A common woman who worked the stables. Being fools, we believed we could keep our affair hidden."

"Did your father kill her?" I asked.

"Yes. Sent her to the Empty, as is tradition. And our child?" Phaedrus swallowed. "I barely managed to get him to the Guild before the same fate befell him."

Something spun in my stomach, and I sat back. Could it be. . ?

"My second mistake was compassion." He said, a hint of humor in his tone. "When my father died an untimely death, I rejoiced. With his mantle and power, I believed I could change my city for the better." He chuckled bitterly. "You're clever. I needn't tell you why I failed."

No lord would give up a cent of their treasury to feed the hungry. No lord would give away a mile of land to house the homeless. Any law Phaedrus tried to pass was doubtless thwarted by every noble who called Cynthus home.

And Seth was right. It was easier to ignore the brothel recruiting children than lose the money it generated. Easier to excuse the man beating his wife than start a fight. Easier to take the gold the lord offered, and seal your lips.

"Nothing will ever change," Phaedrus said. "What little good blooms in this world is suffocated by the darkness. Just as the very land withers beneath the Empty. There are no gods. No pleasant afterlife. This world is a meaningless farce. Let it fall into nothing."

Wiping the tears from my cheeks, I staggered to my feet. "You don't care that Seraphim might get me killed. You just don't want us to succeed."

"On the contrary," He picked up his drink, swirling the amber liquor. "Duath Nun knows about your magic. And those with it suffer a horrible fate. But Seraphim has grown fond of them. She intends to save those who would condemn you."

"And you won't?"

"I would see you to the shallow wound and tear it wide open." He said, spreading his arms. "And we, too, would know peace."

I dug my fingers into my skirt, studying the man before me. His eyes looked nothing like Eleos' though they shared a hue. Phaedrus' irises reflected no light. Empty. Hopeless.

"Eleos is your son." I blurted out.

"I believe so," Phaedrus confirmed. "The Guild did its job well. I never caught wind of him again. But he looks so much like his mother. . ." He looked away. "I'm not surprised the world has ruined him, as well."

My guess had been right, back in Serifos. Sage-green eyes.

. .

"One thing's still bothering me," I said. "If Ainwir was your teacher, why did he leave to become a con man?"

"Twelve years ago, Seraphim sent back word of Duath Nun's knowledge of your magic." He stood, trailing a hand across the mantle. "I sent Ainwir to find the girl who possessed it."

"Why did he train me? Why didn't he bring me back to you?"

"For seven long years, I didn't know the answer to that." Phaedrus's hand slid off the marble, and he stared at the speck of dust clinging to his fingers. "Even with the Guild's aid, I couldn't pin the bastard down. When I finally captured him, Ainwir said," he turned to look at me. "He couldn't stand the idea of letting me use you."

"Captured. . ." My mind blurred. "But he took a loan out from-"

"From Laverna?" Phaedrus laughed. "You're clever. Surely you know there was never any loan. He paid Laverna handsomely to hide you. The debt? Just a means to ensure you stayed near her, so she might protect you from me." He looked at his fingernails, nose wrinkled. "And it worked. For five more years."

I backed into the table, knocking my glass over. "But. . . but he worked for your family. Found you for me. Why did he change his mind?"

Phaedrus watched the spilled drink trickle off the table. "Because he took your tiny, malnourished hand in his. Nothing more. He brought you all the way to Cynthus' border, telling himself it was just another job." His eyes flicked up. "But he turned back at my doorstep."

Releasing the table, I staggered forward as memories rushed back to me. Ainwir had smuggled us out of *Cynthus* in a corpse cart. That foggy remembrance had been the day he betrayed his master and saved my life.

"Small wonder he took you on as an apprentice." Phaedrus continued. "Anyone who could melt Ainwir's cold heart had a promising future as a con man."

I should have felt something. Grief. Sorrow. Maybe I couldn't anymore.

I'd lived a thousand lifetimes during Phaedrus' assault, and in each suffered unimaginable horrors under the gods' uncaring gaze.

Raising my head, I remembered the last piece of the puzzle. "I still don't understand. Why do you call me Elpis?"

"That is what the people of Duath Nun call your kind," Phaedrus reached for the fire, as though intending to grasp it. "Its translation feels far more appropriate, than merely attributing you to the Maiden."

"But you say it like a name. A title."

"Because it is." Phaedrus paused. "The manor is yours." He gestured to the door. "Your magic is potent, but quite useless in a fight. I wouldn't press your luck with the guards."

"I don't intend to try," I said blankly, walking to the door and pausing in its threshold. "Thank you," I said stiffly. "For telling me the truth."

He nodded, sharp gaze following me down the hall. I returned to my room and shut the door behind me.

For a while, I stood there, emotionless, still as a statue, silently reflecting on everything I'd learned. The fog lifted from my brain, and the gears started spinning all at once.

Five long years had passed since Phaedrus found Ainwir. Time enough for my master to have sailed to Duath Nun and started a family. But I knew he hadn't.

The Guild had a saying. When someone vanishes, look instead for their corpse.

I fell to my knees, broken. Ainwir hadn't found me by chance. Hadn't betrayed me.

My eyes burned and tears flowed down my cheeks, one by one, until the dam burst and a racking sob burst from my chest. For I knew the truth Phaedrus had not voiced.

Ainwir had *loved* me.

And he was long dead.

THIRTY TWO

I SAT ON THE COLD floor long after the moon had risen into the sky. A strange mix of emotions boiled within me. Despondence weighed down my limbs like heavy steel; even rising seemed a pointless feat. But anger simmered within, heat building at the base of my throat.

Bowing my head, I let the weight drag me down. My fingers were still shaking from all the pain I'd experienced—both my own and others'.

A voice not my own whispered against my skull. "*Lady Aethra?*" Eleos' voice.

My head snapped up. "*Eleos? Are you alright?*"

"*. . . yes.*"

Though I could not see his face, I could tell he was lying.

"*No wonder I couldn't read Lord Phaedrus.*" He continued. "*I chalked it up to training. . .*"

"*None of you got a good look at him,*" I said, "*It's my fault.*"

"*It doesn't matter now.*" Eleos sounded strained and weak. "*I forged a connection between us before I passed out. To say goodbye, if nothing else.*"

I pulled my knees up and leaned against the door. "*Phaedrus made me feel your pain. Someone. . . someone killed your sister, didn't they?*"

Nothing came in response.

"Is that your secret? Because, if so–"

"I have no proof." Eleos' voice sounded fainter. "Her husband claimed she died in her sleep. Father and I knew better. Knew they'd been having arguments. Knew he was violent when drunk." He paused. "At the time, I was certain he'd gone too far. Choked her. But he was second in rank only to my father in the clergy. So everyone patted him on the back and offered their condolences."

"What did you do?"

"I didn't kill him, Aethra. I wormed my way into his mind, made him pick up his own blade, and forced him to rip it across his throat." Eleos hesitated. "I took joy in it. The horror on his face. The power I had over him."

I swallowed. My throat was cracked and dry. "Anyone would feel the same, Eleos."

"Maybe. But that was only the first of my sins." He paused. "I can't hold this connection much longer. Know this: Phaedrus is a psyche—born of compassion. He won't hurt you."

I wanted to protest, but I couldn't. Phaedrus wished to destroy the world and everything in it because of his overflowing compassion. And if my hunch was correct. . .

"Don't be reckless, Aethra," Eleos said. "I can feel your thoughts."

"Hold on." I thought, standing. "I'm coming."

"I should have known. Be careful." Eleos' voice faded away, leaving me alone.

Wiping my face, I grabbed my satchel from its hook. Flipping through the contents, I found the prize I sought: the pants Seth had stolen for me. Worming out of my dress, I tossed it aside and pulled the pants on, then yanked a simple tunic over them. Binding my hair back, I wrapped a cloak around my shoulders and attached my coin purse to my belt.

Ainwir had taught me how to block psyches out. Closing my eyes and breathing slowly, I forged walls around my thoughts to keep my intentions hidden.

Slipping outside, I hurried down the hall, peeking into the parlor. Lord Phaedrus stood before the flames, staring into them as though watching a fond memory dance in their light. Clearing my throat, I knocked on the door frame.

Roused from his trance, Phaedrus turned, raising an eyebrow. "Going somewhere?"

"You said I had the run of the manor," I said. "And you aren't the kind of man to kill dogs. Is Whisper here?"

He nodded. "I put him in the stables, for now. Were you fond of him?"

"Yes. I'd like to see him, if that's okay."

Phaedrus' eyes flicked over my face, but if he read my intent, he didn't act on it. "Seraphim and I had a dog just like that, once."

"When you were kids?"

"Yes. Lord Kasos' father shot him while hunting. Seraphim was inconsolable for days." He tilted his head. "I'll never forget how it whined as it died. . . unable to understand why."

Despite all this man had done to me, all he had said, my heart ached for him and the image he placed in my head.

"Go on." Phaedrus waved me off. "Take whatever courage you need for the days to come."

I stepped away, but my muscles locked up, forbidding me from leaving. Returning to the doorway, I hesitated before speaking. "I'm sorry. For all you've suffered. I wish. . ."

"Strange." Phaedrus smiled faintly. "That you were not gifted the powers of a psyche." He turned back to the fire and his memories.

Pulling myself from the doorway, I walked down the hall, nervously glancing at every passing servant. As I descended the grand stairwell, I counted four guards patrolling the bottom floor and two more watching the outside entrance. They observed me, but did not stop me.

Finding my way to the side entrance, I stepped out into the dark yard and followed the paved stone path leading to the lord's personal stables. Grabbing the low wooden fence wrapping the horses' field, I swung one leg over and dropped down on the other side, imagining how easily Seraphim and Seth would have vaulted it.

A familiar hound raced toward me before I'd taken two steps. Whisper sniffed me vigorously, tail flailing like a weapon of war. Grinning, I dropped to my knees and ran my hands through his wiry fur, wincing as he covered my face in wet licks.

Pushing the hound off me, I stood, searching the yard for guards. A tower rose in each corner. Faint lights glowed at their peak and in the turrets, signifying patrols keeping watch over the area. Down the main path, iron gates barred the entrance, watched over by more heavily armored guards. Thick, tall stone walls encircled the entire manor, with nary a crack to slip through save for that main gate.

With men watching from on high, I could scrabble up maybe two inches of wall before they descended upon me to drag me back. And if I got caught fleeing, Phaedrus would confine me to my quarters.

Grabbing a broken branch, I paced back and forth, pretending to play with Whisper. Throwing the stick across the field, I watched the hound sprint after it.

Think, Aethra. I ground my fingers into my scalp, trying to force my brain to work harder. Phaedrus thought my magic could push away the Empty, or aid its growth. Could it do nothing else?

Whisper dropped the stick at my feet, and it broke into pieces. Staring at the fragments, my mind snapped into clarity. "C'mere, boy," I called, running toward the stable doors.

Closed and locked. Glancing over the barn, I searched for an open window or gap, but found none. Gathering myself, I shook my hands and focused on the left stable door.

The Empty destroyed *everything.* Disintegrated it. The herald of despair, it washed away life, color, and hope. To destroy it, I had to give in to its nihilism. But to summon it, to wield the Empty in *defiance* of it. . .

I needed *hope*.

There was no escape from this manor. We were all trapped. But I was the sole beacon of hope that yet remained.

A wave of hushed, stagnant air washed over me, and magic bloomed in my breast, begging to be set free. Silent, instant, the stable door crumbled into dust.

Gasping, I stared at my handiwork. Whisper flinched away, head lowered, hackles raised. My lips tugged up into a grin, and a laugh burst from my chest. "Stay with me, Whisper," I called, ducking under the chain dangling from the broken door.

Adjusting my eyes to the shadows inside, I found a blonde horse with a stark-white mane. "Athena," I whispered, running a hand down the mare's neck. "Come on, girl." Grabbing a lead from the wall, I wrapped it around her neck and led her outside.

There was no time to properly saddle her. Eyeing the bulk of her bare back, I shimmied back into the stables, found a step ladder, and dragged it to sit beside her. Stepping up, I grabbed onto her mane and pulled myself onto her back. My legs floundered and kicked, but I managed the feat.

If Percy ever wrote a ballad about us, I hoped he'd leave out the heroine's inelegance. Grabbing Athena's mane, I dug my knees into her side and took a deep breath. Once I started down this path, all hell would break loose, and there would be no going back.

"Alright." I patted her neck. "Let's go."

Yanking her mane, I directed her toward the northern wall between the gates and the corner turning south. Kicking my heels into her flank, I drove her into a gallop, calling for Whisper to follow. I grabbed onto her neck as she leaped the fence, the hound a pace behind her.

We galloped across the field, in full sight of the guards, heading straight for a dead end.

Focusing on the sensation I'd summoned earlier, I thrust my hand toward the wall, grimacing as the swell of magic swirled within me, begging to be released. Another wave of stagnant, silent air consumed the field before a small section of the wall crumbled into dust, the grass withered and died, and deep gouges formed in the earth.

I heard the guards shouting before we reached the gap. Athena tore through the broken wall, drawing the gazes of every guard in the vicinity. Glancing behind me, I saw the men on the walls pointing, one drawing a bow before remembering his orders and scrambling to ring the alarm bell instead.

Chimes rang behind me as Athena galloped into the city. More guards patrolling the streets sprang to attention as we blazed past, shouting and drawing their weapons. I flinched as an arrow soared over my head.

These men had no orders to spare me.

Phaedrus said Seraphim and the others were in the dungeons—those would be near the old gallows, in the city center. Using the towering lighthouse as a guide, I navigated Athena through he narrow, winding roads, praying I was heading in the right direction.

Hooves clopping on the cobblestone roads, Athena leaped over an empty wagon and turned into a wide, open field. A raised platform stood ahead of us: this was the place. Eyes flying around wildly, I noticed a large stone building to the west, windows stained and walls worn. That must be the dungeons. Spotting a hitching post nearby, I drove Athena toward it.

Throwing myself off her back, I tied her up and darted away, Whisper at my heel.

Scanning the two-story building, I spotted a cluster of thick bushes under a broad-leafed tree. Sliding into the dirt at its trunk, I ducked beneath the bramble, and Whisper crawled in behind me.

He must have hidden like this with his master countless times.

Holding my breath, I pressed myself to the ground, hoping I was concealed. Watching the streets like a hawk, I counted the guards who ran by, some mounted, others on foot. Lanterns glowed where they passed, and I heard the occasional voice barking orders.

Lifting my head, I strained to overhear, and while I couldn't make out all the words, I caught enough. One asked where I'd gone, the other didn't know.

Phaedrus wouldn't have mentioned me. He didn't want me hurt or imprisoned. To the guards outside his manor, I was a no-name woman breaking the minor law of riding a horse too fast at night.

Gradually, the activity in the square dimmed, but Phaedrus's men would doubtless be scouring the city for me soon. "Stay here," I whispered to the hound, rising and brushing myself off.

I had to bullshit the rest of the way.

Pushing the heavy stone doors open, I entered the dungeon, boots echoing on the tiles. Dim light guided my way forward, and I passed a stairwell leading up. Judicial offices, probably. The last place I wanted to be.

Finding the office I sought, I sheepishly stepped through, catching the attention of the guard sitting inside. He shot to his feet, voice tired and muffled inside his helm. "Sorry, lady. Visiting hours are over."

Knitting my hands nervously, I approached him. "I know! But my father won't let me come see him, and I can't slip out during the day. . ."

I batted my eyelashes, played my best whimpering maiden, and pulled the coin purse off my belt, forcing a tremble into my fingers. "Will this be enough to convince you?"

The guard stared at my offer, took the pouch, and made a rough count of its contents. "Do you know which cell block he's in?"

"I. . . I'm not sure. I'll know him when I see him."

Sighing heavily, the guard felt the weight of the bag and set it down. Grabbing a lantern from a hook on the wall, he beckoned. "This way. We'll find him."

Hiding a grin, I scurried after him, holding my cloak tightly around my arms. The guard led me to a heavy iron door and paused to unlock it. Ushering me through, he locked it again once we stood on the other side. Pocketing his key, he guided me down a set of stairs into dark halls.

"Keep your eyes out," he instructed.

Nodding, my eyes flashed between every cell, peering through the iron bars. Some were empty, others held men and women I'd never laid eyes on. Surely they were here. They had to be.

A shout echoed somewhere to our north. I couldn't make out what they said, but the following words carried clearly. "I don't care!" A man snapped. "My son will be prosecuted, not made a victim of your superstition."

Percy. That was his father's voice. Eyes widening, I gazed down the hall from which the voices had come. Stepping back, the guard changed courses, leading me east. "Let's go this way, first."

Shit. Were they all imprisoned together? Eyeing the guard's tabard, I wondered how easily I could pick his pocket.

. .

Gnawing on my lip, I kept checking each cell until I found a familiar face.

A young man with wavy brunette hair was tucked in the corner of a dim prison, knees pulled up, head resting in his hands. The flower patterns on his bracers were all too familiar.

I tugged the guard's tabard. "That's him!"

Sighing, the guard gave me space. "Make it quick."

Eleos raised his head when he heard my voice, and his eyes flew wide. Leaping to his feet, he ran to the bars, bit his tongue, and glanced at the guard. When he spoke, his voice was hushed and calm.

"Aethra." He said, lopping off my title. "You came."

"I said I would, didn't I?" I said, studying his face. A slash traced from his neck to his cheekbones, and bruises darkened his skin.

Eleos's eyes slid off me onto the soldier behind us. Tapping his foot idly, the guard pointedly looked away, offering us privacy.

"Cry," Eleos whispered. "Sob. Break down. Something pathetic."

"What? Why?"

"Make him have sympathy for you." He stared at me pointedly, waiting for me to catch on.

Oh. *Oh.* Psyches could change people's thoughts when a kernel of genuine emotion was seeded in their minds. Pressing a hand to my chest, I steadied my racing heart and prepared to put on a show.

Backing away from the cell, I buried my head in my hands and released a pathetic, simpering moan. Hearing me, the guard rushed over, reaching out to check on me. His eyes fogged behind his helm, and he wobbled on his feet, confused. Eleos reached through the bars, only managing to brush the man's forearm, but it was enough.

A strange light entered the guard's simple brown eyes. He grabbed my shoulders. "What can I do to help?" He pleaded.

"I need to find Seth and Seraphim," I said quietly. "And I'd like you to open his cell."

Nodding, the guard pulled out a ring of keys and fitted one into Eleos' lock, clicking the door open. Stepping into the hall, Eleos grabbed the man's arm, meeting his gaze for a moment before uttering a quiet whisper.

"Why don't you take a break? You're exhausted."

The guard nodded, eyes drooping until he fell to a knee. Eleos grabbed him before his metal armor clanged across the floor and gently lowered him to the ground. Grabbing his ring of keys, he turned to me.

"This way." He jogged down the hall, pausing at an intersection to glance around. His head snapped back behind cover, and he motioned toward the eastern corridor. "Our chthonics are there. In high security."

Leaning beside him, I saw a door further down the hall, watched over by a guard reclining against the wall.

"What now?" I asked.

Eleos thought for a moment before turning around. "We get Percy first."

Following him back down the hall, I caught up and hissed in his ear. "His father's there!"

"I know," Eleos shot back.

Gritting my teeth, I glanced at the sleeping guard as we backtracked. Rounding back to the northern cell block, I heard Sir Percivus' voice carrying from ahead, though the second voice was gone.

Eleos pulled me behind a pillar, and we listened.

Sir Percivus sounded more upset than angry. "Don't you think it bothered me, too?"

"Bothered?" Percy tsked. "Not the word I would use. I'd choose, mm, *destroyed*? Or maybe-"

"This is exactly why you're here." His father snapped, anger overtaking his tone. "You take nothing seriously, you flit between women and duties, treating them as disposable frivolities."

"I had a feeling you'd say that. You can go now."

Silence fell over the hall. Daring a peek from behind the pillar, I saw Sir Percivus' lantern outside a cell, barely illuminating the officer in his brilliant red surcoat. He took a hesitant step back, fingers twitching on his lantern.

Regret. I could read it in his body language like an open book.

"I never meant. . ." He said, the anger gone. "Your mother and I. . ."

Eleos' eyes flashed. "There it is." He muttered.

Sir Percivus shook his head, as though doffing a headache. When he looked up, his tone shifted toward grief. "I would have given anything to save you."

Darting out from our cover, Eleos crept toward the officer, hardly making a sound. Sir Percivus only noticed Eleos' approach when the scholar was upon him, and by then, Eleos had already reached out and brushed the man's arm.

Staggering back, Sir Percivus shook his head, blinked a few times, then faced his son. "But there's still time, yet." Turning to Eleos, he stepped away. "There's still time yet."

In a daze, the man walked away, passing me with nary a sideways glance. Catching up to Eleos, I met Percy's bewildered gaze as he leaned against his bars, watching his father go. Eleos shoved a key into the lock and yanked the door open.

Frozen to the spot, Percy gaped at Eleos. "Was that. . . Was that you, or. . .?"

"Do you want the answer to that?" Eleos asked.

"No." Percy shook his head and grabbed his hat from the stone bench. "No, I don't." Fixing the feathered cap over his hair, he gasped when he saw me. "Aethra!" He laughed, slapping my shoulder. "You clever little she-devil, how in Callesis' boundless luck did you get here?"

"There's an army after me," I whispered. "We should hurry."

"Right." Percy nodded. "Right. Where are the others?"

"They're-" Eleos wobbled on his feet, blood trickling from his nose.

"Are you alright?" I asked, worried.

"I've used too much magic." He wiped his nose. "This way." Eleos spun on his heel and jogged away.

Pushing Percy ahead of me, I took up the rear, watching the halls for patrols. We rewound our way to the eastern wing.

Eleos grabbed my collar, yanking me behind a pillar. "Guard." He mimed at Percy. "Take him out."

Nodding curtly, Percy hurried around the corner. Pushing me, Eleos bade me follow.

I took two steps before the most excruciating sound ripped through my ears. It sounded like a violin, but I'd never known the instrument could produce such a wretched, deathly noise. Out of tune, whining and sharp, it pulled on a high note, sending shivers down my spine and forcing my hands to my ears. Gods, were they bleeding?

Someone grabbed my hand, and the noise stopped.

"Sorry," Percy muttered. "Hurry. I can't keep this up long."

Lifting my head, I saw the guard curled up on the ground, hands pressed to his bleeding ears. Pulling his key ring out, Eleos flipped through them, trying a few before finding the correct combination. Leaning against the heavy doors, he pushed them open. Percy and I stepped over the disabled guard and followed him inside.

A pitch-black chamber greeted us. Grabbing the torch hanging beside the guard post, I held it up to illuminate the cells.

Protected on all sides by thick stone walls, the cells allowed no light through. Eleos fitted a key into the rightmost cell, then tossed the ring to me.

"Get Seth." He ordered, pushing the door open.

Running to the opposite cell, I shoved the lock in and clicked it open, holding up the lantern to see inside.

I shouldn't have been surprised by the way chthonics were restrained. Bound in a standing position, thick ropes tied Seth's hand, preventing his fingernails from brushing any part of his skin. A thick gag wrapped his mouth, so he couldn't dig his teeth into his lip.

Heart flipping in my chest, I pulled my little paring knife from my belt and sawed through his gag. Spitting the remnants out, Seth bit down hard on his lip, drawing blood. I stepped back as the droplets flew from his mouth, forming into a bloody dagger. It whipped behind him, severing the rope holding his hands in place.

Yanking his arms free, he stalked toward me and gripped me by the shoulders, pressing me up against the cell wall. "I'm going to fucking kill him." He seethed.

I probably looked like a frightened child. The intensity radiating off him reminded me of our first meeting, when hate had filled his voice and movements. When he'd ruthlessly murdered that officer.

Exhaling shakily, Seth pulled me toward him, burying me in his arms. Pressing my head against his warm chest, I allowed myself a moment to breathe. To feel like my hope hadn't been misguided.

Gods, but finding him alive and well lifted a heavy burden from my heart.

"Um." Percy's voice broke the moment. "Um!" He repeated.

Fire blazed through the hall behind us, and I broke from Seth's grip, stepping outside. Seraphim strode past, scythe of blood and fire forming in her grip. The guard outside had awoken, one hand on his weapon, but his courage fled at the sight of her.

Scrambling back, he fled down the hall into darkness.

"Well," Seraphim turned to me, faced bruised and bloody. "Time to make our daring escape."

THIRTY THREE

FLAMES BURST FROM THE DUNGEONS' doors, shooting out into the night like a pair of phoenix wings. Seraphim strode down the steps to the courtyard, bloody scythe in hand, facing the knights gathered outside.

Several armored men, clad in the silver and blue of House Cynthus, blocked each entrance to the square—there would be no escaping without a fight.

Seraphim turned her head, eyeing the western road. Slashing the scythe across her wrist, she thrust her wounded arm forward, and the blood surged through the air. Flames crackled to life as the blood solidified into two spinning scythes.

Seeing the whirling death heading their way, the men scrambled. Stone fractured where the scythes impaled, bursting into pillars of flame.

"Get to the harbor," Seraphim ordered.

Nodding, I darted past her, whistling for Whisper. The hound burst from its hiding place and dashed to my side, skirting between my legs to reach Seth. Skidding to a stop, I whirled around, staring past the men and flames toward the hitching post where I'd left Athena.

Seth followed my gaze and cursed. "I'll get her. Go." He shouted, spinning on his heel and darting away.

I moved to follow him, but Eleos caught my arm and dragged me away. "He's going to get himself killed if he has to protect you, too." He pressed a scabbard into my hand, filched from a passed-out guard.

Shoving the sword into my belt, I squeezed between the pillars of flame left by Seraphim's magic. Trusting Eleos's sense of direction, I kept pace with him as he slid down a steeply sloping path.

The lighthouse glowed with fire in the distance, a beacon to light our way. Gut churning, I glanced behind me, wishing I hadn't left the others behind. Percy ran into my back as we reached the bottom of the hill, nearly knocking us both over.

"I know what you're thinking." He said. "If Seraphim can't handle it, *no one can.*"

"But-" I cut off, gazing back up the slope. Several knights appeared above us, spears drawn as they gave chase.

"Time to go!" Percy shoved me, and I obeyed.

Alarm bells rang above us, resonating throughout the city. We ran for our lives, darting into alleys when resistance appeared, weaving through narrow roads to lose their pursuit. Salt carried on the breeze, and the crash of waves sounded on the horizon—we were nearly to the sea.

Eleos squeezed through the narrow crack separating two buildings, and I followed. We emerged on an ancient stone dock, where the ocean crashed into the piers, sending white foam into the sky.

Clinking armor and pounding footsteps sounded to my right, and I barely had time to turn my head before a guard was upon me, thrusting his spear toward my flank. Skidding backward, I tried to avoid the attack, but his spear grazed my side, drawing blood.

Grabbing the sword Eleos had given me, I yanked it loose from its scabbard, thrusting it forward into the defensive position Seth had beaten into my head.

Every muscle in my body quivered as the man charged again, this time trying to sweep the spear across my feet. I tried to block it, thrusting forward. Steel rang against steel. Pain rang through my arm, but I managed to knock his attack aside.

With my attacker thrown off balance, an opening appeared for me to step back, escaping his reach. Raising my sword, I prepared for him to charge again.

A spear whirled past me, striking the guard in the thigh. Blood spurted from the wound, and he gasped, falling to a knee. His weapon clattered to the ground, and Eleos slid past me, snatching it up.

"Not bad," he said, twirling the spear. "Maybe you'll be a warrior after all."

"I thought you couldn't fight!" I chattered, nerves running up and down my limbs like lightning.

"This way." He shouted, running off.

Another guard lay unconscious behind me. Swallowing, I waited for Percy to squeeze through and pushed him ahead of me, watching behind for pursuit.

The ship we were supposed to take was moored in a cove beneath the lord's manor. Here at the south shore, we couldn't be further from our goal—only an array of fishing boats bobbed along the docks.

Eleos halted before the only ship in sight with two decks. Percy ran to his side and doubled over, panting. "Why did you stop?" He gasped.

"I think this is our escape route," Eleos said calmly.

"What?" Percy repeated. "Only one ship can survive the Lethe, and I don't think this is it!"

"Want to run back up to the manor and steal the keys?" Eleos looked up sharply, listening to the alarm bells. "We don't have time. It's this or nothing."

"Wait," I said. "Seraphim crossed the Lethe—traveled to Duath Nun and back. How?"

"With a better ship than this," Eleos said. "There's another way to avoid the storm—but it's more likely to claim our lives."

"*More* likely? *Gods.*" Percy cursed, drawing his dagger to cut the ropes loose.

It wasn't a bad ship. Double-masted with an underbelly, it could probably weather rough seas, but not the deadly whirlpool said to haunt the Lethe.

Standing guard at the pier, I glanced up and down the dark docks, hoping to see Seth, Athena, *anything.*

Something moved out of the corner of my eye, and I turned to see blood-red vines streaking across the docks toward me.

The vines shot up, wrapping around my wrist while another grabbed my ankle. Both pulled, yanking me off my feet and twisting the sword from my grip. I hit the ground with a heavy thud and was dragged across the rough ground.

Phaedrus stepped from the building's shadows, the scarlet blood streaming from his palm a match for his hair. Grabbing my collar, he hauled me up. Sage-green eyes peered at me. Not with anger, but sorrow.

"You're as slippery as Ainwir." He said. "He would've been proud."

My mouth twisted into a sneer. I'd never wanted to kill someone before. Not until now.

Phaedrus' eyes darted behind me, landing on Percy and Eleos.

"If you so much as *touch* them. . ." I snarled.

Eyes flaring open, Phaedrus threw me aside and leapt back. A greatsword of dripping scarlet whirled between us. Had he not released me, it would have severed his arm.

Seth dashed in front of me, a crimson longsword gripped in one hand, and a scarlet dagger in the other. The floating great sword impaled the wall behind Phaedrus before launching out of the stone. Vines sprang from the ground in a rush of blood, blocking the greatsword from cleaving through the nobleman's neck.

A shower of blood rained from the clash of two chthonic spells. Red splotches darkened my vision.

"*Get the hell away from her.*" Seth snarled.

The sound of galloping hooves pounded toward me, and I desperately rubbed my eyes, stumbling backward.

My vision cleared. Athena halted beside me, Seraphim mounted on her back. Leaping off the mare, Seraphim grabbed my arms and turned me toward the boat. "Get aboard! We'll be right behind you."

Panicked, I searched for Seth. He stood amidst a sea of red flowers and deadly vines, chopping aside the striking whips with his blades while advancing toward Phaedrus.

One tendril found its mark, tearing across Seth's upper arm. Blood rushed from the wound, quickly gathering into a new blade—a thin rapier that darted toward Phaedrus, grazing his cheek.

Seraphim whirled me around and pushed me. "Go!" She ordered.

Slapping Athena's rear, I aimed her toward our boat. She took off running, with Whisper at her heels. Eleos ducked out of their way, grabbing my fallen sword to saw through the anchor's ropes. On the deck, Percy fought with the mast, trying to unfurl the sails.

Forcing my attention away from the battle, I ran for the ship.

My head spun, and I tripped. Unwelcome emotions pounded in my skull. Overwhelming, all-consuming.

Phaedrus' voice caressed my aching mind like a pleasant breeze. "*She's hidden too much from you. And now, she sends you to your death. To their deaths.*"

I fought against the anger boiling in my gut. Against the sore ache of betrayal. These weren't my emotions.

Phaedrus spoke again, his voice irritable. "*She knows what Duath Nun does to your kind. They torment you. Torture you. Condemn you to a fate worse than death.*"

My arms moved without my consent, fingers seeking the hilt of my blade.

"*Kill her for those she's murdered. For the suffering she would inflict upon you.*"

Drawing the blade from its scabbard, I raised it over my head and brought it down on Seraphim. Her back was turned. Hearing the steel ringing through the air, she spun. Too late.

The sword raked through her forearms as she raised them as a shield. Blood rushed from the wound, coating my blade and her sleeves. My heart pulsed with horror.

What was I doing?

Seraphim staggered back. Her scythe reforged from the fresh wound, catching alight with flame. She effortlessly blocked my second strike, though I saw her eyes flare in pain as the weight of my attack bore down on her wounds.

Someone called my name in the distance. I screamed inside my skull, unable to speak, unable to stop myself from pushing against her, trying to break her guard.

Seth yelped in pain. I wanted to search for him, but my head wouldn't turn. I saw one thing: Seraphim, weakened, a moment from breaking.

Though her arms quaked, Seraphim's voice was calm. "You're stronger than he is." She said. "I know you don't think so. But we do."

Biting my lip until blood trickled down my chin, I watched as she lost her grip on the scythe and fell to a knee. My sword swung wildly as I broke her guard, before sweeping back up to bring down on her neck.

Eleos grabbed my arm, drawing my attention away from my prey. "Lady Aethra." He said calmly. "Stop. Don't let him in."

My mouth twisted into a grimace. How dare he? Lies after lies, hiding the truth. He'd taken my heart and torn it to pieces. Twisting my blade, I shifted course to strike him instead. To get him out of my way.

Eleos gazed at me with soft, sage-green eyes. He didn't move. Didn't defend himself. Nor did I feel his magic slipping into my mind.

He trusted me.

My sight dulled. The world drained of color. If I killed them, everything would have been for naught. I'd never look back at myself and be glad for the road I tread. We'd never succeed.

Guilt would tear me apart every day until the world ended.

Everything we'd suffered—*pointless*.

Screaming, I felt the hostile grip on my mind wither. Flinging the sword away, I dropped to my knees as magic surged in my chest. Rushing tempests burst from my breast, enveloping the world in soft blue light.

Flowers sprouted around me, covering the dock in a thick, lush meadow of pale blue petals. The bloody vines were overtaken, their scarlet flowers consumed and replaced. Phaedrus staggered back, staring at his bleeding palm in horror as his spells died beneath the flower's touch.

Bewildered, Phaedrus dropped his guard, boots sinking into the meadow. Seeing an opening, Seth raised his longsword and threw it toward Phaedrus' heart.

"No!" Seraphim shouted.

Blood from Phaedrus' palm gathered into a fiery shield, deflecting Seth's blade the moment before it struck. It shattered into a rain of scarlet, coating the meadow with blood.

"Onto the ship." Seraphim barked. "Now!"

Alarm bells rang. Incessant. Growing louder. Thundering steps and galloping hooves approached. We would be boxed in.

Head ringing, I tried to rise to no avail. I saw knights streaming toward us, Phaedrus' men come to reinforce their lord.

Cursing, Seth rushed to my side and picked me up, carrying me onto the deck. Eleos was a step behind, supporting Seraphim. Herding us aboard, Percy slashed the last thread holding the rope together. Wind caught the sails, and the ship surged away from the dock.

Seraphim dropped to her knees, and Eleos knelt by her side, tearing off his cloak to bind her forearms. Setting me down gently, Seth whirled around to watch the dock.

Several guards had reached the field of flowers, and while many stopped to gape in confusion, many more did not. Raising their spears and bows, they aimed for our ship.

Spears whirled through the air. With a thud, one impaled the mast, splintering a chunk of wood off. The other sailed toward me. Lunging forward, Seth grabbed his floating greatsword from the air and cleaved through the lance.

The shaft splintered, raining wood into the sea. Flinching away from the impact, I was taken off guard when Seth tackled me. My back struck the deck with a painful thud. Arrows whizzed overhead, lost in the waves.

I tried to rise, but Seth pushed me down, shielding my body with his. Twisting my neck to search for the others, I glimpsed Eleos by Seraphim, head ducked as he tended her wounds. Percy cowered at the helm, one hand clutching his hat, the other wrapped protectively around Whisper.

"Are we alive?" He shouted over the crashing waves.

"Not yet," Seraphim lifted her head. "Now we face the storm."

THIRTY FOUR

WATER STRETCHED AROUND US IN all directions. Somewhere ahead, great mountains would close in, forcing us through the infamous Lethe Strait.

Trapped aboard a ship not meant for those waters, death surely awaited us.

Eleos parted my torn tunic, examining my wound. He looked exhausted. Blood dripped down his nose, and a drop ran from his eyes like a morbid tear. "It's not bad." He said. "Put pressure on it." Balling up his scarf, he offered it to me.

Flinching, I pressed it to the gash on my ribs. Nerves danced in my chest as I watched Seth lean against the mast and roll up his sleeves, checking the wounds Phaedrus had given him.

A nasty gash tore his upper arm, soaking his tunic with blood. Pressing a hand to the laceration, he closed his eyes and leaned back, unconcerned with the injury.

Eleos followed my gaze. "That's how chthonics are. *Reckless.*"

"I guess I'll have to tend his wounds if he won't," I said.

Eleos tried to summon a smile, but failed. Wiping his face, he exhaled. "I knew I was right."

"About what?"

He glanced away, bashful. "When we first met, I had a feeling you would be our hope."

Smiling, I wiped the smear of blood from his face. "Sweet-talker," I whispered.

A tiny half-smirk appeared on his face.

Eyes snapping open, Seth glared at Seraphim. She lay against the mast, arms wrapped around herself. "You should have let me kill him." He said.

"I couldn't." Seraphim shook her head.

"How could you forgive him?" Seth pushed off the mast. "Better yet, how did you not see his betrayal coming? He *attacked* us in Serifos!"

"Phaedrus couldn't use magic when I was exiled. The masked nobleman you described bore no resemblance to the brother I knew. He was always my ally. Always." Seraphim looked away sadly. "I found a way to correspond with him during my time in Duath Nun. We were of the same mind. At least, so I thought."

"He was on your side," I said. "He told me himself. But somewhere along the way, he changed."

Seraphim fell silent, watching the endless sea. "We were both dealt poor hands. But I never imagined we'd turn out so differently." She eyed Seth sharply. "I have lost *everything*. I will not bury my brother, too."

Lip quivering, Seth glanced away. "Eleos did say he was a powerful psyche. I can hardly blame you for falling for his manipulations." He paused before speaking again. "He'll pursue us."

"He will," Seraphim confirmed.

"Then we should avoid him at all costs."

Relieved, Seraphim closed her eyes.

Giving her space, I joined Percy by the helm. He stared ahead, watching the horizon for our impending doom. "Nothing yet." He said, noticing my presence.

"What does it look like?" I asked.

"Depends on the story." Percy ran a hand under his chin. "Some say beautiful sirens lure ships to their deaths. Others say a swirling storm breaks them in half."

"It's both," Eleos said, joining us. "The ship built for envoys is reinforced to endure the storm, to avoid the sirens."

"Sirens?" I repeated. "I thought those were. . ."

"Fairy tales?" He said. "Not here, they aren't."

Seraphim opened her eyes. "Our boat can't weather the storm. Eleos, you'll need to steer. As for Percy and me, the safest bet is to tie us to the mast."

"Tie us?" Percy gritted his teeth. "What for?"

"The siren's call can't be resisted by normal means," Seraphim warned. "Anyone who favors women will be enraptured by them. Lest you want to waltz into the sea seeking a good time, you'll submit to the rope."

Percy's shoulders sagged. He glanced between me and Eleos. "I suppose I understand why you two can run free. But Seth-"

"Us *two*?" I asked. "Shouldn't Eleos be tied up?"

"I'll be fine." Eleos said. When my brow wrinkled in worry, he squeezed my hand. "Trust me."

Electing to trust him, I nodded. Maybe psyches could resist the siren's lure.

Seraphim turned to Seth. "Both times I crossed, I had a much better ship. I followed the storm and kept it from falling apart with my blood." She wiped her mouth. "The whirlpool covers the entire strait—it's weakest by the sirens, but deadly nonetheless. Seth—you're in better condition than I am. You'll need to patch the holes, keep us in one piece."

"What?" He questioned. "If the sirens' lure is so powerful, won't I saunter off the deck?"

"Aethra." Seraphim looked at me. "Your job is to prevent the untimely death of our assassin."

"How?" I asked, raising my arm to compare the size of my biceps to Seth's. A blind man could probably spot the considerable gap.

"I have faith in you." Seraphim winced. "Take a moment to rest. It'll be upon us soon.

Rubbing his forehead, Percy removed his hat and shoved it into his bag. "Well. I suppose I need to find some rope."

Eleos whistled. "C'mon, Whisper. Let's get you below deck."

The two men peeled away from the bow, leaving me alone. Glancing at the calm seas ahead, I searched for the whirlpool before finally turning away. Grabbing Athena's lead, I led her through the door into the tiny captain's cabin. She'd probably be safest, there.

Running a hand down her neck, I locked her inside and stepped out. Seth paced around the mast, raptly watching the seas.

I limped to his side. "Let me see your wounds," I demanded.

"I'm fine," Seth said, pacing.

Grabbing his arm, I tried to stop him, but it was like pulling a pallet of stones. My hand slipped from his rigid muscles.

"That was cute, princess," Seth said softly, offering his arm.

Relieved, I tore a chunk off my cloak and tied a tourniquet around his upper arm. "Chthonics can still bleed out," I said.

"Are you worried about me?" He asked, wearing a sly smile.

"Yes," I said, exasperated. "I've never. . ." The words slipped from my grasp.

I'd never been scared to lose anyone before. Ainwir had seemed larger than life, the father I'd looked up to. Not once had I feared for him; in his shadow, I'd felt safe.

In the years following his disappearance, I'd opened my heart to no one. I had been utterly alone.

But now? Gods, I didn't want to lose anyone on this ship—Seth, least of all.

Seth ran a hand across my cheek. "Don't worry so much. Chthonics clot quickly. It'll take more than a scrape to kill me."

Taking his hand, I closed my eyes and leaned against it.

"Good job, by the way," Seth said. "Rescuing us damsels in distress."

Chuckling, I looked up at him. He wore an expression so starkly different than his usual countenance, I almost didn't recognize him. Soft, warm, genuine.

The wind tousled his waves, and moonlight brightened his face. He looked more than handsome. He looked. . .

Divine.

A dark shadow covered the moon, drenching us in darkness. Seth looked up sharply. The wind picked up, and lightning streaked across the sky, illuminating the sea.

"It's upon us," Seraphim shouted. "Percy. *Now.*"

Eleos raced for the steering wheel while Seth scrambled for the rope Percy had pulled above deck.

Pushing the bard toward Seraphim, Seth tried to cheer him up. "Think of the positives. Didn't you like being tied up?"

"Normally," Percy said, grimacing as Seth wrapped a rope around them. "But as I understand it, this rope is *keeping* me from the fun."

Chuckling, Seth yanked the rope, tying a potent knot.

Unsure what to do, I hovered nearby, watching the bow. Towering cliffs rose to the north and south, funneling us into a narrow strait. Wind whipped through my hair, churning the waves and pounding against the sails. Our ship lurched, and Eleos strained to keep it under control.

Music echoed in the distance—a faint itch at the back of my ears. Rubbing my neck, I turned back to Seraphim. "Are you sure I'll be okay?"

"So long as you aren't secretly attracted to women," Seraphim promised, closing her eyes.

The music grew louder, rising above the thunder and crashing waves.

"Shit." Seth winced. Stalking toward me, he took my arm.

"Seth," I said, "I don't have anything to prevent you from lusting after a bunch of fish."

"Yes, you do." He said. "*You.*"

A distinct voice carried on the wind, haunting and inhuman. Staring down the bow, I saw the storm Seraphim had warned us about: swirling waters gathered into a whirlpool the size of a small outpost, pulling everything into the depths. Only one thin length of the sea was free from the deadly vortex—but the music intensified as we approached it.

A dazed fog clouded Seth's gaze. Ripping the cut on his bicep, he let blood flow down his arm. Wisps of scarlet drifted away from him and blanketed the hull, like a protective tarp cast over a wagon.

"Aethra!" Eleos shouted.

Twisting my neck, I looked up at him. His knuckles whitened from gripping the wheel, fighting against the maelstrom's pull.

"Distract Seth!" He called. "*Quickly.*"

Grabbing my waist, Seth pulled me to the center of the deck. "Not even the goddess herself could tempt me if I have you."

I opened my mouth to protest, but he crashed his lips against mine. Something feral twisted inside me. Pressing my mouth to his, I twined my fingers into his hair, pulling him closer, feeling the heat of his body against mine. His fingers dug into my back, trailing up my spine and grabbing my curls.

The ship lurched, tearing us apart. I could see the whirling storm out of the corner of my eye, the terrifying way we drifted towards it, pulled and bucked beneath the furious waves. The singing grew louder and louder, female voices resonating over one another, their words impossible to understand.

Turning my head, I caught sight of the creatures lounging atop their rock. Enormous serpent heads watched us, anchored to the decaying body of what might have once been a woman. Her sallow eyes locked on mine as she sang, tattered dress hanging from her emaciated form.

She was a keres. To my eyes, she appeared a twisted monster. Seth glanced toward her, eyes glazing over. An expression of unbearable desire and *need* took over him.

Fighting against her song, Seth snapped his head away and stared at my face before pushing me against the wall beneath the wheel. My head struck the wood, and he kissed me again, sliding his tongue into my mouth. His hands traced down my back to my thighs, before rising again.

I released an involuntary moan as he grabbed my thigh and pulled it around his waist, fingers digging into my rear. I hadn't thought it possible to be consumed by fear in the middle of a life-threatening sensation, yet also desire nothing more than for him to rip my clothes off and take me right there.

Seth lifted my other leg, and I wrapped them around his waist, oblivious to everything save his lips against mine.

Unease twisted in my heart. Nostalgia intertwined with it, causing my breast to pulse with painful beats. Seth tilted my head, running kisses down my neck toward my breasts, parting the laces of my tunic with his teeth. The pleasure from his touch vanished when I saw the water.

Terrible darkness lurked beneath the sea, consuming my attention.

The Empty. It hid beneath the waves. If we sank, or someone fell overboard. . . My eyes shot up, meeting the keres' as we sailed past.

Everyone who touched the Empty turned to dust. So who were they, the sallow-eyed wraiths who beckoned us to give up? Something. . . *familiar* shone in her sunken eyes. An overwhelming wave of sympathy and grief tore through my heart.

It almost felt like. . . like she was begging me to save her.

Our connection snapped. The ship surged past her.

Eleos cursed, and I looked up sharply. Something slammed into the hull, shaking the boat. I lost balance and hit the deck, grabbing for something to hold onto. Seth caught me first, and we rolled over each other until his back slammed into the railing.

I landed beneath him, and he stared into my eyes with fiery desire. Not merely lust—something deeper lurked within.

Extending his hand, he gritted his teeth, focusing on me as he held his spell. Grabbing the sides of his face, I forced him to look at me, and only me.

"Godsdammit." He cursed. "I didn't want to fall for you."

"Neither did I," I gasped.

The ship lurched, and the song ceased abruptly. Powerful wind tore into the sails, propelling the boat through the water. Seth panted and sat up, blood dripping down his arm.

"Are we in one piece?" He asked, voice hoarse.

"For now," Eleos gripped the wheel, knuckles white. "If you hurry to patch it."

Snapping from my reverie, I raced to the mast and sawed through Percy and Seraphim's bonds. Dazed, Percy stood, wobbling on his feet as he ran for the stairs. "Oh gods. Where am I?"

"Hull. Hole." I managed.

Shaking himself out of his stupor, Percy flew down the steps, cursing when he noticed the damage. A rock or reef must have torn through the side—a thin webbing of blood sealed the gap, preventing the sea from spilling in. Grabbing a plank from the corner, I slammed it against the wall, waiting for Percy to nail it into place.

Seth followed us downstairs, face twisted in concentration as we made desperate repairs. Falling to a knee, he lost the magic, and I stepped back, hoping our makeshift attempts had been enough.

Water trickled through the edges of the planks, but the worst had been pushed back.

Breathing out, I grabbed a rag and stuffed it around the edges, hoping to slow the tide.

"Whew," Percy doubled over. "I don't remember much, but considering Seth is alive, and not at the bottom of the sea, I imagine you just made him a *very* lucky man."

I glanced at Seth, cheeks flushing when I met his gaze. All this time, I'd thought he wanted something fun, something fleeting—nothing more. But that kiss had revealed the truth.

I expected to see relief in his eyes. Relief for the tension between us to finally have been released. Instead, I glimpsed deepest sorrow. Regret. *Grief.*

We'd survived the Lethe, but Seth looked at me as though he'd just lost me.

THIRTY FIVE

NIGHT SETTLED OVER THE OCEAN. A faint breeze stirred the sail, propelling us onward through calm waters.

Exhausted, I trudged below deck, glancing at Whisper and Athena, who were curled up in the corner. Checking the roughly patched hole, I shoved the soaked rags deeper into the gap. Wiping the sweat from my brow, I found a quiet spot and slid down with a groan, resting my head against the hull, listening to the sea outside.

The poor animals still looked distressed from our brush with death. Whisper had been hiding beneath Athena for hours.

Eleos joined me, sitting in the darkness beside me. Grateful for his presence, I leaned against his shoulder. A smile spread across my lips. "I can't believe I saved you from the dungeons."

He chuckled. "I'm not exactly a knight in shining armor. Scholars and priests play damsels all the time." His happiness faded. "I'm sorry I couldn't protect you. Suffering a psyche's control is. . . horrible."

Remembering his confession, I glanced down. "Have you controlled someone? Since. . . since him?"

"Yes," Eleos admitted. "Many people. But that was long ago, and I haven't used that foul magic in years."

Nodding, I pulled my cloak around my arms. "I trust you, El. Whoever you were back then, you're not anymore."

"I. . ." He sighed. "I hope not."

"Chin up." I nudged him. "We're going to save the world. It's only an ocean away now."

Running a hand down my arm, he found my hand, knitting his fingers through mine. "I still have hope that we will."

Tilting my head, I studied his face. "Your past isn't why you think you're broken. I still don't understand."

"Haven't you noticed?" He looked away. "I don't feel what men are supposed to. I don't look at you the way Seth does." He glanced down at our intertwined hands. "For me, this is enough."

"You prefer men?"

"No." He shook his head. "Lust consumes every man I've met. But not me. Not for any woman I've seen, not for any woman I've courted."

Oh. "I'm sorry if I made things awkward for you," I said. "When I-"

"Don't misunderstand," Eleos interrupted. "I don't see you the way I see the others. What I feel for you is. . . much deeper than that. But I'll never be able to give you what you deserve. Never love you the way you want to be loved."

Lowering my head, I reflected on our journey. Eleos hadn't known how to compliment my breasts, had never ogled me, never made a move. Not once had his hand wandered during the night we'd shared.

He loved me for who I was.

"I don't want to do anything to make you uncomfortable," I said. "But I don't know how to. . . where do we go from here?"

Eleos studied me for a moment. "To see your smiling face every day would be a blessing I don't deserve. And it would be enough. More than enough."

"Eleos." My mouth warbled.

He leaned his head against mine. "Did you see Seraphim and Percy when we passed the sirens?"

"No. What did they look like?"

"Pathetic. Percy, in particular."

A laugh burst from my lungs. "You really don't care about sex?"

"It repulses me, actually." His head snapped up. "Not to say you repulse me."

"Don't dig a hole, El."

"Right." He chuckled. "Were you mad? That Seth was tempted?"

A low chortle rumbled from my lips. "No wonder you never seemed jealous of him. . ."

"He isn't half the lady-killer I am, Lady Aethra. Why would I be jealous?"

Happiness bloomed in my chest for the first time in my life—not brought on by Eleos' spells, or fleeting vice. The warmth enveloped me, and a smile tore across my lips. Leaning my head against his, I closed my eyes.

Ainwir loved me. Eleos loved me.

Maybe I wasn't worthless after all.

THE SEA SEPARATING Duath Nun from the Merchant Isles was surprisingly small, for how well it had kept the two nations apart. After a few days at sea, land appeared on the horizon.

Standing at the bow, I watched Duath Nun draw closer, hardly able to believe just how different it appeared.

Great mountains rose on the horizon, the color of sand. Lush vegetation swayed by the shore, verdant and green. From the waters grew countless feathery reeds that bucked beneath the wind.

Our ship slammed into the bank, scraping across the seabed. I flinched, listening to the delicate wood grind and groan.

"Well," Percy said. "I don't think we'll be making a return journey."

"Not on this." Seraphim agreed, hugging her wounded arms to her chest as she climbed over the deck. "Phaedrus will be right behind us on his fancy ship, though."

Seth glanced at me, and I expected him to offer me a hand down. Sighing, he turned away and climbed down after Seraphim. Whisper leaped after him, grateful to be off the deck.

After everything we'd been through, was he really going to give me the cold shoulder again?

Eleos approached me, offering a hand instead. "Need help, for old time's sake?"

"I've got to set down a ramp for Athena anyway," I murmured, heading below deck. Eleos helped me drag the bridge and throw it overboard, allowing Athena to safely descend to the beach.

Percy greeted the horse when she found her footing. "The last of the horses. I can't believe you made it this far."

"Thank princess," Seth said. "She got too attached."

"Athena saved us at Red Bluff," I called. "I could hardly abandon her, now."

Descending the ramp, I took my first step onto Duath Nun's soil. Or, *sand*. A strange sensation enveloped me, like I'd passed through a barrier, or broken the surface of the sea. Disoriented, I spun in place, but everything looked normal.

Dismissing the odd feeling, I ran a hand down Athena's neck. Grabbing her lead, I guided her after Seraphim. "What now? We're out of supplies and gear."

"There's a city not far from here." She said, pointing. "That's its marker."

Following her finger, I noticed a black obelisk rising from the trees. Ancient and eroding, the faded runes carved on its surface were foreign.

"But we need rest." Seraphim paused, catching her breath. "Or we'll die before we get there." She surveyed the beach. "Let's get out of sight of the shore."

Glancing behind me, I watched the sea until I could see it no longer, wondering when Phaedrus would give chase. Who would he bring with him, and how far would they pursue us?

Deep in the trees, we set up camp. Seth and Percy searched for firewood, while I laid out my cloak for Seraphim and ordered her to sit. She released a heavy groan, wincing with pain.

Checking her bandages to see if they needed redressing, I struggled to meet her eyes. "I. . ."

"Don't apologize," Seraphim ordered. "Evidently, my brother is a powerful psyche. Even more so than Eleos."

"When do you think he became one?"

She studied the fronds of a nearby tree. "When his love died, I'd imagine. Or perhaps when he lost his child. Phaedrus had nothing if not empathy for all things. I'm not surprised Psythos blessed him."

Sinking to my knees, I sat beside her. "He wants to destroy everything. He thinks it's a kindness to end our meaningless suffering."

She chuckled, a short, breathy gasp at first. Then, she closed her eyes and dipped her head, fiery hair hanging in front of her eyes. A laugh burst from her lips, shaking her chest.

"Seraphim?" I asked, concerned.

Shaking her head, she brushed her hair from her face. "Phaedrus and I came to the same conclusion, though miles and years kept us apart." Her pale blue eyes met mine. "Life is meaningless. The gods aren't real, or maybe they abandoned us. We came from nothing, and will return to it when we die."

My face fell. "But. . . but I thought you wanted to save it."

"I do." She said, voice cracking. "It's *because* life is pointless that I find it so precious. Nothing and no one governs us. We are free to live our lives as ourselves and write our own stories. What could be better?"

I didn't understand. I didn't want to think the gods weren't real. I wanted my life to have purpose. For those I loved to carry on after death.

My eyes fluttered close. There had to be life, after death. I needed to see Ainwir again, to embrace and thank him.

"You don't agree," Seraphim said. "And that's okay. You don't have to."

Nodding, I looked down. My life would gain meaning from my sacrifice. And. . . and the Maiden would welcome me, at its end.

"We'll need to make a plan," Seraphim said. "I wanted to prepare supplies and disguises in Cynthus, but. . ." She shrugged. "We'll have to improvise."

"Will the people be hostile?"

"If we walk in like this? Obvious foreigners? Yes, they will." She looked at me gravely. "This place is more dangerous than anything we've faced thus far. We *must* use caution."

Nodding, I looked up at the black obelisk obscuring the moon.

Seraphim nudged me. "Let me sleep. You need to talk to Seth, anyway."

Lifting my head, I saw Seth loitering while Percy started the fire, his scarlet eyes fixed on me.

"Get some rest." I touched Seraphim's shoulder and stood.

Eleos intercepted Seth before I reached him. The scholar gently touched Seth's arm, and spoke a few words. Flashing me a small smile, Eleos returned to the fire.

Seth folded his arms as I approached. "Walk with me?"

"What was that about?" I asked, glancing at Eleos.

"He politely threatened me."

Seth turned on his heel, and I followed him from the camp. Whisper didn't accompany us. Seth remained rigidly silent, shoulders stiff as he strode through the trees.

Catching up to him, I tried to meet his eyes, but he stared directly ahead. "What was he threatening you about?"

"Did you and Eleos work things out?" He asked.

"Yes," I said. "We're friends. Good friends, but. . . not anything more."

"Good," Seth said in a clipped tone.

Chewing on my lip, I searched for something to say. We broke from the treeline and walked across the shore. I stared at the horizon, marveling at the beauty of the moon shining on the sea.

A lone tree grew near the waters, and Seth finally paused beneath it. Sighing, he turned to face me. "Why couldn't you have been insufferable?"

"And here I thought I was," I said, shivering under a cold breeze. "So are you going to ignore me like. . ." I cleared my throat. "Like after our. . . *bonding* in the cave?"

"No." He reached out, fingers trembling. They brushed my face, settling onto the curve of my cheek. "I've lost everything that mattered. I was trying to keep you at arm's length, because I don't have the strength to lose any more."

I took his hand, pulling it from my face. "Phaedrus forced me to feel your emotions. Your grief. I think I understand." I looked away, ashamed. "From now on, I'll keep my distance."

"No." He grabbed my arm and pulled me closer. "The further you walk away, the more I'll want you. There's no use playing pretend. After what happened on the ship, I won't be able to resist." His eyes darted away. "And Eleos made it clear he'd make me suffer, if I broke your heart."

"Oh," I breathed. "That does sound like him."

"Heh," he smiled. "I'm a little jealous of you two, sometimes."

"Eleos called my mind a *hellscape*. I don't think you want to hear my thoughts."

"I want to know all of you," Seth said. "And I want it to belong to me, alone."

My heart hammered against my chest, and heat bloomed in my core when I remember the way he'd touched me on the ship.

"I wanted you to take me, right then," I admitted, flushing. "Despite the circumstances."

He smirked. "Nothing's stopping me from taking you right now."

Wrapping his arms around my waist, he pinned me to the tree, pressing his lips to mine. Sinking into his embrace, I knotted my hands around his neck.

"Mm." Pulling away, Seth held up a finger and reached into the satchel at his waist.

"What?" I gasped.

"I can't have you thinking I'm some classless brute." Pulling out a flask, he popped it open. "I took this from the good lord's estate. I grabbed it before we left the dungeons." He offered the drink. "Shall we?"

"You want to get drunk first?"

"No!" He frowned. "I want to toast. To our lives, and the glorious ravishing I'm about to demean you with."

Laughing, I accepted. "Fine. I could use a drink, anyway." Lifting the flask to my lips, I took a heavy swig before wiping my mouth.

A pleasant brandy raced down my throat, but notes of burning carried with it.

The joy washed from Seth's face as he took the flask back. Worried, I reached out to him. "What?"

My hand swiped the air as I lost balance. The world flickered, and I nearly fell. Seth stepped back, escaping my reach.

"Don't worry." He said. "It's a paralytic. You'll be fine by tomorrow."

Trying to breathe, I managed a single word. "Why?"

"You don't understand what Duath Nun does to women with your magic," Seth said, voice cracking. "It's torture. It's worse than death. and I. . . I can't let that happen to you."

Wincing, I fell to a knee as I lost sensation in my limbs. Phaedrus had uttered those same words.

"I should've done this earlier. I'm sorry." He said, kneeling. "Phaedrus' ship left right after we did. I saw it behind us earlier today. It'll be here in a few hours." He glanced away. "I'll claim we were separated. Whisper will search for you in the wrong direction. We'll enter the Acheron without you and seal it closed."

Trying to lift my hand and failing, I stared into his eyes, panic thrumming in my heart.

"Phaedrus won't hurt you," Seth promised. "We know that. And as much as I hate him." His mouth twisted into a snarl. "I hate my father more. I won't let him take you, too."

Seth stood, and the wind billowed through his cloak, blocking my sight of the shore with its black fabric.

"I can't lose you. I *won't*." He said, swallowing a sob. "If we survive? I'll come back for you. I promise." Taking one last look at me, Seth turned on his heel and walked away.

Falling onto my side, I tried to twitch my fingers, but my body wouldn't obey. Barely visible, a speck beneath the moon's light, I saw a vessel approaching the shore, its flag bearing the silver and blue sigil of House Cynthus.

How bitter, and ironic for me to forgive Ainwir only for the man I loved most to betray me once more.

To be continued...

In the

Serpent Prince of Hades

About the Author

Riley Knight lives in the northern farmlands of Alabama, with her husband, two dogs, and a cockatiel named Seoras. Most hours of the day are spent in the pages of her books, or others, wishing she had magic and could go on quests.

https://rileysknight.com
https://instagram.com/rileysknight/